Monsters Monsters Monsters Monsters

Contents:

Dump Truck — 7
Jeff Strand

The Boy Under the Bed — 12
Gerri R. Gray

The Elephant — 19
Ksenia Murray

Indoor People — 33
Cayce Osborne

Caretaker of a Thousand Houses — 48
Mark Wheaton

The God Whisperer — 80
Richard Clive

Male of the Species — 105
Tom Vandermolen

Creature Feature — 132
Chris Preston

Daddy — 149
P. Mattern

The Hidden — 163
Jeff Oliver

At the Wake of the Medusa — 183
Scotty Milder

Brain Rape — 206
Carson Demmans

Slime — 215
Jane Nightshade

The Widow and the Fortune Teller — 232
Douglas Ford

Curse of the Blood Moon: The Hospital — 246
Alexander C. Bailey

Bloodline — 272
Ricki Whatley

The It Factor — 299
Krissy Eliot

Other HellBound Books — 232

Monsters
Monsters
Monsters
Monsters

HellBound Books Publishing

Dump Truck
Jeff Strand

Amy had been watching all morning, and when the dump truck finally pulled into her driveway, she let out a squeal of delight. She couldn't believe it! This was really happening! She hurried to the front door and ran outside to greet the driver.

The driver got out of the truck and glanced down at his clipboard. "Amy Beamer?"

Amy gave him an enthusiastic nod. "Yes, that's me!"

"Sign here."

She took the pen and clipboard from him and signed. She let out an involuntary giggle as she handed it back to him. The driver glared at her, which seemed kind of weird. Why shouldn't she be excited?

"Where do you want 'em?" he asked.

"Just back it up into the garage," she said. "I spent all day yesterday cleaning it out." She could now easily afford to pay somebody else to clean her garage, but she didn't want to start spending the money before it arrived.

The driver frowned. "What safety precautions have you taken?"

"Excuse me?"

"Is the garage reinforced?"

"No," said Amy. "I mean, it's just a normal garage. It's a safe neighborhood. I didn't think I needed security guards or anything."

"Was a safe neighborhood, I guess."

"What?"

"It's not so safe anymore," said the driver. "Obviously."

"Because of thieves?"

"Nobody's gonna steal what's in there."

"Okay, I'm confused," said Amy. "Explain to me why the neighborhood is no longer safe."

The driver stared at her for a moment. "Are you joking with me?"

"No, I'm not joking with you. I was having a great morning and you're kind of yucking my yum. I get that people might try to steal the money, but that doesn't make the neighborhood less safe."

"What money?"

Now Amy wanted to grab him by the shoulders and shake him until a few of his teeth rattled free. "The genie granted me one wish, and I asked for a dump truck full of money! That's the dump truck, right? That's why you're here, right? Right?"

"Oh..." The driver glanced at his clipboard again. "Okay, I see what happened. There weren't enough available characters on the order form, and 'Dump Truck Full Of Money' became 'Dump Truck Full of Mon,' and from there you can pretty clearly see how the shipping department assumed that the wish was for a dump truck full of monsters."

"What?"

"Didn't you wonder why your money was making so much noise? All the howling and pounding and snarling and roaring?"

"Why would they think I wanted a dump truck full of monsters?"

"They must have assumed you were a raging psychopath planning to unleash your wrath against your neighbors. That's what I thought. It's why I had a judgmental tone earlier."

Amy was in a state of shock. She'd worn an outfit specifically chosen to roll around in the gigantic pile of money. "Can you take them back?"

The driver shook his head. "There are consequences if I don't make the delivery. I will be hanged by the neck until dead, as will every member of my immediate family. When you become a driver for the genie, you vow that you will make every single delivery."

"But...but...but...but..."

"Nah, I'm kidding. This kind of thing happens all the time. You'd think they'd add more spaces to the form. A lot of time with the sex wishes they'll only have the first few letters of the name, and the shipping department will make its best guess. They're not always good at guessing."

"Apparently not."

"Just last week this guy wished to have sex with Mary Pickford. Now, clearly what he meant was that he wanted to have sex with a magical version of Mary Pickford from her time as a superstar in the silent film era, but the shipping department went with the literal version of the wish. Since she died in 1979, you can imagine that the delivery was very disappointing for him."

"Maybe the genie shouldn't outsource the wish delivery," Amy said.

"You're not the first person to say that. Nobody asks me to help make these executive decisions. I'm just the delivery guy. Anyway, I'll need you to sign another form, and then it'll be six to eight weeks until your replacement wish gets here. Sorry about the inconvenience."

"But I placed a huge order for heroin!" Amy told him. "What am I supposed to do when the drug dealers arrive and I can't pay them?"

"Are you joking, like when I said I'd be hanged if I didn't make the delivery?"

"Yes."

"That was a pretty good one. Most people aren't in a joking mood when this happens, generally because they're really, really horny." He reached inside the truck and handed another clipboard to Amy. "Sign and date at the bottom, please."

"What kind of monsters are in there?" Amy asked.

"Oh, a little of everything. Scaly ones. Furry ones. Slimy ones. Claws, teeth, suckers, spikes, and so on and so forth. Swamp monsters. Desert monsters. Snow monsters. Space monsters. The classics like zombies and mummies, and stuff you've never heard of before, like a venomous esophageal glow-worm. Some believe that man is the worst monster of them all, so we threw in a serial killer. It's a pretty good selection."

"Hmmm."

"Just sign here," said the driver, tapping the form.

"Do you have to take them back?" Amy asked.

"I don't have to, no, but then I wouldn't be able to exchange it for the dump truck full of money."

"I'm just saying that vengeance against my neighbors doesn't sound so bad. They've always been kind of snotty. I was planning to rub my vast wealth in their faces, but maybe setting a bunch of monsters loose on a killing spree would be even more satisfying."

The driver smiled. "This is another joke, right? Like the hanging and the heroin?"

Amy shook her head and gave him back the clipboard. "No. I want to keep them."

"Okay, look, we've only just met and it's not my place to tell you how to live your life. But unleashing that kind of carnage will change you. It'll haunt you. You'll look in the mirror, and you may not like what you see."

"You're right," said Amy. "It's not your place."

"There will be innocent bystanders."

"Are any of us truly innocent?"

"The cops will come after you."

"My new pets will protect me."

"Please," said the driver. "Don't do this. You don't know how relieved I was to discover that you'd wished for a dump truck full of money instead of a dump truck full of monsters. As bloodthirsty as you may be right now, I swear to you, you'll never get the sounds of your victims' screams out of your head. Never."

"Good," said Amy. "The sound will bring me peace."

Weeping, the driver opened the back of the dump truck, and lo, the monsters did spill forth, and lo, the loss of human life was vast. Amy cackled with laughter and wondered why she hadn't wished for this in the first place, because monsters were so much better than money.

The Boy Under the Bed
Gerri R. Gray

The hysterical scream of a child echoed through the cobweb-shrouded corridor of the derelict castle. The flames of the torches on the stony walls flickered, and then a second scream, louder than the first, sounded. There soon came another scream, followed by yet another one.

A gargantuan humanoid beast, awakened by the screams, darted down the corridor in the direction of the child's bedroom, his razor-sharp talons scraping along the wall. Scales covered his body in armored plates, and dark green dreadlocks, like thick ropes of seaweed, hung from the back of his elongated head.

The moment he opened the door of the bedroom, the screaming stopped.

The beast's lips, black and slimy like a pair of eels, peeled back to reveal a row of needle-like teeth that were as dreadful as they were sharp. His reptilian eyes zeroed in on the terrified child in the bed for several seconds, and then he spoke.

"Damn it, Gruelian! It's the middle of the day and you should be sleeping! What's the meaning of all this screaming? Did you have another pleasant dream?"

The child sat up and shook his head from side to side. Tears were flowing from all three of his eyes, staining the dark green scales on his cheeks.

"No, Father. It wasn't a dream. There's something underneath my bed. Something too horrible for words! Its face is pale like a lifeless squid and splattered with brown dots, and the fur growing out of the top of its head is fiery red!"

The father beast crossed his arms and shook his head with disgust. "Oh, here we go again! I suppose the next thing you're going to tell me is that you saw the little boy that lives under your bed?"

The curved horns protruding from the sides of Gruelian's head like a steer drooped a bit as he nodded, fear of his father's wrath merging with his fear of the boy under his bed.

"We've been through all of this before. How many times do I have to tell you, Gruelian, there's no such thing as little boys? Humans don't exist. They're nothing but a figment of your overactive imagination."

"But I didn't imagine it," the distraught monster-child protested. "The boy... it really does exist. I've heard it moving around and I've seen it, too, with my own three eyes. If you take a look under my bed, Father, you'll see it for yourself!"

"This is utterly ridiculous!" the father beast growled before taking a quick peek under his son's bed in the hope of calming his fears. "There, are you happy now? I looked, like you asked me to, and I didn't see a thing. There's no little boy living under your bed."

"It must have ran into the closet when it heard your footsteps approaching," Gruelian reasoned. "Please,

Father, take a look in the closet. I'm sure it's hiding in there."

The father beast's eyes glowed an angry red and a small flame shot out from one of his flaring nostrils. "No! I've had enough of your nonsense for one day! When I was your age, son, I was already breathing fire and terrorizing dwarfs. It's high time for you to start acting your age and not your hoof size!"

Gruelian sniffled and wiped the tears away from his trio of eyes. "I'm sorry, Father."

The father beast grunted in disgust and started for the bedroom door; but, before exiting the room, he stopped and turned to look at his teary-eyed disappointment of a son. "You know, Gruelian, if this abnormal behavior of yours keeps up, you'll leave your mother and me with no choice but to send you to a child psychiatrist. Do you understand me? Now, stop all of this boy nonsense and go back to sleep!"

A sinking feeling began in the pit of Gruelian's stomach as he watched his peevish parent exit the bedroom, shutting the door behind him. With resignation, he lay back down, pulled his fleece blanket up to his pointed chin, and listened to his father's footsteps recede down the corridor until they vanished away into grim silence. He shut his eyes and attempted to go back to sleep as his father had ordered him. But just as he was starting to drift off into slumber, he was startled awake by a creaking sound. He opened his eyes and turned his head in the direction of the noise, horrified by what he saw.

The door of his bedroom closet was slowly opening.

Paralyzed by fear, Gruelian watched as a ginger-haired, freckle-faced boy of about nine years of age emerged from the closet and proceeded toward his bed. His heart pounded a frenetic pace as the boy drew closer, and his fangs began to chatter. He pulled the blanket up over his head and shut his eyes, tightly.

"Go away!" Gruelian's voice rang out with dread. "You aren't real."

"Oh, yes I am," the boy replied with a slight air of indignation, his fists on his hips.

Gruelian was utterly astonished. He could scarcely believe what his pointed ears had just heard. He lowered his blanket and gawked at the boy standing at his bedside.

"You can speak?" he asked.

The boy chuckled with amusement. "Of course I can speak, you silly monster."

"But… but… you're a human! How are you able to speak?"

The boy rolled his eyes, which were the color of a hangman's gibbet. "All humans can speak. We're the ones who invented language. Don't you know anything?"

Gruelian shook his head. "I don't believe you. Humans can't be trusted to tell the truth. And besides, they don't exist… and that includes you. You're nothing but a figment of my overactive imagination. My father told me so."

The boy let out another chuckle. "Is that a fact? Well, I've got some news for you, monster. Your father is wrong. He's either not telling you the truth, or he doesn't know what he's talking about."

Gruelian's three eyes widened with fear, and the horns at each side of his head quivered with trepidation. "Shhh! Don't let my father hear you say that! He doesn't like to be contradicted."

A smug expression came over the boy's face. "I'm not afraid of your father."

"Well, you should be," Gruelian warned. "My father is the fiercest fire-breathing monster in all the land!"

The boy reached behind his back, and to Gruelian's horror, brandished a large silver dagger that had been concealed in a leather sheath attached to the back of his belt. His eyes twinkled with impishness that soon turned menacing. "And I'm Marcus the Brave—the fiercest monster-slayer in all the land!"

"M-m-monster slayer?" Gruelian nervously stuttered, his panic-stricken heart beating a mile a minute.

"That's right," the boy replied, proudly. "I've killed all kinds of monsters with my trusty dagger, then I mount their ugly heads on my bedroom wall as trophies. They don't stand a chance against me!"

"But why?" Gruelian asked, confused. "Why would you want to kill innocent monsters who've done no harm to you?"

The boy rolled his eyes in response to the young monster's naïveté. "Because killing things is what humans like to do. It makes us superior." He pressed the blade of his dagger against Gruelian's twitching throat. "Now hold still so I can make a clean cut."

The terrified monster shut his eyes, and in a desperate attempt to make the little boy disappear, began chanting, "You aren't real. You aren't real. You aren't real."

He suddenly felt an intense burning sensation as the sharp metal began to slice through his flesh. He grabbed the boy's wrist with his claw-like hand in an attempt to pull the blade away, and bellowed out a ghastly scream that echoed throughout the castle.

At that moment, Marcus awoke to find himself in his own bed. Groggily, he sat up and rubbed the sleep from his eyes. A sinking feeling of disappointment engulfed him upon the realization that his monster slaying mission was nothing more than a vivid dream.

But it couldn't have been a dream, he thought. It was too real.

His ears suddenly detected the sound of footsteps rushing down the hall toward his bedroom. The door swung open and the light clicked on.

In the doorway, clad in a pink quilted housecoat and even pinker fuzzy slippers, stood Marcus' mother—a slightly plump, thirty-something woman with flaming red hair wrapped around pink plastic curlers. Her round face bore a worried look as she peered into the bedroom.

"I heard a loud scream come from your room," she announced, her tone one of motherly concern. "Are you all right?"

"I'm fine, Mom," Marcus replied. "It wasn't me who screamed. It must have been that monster that lives under my bed."

The boy's mother crossed her arms and flashed her son a look of disapproval. "Here we go again. If I've told you once, I've told you a thousand times, there's no monster living under your bed! Monsters aren't real. They exist only in your imagination."

"But, Mom…"

"Don't 'but Mom' me. I don't want to hear any more talk about monsters under beds, and I don't want you watching any more of those silly monster movies on T.V. with your older brother. They always end up giving you bad dreams."

"But, I'm telling you, the monster under my bed is real!" Marcus insisted, his eyes begging to be believed. "It's not something that I dreamed. It really is there! I'm not making it up. You have to believe me, Mom! If you take a look underneath my bed, you'll see it for yourself!"

Heaving a weary sigh, the boy's mother shook her head and then started out of the room. She paused for a moment and turned back to her son.

"It's the middle of the night, Marcus. I have to get up early in the morning for work, and you have school. Now, stop all of this damned monster nonsense and go back to sleep!"

With that being said, she switched off the light and left the room, shutting the door behind her. Her footsteps echoed down the hall until they faded away and an ominous silence enveloped the house.

Marcus shut his eyes, determined to return to the dream and finish slaying the monster in the castle. But the sound of a creaking floorboard prompted him to open his eyes and sit up. From the relative safety of his bed, he nervously glanced around the room. There were no monsters in sight, and no monster heads mounted on the walls. However, a metallic object on the floor, illuminated by the moonlight that crept like silent cat paws through the window, caught his eye. A rush of adrenaline surged through his body when he recognized what the object was: It was the monster-slaying dagger from his dream.

He felt compelled to climb out of bed and retrieve the weapon. His hands begged to hold it as they had done in his dream and to feel its power over life and death.

With his eyes on his prize, he swung his legs over the side of his bed. But just as the bottoms of his feet were about to touch the floor, a claw-like hand, covered completely in scales of dark green, shot up from the shadows beneath the bed and wrapped itself tightly around one of Marcus' ankles. Before the young monster slayer could emit a cry for help, the monstrous hand pulled him from the mattress and his body landed on the floor with a thud. The blood in his veins turned as cold as ice.

With all the strength a young lad of his age could muster, he struggled against the hand that held him captive, at the same time stretching his arm as far as it would go in the direction of the dagger, which sat just inches away from his fingertips.

A second claw-like hand reached out from its hiding spot and wrapped itself around the boy's other ankle. Marcus felt himself being reeled in like a fish. He opened his mouth to cry out that he was the fiercest monster slayer in all the land, but before his words could form, he disappeared into the darkness underneath the bed, never to be seen again.

The Elephant
Ksenia Murray

Andy stood on the side of a derelict highway. He watched as a large RV approached him from the distance; he stuck his thumb out and hoped that this one wouldn't ignore him too. Andy had been walking along the highway for hours, his ratty old backpack straps dug into his shoulders with the weight of clothes and other personal belongings. His throat was as dry as a sponge on a sunlit windowsill and stomach as empty as a newly changed trashcan. The RV grinded to a halt about twenty feet away from where Andy stood. The vehicle was covered in faded blue paintings of clowns and elephants, the front left headlight seemed to be smashed out and a thick black smog emitted from the tailpipe.

Andy ran up to the passenger-side door, out of breath. He had trekked this highway for several miles while the vehicles that drove it ignored him. Andy's body jolted in excitement. His clothes were covered in the desert sand that the wind had blown around. They were ragged and he smelled of rotten beef. Andy knocked on the door twice and took a step back. The RV shook as someone made their way from the back to the front. An old woman appeared at the door and opened it.

"Where ya headin'?" she asked, her voice low and the stench of cigarettes and piss wafted his way. Her face was covered in peeling blue paint; large white circles surrounded her eyes and a huge white smile was painted ear to ear. It fell off in chunks, exposing her tanned, leathery skin underneath. She wore a large blue dress that was covered in stains and glitter. Andy sniffed and recoiled.

"Anywhere but here, ma'am. I'm just looking to get off of this highway and into a town somewhere."

The old woman's piercing brown eyes stared down at him, her eyes darted back and forth from him to the empty highway; she tutted and slammed the door shut. Andy sighed and stepped away from the RV. Loud voices filled the quiet air as she spoke with whomever was inside. A few moments later, the older woman opened the door again.

"Get in."

Andy smiled, "Thank you, ma'am."

He climbed the worn, rusted steps into the RV. The old woman said nothing when she shuffled to the back of the bus. There was a middle-aged man who sat in the driver's seat. His hair dark brown and skin not quite as leathery as the old woman's, it seemed from the missing paint on his face. He stared straight ahead at the road before them.

Andy closed the rusted door behind him with a loud thunk. He looked around and saw five people crammed into the RV like sardines. There was the old woman who sat in the back on an old floral couch. Next to her was a younger woman in a blue leotard, her nipples showing through the thin fabric and her face painted in the same fashion as the older woman. Her hair was bright red and her nails were dirty. There were two men who sat next to each other on the opposite side of the women on a worn leather couch. They had the same faded face paint as the others but they weren't wearing shirts and their leather pants were blue. The last person that Andy noticed seemed to be a small child in a blue tuxedo, again with the same face paint as the others. The boy waved at Andy and motioned for him to sit in an empty stool next to him.

"Sit there," the old woman commanded. He nodded and walked to the back of the RV and sat on the stool next to the boy. Andy dropped his backpack next to the seat on the dusty rotted floor. His muscles ached and he sighed as the RV pulled away from the side of the road. The engine roared and shook; it sounded as if it didn't have many miles left to it before it would decide to turn off never to be turned on again. The noise of the bus was almost deafening, and Andy looked around the RV and noticed that the furniture was drilled into floorboards. When the passengers moved, dust would fly into the air, which made Andy sneeze. The faux wood floor had several boards missing, and the pieces that were still there were covered in a black mold. There was a small round table which had molded fruit on it; flies had made happy homes within the fruit.

"What do you want?" the man to his left asked.

Andy looked over at him and the man didn't return his gaze. "Just wanting to get the hell out of this shitty place. Anywhere is better than here."

"How old are you?" the young woman asked, her eyes darted around his face.

"Seventeen."

"Aren't you supposed to be living with your mommy and daddy?" she asked. Her voice high pitched and sounded a lot younger than what she looked.

"I guess so. I don't like it there though and I'm ready to start my life."

The women laughed and shook their heads. They stared at each other for a few beats before looking back at Andy.

"What's so funny?" he asked.

"You are a child. A baby. A cub. I reckon that you won't be able to make your own way," the old woman replied.

"Excuse me? I'm fine. I can take care of myself." Andy said, his face grew red.

The old woman waved her wrinkled hand at him. "That's what all ya'll youngin's always say. I bet once we drop you off wherever the fuck you're going, you'll be calling back home crying to ya momma wanting to go back."

"You have no idea what you're talking about!" Andy raised his voice; his face was beat red and his eyes bulged.

"Oh, calm down boy, ain't no reason to get ya panties in a twist. I'm just a measly old woman who knows a lot about the world. Maybe you'll make it and then be happy that you proved me wrong."

Andy took a deep breath and shook his head. "Sure."

"See? Just take my words with a grain of salt and you'll be fine." She reached over across the young woman and patted his leg.

"What's yer name?" the young woman asked.

"Andy, and you?"

"I'm Marjorie, this is grandma Ethel," she put an arm around the old woman's shoulders. "Them over there are my uncles, Tim and Tom. They be twins. That's Josh, my younger brother," she pointed to the boy sitting next to Andy. "And the one driving this home of ours is my papa. You can call him Fred."

Andy nodded "Nice to meet all of you."

Marjorie's brown eyes lit up. "Nice to meet you too! It's so awesome to meet people with manners. We haven't seen anyone with manners in a long time."

Andy relaxed and glanced around the bus. "So, where are ya'll headed to?"

"Anywhere." Tom answered.

Andy raised an eyebrow but before he could speak up, the old woman answered. "We're a traveling circus. We show up wherever we're needed and then we move on."

"Where's the next performance?" Andy asked.

The old woman laughed. "You're quite noisy. No wonder you had to leave your momma's house, she ain't raised you with no decency. Anyway, we just stop wherever Fred decides to. It's always a mystery."

"You don't schedule performances?" Andy asked incredulously.

"Oh, hell no, schedules are for losers who can't live life as it is. We stop, perform on the side of the road or in alleyways, or maybe a park or a suburb, and then we move on. It's quite fun living life with no rules and doing whatever we want; when we want to." Marjorie answered for her grandma.

"Interesting," Andy said. He leaned his back against the mildew-covered wall and let his body relax.

"We're performing tonight if you'd like to watch. Or hell, you could even join in! I know you ain't got no money and you'll need some if you're ever gonna make it out in this world on ya own. What do ya say?" Marjorie asked. Ethel looked over at Marjorie and whispered something that Andy couldn't make out; Marjorie answered and her grandma nodded.

"Um, how much are you willing to pay? And what would I be doing?" Andy asked.

"How about a hundred bucks? Seems fair for one night of work. Then after that, we'll set ya free," Ethel answered.

Andy took a deep breath and asked again. "Okay, but what will I be doing?"

"We don't know yet. We'll find a job for you once we stop," Ethel said.

Andy nodded and rode in silence. Josh, the boy who sat next to him, kept poking him in the ribs. Andy smacked the boy's hands away and he grumbled as he folded his arms across his chest. Josh had grown bored of poking Andy when he decided to ignore Josh. With a whine, Josh turned to bother Marjorie instead. After a few minutes, Andy closed his eyes and fell asleep.

A couple of hours later he awoke to find the RV at a complete stop. He looked around and saw that everyone else had left. Andy stood up and stretched, his bones cracked and his body shook; he yawned and grabbed his backpack. As he climbed out of the RV, the darkness enveloped him and the night bugs made their noises. He was in a park dimly illuminated by streetlights and the RV was parked in the middle of a grass field, the tracks from where Fred drove the RV still visible even in the poor light. He looked around and saw a large makeshift tent set up about fifty yards away, bright blue with aqua fairy lights draped over it. There was a small wooden sign that just said "Circus" placed outside of the entrance.

Andy walked over to the tent with his backpack slung over his shoulder. He grabbed a hold of the tent flap to open it when he was interrupted by Marjorie.

"Here ya go!" She squealed, handing him a glass of misty clear liquid that had a blue hue to it.

Andy let go of the tent flap and grabbed the cup. He smiled over at her, his yellowed and stained teeth glowed underneath the lights. "What's this?"

"Water! Well, water and a dash of something fruity. I absolutely hate drinking plain water. It's so fucking gross, right?" She smiled just as wide as Andy was back at him. Marjorie raised her eyebrows and wiggled them.

"How did ya'll get set up so fast? How long was I out for?"

"Long enough! We do this every day so we're used to set-up and tear-down. We might as well be robots with how fast we work!" Marjorie's face paint was fixed- no more cracks, chips, or pale flesh broke through the thick blue veneer of the paint. Her painted white smile was much brighter than it was earlier.

"That's pretty cool. So, what are ya going to have me do? Your grandma said she'd pay me to work tonight?" Andy asked and he took a sip of the water; it tasted of mildewed blackberries.

"Don't worry about it! We're all set up now," she answered and patted his shoulder. Her hand was thin and bony and Andy imagined her porcelain skin underneath the paint.

"Well, how am I being paid if I'm not helping? Am I performing?"

"Woah woah woah, slow down there partner! You've got your panties in a twist again. My grandma was right, you do ask too many questions!" She leaned over and gave his cheek a kiss. Andy blushed. "We decided, as a family, to go ahead and pay you anyway. You looked so peaceful sleeping that we certainly didn't want to wake you up! Now, why were you hitchhiking anyway?"

Andy took a big gulp of the water; it coated the back of his parched throat. The liquid danced on his tongue and his mouth was rejuvenated with moisture. He licked his lips, his throat no longer dry as dehydrated flowers. "Well, I got into a fight with my family."

"What about?" Marjorie asked while she cocked her head to the side.

"It's complicated-"

"Nope! You're not weaseling out of this question! Inquiring minds want to know," Marjorie interrupted.

Andy's neck and face turned scarlet red and he finished his drink. Marjorie yanked the old cup out of his hands and sat it on the lush green grass in front of them.

The sky was clear and painted with a few stars; the wind blew gently and rustled his brown, matted hair. "Got into a fight with the pops again. I had to dip out of town."

Marjorie nodded her head and shrugged. "I know how that goes, trust me! Living in an RV with your family isn't all sunshine and rainbows. What was the fight about?"

Andy clicked his teeth with his tongue and shook his head.

"Come on, you can tell me! We're practically family now," Marjorie leaned over and ran her fingers through his knotted hair, her spindly fingers caught in one of the knots. She retreated her fingers from his dirty hair and caressed his cheek gently.

Andy froze and looked around the park. "Got caught stealing from my pop's business. I needed the money for food."

Marjorie tutted and shook her head. "Poor thing! If papa decides to hire you full time, you'll never have to worry about food, drink, or shelter ever again! We stick with each other through thick and thin, no matter what."

Andy smiled and looked down at the ground. "When should we head inside?"

"Right now! The show is about to start and I don't want you to miss it!" Marjorie grabbed his hand and pulled him behind her.

"Really? There's no one here," Andy glanced around the abandoned park once more.

Marjorie ignored him and grabbed the tent flap and pushed him in. Inside there were several benches set up near the opening of the tent. The benches were finished with a fake cherry color and the stage consisted of a broken particle board thrown on the ground haphazardly. The grass was yellowed and dead within the tent and crunched beneath everyone's feet. To the left there was an antique blue popcorn machine with faded paint and no popcorn; to the right was a a small shopping cart with three blue balloons tethered to it. The shopping cart was filled with bags of blue taffy.

"There's no one here," Andy muttered under his breath as he stepped inside.

"I said don't worry about that!"

"Where is your family? Shouldn't they be setting up right now?" Andy walked forward toward the stage and Marjorie grabbed his hand and pulled him closer to her once more.

"My darling Andy, everything is already set up." At that moment her family filed into the tent behind them. Josh pushed Marjorie aside who had blocked the entrance.

"Glad to see that you're finally awake, Andy. The show is about to begin," Fred, said, speaking for the first time. His voice was deep and gruff, like the sound of pebbles sliding across gravel. He placed a hand on Andy's shoulder and guided him to sit on the bench in the front row. The rest of the family followed suit and sat down next to him. Marjorie sat next to him and grabbed his hand tightly; her hand was small in his, but surprisingly strong. Marjorie's skin was supple, not dehydrated as Andy had previously assumed.

"Here, let me take your bag from you," Fred said, reaching in front of Marjorie, motioning for Andy to give it to him. He did.

"Quiet now Papa, the show is about to start!" Josh squealed. Fred laughed.

"How is the show about to start when we're all just sitting here?" Andy asked. At that moment his stomach recoiled something fierce. It felt as though he had just dropped off the first hill on the tallest rollercoaster known to mankind. It grumbled audibly and bile rose in his throat and burned his esophagus. He wrapped his arms around his stomach, hunched over, and moaned.

"Just watch boy," Fred stated and reached over and smacked him upside the head. Ethel looked over at Andy and tutted; she rolled her eyes and looked over at Tim and Tom. She nodded at them and at once, bright lights showered down upon them. The lights were bright blue and danced around the room. The family soaked up the lights, their faces glittered. A big, deep, booming voice came over the speaker system that Andy hadn't noticed earlier.

"Welcome to the Turner Family Circus! My name is Tom and I'll be your host for the evening. First up, we've got Binny the Mysterious Clown! Now, I know he ain't much to look at, but he sure has personality to make up for it!" Fred's voice filled the tent.

Andy looked over and saw Fred sitting next to Marjorie; his mouth wasn't moving and he stared straight ahead. Andy opened his mouth to say something but Marjorie shushed him and placed a finger to her mouth. She pointed to the stage. His stomach turned harder than before and it became a battle of wills to keep the vomit from spewing forth.

"Do you have any water?" Andy whispered. Marjorie stared at the stage.

An old man that Andy hadn't seen before hobbled out onto the particle board stage. His face was painted in the exact same way as the family, blue skin and white smile, except the paint was somehow peeling in some places while still and running down his neck in others. His blue eyes were hollow and his arms hung by his side, not moving. He wore a robin blue shirt with big suspenders that held up matching blue pants. His mouth was closed and his glittered circular clown nose started to glow.

"Oooo, I love clowns!" Marjorie squealed. Andy focused his eyes on the clowns glowing nose; he took deep breaths and squeezed his hands into fists. The clown didn't move at all, just stood still as three glowing orbs appeared out of thin air in front of him. The orbs were dark blue and had a light blue fire that surrounded them. The balls moved up and down, in circles and in squares, up to the ceiling and down to the floor. One ball dropped and bounced along the particle board and disappeared. Fred grunted and the man shook.

Josh stood up and clapped, "I love it when he juggles!"

The two orbs in front of the old man started to dance around him; enveloped in with a blue sheen. The clown suddenly moved his arm, grabbed his big blue nose and honked it. Josh squealed and stomped his little feet into the dead grass. The old man's skin started to sparkle like college girl's shimmery eyeshadow, his white mouth glowed a luminous yellow, and his body began to shake like a cell phone on vibrate.

"Ooo, this is my favorite part!" Marjorie squawked. She grabbed one of Andy's fists and squeezed it tightly. Andy looked over at her, his vision started to blur as if he was tipsy on alcohol.

"Yay!" Josh yelled once more, his eyes never leaving the clown's face. Blue lights shot from the clown's eyes, nose, mouth, and ears and danced off of the old man's expanding body; his body vibrated loudly across the tent and his blue nose popped off of his face. Happy music blared from the sound system as the old man started to dance. The clown hopped around as glitter fell off of his body and lights danced across the tent. Josh started to clap when glitter flooded from the clown's nose and covered the decrepit stage. The old man wheezed and blue glitter spewed from his mouth and sprayed everyone in the tent violently.

"Again! Again!" Josh chanted. The clown cried tears of glitter and in a single moment burst into blue flames, which ignited the back of the tent in a blue fire. The light from the flames licked everyone's body and illuminated Marjorie's face.

"Wow that was absolutely astonishing! I wonder how he does that?" Marjorie asked to no one in particular.

"What…is…he…okay?" Andy coughed out; he doubled over and spewed bile onto the grass in front of him and drenched his worn black sneakers. His bile glowed green under the blue flames.

"Don't worry about old William here, he does this every night. He'll be back tomorrow!" Marjorie answered while idly rubbing Andy's back. No one looked over at him as he wretched yellow oozing mucus.

Ethel shouted, "Next is my favorite part! The acrobat! Say hello to Chastity!"

Everyone, sans Andy, clapped and cheered when Chastity walked onto the stage. She wore a bright blue sequined leotard with matching blue ballet shoes and opaque white tights. Chastity's blue face was as worn as the clowns and her blonde hair pulled into a tight sock bun on the top of her head. Her brown eyes were lifeless and didn't move to look around the tent; all she did was stare straight ahead as she began her routine.

"Hell yeah!" Fred cheered as Chastity's feet left the particle board and she hovered in the air. Her legs moved into a full split and she touched her toes in a mock toe-touch.

"She's so fucking sexy," Fred said.

"Papa, shut up! You can't say that, you're married!" Marjorie yelled.

"Your mother's been dead for a century, get over it! A man has needs and I want Chastity," Fred said and grabbed his crotch through his jeans; his dark brown eyes grew black as he stared at Marjorie. Her hand trembled and she continued to rub Andy's back.

"Yeah, yeah, okay, whatever," she whispered and rolled her eyes to the ceiling.

Chastity floated even higher into the air, spinning as if she was a ballerina at the Royal Opera House. The blonde bun shimmered under the blue-flamed light and her eyes stayed open and never moved as she twirled. The lights bounced off of her sequined leotard and enveloped the room in a disco-ball like light show. She stuck her arms straight into the air as her body moved in a mock cartwheel.

"I think I need to leave…" Andy whispered. He wiped the vomit from his mouth and onto his dusty shirt and stood up.

"Shhh…" Marjorie cooed, elbowing him in the stomach and pressing him back onto the bench.

The acrobat danced around the tent above their heads, doing a black-flip right above Josh. He cheered happily and tried to reach up and touch her with his dirty finger-tips. She dogged his touch while she did a split leap over their heads. Chastity slowly lowered herself back onto the dead grass and completed a handspring; Fred stood up on his feet and clapped loudly.

"That's my baby girl! You're so lithe and smooth…" Ethel grabbed his arm and pulled him back onto the bench. Andy looked up at the right time to watch as Chastity's body exploded into blue glitter. Everyone but Andy clapped and cheered, hugging each other with their glitter covered bodies. Andy cried and whimpered; he moved his mouth but no sound came out.

"Oh dear, it looks like Andy is ready for his first performance!" Marjorie squealed as she pushed Andy off of the bench and into his vomit puddle.

"We don't have an outfit for you just yet hon, but don't worry, tomorrow night you'll have the right attire for the event!" Ethel stated.

"Jesus Christ, do we have to watch him perform covered in vomit?" Fred asked.

"Now go on and stand up," Marjorie commanded. Andy's body did as it was told; the tears dried on his face leaving a streak of bare face against the glitter covered cheeks. His knees cracked and his back straightened.

"Go onto the stage," she commanded again.

Andy walked onto the particle board; the wood groaned. He stood there and stared at the family in silence. His once vibrant brown eyes and ruby cheeks were as grey and dull as dead fish that washed up onto shore. He no longer smelled of body odor and vomit, but of blueberries and cinnamon.

"Have you decided what his part will be?" Ethel asked Marjorie. She stared over at Andy and cocked her head to the side for a few beats.

"Yes, he'll be the elephant!"

"Yay! I love animals!" Josh screamed.

Indoor People
Cayce Osborne

This autumn night is like something out of a movie—a romcom from the 90s starring Meg Ryan, probably. Rays of sunset light filtering through the burnished trees, the smell of cider in the air; so perfect it feels contrived. But I'm not Meg Ryan. My feet ache and my hair is pulled into a limp, hasty ponytail as I hurry after my two boys, eager for our annual Halloween door-to-door pilgrimage. Brody, dressed as the Incredible Hulk, is eight and stoic. Charlie, a little gray mouse, is five and timid. All night I've been waiting at curbs and leaning on fences (calling after their masked heads: Remember to say thank you!) as they charge up and down every set of front steps in a four-block radius.

I can't remember the last time we had good weather for Halloween. Two years ago, we were treated to a foot of snow. I took the kids out in boots and snow pants, costumes tugged over parkas and masks over stocking caps. Passing other families on the sidewalks, all of us lumpen, disfigured creatures of the night.

Despite Wisconsin's appetite for weather-related cruelty, it's gorgeous tonight. And the trick-or-treating has been easy, almost languid. As we approach our last house—the new neighbors—I'm tired but gilded with nostalgia. There is a special magic in shepherding your own kids through a tradition you remember fondly.

The boys' pillowcases stretch to the ground with the weight of their booty. Brody, confident in his older brother role, leads the way to this final front door. The entrance is outlined in plastic ghost lights. He punches the doorbell with a foam Hulk fist. The round button glows like an orange eye in the darkness; it is a gatekeeper, glaring. Charlie tries to shove his way in front as the boys jostle for prime treat-grabbing position. They calm when I step up beside them, the angry buzz of the bell echoing behind the door—reverberating like it's traveling down the throat of a cave rather than through the avocado halls of a 70's pre-fab.

I put on a neighborly face, the only costume I've worn tonight. The new resident (Hot Neighbor, I've dubbed him) and I have crossed paths a few times, chatting briefly while retrieving our cans on trash day or waving as we raked leaf piles toward the curb. We aren't well acquainted enough to politely ignore each other yet.

He's a single parent, like me, with one child I have yet to see. He hasn't told me this—I don't even know his name—but neighborhood gossip has filled in the blanks. The elderly busybody across the street told me she saw an elaborate crib and a neon green climbing dome being unloaded from the moving truck, followed by Hot Neighbor carrying a not-toddler but not-teenager-sized child into the house. The kid clung to his chest, covered with a blanket. It was dirty, with a scatter of rainbow polka dots—the blanket, not the kid.

During my last curbside run-in with Hot Neighbor, I mentioned my boys like to play on the swing set in our backyard when the weather is nice.

"You guys are welcome to join anytime," I said, hoping the catch-all guys would make up for not knowing names, or whether he had a son or daughter. A shameless attempt to get more details about him, yes, but also an honest invitation. My kids are not great at making new friends, and a built-in buddy next door had serious playdate potential.

He held my gaze a beat too long, unblinking, and shrugged: "We're indoor people."

I remember that brush-off as he opens the door, and my face flushes. His house smell—aggressive lilac air freshener masking a hint of rotten egg—wafts toward me. I force my feet to stay put; they want to step back but politeness holds me steady.

He recognizes me and a smile spreads across his features like a puddle of syrup on a plate. Sticky sweet.

"Howdy neighbors! Nice costumes, boys." He brandishes a bowl of full-sized candy bars, bicep bulging under the weight: Snickers and Take 5s and Butterfingers. The boys choose one and then look up at me, seeking permission for gluttony.

Before I can give it, he does: "Why don't ya take one of each kind?" They grab before he can finish speaking. "Both of y'all, yeah."

I bite down on an apology. Some days ice-breaking my kids' way through the world is too much, and I need to let the small stuff go. On this golden Halloween night, when permission to be greedy is implied, it's all small stuff.

"You look like you could use a little trick-or-treat too, neighbor." I'm distracted, busy monitoring the boys' manners, when I realize he's talking to me. His speech is full of broad Midwestern vowels, incongruously twined with a honeyed drawl—Matthew McConaughey if he'd moved to Green Bay as a teenager. Or an alien who learned to speak human by watching episodes of Fargo and King of the Hill.

The combination, like everything else about him, shouldn't be charming but is. I sink into each word, quicksand drawing me below the surface. His eyes are a rich brown. As I look up at him his smile widens and his eyes glow, irises pulsing the same orange as his doorbell. It's the lights hung overhead, I tell myself, and the Halloween spook in the sugar-laced air. Nothing more.

From inside the house, a television rises to full volume, canned applause pouring from tinny speakers, before falling back to silence. A rollercoaster of sound, fitting for the evening's funhouse atmosphere. I can't see past him into the house, but not for lack of trying. His position in the wood-paneled entryway blocks anything, or anyone, behind him. The fake flower smell intensifies. I breath through my mouth.

"Did you and—did you guys go trick-or-treating?"

"Naw. We like to stay in. See all the costumes that come to the door, ya know." Gaze still glued to mine, he reaches into his back pocket to retrieve something and extends his fist toward me, over my boys' heads.

They're debating what candies to eat first.

"Mom's rule is, we get three tonight," Brody reminds his little brother. "You should pick all big ones." He points to the full-size candy bars, his half-mad grin already anticipating the oncoming sugar rush. "That's what I do."

"A treat, for you," my new neighbor says. An urgency in his voice tells me he's irritated my attention strayed. I put my howdy-neighbor costume back on, and smile up at him. As a reward, he peels open his fist, finger by finger, to reveal an expertly rolled joint the thickness of a No. 2 pencil.

I haven't smoked since I had kids, but I'm compelled to take it—politeness and a need to seem cool are equal motivators as I scoop it from his palm. A zing travels from fingertips to groin as our hands brush. The sensation lingers.

The boys want to go home, ramming my hips and knees—the back of a tiny skull, hair mussed by mask elastic, butts my stomach. I nod farewell to the neighbor, stepping backward.

"Appreciate it," I say, the joint now clutched in my own fist. I raise it in salute. Not wanting to go but having no excuse to stay. I trip over Charlie's feet as we retreat. So much for looking cool in front of Hot Neighbor.

We're halfway up our driveway when the whining begins: "Mom-my! My mask is gone."

I look at Brody, still fully Hulked. Charlie's moony face glows in the night, cheek smeared with something sticky and blue that tells me he's already snuck a piece of candy. He's wearing the furry, gray mouse suit my ex-mother-in-law sewed for him. A pair of ears, their pink insides like tongues, sit askew on his head. His mask is nowhere to be seen. I pull open the corner of his pillowcase, turn around to search the shadowy driveway and sidewalk behind me. Nothing.

"When was the last time you had it?" I mentally retrace our steps, but I don't remember seeing him without it all night. "Think."

"I don't know." The whining kicks up to a higher pitch. He's tired. "Thinking hurts my brains!"

"Ok, ok, let's go inside. You can pick your candies, and I'll come back out and look for a little bit while you're eating."

Charlie trudges into the house, pink felt mouse tail rasping on the cement behind him.

I dump their hauls on opposite ends of the living room rug and paw through, on the lookout for anything odd or unwrapped: lumpy popcorn balls, homemade peanut butter truffles, stray pieces of candy corn. When I've cleared any suspicious treats, negotiations begin. Twizzlers traded for Laffy Taffy, Whoppers for Milk Duds. Brody picks up a tiny box of SunMaid raisins from next to his knee and tosses it into Charlie's pile. It stays, unnoticed.

I leave, knowing they will sneak-eat more candy than allowed (also a Halloween tradition). Jogging down the sidewalk the way we came, there is no sign of the mask. A light gray plastic shell with a rosy tint on the cheeks and pointy nose, it should stand out among the crunch of fallen leaves and dying grass like a fractured bone poking through skin.

On the walk home, I steel myself for the battle that bedtime will surely become. I study Hot Neighbor's house as I pass. The ghosties around the entrance are no longer lit, and the eerie doorbell has gone dark. A few lights glow from somewhere deep inside the house, but my eye is caught by the front right window, a deeper black square in the night's darkness. The longer I stare, the more certain I am I've just missed a flash of movement. A twitching curtain, perhaps, or a shadowed figure receding deeper into the black.

There is nothing, now. Probably never was. I've seen too many macabre decorations tonight. Spooky houses with cardboard graves and fog machines and dangling skeletons and papier-mache bats. I'm manufacturing terrors where there are none. As usual. Single motherhood is full of sinkholes and boogeymen.

My house feels empty. The front door draws closed behind me, creating a vacuum of quiet. It's never quiet while the boys are conscious.

"Boys? Where are you?" The ice maker dumps a load of cubes into the waiting freezer tray, making me flinch.

No one answers.

Heart lurching with pure wrongness, I run to the living room.

There are my boys, still half costumed, mouths too full of chocolate and caramel to answer. In their candy thrall, they likely didn't even hear me. Charlie gives me a gooey smile and my pulse slows. His teeth are outlined in brown liquid. My stomach lurches, remembering a similar sight from childhood: my chew-addicted Uncle Alvin, spittle cups left all over his house when he'd visit for the holidays. His diseased grin, and the time I drank from one of his cups thinking it was my root beer.

"Bedtime!" I announce, shrill in the too-quiet. I'd planned to let their sugar rush die off before wrestling them under the covers, but the sudden need for a break from the weight of motherhood, to be alone, to shrug off the day, is too much. "Now. Let's go!"

The tooth-brushing ritual takes an eternity, but this is not a night we can skip. I take their toothbrushes in my own hand when they finish, scrubbing the bristles over candy-coated molars. There is no way they are settled enough to sleep, so I confine each to his bedroom with a warning to play quietly until they feel sleepy. Divided, their frenzy will die much faster than if they were feeding off each other.

"School tomorrow, remember," I say, inwardly cursing the mid-week holiday. "I'm gonna lock the house up and put some stuff away and I want you to be ready for tuck-in when I get back."

I pad through the living room—stopping to steal a candy bar from each boy's pile and a lighter from the shelf next to the candles—and sneak out the back door to our small brick patio. It's not until I'm breathing night air again that I realize I've decided to smoke the joint. Perhaps I'm hoping Hot Neighbor will be in his backyard doing the same, and we'll see each other, gazes colliding, holding for too long, and he'll give me that ooze of a smile, and... I don't know what. But something.

Beyond our back fence a wide greenway runs along the highway. On this Halloween Wednesday I expect traffic to be lighter but should know by now, after living in view of I-39 for three years, that this roadway is a living thing. Blood always pumping, throat always roaring.

I light the joint. When the smoke clears, I look toward Hot Neighbor's house again. A low row of scraggly bushes runs between our properties. His backyard is empty, the house gone full dark. Each window a square of black velvet. His sliding glass door is wide open, exposing the innards of the sleeping house. No—my eyes are playing tricks on me. It's closed, surely. He probably just keeps his door glass a lot cleaner than mine. Our neighborhood isn't dangerous, but everyone still locks up at night.

I take another puff and relax onto a plastic lounge chair, one of the last things my husband bought for the house before he split. I watch the highway; the passing of cars is hypnotic. I wait for the pot to lull me further, deeper. I eat a tiny Twix and consider the Three Musketeers still in my pocket. When I reach for it, I realize I've already eaten it. My stoned giggle drifts toward the sky.

Is that a hint of sulfur I smell? No, just the pot smoke, drying my eyes and hanging thick and fragrant.

The scream of a passing semi and the hiss of its air brakes make me jump. In its wake there's a reprieve from the traffic, a furrow of silence. I watch the place on the highway where the truck has disappeared from view and a small figure materializes in the exhaust. It is standing on the far side of the road, outlined against the concrete noise barrier that protects the upscale neighborhood opposite mine. My stomach plummets at the thought of any living thing—an animal standing on its hind legs, a tiny adult, or oh-fucking-hell, a kid—attempting to cross the interstate. I jump to my feet.

Do I wave, or will that entice them to cross?

Do I yell, even though the chances of being heard at this distance are slim?

I bounce on the balls of my feet, heart pounding.

The figure shimmers like hot pavement and I squint, taking a few steps closer, trying to pull more details out of the night draped between us. A pale, glowing face; the sodium vapor lights show me a curve of cheek and a high forehead. Stubby legs—a little kid, maybe three years old, unless my eyes are tricking me. A solid, barrel-shaped torso, with the adorable sturdiness unique to toddlers. I'm mid-yard now, next to the boys' outdoor play structure. A breeze pushes the swings and their rusty chains squeal in protest. I rub my scratchy eyes but it doesn't help. My vision blurs.

A line of cars snakes along the highway, no gap big enough for me to see though. I lean against the chain link fence that marks the back of my property, watching.

When the road clears, I blink away what my brain can't quite process: the figure is halfway across, climbing on top of the median. Pacing back and forth along the narrow cement wall between the two directions of traffic. Its every movement telegraphs frustration, impatience. I feel its need to cross further, to come closer.

My head shakes back and forth along with each step: No. No. No.

My initial assumptions were both right and wrong: the figure is small, yes, but not childlike. Its movements are deliberate and practiced, lacking the frenetic reflexes of a child adjusting to a growing body. The arms are overly long, like a sloth's; shaped like human arms, but stretched to funhouse proportions.

And—oh, jesus—I could swear it's wearing…

I stare down at the joint still burning between the tips of my fingers.

What the hell is in this stuff?

I retreat to the corner of the house, stubbing the joint out in the bare dirt of a planter, my failed effort at growing a hibiscus. If something can't yell at me to feed it, I can't seem to keep it alive. My husband was the gardener.

I don't let myself look back toward the highway until I've sat down again. I inhale deeply through my nose, out through my mouth, willing my head to clear. But the figure is still there, closer now, in the middle of the greenway on my side of the road. Moving in my direction. Coming closer. The only barrier between us is a 15-year-old chain link fence, permanently buckled from the annual press of drifting snow.

Even though this child-sized thing walks upright, it skitters—insectile and unnervingly swift.

As it nears the fence it gets down on all fours, long arms becoming extra legs, and crouches. Preparing to jump.

I bolt to my feet, hand on the back of the lounge chair for support. Without it, I would collapse.

It's true, what I saw before. What I didn't want to believe.

That thing is wearing my son's mouse mask. Without the rest of the costume—the cutesy, furry ears and bulky gray suit—the mask is terrifying, vulgar. The sculpted, rouged cheeks like an antique porcelain doll's. The un-doll-like mouse nose, more of a snout, comes to a phallic point in the center, a pink bulb perched at the end. A thatch of black whiskers sprout from each side, splayed like spider legs. There are no ears or hair peeking from behind the mask, no hint of humanity. It looks like an inanimate costume come to life.

It has seen me watching it. It has noticed. The mask's eyes are black holes. Their bottomless gravity is trained on me. Only me.

It pulls itself to standing again and one spindly arm raises, claws curved like tiny, deadly scythes. It grasps for the top of my fence, and misses. Lurching forward, it tries again.

This time it does not miss.

I stumble backwards—no, no, no—and crash into the siding, the house's bulk a comforting presence against my trembling spine. The sliding door is off to my left, but I'm frozen, the thing's soulless gaze pinning me in place. It nods, and a flash of glistening white shows through the mask's shifting mouth slot.

Gnash is the word that springs to mind.

The better to eat you with, my dear.

That's all I need to get moving. My hand scrabbles at the door handle, the scraping of fingernails a desperate sound in the crisp night. The masked thing raises its claws in a wave, and I have to stop myself from guessing what sound those talons would make—whipping through the air, tearing across my skin, striking bone.

I hook my thumb around the door handle, unwilling to turn my back on the creature, wrenching my hand and wrist painfully as I slide the door open.

I dart inside and slam it behind me, flipping the lock and pulling the blinds closed. Running through the house to the front door, I pray I remembered to lock it. The thing appears at the side window as I pass, mask pressed against the glass, claws splayed on either side of its head. No way it should've been able to get there so fast, or to track my movement through the house from outside.

Not if it's...human.

I laugh at myself, a crazy, fear-soaked cackle. No way in hell that thing is human.

Yes, hell. That's exactly right.

The front door is locked. We're safe. It can't get in.

Can it?

I inch back toward the side window, trying not to make a sound. The hell-thing is gently headbutting the window with the mask.

Tap, tap, tap.

I pull all the curtains closed, flip on every light in the house, huffing in relief once I'm done. I'm back in a sane space (I tell myself). A bright, familiar world. Home. Where stubby demons with clawed forelimbs don't exist. Where Halloween is made-up silliness, a childhood nirvana complete with endless candy, all treat and no trick.

I hurry toward the bedrooms. The gap under Brody's door is dark; he must have put himself to sleep. Charlie still has a light on. Wrenching sobs drift from his room. I open the door to see what's wrong. He's in bed, curled into a ball. He wraps sweaty arms around my neck the minute I kneel next to him, burrowing his wet face against my collarbone. One of his night terrors, probably. Charlie's little boy smell—part damp fur and part grass clippings, like a puppy—is comforting. Almost enough to convince me everything I've seen tonight is a drug-induced hallucination.

By the time we're both calm again, I can't keep my eyes open.

It was the pot, right? Or whatever else the joint was laced with?

And the Halloween atmosphere, and the poor sleep the last three nights, and the tumultuous year of divorce and drama. Everything, converging, making me crazy, making me irrational. Making me the person my ex insisted I had become.

I skip my usual face-washing routine and brush my teeth quickly, trying to remove the skunky flavor of pot from my mouth. I pause in the hallway; listening for tapping, for the scrape of claws on the outside of the house, for the creak of a door. The night has gone silent, except for a faint…something. I tell myself it is the wind playing with the swing set.

I change into my pajamas, ready to put this night behind me and dive into the oblivion of my prized pillow top (I fought hard for it in the divorce) when Brody's door opens.

"Mom?" His voice is as thin as a blade.

I hang my head in surrender, preparing to meet whatever nighttime crisis has woken him.

"You found it!"

"Found what?" I say as he rounds the corner into my bedroom.

He's holding the mask.

"Charlie's—"

I knock the mask out of his hand and stomp on it. Smashing the memory of that skittering, impossible, nightmare thing. The thing that was wearing it and now is not.

"Mom! What are you doing?" Brody is looking at me like I've gone mad—because I have, I must be mad to be thinking what I'm thinking, to have seen what I've seen and believe it. "What in the H is wrong with you?" He's yelling now.

The light blinks on under Charlie's door.

Well, shit.

I can't form words, not even to tell Charlie to stay put or beg Brody to run, because there is something behind Brody now, a shadow, stretching grotesquely down the hallway. Long arms. Coming closer. The shadow is tall and thin, but I know better. I know when it reaches us it will be small and vile and deadly with claws for hands and gnashing fangs for teeth.

But there is something I don't know. Something important, and terrifying.

With the mask smashed under my feet, I don't know what face the hell-creature will be wearing when it finds us.

I slip into the hall and open Charlie's door, shoving Brody ahead of me, slamming it when we're all inside. I push the dresser across the room to block the doorway. Charlie screamed when we barged in, one staccato shriek of surprised fear, but now he's grinning like we're about to have a family slumber party.

I turn to Brody. "I—I need you to listen, now. For serious." He nods, eyes like headlights on full beam. "Take your brother and run. Don't let him out of your sight, whatever you do, and don't come back to this house unless I bring you back here myself. Out the window now, hurry."

One advantage of living in a ranch is that all the bedrooms are on the first floor. I ease open the window and help the boys through, lowering them quietly to the ground. One at a time. Their sweaty little hands slip through mine, and I let them go. It is the hardest thing I've ever done.

"I want you to run," I remind them, my upper body hanging out the window. "Quick like bunnies." Brody opens his mouth to ask questions, but I cover it with my palm. "Do not stop until you get to Ms. Nelson's house at the end of the block. You know it right? The one with the yellow front door?" She'd been Brody's first-grade teacher. "Pound on the door until she lets you in and—and don't stop for anything else. You hear me? Not for anything or anyone. Go."

I don't ease back inside and pull the sash down until they take off, Charlie's wide eyes turned back toward me as Brody pulls him around the side of the house to the front yard.

I am alone. Or, more precisely, I am the only human left in the house.

Into this pool of silence drops a single sound: claws, skittering against the bedroom door. Relief pumps through my heart and floods my extremities because that thing is still here. It didn't follow the boys. They will get away. To safety, to survival.

I need to keep it that way.

Keep the thing here, with me.

The claws go still and my terror flares. The creature is no longer content to wait. Its need pulses through the hollow laminate of the door. I move the dresser out of the way and put my hand on the knob.

"Trick or treat, asshole," I whisper, flinging it wide.

Waiting for me in the hall is the last thing in the world I expect.

Hot Neighbor, leaning casually against the wall next to the boys' framed school photos, sexy grin on display.

"What the actual fuck?" I scream in his face.

His grin slips. We all wear masks, and for a minute, I see behind his.

The rotten stench of sulfur chokes the hallway, making my eyes water.

He collects himself; the grin returns. "Sorry neighbor. I tried to keep him indoors. But ya know, when he takes a shine to someone, there's not much I can do."

The last thing I hear is a sharp clack, the bone-on-bone collision of teeth, as my hot new neighbor steps aside to let his little creature take me.

Caretaker of a Thousand Houses
Mark Wheaton

"Vaccination card, Edwin."

"Sorry," I say, taking the laminated card from my pocket and holding it up for Gina to scan. "Anybody ever checks these?"

Gina scoffs and waves me into the grocery store. The place is immaculately clean. The shelves are full of food and every item is perfectly faced. Yet there's not a single customer.

"How long did this take you?" I ask, nodding to my reflection in the waxed floors.

"I did all that yesterday," she says. "No one's been here since except Alvis to pick up deliveries. What do you need?"

"Cleaning supplies."

"You bring me anything? Or are we heading to Aisle 3?"

I hand over a canvas bag. Gina looks inside at the pile of fresh zucchini, two kinds of cucumbers, three kinds of tomatoes, and kale I harvested from my garden an hour earlier.

I expect a compliment. She jeers and holds up a zucchini in a gloved hand. "I haven't finished eating the ones you brought last time!" she exclaims.

"You can store them," I suggest. "Chop it in a food processor, press out the water, then freeze."

"My sister's down in Bullhead," she says with a shrug. "Maybe I'll bring her some. Follow me."

She pulls a cart from a rack marked 'sanitized' and rolls it over to me before leading me to the back of the store. At the height of the pandemic, people still thought that protected them.

"What're people even ordering these days?"

"Junk," she says. "Cereal. Frozen pizza. Chips and more chips. Soda. Cookies. When we get produce, it sits then goes in the dumpster. At least we're saving Summerlin South's rat population from extinction."

It's my turn to scoff. Three years ago, Summerlin West was Las Vegas's fastest growing suburb. Subdivisions with names like Copper Place, Timber Creek, Mill Run, and Champions Forest sprang up in a matter of months lined with thousands of nearly identical, beige and stucco, three- and four-bedroom modular homes. Though the houses cost nearly a million apiece, Vegas's economic boom seemed to suggest they'd be snapped up before even the foundation was poured by investors, snowbirds, and folks fleeing the housing gluts in San Francisco and Los Angeles.

Then came the pandemic.

Now the subdivisions stood empty with only a handful of full-timers and as many renters. Given the downturn, the casino hotels and condos closer to the Strip used rock bottom prices to lure tourists, all but killing Summerlin West's prospects.

Which makes my job as the assistant property manager to a large percentage of these houses that much easier despite being asked to listen to the occasional sob story about crashing property values wiping out someone's savings.

"You have any occupieds this week?" Gina asks as we reach the back.

"Six. Three families, two couples, then a single."

"A single that'll turn out to be twenty teenagers throwing a rager."

I grimace. Despite Red Rock Properties' best due diligence, this happened twice this past spring.

"Nah, it's some professor who travels a bunch," I counter. "All five-star customer reviews from past hosts. Seems legit."

"Professor of what? Meth production?"

"Hope so. Think he'd trade for zucchini?"

Gina laughs and leads me through the swinging doors to the stockroom. While there are cleaning supplies out on the shelves, the good stuff is in the friends and family cage. I grab various detergents, several bottles of spray disinfectant, bleach, and a several sleeves of wipes. Gina zaps each with her wireless scanner. I pay with Red Rock Properties' credit card.

"Indrani's birthday is tomorrow night," Gina says as she helps me load the supplies into my truck. "Any chance we can bum a pool?"

"To throw a 'rager?'" I joke.

"It'll be like six of us," she says. "No one'll go inside. Backyard only."

"Use 2674 Morenga in Fairmont East," I say. "Security camera is still busted. The street number backwards is the gate code."

"You're a sweetheart," she says, loading in the last box. "You're invited, of course."

"Nah, gotta get my strawberries in the ground," I say, realizing immediately how lame I sound.

"Strawberries, huh?" Gina says. "You really can grow anything out here, huh, Edwin?"

"Trying to," I admit before heading off.

I've been into plants since I was a little kid in my grandma's garden back in Texas. She taught me how to cultivate things like Virginia creepers and sunflowers. I got so good at it, I started selling cuttings and seedlings at garage sales. After high school, I got into the biochemical engineering program at University of Nevada, Reno hoping to go into biofuel as I've always had a knack for creating robust corn strains. But like with Las Vegas real estate, the pandemic came along and busted my plans. I ended up taking the property management job in Summerlin West.

"It's lonely work," Red Rock's owner, Carlos Ruiz, told me during my interview. "You're basically a concierge for a thousand empty homes. Sounds easy but after driving up and down those empty streets day after day, week after week, wishing you had some client in your ear demanding more toilet paper or something, you start to crack up."

"I work with plants," I'd admitted. "Used to long silences."

"What kind of plants?" Carlos asked as if my future depended on it.

"Corn?" I replied with a shrug.

"I hate corn," he said, then started me at $15 an hour.

Red Rock oversees the five largest subdivisions in Summerlin West: Wimbledon Estates, Duncan, Fairmont East, Fairmont West, and Crescent View. They're like the five points of a star with nothing in the center except a couple hundred yards of scrubland. There are around 200 houses in each. Carlos has gardeners, maintenance workers, and housekeepers to look after the day-to-day chores, including keeping up the long-term empties.

I handle our rare occupants.

After leaving the grocery store, I head to a house in Duncan. A pair of women in their forties checked out this morning. They're to set the alarm when they leave which sends me an auto-text. I go in first to make sure the place is in order. See what supplies need to be restocked. Check if anything's been stolen or damaged, then I call our housekeepers who get it ready for the next occupant.

Unsurprisingly, the women left the place in impeccable condition. I've noticed this with a number of our renters. Because of the recent pandemic, they're extra careful to clean up after themselves. They're mindful of the next guests and even avoid going into rooms they don't need or using too many appliances.

I glide through the house like a ghost, checking every drawer and cabinet. Searching for things that aren't there. Being a plant guy, a term I use as it's feels comfortably ambiguous and somewhere between gardener and actual botanist, I'm used to noting minute differences from day to day. Maybe that's why I'm good at my job.

I'm done in twenty minutes and alert the housekeeping service. I'm about to head back to the office when Carlos calls.

"I shut off the gas at the house on Kolesnik this morning when I installed the new hot water heater," he says. "I relit the pilot on the stove but forgot the one in the heater. Not that I expect the guy to crank it up when it's already 100 degrees outside, but can you go by and relight it before he arrives?"

"He" refers to the professor. It's already noon. Check-in is now. If he's on time, I'll never make it.

"No problem," I say anyway.

Kolesnik Street is at the back of the Crescent View. It's only five minutes away but singles tend to check-in the minute they're able. I'm two blocks away when my cell vibrates. It's the auto-text telling me the alarm at the Kolesnik house has been deactivated.

It wouldn't be that big a deal if not for the virus. We have a "pandemic guarantee" that promises our renters that no one has gone in for seventy-two hours before their arrival. Of course, Carlos was there all morning installing a water heater, so that's moot but the client can't prove it. If I roll up and explain why I need access, he can ask for his money back.

No need to make trouble.

There's a large beige RV parked in front of the house. I'm about to pull past it to do a U-turn when a tall, thin man in his late fifties emerges from the side door carrying a couple of boxes. He eyes me curiously. He's probably wondering who would be coming down a street otherwise completely devoid of life. No cars in any driveway. No trashcans at any curb.

"Hey, there," I say, pulling up the curb. "Welcome to Summerlin West. Wanted to make sure you had everything."

He makes a show of putting on a mask which guilts me into raising my own.

"I'm all good," he says. "Place looks perfect. Street's pretty empty, though. Anyone else around here."

"Not at all," I say. "You've got almost the entire subdivision to yourself. If that's too lonely for you, I could probably mo—"

"No, that's perfect," he interrupts, prompting me to think Gina may be right that he's a drug cooker. "I'm all for peace and quiet."

"Not here for the gambling?"

"Nah," he says, scoffing. "Spent a bunch of months in the national parks, but they're starting to fill up again. This looked my speed."

"Yeah, we're our own little island out here," I say. "Enjoy your stay. Let me know if you need anything."

"Sure thing," he says. "What's your name?"

"Edwin Penck."

"Tom Moro," he replies. "Take care, Edwin."

I nod and head away. The rest of the day's check-ins arrive over the next couple of hours. I get calls about extra bed sheets and how to use TV remotes. It's easy stuff. Five o'clock rolls around and I head to my little paradise in Fairmont West.

Fairmont West went up the fastest of the subdivisions. Which means, the houses there are the most screwed up. Crap electrical work. Crap appliances. Windows put in backwards. Pools without working filters. In one of the houses, the plumbing work was so shoddy it erupted one day and flooded the house with sewage. It destroyed all the flooring on the first story and seeped into the walls. It was slated to be torn down and rebuilt, but that still hasn't happened.

The thing about shit no matter what the source is that it makes for really strong fertilizer. Once it was understood that the house would remain unoccupied, the gardeners mowed the front yard for appearance's sake and left the rest alone. At some point, I was next door and looked over the fence. The backyard was filled with wild, uncontrollable plant growth. The combination of sun, sewage-rich earth, and the automatic sprinkler system no one remembered to turn off had created an Eden.

I snipped the wires to the security camera overlooking the backyard and commenced to planting, the apartment I rented in Spring Valley having no yard of its own. In six short weeks, I harvested my first tomatoes. Even better, I transplanted some of the corn strains I'd been developing up in Reno, keeping my hopes alive I might one day return to my research.

As the sun sets now, I take the strawberry plants I've been growing in a window box from the truck along with a spare hose and weave from the front yard to the back. Southern Nevada is unmercifully hot during the day but cools into a desert by night. If you're not on the hook for the water bill, a nightly soaking is all you need to keep things growing.

Two hours later, the strawberries in the ground, I lift a celebratory beer to my lips. My phone vibrates announcing a text. It's from Gina.

GINA: Something's going down in Wimbledon Estates. We can hear it all the way over here.

If Fairmont West is the westernmost point of the Red Rock subdivision star, Wimbledon is the point aimed north. I boost myself onto the rear wall and look over. Most houses are lit only by the uniform, second-floor security lamps that go after dark. One glows brighter. It's the house I installed one of the families in this afternoon. What were their names? Schroder? Schraeder?

Jagged shadows dance across the back of the home suggesting they're in back, likely in the pool. Nothing out of the ordinary.

EDWIN: What did you hear?
GINA: Don't know. Something moving.

That's when the motion activated security light in the backyard two houses up from the Schraeders goes on. Followed by the one next door.

Then the second-floor bedroom window of the Schraeder house explodes outward. Worse, something or someone falls through it. A scream echoes across the night.

I vault the wall and run toward the sound. There's movement and shouts from Fairmont East we well, likely

Gina and her friends investigating. There are more shouts from the Schraeder house.

Then three loud gunshots.

I throw myself onto the ground. I doubt anyone's shooting at me, but I don't take chances. There's a fourth shot. Somebody at Gina's yells something I can't hear.

Silence. All is still.

But only for a moment. The motion activated security lights next door to the Schraeder house glow to life. Then the ones next door. Followed by the ones next door to that. Someone is on the move.

A shadow, barely more than a strobe of black, appears on the wall of one of the houses before vanishing into the darkness of the scrubland between neighborhoods. Whoever it is, they move with surprising agility, likely juiced with adrenaline if they're behind these gunshots. A robbery? Who the hell knows?

The motion activated security light on the house four up from my garden comes on followed by the one next door. Whoever it is has come over to my subdivision. I press myself into the dust as more lights come on. When it's the light over my garden, I hold my breath.

I'm a good twenty yards away. Well outside its halo. But whoever it is has stopped. They're on the wall looking out into the night. How could they know I'm here? Did they see me?

There's a sound like rough breathing. As if something large and monstrous is back there, sniffing in the night air. Like a bear or a large hog. A wolf? I'd never heard of anything like that wandering in from nearby Red Rock Canyon, but it didn't seem human.

Maybe some junkie with half their brain gone on their drug of choice. I hold still, praying they don't see me. There's new shouting from the Schraeder house now. Red and blue flashing lights illuminate the scrub as the police arrive.

I finally turn to my garden wall. There's nothing there but night.

"Did you see anything in Wimbledon Estates last night?" Carlos asks the next morning when I check in at the office. He doesn't have to explain. The murders at the Schraeder house are all over the news. "Cops have been in here all morning looking at security footage, but I told them one of my guys might've seen something."

I shake my head. If I say yes, I'll have to explain not only about the garden but probably about how Gina and her friends knew the combination to the lock on the Fairmont East house. I'll be fired by midday and my garden, including my corn strains, plowed under by nightfall.

All that when the police already have our cameras, witness statements from people who actually saw something, and the crime scene. What am I going to add?

"They said the dad, Mr. Schraeder, got laid off a few months back," Carlos says. "There was some fight, probably over money. He went nuts. Got a gun from his truck and didn't stop shooting until his whole family was dead. How's that for a mess?"

"Not great," I agree.

"Worse, there's blood and brains inside and out," Carlos continues. "I put in a call to a trauma scene cleaning team from Vegas to come in once the cops release the scene. They do all the casino hotel suicides. Already said we'd probably have to replace the carpets."

"They see anything else?" I ask, letting this image settle in my mind. "On the footage?"

"Nah, they bitched about the quality of the video and said we should've had cameras inside the houses. Which, of course, is illegal."

"They look at any footage from the houses next door?" I ask, though I figure he would've led with, Oh, and they saw a giant, blood-covered bear-slash-junkie exiting the premises, too, but decided they'll pin it on the dad anyway.

Carlos shrugs. He's bored with the topic now that he's aired his grievances. I'm off the hook.

I stop by one of the unused desks out front on the way to my car. With so few renters, who needs sales agents? I login using Carlos's own password and check out the security footage myself.

I'm surprised to see the footage from the Schraeder's house missing. The police must have taken it as evidence but then what? Had Carlos destroyed it? Put it behind another firewall? Whatever the case, I can't get it. So, I click on the security feeds to the houses immediately east and west of the Schraeder house.

If possible, what's recorded there is worse. Instead of seeing a shooting directly, I catch it in bursts of light and passing shadows. There are reflections on a glass table showing the muzzle flash of what seems to be a shotgun and then a body, seconds later, flying through the upper window of the house as reflected in the still waters of the pool next door.

The body looks like an adult male. When there are more shots later, I wonder if it really was the dad killing his whole family. There are more moving shadows. One last burst of muzzle flash. Then all is still until the police arrive.

Never in the footage do I see a bear or a wolf.

I search the footage near my garden. There are more reflections. More moving shadows. Again, no junkie or no animal. It likely only stopped once and that was on the wall behind me. I kick myself for disabling the camera there.

I wonder if my mind was playing tricks on me. Spend enough days in the empty, sunbaked desert and something's going to give.

My cell vibrates. It's one of the families in Crescent View calling. I wonder if they've heard about the shooting.

"Our back door is jammed," a woman, Meredith-something, says. "Worked fine yesterday but now we can't get to the pool. Is there another way into the backyard?"

"I'll be right over," I say.

I arrive ten minutes later to a pair of little girls with disappointed looks on their faces, their moms behind them, staring through the front window. I wave, slide a mask over my face, and head around to the side. There's a gate, but I guess they didn't notice it or that the combination to its lock is in their guest binder. Oh, well.

I unlock it and head into their backyard. When I see the back door in question, it takes all my will power not to scream.

Long, deep gouges have been carved in the door, its frame, and even the cement stoop under it. The door is bent in several places and the paint torn off in strips. I've had to replace a few of these doors. They're galvanized steel. This looks like it was done with construction equipment or the jaws of life.

I run my fingers over the damage. A handful of short, yellow and black hairs come off into my hands. They're stiff and wiry like from a brush with steel bristles. I'm about to pocket a few when I notice I'm being watched by the family. I can't let them see this.

"Door's warped shut," I say as evenly as possible. "If you haven't unpacked everything, I can move you across the street. It's been empty for a few weeks. Sorry about the inconvenience."

The moms deliver a matching exasperated look. I take this as a yes and hurry away.

My whole body's shaking. I try to control my breathing to keep from hyperventilating. So, maybe I did see something—something capable of doing this. I have to call the police. No, I have to get this family to safety first then call the police. I try not to imagine what would've happened to these folks if whatever attacked the Schraeders came here next—

The professor. He's only four blocks away. If this would-be home invader were kept out here, his house would be next. I leap behind the wheel of my truck and drive over. *Please be alive,* I pray to no one in particular. *Please be alive.*

When I'm a block away, I turn up the alley instead of going to the front of the house. On the off-off-off chance nothing happened, I don't want to alarm the guy. I park a few houses down and head up the narrow lane.

It's broad daylight. I've been down this alley a hundred times. The same beige, empty, three- and four-bedroom prefab houses stare back at me as always, but it feels more ominous now. As if each had borne witness to something terrible but refused to give up their secrets.

Could a creature be hiding in one of them? Watching me even now?

I count down the houses until I reach the back of where the professor is staying. From the alley, I can only see the upper floor windows. At least they're still intact. I boost myself onto the back wall for a better look, hoping I've wound myself up over nothing.

But what I see next is far worse than any busted door.

The house looks as if it's been struck by a localized tornado. The backyard furniture is torn to pieces with half of it bobbing in the pool. All the first-floor windows are shattered. The back door is off its hinges. The security camera above it hangs limply from its perch.

What I can see of the inside is just as bad. All the furniture in the living room has been bashed to splinters. All the appliances and dishes from the kitchen lay broken on the floor. A group of teenagers handed bats and paid to demolish the place couldn't have done worse.

"Professor?" I ask the ruins.

There's no response. I picture his dead body beaten to a pulp in the garage or on the stairs. I want to leave. Let the discovery of the corpse be someone else's job. But I already screwed this up once. If there's a chance he's still alive, I can't wait for an ambulance.

I hop the wall and hurry into the house. The damage is even worse close up. The walls have the same deep gouges slashed into them as the back door of the other house. Glass crunches beneath my feet, though if it's from the shattered television, a window, or one of several smashed picture frames, I can't tell.

Something is stabbed through the door leading to the laundry room. It takes me a second to realize it's the bannister from the stairs. It's been torn from the wall and driven through the door like a spear. I don't even want to think about the amount of strength that would've taken.

Somehow, the front windows remain intact. The professor's RV sits at the curb looking untouched.

The stairs creak. I glance back. There's an animal there. It's huge. As a large as a bear but a different shape. It has the head and coloring of a cheetah but the bulk of something much bigger and stronger. Its claws are curved and thick like an eagle's talons. Its fangs are so long they protrude from its mouth to hang over its bottom lip.

I'm still marveling at the sight when I realize its stillness isn't fear. It's readying to pounce. A guttural growl echoes out from its belly as saliva sluices through its teeth and onto the carpet.

I run. It takes four long strides to get out the back door and twice that again to make it to the back wall. I hear it behind me, crashing down the stairs and across the broken glass. I have no illusions that I can outrun this thing, but my fear is in control.

I'm two steps down the alley when it vaults the wall. It's silent which is unnerving. There's no roar. No sign of anger. It's doing what predator's do when faced with easy prey.

My one hope is the truck. I make it to the driver's side door and swing it open. The beast-cheetah springs at the truck's hood, slamming its front paws into the windshield with such force it bashes out the safety glass. The creature awkwardly crashes into the front seat, baring its fangs at me.

I slam the door shut and keep going.

If I run through the neighborhood, I'll lead the thing straight to the two moms and their daughters as they switch houses. They'll be torn to pieces. My only option is to vault the subdivision's back wall and lead it away into the scrubland between neighborhoods.

In other words, open ground.

I don't look back as I break for Fairmont West. There are no occupieds there. It can feel free to tear me apart in peace. But hey, if the last thing I do on this planet is lead this monster away from a few innocent people, so be it. I can practically feel its claws stabbing into my shoulder blades.

It's not until I'm halfway across the scrubland that I look back. The monster isn't there. The only evidence that it even followed me is a dissipating plume of sand it kicked up as it ran.

I'm alone.

Terrified it went after the kids, I retrace my steps. I was exhausted but pick up speed as I go. My cell vibrates. Oh God. Is it one of the moms? I answer quickly.

"Hello?"

"Hey, man," says the easygoing voice of Professor Moro.

"Hey!" I say. "You're okay?"

"Yeah, yeah, guess you saw the damage—"

"You have to get out of there," I yell. "There's some kind of wild anim—"

"Yeah, sorry about my friend," Moro interrupts. "He can get a little rambunctious as you saw. But I called him off."

"Called him off?"

"Yeah, maybe you can come back and let me explain?" he asked. "Being that you're partly to blame for this mess."

"Blame?"

"Yeah, the Schraeders. And almost those two cute kids. Anyway, come over. We'll chat," he says. "But don't keep me waiting."

He hangs up. I stop running.

I glance around to any of the hundreds of empty houses within view. I could hide in any one of them. Call the police. Have them deal with Professor Moro and…whatever that thing is.

But something tells me it won't be so simple.

I wander back to the house on Kolesnik Street. Professor Moro is sitting on the steps of his RV sipping from a coffee mug.

"Think this meets the insurance deductible?" he quips, shooting a thumb over his shoulder to the house. "And I'll be long gone before you can charge my credit card or come after me. The past few years have taught me more than enough about how to disappear."

I scan the RV and the house, looking for signs of the beast-cheetah. For a second, I wonder if it's Moro himself.

"Why'd you call off the monster?" I ask.

"'Monster?'" Moro says with a chuckle. "You mean João? He's usually pretty docile and easy to control. What's amazing about cheetahs is they can run really, really fast as they've got that highly evolved respiratory system. Only, they can't do it for more than short distances. They overheat. Controlling João's environment is how I control him. The house stays somewhere around ninety degrees or higher, he's a happy kitten."

"You didn't control him last night," I say.

"That's on you, buddy," Moro says, tone all but freezing over.

"Yeah? How's that?"

"When I came by to check this place out two days ago, heater worked fine," he said. "Didn't come on last night, though. I put it together once I saw the new water heater. You were coming by to relight the pilot, huh, but I beat you here."

"I don't know what you're talking about," I lie.

Moro gets to his feet. He looks pissed. Despite being twice my age, he's wiry and lean. I still think I could take him in a fight. Then I spy the pistol in his waistband.

"Why don't you tell that to the family of five laid up in the Clark County Morgue?" he says. "I know you were out there last night. I'm sure the police would like to know that, too, especially if someone came along and poked holes in their already flimsy case."

"Are you threatening me?" I ask.

"Kind of?" he admits. "But I'm also hoping you might help me out. I looked you up. You're a scientist. Better yet, a geneticist."

"And you're a murderer," I say.

"No, I got cocky," he says. "Checked something once I should've checked twice. But I'll let you make it up to me. Come on."

He opens the RV door. A raise an eyebrow.

"João is inside the house under heavy sedation if that's what you're worried about," he says. "Now follow me before I wake him up."

I follow him into the RV. It's about as shocking as walking into his demolished house but for entirely different reasons. The outside looks like an old, past its prime motorhome. The inside looks like a state-of-the-art surgical suite with seemingly endless built-in cabinets and drawers, multiple refrigeration units, a number of computer and video screens, as well as several lights and multiple cameras set up over a long examination table.

"What is all this?" I ask.

"Watch," Moro says, tapping one of the screens.

A video appears showing a man about Moro's age sitting in a chair. It takes me a moment to realize he's in the RV, the chair being the examination table folded in a different configuration. He is hooked up to several machines and has an IV running into his arm. I only recognize a heart monitor and oximeter.

"João?" I ask.

"My great explorer into the unknown," Moro says.

João taps a pedal with his foot. Only then do I notice heavy restraints on his ankles and wrists. A brown liquid moves from the IV tube into his body. Nothing happens for the first second or two. João's face contorts but not necessarily from pain. His muscles shift across his face as if involuntarily. His skin color changes from tan to blue to slate gray then almost a translucent white. His flesh undulates and seems to cave in as if his skeleton has lost its structural integrity.

Now he's in pain. His face twists and warps as he grits his teeth in agony. His hair falls out. His organs become visible under the surface of his skin then fade. His eyes vanish. It reminds me of watching a sea cucumber turn itself inside out to eject its internal organs.

"What's happening to him?" I ask, realizing I'm more curious than horrified.

"Genetic alchemy," Moro explains. "Most people know that we shed close to 40,000 dead skin cells every minute. Almost 50 million a day. What they don't consider is we're doing that with all our cells, constantly reproducing and rebuilding, replacing aging cells with new ones in an endless and ongoing cycle. The DNA embedded in each of these cells tells it what to express. Is it a blood cell? Skin cell? Muscle tissue? Nerve tissue?"

On the video screen, João, or whatever João has become, begins to settle. New hair sprouts across his body. Rolls of fat bulge around his neck as his limbs shorten.

"What we discovered in our research was a facility by which we could not only make this entire process of cellular reproduction happen all at once but also how to recode their DNA to express something new," Moro continues. "Through that, a new hybrid emerges."

I expect to see the cheetah-monster on the screen, but it's the wrong shape. It has cloven hooves, a short snout, and a vast belly. Its eyes are small and beady. Its forehead is sloped and its brow thick.

"You turned him into a pig?" I ask.

"Into an incubator," Moro corrects, switching the video. "This is two weeks later."

The surgical suite is covered in plastic sheeting in this video. Moro, in scrubs, opens up Pig-João's lower torso. Rather than two kidneys, Pig-João appears to have eight. Moro removes six of them.

"These were transplanted into half a dozen people across the country," he explains. "While pig kidneys injected with human stem cells are often modified for transplant into human patients, there's a high rejection rate. None of ours were rejected because each was as a perfect genetic match. It was as if the patients replaced their own diseased kidney with a spare they didn't know they had."

"That's…incredible," I say, meaning it.

"Humankind will owe us such a debt one day," Moro says, marveling at his handiwork. "You don't need invasive technology and expensive technology to advance the species. Nature has long given us access to all her tools. We simply had to learn how best to use them."

He flips between several video streams showing people of all ages going about their daily lives. They're with their families. At work. Celebrating birthdays. One is even running a marathon. It looks like some kind of car commercial.

"Our patients," Moro says. "They were all going to die without our help. We saved every last one though many in our field refuse to approve of our methods."

"Pigs tend not to kill people," I say. "Why the change?"

"That's a product of our current moment," he says. "We've endured a pandemic that may have killed hundreds of thousands around the world but is leaving in its wake millions of survivors with all kinds of unheard-of respiratory issues. With more airborne pathogens surely around the corner, the need for lung transplants is already outstripping the demand for almost all other organs combined, particularly when so many need both replaced to resume a normal life."

"And what better lungs in all the animal kingdom than a cheetah's?" I offer.

"Precisely."

I feel like I'm in a strange dream. As Moro explains it, everything seems perfectly logical and in its place. Admirable even. Except for the slaughtered family.

"That's the difficulty of going it alone," Moro says as if reading my mind. "One careless error and lives are lost. Which is why I need your help. I need an assistant. Someone who understands the risks but also the endgame. We're on the cusp of an earthshattering breakthrough. It's not only about the lives we can save today but the millions we can save in the future. We are the caretakers of the future. The research we do in this ridiculous RV could well lay the foundation for an entirely new branch of medical science."

He waits for my response. There's a part of me that wants to say yes. That knows I'm looking at something otherworldly and as impactful for the coming future if not more so than my fledgling biofuel research.

"There's too much risk outside of a controlled environment," I say, shaking my head. "People died. Shouldn't you at least take the time to reconsider your safety protocols?"

The light goes out in his eyes. In that instant, I realize the Schraeders might not be the first to die. Moro nods. "I understand your reluctance. There are other ways you can help my research."

He takes a step toward me. I look to his gun but instead see a reflection of the syringe he's holding behind his back in his right hand. I plant my hands on the cabinets on the opposite sides of the RV, swing both my legs back, and kick him with all my strength. He flies backward, nailing his head on the driver's seat. I launch myself out the door.

I get maybe two feet when the sky darkens overhead. It's João, the cheetah-beast. Rather than sedated, he's actually waiting on top of the RV. His teeth are bared, his claws protracted. He leaps at me.

I drop and roll to the side. Somehow, he adjusts in mid-flight and land on me anyway. I raise my arm in time for him to sink his fangs into my wrist instead of my throat. Blood splashes across my face as he claws at my chest.

I scream. I try to wriggle free, but he's too heavy. I punch the beast in the side of the head. It doesn't let go. I hit him a second time and the jerking motion rakes his teeth down through my flesh. No one's calling him off this time.

I get an idea and sweep my legs around as quickly as possible. I'm not trying to kick the cheetah away but to knock him off balance. It works. The beast's hind legs buckle. I roll over as quickly as I can and smash the back of my head directly into its face.

The creature flinches back, blood erupting from his nose. I pull away as best I can and manage to get out from under him. I have to make a split-second decision. I won't get away on open ground this time. I fly toward the house, praying the front door is unlocked.

I'm through it less than an instant. But before I can slam it shut, João springs at me. His claws miss my torso but hook into my leg. I spin around screaming. The pain is tremendous. I kick at the paw reaching in between the door and frame until it lets go. I kick the door shut but know it won't hold long.

I remember what brought me here the day before and get an idea. I limp to the kitchen and turn on the burners on the stove then blow out the flames. As I yank out a drawer to look for matches, João smashes through the front dining room window.

The drawer is empty. Damn.

João leaps into the kitchen only to slip on the slick linoleum floor when he lands. Doesn't matter. I'm three steps to the back door. Only every third house has a propane barbecue grill. Red Rock tries to rotate them to make sure the occupieds have one, but I didn't get around to it with the professor's house which means there's only a one in three chance there was one already here.

I reach the backyard. Bingo. Propane grill. I thank my lucky stars as I duck alongside it, spin the gas valve below, and ignite the burners. Then roll it toward the house's open back door.

The explosion tears through the back of the house sending bricks and other debris raining down around me even as I'm blown into the swimming pool. I push myself down into the water, fighting to get to the deep end but am struck repeatedly by heavy objects. One blow to the head and I'll drown instead of getting torn apart.

Something large splashes down in front of me. It's João, his fangs bared inches from my face. I scream out a wave of air bubbles only to see it's only the cheetah's man's limbless torso. His fur has been almost entirely burned away. Several wooden splinters, each the size of a javelin, are embedded in his back.

I'm about to swim away when I notice something even odder about the cheetah's anatomy. It has female genitalia and no sign of surgical alterations.

The house is still smoldering as I clamber out of the pool. I hurry through the house, but Moro and his RV are long gone.

I go into hiding, picking an empty house in the dead center of Wimbledon Estates with windows looking out over every possible approach. Carlos calls repeatedly, but I don't answer. Even Gina texts to ask about the explosion. I tell her I don't anything. I clean and dress my wounds as best I can.

I call the police only to hang up before anyone answers. What am I going to say? The renter on Kolesnik Street had a guest that was half-animal that actually killed the Schraeder's? And now I've killed it? But no, Professor Moro is nowhere to be found and what-do-you-mean-did-I-actually-kill-the-professor? I was at a loss.

How do you report a crime when everything you say implicates yourself?

I have to think of a better way. I head to the kitchen, but the cabinets have little more than condiments and a couple of cans of chickpeas. Chickpeas? Really? I eat them anyway. I'm starving. I want to get to my truck, but it's trashed. Another reason not to call the police. I left my vehicle at the crime scene.

I'm really, really bad at this.

I plug my phone into one of the cheap, alarm clock chargers we put in every house and go online to see what I can find out about Professor Moro. There's plenty though much of it is out of date. Maybe I'm not the only one looking for him. Turns out he's from Montreal, did his undergrad work at McGill, grad at MIT, doctorate at

Caltech, and a post-doc work at UC Berkeley. Hm. Impressive. For several years after, he seems to have been at the forefront of genetic research, working in concert with groups like the National Institutes Health on stem cell research.

A Professor João Guimarães begins sharing credit for Moro's achievements around this time. He's from São Paulo and attended the university there getting a degree in molecular biology before joining Moro at the Berkeley Labs. About five years ago, however, the records end. There's nothing on what happened to Moro. There's a single reference on one of Berkeley's pages announcing that Professor Guimarães is on an extended sabbatical.

If I expected scandalous articles about scientists pushing the boundaries of ethics and facing censure, there are none. Maybe Moro overstated his enemies. Maybe he imagined them.

I wait all day to hear from Moro. By the time the sun sets, there's still no sign of him. I can't imagine he's actually gone. All I do know is I have to get out of here. I think about heading up to Reno, but if Moro comes looking for me, that's the first place he'll look. I want to avoid Texas as well to keep him from following me back to my family and friends.

My best bet is to rent a car and keep driving. Luckily, I'm already in Vegas. It takes me ten minutes and a credit card to rent a Honda online. I just need a ride to the airport to pick it up.

I consider an Uber but am paranoid about even that. If Moro is watching and sees a strange car heading into the Red Rock neighborhoods, he could follow it. So, I text Gina instead and ask if she can pick me up after her shift. I offer twenty bucks. She takes it.

EDWIN: Pick me up in Fairmont West, okay? Want to grab a couple of things from my garden.

GINA: No prob. Address?

I text it to her. Then I pass out on the bed for the next three hours.

When I wake up, the sun is down. I check my phone. Only calls from Carlos. None from Moro. It's time to go. Using the cover of darkness, I slip from Wimbledon to Fairmont to retrieve my all-important corn plants. I consider leaving them behind but know I'll regret it.

What had Moro said? We are caretakers of the future.

The night is silent and still. I stick to the shadows, avoiding the pools of light cast down by the streetlamps while also dodging the motion-activated ones on the backs of houses. I finally hear sounds when I'm almost to my garden and spy a number of work lights up at the Schraeder house in Wimbledon.

I make out a few hazmat suits. Guess the trauma scene team is already at work.

I slip over the garden wall and dig out the corn plants, placing each in plastic pots for transport. I consider asking Gina to stop by my apartment in Spring Valley to grab clothes, but Moro might be there, too.

For some reason, this reminds me of something he said. There are other ways you can help my research. What had he meant by that? I'd assumed there was some kind of poison in the syringe. What if it was something else?

"Edwin? Is that you?"

I'm so startled I almost jump over the wall. But it's not Moro. It's Carlos.

"Holy crap, man," Carlos says, stepping into the garden. "Whoa. This is all you?"

"Yeah," I say reluctantly. "How'd you find me?"

"Was worried about you!" he says. "Fire department found your truck near the explosion. Thought you might've gone up in smoke. Did what you said and checked other security camera feeds until I saw you come over here. You forget how to answer your phone on a day like today?"

"I'm sorry, Carlos," I say. "It's…it's been nuts."

"You're telling me," he says, staring out past the wall. "Aw, crap. What now?"

"What?" I ask.

"The trauma scene people are coming over here," he says. "Bet there's some new problem. Man, they're in a hurry, too."

I bolt upright. Carlos is half-right. The trauma scene team, maybe ten individuals in all, hurries across the scrubland from the Schraeder house, likely alerted to our presence by Carlos's voice. But they're not people anymore. They're on all-fours, kicking up dust as they come.

More cheetahs? I wonder. But then a strange, braying cry echoes over to us. It sounds like a cackling donkey. They're not cheetahs. They're hyenas. Their hazmat suits fall to shreds as they draw near.

"We have to get out of here," I say.

"What're you talking about?" Carlos asks.

But then he sees the first couple of hyena-people nearing the back wall. "Holy crap!" he yells.

We race out of the garden, through the gate, and to his truck. The hyenas are over the wall and hot on our heels by the time we get into the cab. I slide behind the wheel.

"Keys?" I ask.

"Ignition!" Carlos cries.

I start the truck and peel out of there as the first hyena charges the truck. It slams its head into the passenger side door with enough force to almost rock us over. A second hyena leaps onto the hood, clawing into the metal as it peers at us with black beady eyes over a toothy, terrifying grin.

I hit the brakes. It flies off.

"What are these?" Carlos asks, terrified.

I say nothing, wheeling the truck around and slamming into a third one as a fourth tries to bite out the left rear tire. It gets its teeth into the rubber and chomps down. The tire blows, but I spin the wheel and run over it. Its decapitated head rolls alongside us for a few yards before spinning away.

They come after us, running as fast as they can. After a block or two, they fall back.

"What's going on here, Edwin?" Carlos asks.

"I wish I knew," I say, exiting the subdivision.

The flat tire is so shredded now the radials send up sparks. I don't care. I have to get to Gina. Have to warn her about what's happening.

The grocery store is only a few blocks away. I pull into the parking lot even as Carlos looks around. "What're we doing here?" he asks.

"Warning my friend," I say.

"No, no, no," he says. "We have to get to the cops. Get a SWAT team."

He points to the Summerlin West police station on the other side of the street.

"Be my guest," I say.

He scoffs and jogs across the street. I hurry across the lot to the grocery store. Summerlin West is eerie enough when there's not another soul around. But the extreme cool of the night makes it seem like another planet after the scorching heat of the day.

I'm almost to the front entrance when I glance back to the police station. Moro's RV is parked a block past it, hidden on a dark street. I freeze.

A scream pierces the night.

A second later, Carlos's severed head comes flying out the front door of the police station. Blood spirals in every direction from the tattered skin that used to attach his neck to his torso. A thunderous whooping sound echoes out next. A half-man, half-gorilla clambers out of the station advancing sideways, knuckles against the concrete. What's left of a police uniform hangs from its body.

I expect more gorillas to follow but underestimated Moro. A veritable menagerie emerges next. One is part wolf, another has the wrinkles and horn of a rhinoceros, a third, the face of a tiger. The last one is bipedal but with the scales and snout of a crocodile.

They look right at me. I race into the grocery store.

"Gina!" I yell as soon as I'm in. "Where are you?"

No one responds. The vast, brightly lit building is as silent as the night. I jog down the aisles hoping to catch sight of her. Nothing. I get all the way to the produce aisle before I see a quaking mass of flesh, half-covered in fur, laying on the ground. It's Alvis, the store's delivery guy.

"Edddd…wwwiinnnn," he croaks.

"Jesus Christ," I whisper. "Alvis."

I kneel over him, unsure what to do. The front doors of the grocery store slide open. The beast cops enter, seeing me immediately. Alvis touches my foot with a weak hoof.

"It's not as painless without sedatives."

Moro steps out of the shadows near the stockroom door. Gina is beside him. His hand it tight around her neck. A syringe is in her arm, but the plunger is raised.

"Edwin?" Gina asks, voice shaky. "What's going on? Is Alvis okay?"

"He'll be fine," Moro says. "If your friend Edwin here agrees to help me. Then everyone goes back to normal."

"Like your partner, João?"

A ripple of recognition passes through the police behind me but also Alvis.

"What're you talking about?" Moro asks.

"I saw the remains of that cheetah-person," I say. "João's DNA may have been used to make her a cheetah, but I'll bet João's own body is long gone. How much of genetic material do you even have left? Or have you lost him in here?"

It's a gamble, I know. But the animals around me listen. Intently.

"I can get him back," Moro growls.

"Really? How long has it been since you've seen him?"

"Kill him," Moro orders the beast cops. "Kill him now."

The tiger-man lurches forward then stops himself. The other beasts don't move.

"Was I next? A new baseline host body to replace João?" I ask. "But every time you do it, that host's DNA sticks around a little, degrading and corrupting what's left of João's genetic code. You don't know how you'll get him back, do you? And you're so desperate you don't even blink when your ex-partner kills people."

"João, wherever you are in here trapped across multiple bodies, you're more human than Moro is now," I say, turning to the beasts.

The gorilla looks at his fellow animals then to Moro.

"You think evolution is a smooth process?" Moro asks. "Those who push it forward always do so on the backs of those left behind. It's always been that way."

The gorilla roars at Moro. The scientist, for the first time, looks scared. He turns his gaze to me, sneers, and pushes down the plunger on Gina's syringe.

"No!" I yell.

He shoves her forward and dashes into the stockroom. I race toward Gina, but the rhino knocks me aside as it goes after Moro. I fly into a display of bananas as Gina transforms. I try to see her, but the minute she's whole again, she disappears.

I rest my head on the floor, staring into the store's bright fluorescent lights. I hear a shout and an agonizing groan. Moro steps out of the stockroom, half his face missing, and several large gashes opened across his chest.

Gina, now half-leopard, follows silently behind him. When he drops to one knew, she bats at his neck with an outstretched paw and snaps his neck.

Five years later

"Good day, welcome to the João Guimarães Memorial Clinic, Mrs. And Mr. Dalmaso," I say, greeting our newest patient and her husband as they are offloaded from the Air Ambulance newly landed on our island's private airport. "I hope your journey was a pleasant one. Can get bumpy over the South China Sea. If there's anything I can do to make your stay better, please let me know."

Mrs. Dalmaso nods idly, still sedated from the flight. Her husband nods to the thick jungle surrounding the single runway.

"Are we safe here?" he asks. "When we flew over the island, I saw all kinds of wild animals down amongst the trees."

"Quite safe," I assure him. "We endeavor to create an equitable ecosystem here, one that balances the needs of the humans and all plant and animal life we share the island with."

He looks about to scoff when Mrs. Dalmaso pulls down her oxygen mask.

"Are you my doctor?" she asks.

"No, I'm the co-founder of the clinic and the head of its research division," I explain. "Your doctor, Dr. Chauhan, comes to us through an sxchange program on the mainland. To maintain our independence, we allow certain reciprocities with the nearest governments."

She seems satisfied with this answer. The Air Ambulance's pilot, Alvis, shuts down the engines and steps out of the plane, offering me a wave. He has chosen not to retain any of his goat DNA and is fully human again. Gina, now in the fourth month of her pregnancy, waves at him from her office window inside the clinic.

"Shall we?" I ask.

Alvis and I wheel Mrs. Dalmaso into the admissions center. "I've already checked and entered your paperwork," I assure the Dalmaso's. "All you need are your wristband trackers and you're good to go. They monitor you twenty-four hours a day and record your vital signs."

"Mine, too?" Mr. Dalmaso asks.

I nod, about to explain when we're joined by João.

"My God!" Mr. Dalmaso exclaims, staring up at the eight-foot-high horned beast. "What is that?"

João, who cannot speak, smiles warmly at Mrs. Dalmaso as I place a hand on his hoof.

"This is João," I say gently. "A dear friend and co-author of the procedure that will deliver your wife's new lungs and new heart to her. They are working within his chest at this very moment."

"His chest?" he asks, incredulous.

"Would you like to hear?" I ask.

Mr. Dalmaso recoils. Mrs. Dalmaso does not. João slowly leans forward, careful not to touch her with his horns, as he brings his chest to her ear. His twin ox's hearts beat as one, his chest rising and falling. Her eyes widen in amazement.

"But if my heart is within João," she says, "what happens to João after? Do you die?"

"Nooo," he whispers in a guttural voice, lifting a file from the receptionist's desk. He shows her a photo of a child inside. "I grrrrooow kiiiidneeeys. For booooy from Camerooooon."

Mrs. Dalmaso stares at João with new appreciation.

"Yoooou will doooo soooo wellllll," he says, putting a hoof on her hand.

"We will do so well," she says.

"We," he agrees with a grin.

João wheels her away, her husband in tow. I angle my ear in their direction, singling out her troubled heartbeat. It was erratic for a second or two but is now easing toward normal. I can hear its broken rhythm, what has brought her here in the first place, and am glad we can help her.

Her husband's heart betrays his anxiety. We'll have to do something about that though it's her maiden name and the fortune she inherited because of it that we hope to add to our wall of benefactors as we inch toward legitimacy.

Despite our best efforts, the world continues to spiral into chaos. Professor Moro was a visionary and right to believe that only the few would understand what had to be done, but he didn't think big enough. This isn't about creating hybrids to help the human race limp along. Instead, we allow natural selection to apply to all animals equally. This way only the strongest genes in not simply the species but the entire kingdom are allowed to face the challenges of tomorrow.

Only then will we truly be the caretakers of the future.

The God Whisperer
Richard Clive

The plan would go like clockwork. That's what Tucker had said.

'Easy money. They're scientists. They won't put up a fight.'

But now, sitting in the dark, in the passenger seat, sharing the beat-up Land Rover with two other men, Will had doubts—*big ones*.

"Fucking dogs," said Tucker, an ugly scowl etched into his thick features. Even in the murk, his knuckles appeared white as they gripped the steering wheel. "Nobody said shit about guard dogs." He slammed his meaty fist into the dashboard.

The engine ticked as it cooled. The headlights were off. Tucker nursed his knuckles. The Land Rover was parked on a hill beside a dirt track, beneath the black bulk of the Grampian Mountains, the car surrounded by a sea of strange-looking toadstools.

Above them the constellations glittered. The farm buildings were scattered sporadically across the valley below, yellow light leaking from the occasional window. The bone-white moonlight revealed two squat shadows patrolling the perimeter of the fences that enclosed the farmland.

Pacing back and forth, the dogs settled their attention on a corner of the fence that was parallel to the car, some twenty feet beneath them. The animals whined and yelped. Then they began to bark.

"They look big," said Jones from the backseat.

Tucker ignored him. His eyes were searching for a way around the dogs. There was none. One narrow drive served what had once been a farm, now protected by a heavy gate and looping barbed wire. The back way was the only way—down the hill and through the fence.

By their boxy-headed silhouettes, Will guessed the dogs were Rottweilers, but it was difficult to be sure.

"Fuck's sake," said Jones. "Will someone throw us a fuckin' bone?"

"None needed," grunted Tucker, producing a pistol from inside his black bomber jacket. "Roll the fuck over, Rover."

On their long journey north, Tucker had proved he was anything but the cool, calculated criminal he'd tried to portray. Despite the intricate planning, the drone footage and the maps, the man possessed a violent temper. When sheep had blocked a narrow country lane, Tucker's face had turned a furious shade of purple. Then their mobile phones had lost their signal, cutting off their navigation, causing the vein at his temple to pulse. When their route was eventually blocked by a closed road, he had erupted in a fit of incandescent rage, and Jones had narrowly escaped a beating.

Hot temper. Cold steel. It was a bad recipe.

Will listened to the barking of the dogs, took a deep breath, then reminded himself why he was here, and of who depended upon him.

Back in that grubby working men's club, it had been Tucker who had convinced Will to take this job against his better instincts. Because the gig seemed easy. And the reward was twenty fat ones. *Each.*

"Exactly what are they researching?" Will had asked whilst sipping a flat pint of beer.

"Mycology."

"*In English?*"

"Fungus," said Tucker. "American company. Discovered some rare shit. Look it up."

Will had.

The area was a site of special scientific interest. The facility was a small operation, set up to monitor, conserve and research the area's unique flora.

The deal: Break into the lab, obtain the fungal specimen and get the fuck out.

Tucker's contact had not divulged the details of what was so special about the fungus. That knowledge was useless, anyway, unless you knew what to do with it.

"So what's the big deal?" Will had asked, tearing pieces from his beermat.

"With the fungus?" said Tucker.

"Yeah."

Tucker scowled. "Who cares?"

"They synthesize that shit, you know, for new antibiotic compounds," said Will.

"I don't care if it's a cure for baldness, bowel cancer or fucking hemorrhoids."

Tucker was right, Will supposed. *Who cared?* If they got their cut, it was irrelevant. It wasn't even immoral, was it? Because these research companies were in it for the money. They'd sit back and let hundreds of kids die of some rare genetic disorder while they haggled over the price of pills.

Now Tucker fed bullets into the pistol's magazine, his thumb sliding in the ammunition with practiced ease. He snapped in the full mag and pulled back the gun's slide, his fingers precise and at one with the deadly mechanisms. For a second, Tucker's hand wavered and the barrel pointed at Will.

"*Christ*, would you keep that thing away from me?" shouted Will.

Tucker remained silent, but his eyes gleamed, as did the gun's black metal, reflecting the dim lights on the dashboard. Will knew nothing about guns. He'd once been to a firing range when he was eighteen or nineteen, but that was a long time ago.

What was that principle —*Chekhov's Gun?* The theory that if you introduced a gun to the first scene of a story, it would go off in the next.

Will briefly closed his eyes and sighed. Bloodshed painted his imagination in crimson shades. "I thought we agreed," he said, finally plucking up the courage to confront Tucker. "No guns."

Tucker looked up from the pistol. His eyes brimmed with disgust. "And how do you propose we reach those labs without being torn to fucking shreds?"

Beyond the dip of the valley below them was a short incline, which rose sharply before the land plateaued. The slope could prove problematic, even for the Land Rover, and they couldn't risk getting stuck, like cavalry in a castle's moat. They had to do this on foot, or not at all.

"Six staff," said Tucker. "Four men, two women. We stick to the plan: cut the fences, *shoot the damned dogs* and get what we came for."

"How do we know what we're looking for?" said Will.

"I'm sure the researchers will help us out once they know we're serious," said Tucker, waving the gun.

"The fungus, what did you say its name was?" said Will.

"The God Whisperer," said Tucker.

Sounded ominous. But didn't they all? Death Cap. Devil's Tooth. The Medusa Mushroom… Stinkhorn. It was something of a tradition, it seemed, to give fungi names that might appear in a children's fairy tale.

"If you use that gun, they'll know we're here," said Will.

"They *already* know we're here," said Tucker, gesturing to the farm buildings with a nod of his closely cropped head.

Beyond his pallid reflection in the windscreen, Will saw the front door of the largest building—the farmhouse—was open. A silhouette stood in the doorway. The man was holding a hand to the side of his head.

"And he's on the fucking phone," said Tucker. "We need to get in there, *now*."

Tucker exited the car, slamming the door behind him. Jones followed, clutching his baseball bat.

Will reminded himself why he was here by thumbing the screen of his phone, on which the gaunt face of his sister Jess appeared. Even without hair, Jess was striking, her baldness only serving to make her eyes sparkle all the more. Her three daughters hugged her waist.

Pioneering treatment in America was expensive, but Jess' girls needed her.

He had this.

Will opened the passenger door and stepped out into the brisk night. Soon these valleys would be covered in snow; there was already an eerie stillness to the land. A quiet wind blew, and he could almost hear the gentle sway of heather, the land whispering beneath the cold stars.

Reluctantly, he followed the other two men, all three of them treading on toadstools. These were evidently not the rare specimens they had come to collect—there were dozens, if not hundreds, of them. The land, Will guessed, must be particularly conducive to fungal growth, hence the presence of the rare and mysterious God Whisperer.

Tucker and Jones were already halfway down the rutted hillside. The grass was crisp underfoot, freezing in the November chill. They staggered sideways down and towards the fence and the raging dogs.

Tucker reached the fence and pointed the beam of his torch at the two muscular beasts on the other side. Their barking had now ceased. Ears back, hackles up, the Rottweilers crouched on their hind legs. The dogs' lips were curled back, revealing salivating jaws. Both animals emitted low growls, occasionally snapping their sharp teeth in the cold air.

Casually, Tucker raised the gun, pointed the barrel through the chain-link fence—and fired. The pistol crack echoed under the brittle night sky. The first dog whimpered and became silent. Tucker fired a second time before the other dog could escape, and the weight of its body thudded lightly on the frozen ground.

Jones was already working on the fence with a heavy set of cutting pliers, his breath frosting while he worked.

Will stood back, watching the action unfold in a dream-like state of disquiet. Two dead animals lay in the grass, bathed in the torchlight, tongues lolling, eyes bulging.

How far would Tucker go?

In the distance, the man in the doorway was still on his phone. Three people dashed from the surrounding white rendered buildings towards the farmhouse.

"Fucking fence," said Jones, struggling with the pliers.

"Hurry," said Tucker. "They're locking the place down."

There was a sharp snap, then another. "*Through*," said Jones, holding up a flap of loose wire.

Tucker ducked through the gap in the fence, stepping over the dead dogs. Jones followed. Will lingered last in line.

The dogs' blood seeping into the ground appeared black in the moonlight. Will wondered how much more would be spilt before this was over.

This was not how it was supposed to be.

In the distance a lone figure was running for the farmhouse, passing a procession of single-story buildings that Will understood to be either storage huts or laboratories. A piece of corrugated roofing, a rusted metal drum and an overturned trailer were the only reminders this had once been a working farm.

"Stop, or I'll shoot," bellowed Tucker.

The silhouette, lit in the gloom by a symphony of strobing security lights, was forty yards from the house's door and the man on the phone.

Tucker pointed the gun at the sky and fired.

The silhouette hit the ground.

Tucker briskly moved forwards, the pistol at his side. "Don't move," he shouted.

But the silhouette did. First, dog-like, it scrabbled on all fours towards the house, and then it was up and running again, arms pumping, heading towards the door, white coat flapping in the wind.

In one sweeping motion, Tucker aimed the gun and fired the semi-automatic weapon three times in quick succession.

The figure collapsed, falling forward.

The door to the farmhouse closed, shutting out the light from within. A second later, all the lights went out, every window turning black.

Will rushed towards Tucker and grabbed his brawny shoulder, spinning the larger man around. The veins in Tucker's neck were bulging cords. His eyes, though, were dull looking. He might have gunned down a deer, not a human being. For Will, even shooting an animal was a step too far.

"Fucking lunatic! You realise what you've done?" shouted Will.

All Will saw was the flinch of Tucker's thick bicep, and he felt the impact of cold metal striking his head. He staggered and fell as the delayed onset of pain hit him.

"You're either with us or against us," said Tucker, his imposing figure looming over him. The pistol was now at his hip. "*Decide.*"

Lying on the frozen ground, Will's head spun, and when he closed his eyes, the starry sky remained, white dots whirling behind the screens of his eyelids. He patted his temple, feeling for blood—it was dry.

"*Well*?" hissed Tucker.

"You... You *shot* them," said Will, struggling to articulate his words through the pain.

"Not without warning." Tucker shrugged nonchalantly and spat a ball of phlegm into the grass. "Get up—let's get this done."

Unsteadily, Will rose to his feet. Nobody was supposed to get hurt. They *had* agreed to tie the lab workers up, but only so they could make their getaway.

Tucker turned and marched towards the spot where the figure had fallen.

Will was bent over, hands on his knees, catching his breath, waiting for his sight to realign, when Jones put an arm around his shoulder.

"No use going against him," Jones whispered. "Got to stay calm, for all our sakes. Remember, it wasn't you. You never pulled the trigger. Let's get this done, and two days from now, you'll be sipping a cold beer on a warm beach. C'mon, man." Jones pulled him up straight by his arm. Will thought he might collapse. Didn't, but the world quivered.

Stood on the periphery of a sensor that activated a security light, Tucker's figure strobed, his long shadow lurching up against the side of one of the low farm buildings.

This side of the fence, the toadstools sprouted from the ground in even greater abundance. Will noticed their vibrant colors and how they covered the land like coral at the shore of some exotic ocean. They looked somehow alien in this bleak and beautiful land of thistle and heather.

When the two men reached Tucker, they found the girl writhing in the dirt, blood pumping from her thigh. She was in her mid-twenties, wearing a thick fleece over a white laboratory coat.

"Pl… please don't hurt me," she begged.

"We're here for the God Whisperer," said Tucker. "*Where*?"

She shook her head, panting, her breath misting. A strand of her blonde hair was plastered to her sweat-glistened forehead, despite the cold.

"Tell me," said Tucker. "*Now*."

The woman was hyperventilating.

Tucker crouched on one knee, grabbed her hair and pulled. "Listen, *bitch*. We're not playing games."

"Please, no," the woman gasped.

Again, Tucker yanked back her hair, twisting it violently. The woman's eyes bulged in their sockets, her skin pulling tight against her skull.

Still unsteady from the blow to his head, Will stormed towards Tucker, but the big man threw out a huge fist, thudding into his crotch. Pain seared from Will's balls, spreading to the tops of his legs and stomach. He collapsed onto his knees.

"Won't tell you again. *Last chance*," growled Tucker, cocking the pistol and pointing it at Will. Tucker lowered the gun, turned his attention back to the young woman and pulled her hair again. "Last chance for you, too, sweetheart. *Where*?"

Her answer was nonsensical.

Tucker pointed to the farmhouse. "*Keys*?" he said, patting her down. He found nothing. "If I have to kick down that door and murder every one of you, I'll do it."

But the woman was unable to speak coherently through her hysteria and pain.

Tucker hit her then with the pistol grip. Her head jolted on impact, and she flopped into unconsciousness. Blood poured from what had been a neat, little nose. He let go of her hair, and she rolled from his arms into a bed of toadstools.

"C'mon," said Tucker, rising to his feet and gesturing to the two other men.

From the cold ground, still wincing from the blow to his crotch, Will stared at the young woman. Left like this, blood leaking from her leg and nose, she'd be hypothermic in half an hour, if not dead from blood loss. Already her skin looked pale and mottled, like marble. Will took off his jacket, knowing he'd be leaving behind traces of forensic evidence, and wrapped it around her. Next, he took off his belt and fastened it around her upper thigh, like a tourniquet. He was conscious of cutting off her blood supply but feared not acting at all. He contemplated dragging her to one of the nearby buildings, but those, he guessed, were most likely locked. His thoughts were interrupted by gunfire.

Tucker was standing before the large farmhouse. It was no fortress, but Will wondered if the small windows and heavy oak door would keep intruders out long enough for the police to arrive. The nearest station was about an hour away.

He'd been stupid and naïve, blinded by pound signs and the promise that nobody would get hurt—blinded by the promise he'd made his dying sister.

Tucker fired a warning shot into the sky. "Open up," he bellowed.

No response.

Again Tucker shouted, his voice echoing across the valley. "Open up and no one else gets hurt!"

His request was met with silence. Only the cold wind answered, scattering rattling leaves through the carpet of fungi.

Tucker marched towards the cottage door and kicked it with all his weight. The door visibly buckled. He pointed the pistol at the lock. The gun cracked. He kicked the door. It bowed, rattling on its hinges, perhaps still secured by a second lock or chain from inside. But it made no difference. He kicked the door once more, and it crashed open.

Tucker's hulking figure strode into the house, screaming obscenities, waving the gun before him in erratic arcs.

***

Will could do little for the girl now. The best thing he could offer was getting this done quickly and efficiently. Please let her live, he prayed—and left her in the frost.

Shivering without his coat, he followed Tucker into the cottage and found a dark hall cluttered with sealed cardboard boxes that were stacked four high against the walls.

Tucker was a dim apparition bathed in the residual light from his torch. He stood halfway along the narrow corridor with its three doors, a scowl warping his face. He was pointing his gun at the head of a small, portly man with a thick moustache, who squinted back through the round lenses of his glasses. In his mid-sixties, the man was balding and wore a white lab coat. Behind him, the cowering heads of four of his colleagues crowded in the doorway of a small kitchen.

"We're here for the God Whisperer," said Tucker. His torch skipped across the crudely plastered, uneven walls, the darting beam scattering shadows, terrified faces leaping out of the darkness. The group shrank away from the torch, their eyes narrowing in the glare.

"Stay back!" shouted Tucker, concentrating the beam on the man in the round glasses. "Where is it?"

The man said, "You're making a huge mistake."

Tucker placed his torch on top of a stack of cardboard boxes, the beam pointing at the fat scientist. He patted the man down, searching him. From the left pocket of his lab coat, he took a jangling set of keys. He held the keys up by the binding ring so the man in the glasses could see them. "You're going to take us on a magical mystery tour," he said, gesturing with a firm nod towards the door and the nearest of the three outbuildings.

Tucker lifted the gun until its barrel was pressed against the dome of the man's head. "What's your name?"

The man looked at him, frightened but quizzical.

"Please, *no*!" screamed a woman from the kitchen.

"Shut the fuck up, or I'll blow his bald head off," shouted Tucker, jamming the gun harder against the man's temple. "*Name?*" he repeated.

"Mackenzie. Dr Elliot Mackenzie."

"Well, *Elliot*, here's what we're going to do: you're going to take these keys, and we're going to explore that lab," said Tucker, pointing out into the cold night air. "Any games, any at all, and I'll spray your brains in the wind. Do you understand?"

The doctor nodded. "Yes."

"Good. Let's go," said Tucker, picking up his torch.

Lingering near the front door, Jones stepped forward, gripping his baseball bat.

Tucker gave Jones a brusque nod and pointed to the group cowering in the kitchen. "Stay here. Take their phones. Any one of them causes trouble, smash their heads in."

"Got you," said Jones, readying the bat and directing his eyes at the shuffling crowd of bodies.

Tucker nodded at Will. "*You* are with me."

Mackenzie walked out through the door. Tucker followed with the gun jammed into the small of the man's back. When he passed Will, Tucker said, "I meant what I said. *Last chance.* Now c'mon, let's get this finished."

Tucker patted Will's shoulder, then pinched him hard before letting go.

***

The three men walked through the darkness, towards the lab.

Again, the wind whispered in the trees, as if conspiring against them, and Will had a strange thought. He wondered if the trees were listening to the erratic beat of his heart, to the thrum of blood in his ears, to the dry rustle of dead leaves. This remote wilderness possessed an eerie, even oppressive silence that was almost symphonic: a beat you could feel, not hear, in the land's inaudible echoes.

Mackenzie led the way, his white coat flapping gently in the breeze. It was obvious he was trying to stall their progress by walking slowly—too slowly for Tucker's quick temper.

Tucker jabbed the gun at the base of Mackenzie's spine, his fingers twitching on the pistol's trigger. Will feared the gun going off; he could see Tucker's teeth were clenched and knew it would take little to irk him.

"Move it," said Tucker.

Mackenzie did.

When they passed the young woman Tucker had shot and knocked unconscious, Mackenzie's mouth fell open. "No, *Jade*," he cried. He spun around to confront Tucker, who stepped back, but the barrel of the gun remained firm, pillowing into the doctor's soft belly. Mackenzie's face reddened, became a mask of exasperated fury.

"If she—"

"She's alive," said Tucker, barely looking at the girl on the ground.

Will checked, and she was, but her pulse felt faint, although he was no expert.

Scowling and turning towards Will, Tucker snarled, "Your coat—?"

"Was the least I could do," finished Will, meeting his scowl, and that's how they stood for several seconds, eyes locked, the night air charged between them.

Finally Tucker turned back to the doctor and said, "The quicker we get this over with, the quicker your friend gets help."

Mackenzie stared at Tucker with deep contemplation. Will could see the cogs of an intelligent mind working behind his eyes. After another long second, the doctor turned and walked towards the building.

The laboratory was one of three converted outbuildings. All were one story, narrow and crudely rendered in white. The door was PVC but solid.

"Open it," said Tucker.

Fumbling, Mackenzie rattled through the keys, searching for the right one, his eyes wavering momentarily back towards the girl. *Jade,* thought Will. He could almost still feel her gentle pulse on the ends of his fingers.

"Door," barked Tucker, reminding the doctor of his task.

Mackenzie placed the key in the lock and opened the door. He stepped into the darkness with Tucker following closely behind.

"Lights," ordered Tucker.

Inside, Mackenzie pawed clumsily at the wall, searching for the switch, tripping over some unseen clutter as he did. When the light came on, Will squinted against its fluorescence. The doctor's eyes blinked behind their little, round spectacles, and Will was reminded of Mole in *Wind in the Willows*.

The lab was one long room: no windows, white walls, polished tiled floors. A stainless-steel worktop ran the length of the room. The worktop was cluttered with expensive-looking scientific equipment, including some Will couldn't identify. What he did recognize was two pairs of binocular microscopes, a plastic bin-shaped container he guessed was a centrifuge and several laptops. A row of potted plants stood under ultraviolet light. The room smelled of chlorine.

"Fridges?" said Tucker, pointing to a row of three at the far end of the room.

The doctor nodded.

Tucker walked to the first fridge; it, like the neighboring two, was sealed with a push-button electronic lock.

"Open them," said Tucker, lifting the gun to the doctor's eye line.

"And what if I do? What if I open every damn fridge, and you don't find what you're looking for?"

Tucker prodded Mackenzie's forehead with the gun.

Turning towards the first six-foot-tall fridge, the doctor punched a four-digit code into a security panel before pulling the door open.

The fridge was packed full of glass vials, test tubes and stacks of petri dishes. Tucker barged the doctor aside and tore into the fridge like a lion into the belly of its kill. Wild-eyed, he searched, checking every label. Glass smashed, and boxes of supplies were tossed to the floor. Unsatisfied, he ordered the doctor to open the other two fridges. When the entire frenzied search was finished, he had still not found the specimen.

Tucker grabbed the doctor by his collar and slammed him against the last fridge, which rocked, tumbling more of its contents onto the hard floor. "Where is it?" he shouted, his face contorted, his feet trampling on a plastic dish, which split underfoot. "The God Whisperer?"

"I have told you—"

"Oh yeah, then we'll tear this whole forgotten shithole apart until I find it."

Mackenzie looked like he was struggling to breathe in the vice of Tucker's grip. At last Tucker eased the pressure, allowing the doctor to catch his breath.

Tucker stepped back, an insane grin splitting his face in two. "How old is that girl, your friend, outside, the one bleeding to death?"

"You bastard."

"My guess—twenty-seven?"

"If anything happens—"

Tucker slapped a hand over the older man's mouth and rolled his eyes upward in a pantomime expression. He removed his hand, rubbed it on his jeans. "No, I guessed twenty-seven because of the white coat. It makes her look older. Don't you think? Whatever you're doing here, I'm guessing you need a PHD—*right*, Elliot?"

Tucker, still holding the gun, nonchalantly scratched his head, sarcastically miming deep thought. "Do you know what? I'd say twenty-four if it wasn't for the coat. *Christ*, Elliot, she's young enough to be your fucking granddaughter, yet you're going to let her bleed to death, out in the fucking cold, like a pig."

Tucker's brief parody of feigned contemplation had given way to his fraying temper. His skin was flushed, his rage close to the surface.

The doctor blinked again, lightly shaking his head as if the situation had descended into hopelessness.

Tucker jammed the gun into the man's temple. "OK, you have three seconds to tell me where to find the magic mushroom, fat boy. If you've not told me, I'm going to blow your prized asset out of your head."

"I've told you—"

"One."

"It's not what—"

"Two."

"If it's money—

Tucker's finger slowly applied pressure to the trigger.

"OK," said the doctor. "*OK.*"

Tucker widened his eyes in mock anticipation.

The doctor said, "What do you think it is we've got here, some kind of cure for cancer?"

Tucker pressed the gun harder against the doctor's head. "Nice knowing you—"

Will hit Tucker a split second before the gun went off, knocking his aim askew and the bullet astray—it thudded into the ceiling above the doctor's head.

Possessed by rabid anger, Tucker turned on Will, spinning around with the weapon, but Will was quicker and knocked the gun from his grip. The weapon skidded across the polished floor and came to rest some five feet away against the base of the worktop.

The two men wrestled and fell to the ground, fighting amongst broken glass and the contents from the fridges. Tucker's breath was hot, sulphurous, tinged with cigarettes. The big man was trying to throttle him, pressing his thick thumbs into the base of his windpipe. Will's vision greyed out. So, this was it. The last thing he'd see in his brief existence was Tucker's grimacing face squeezing the life out of him.

No.

His fingers numb, Will fumbled on the ground and felt something sharp. He picked up the glass shard. His arms possessed the strength of a poorly stuffed scarecrow, but it was enough. He stabbed Tucker in his thigh. The hands that clasped his neck let go. Head spinning, Will gasped, then gulped at the medicinally tinged air of the lab, his throat burning.

Will dived and grabbed the gun before Tucker could recover. He spun around with the pistol as Tucker fell upon him, his hands impossibly large and reaching again for Will's throat.

But now it was Will who had the gun. He pressed the barrel against Tucker's stout neck, dimpling the skin. He put pressure on the trigger and Tucker backed away.

Using his last reserve of strength, Will kicked Tucker's legs from under him, striking him behind the knees, and Tucker fell to the ground.

Will panted in recovery.

On his back amongst the glinting glass, Tucker said, "You're going to mess this whole thing up."

"You nearly killed me." Will leaned against the worktop. It was then, still gasping, that he noticed the doctor edging along the wall towards the door.

"*Stop*," Will shouted. "Or I'll shoot the fucking pair of you."

The doctor was five feet from the door. Tucker was attempting to push his considerable weight from the floor by his palms when the expression on his face changed. He was now patting the ground excitedly with his bleeding palms, ignoring the glistening splinters of glass.

Tucker had found a substantial ridge in the floor. Will met the doctor's eyes. Mackenzie's wrinkled face was a map of defeat, all at once resigned to them finding whatever it was he'd protected so virtuously.

Tucker was hoisting up a section of the floor—a hatch. When the trapdoor was wide enough, Tucker picked up his torch, which had fallen out of his pocket during the fight. He first pointed the beam at the doctor in the lit laboratory, then jerked it towards the darkness below, motioning for Mackenzie to descend the ladder.

The doctor went first. Still holding the gun, Will went next, so he wouldn't have to turn his back on Tucker. As far as Tucker was concerned, though, the fight was forgotten. He seemed preoccupied only with his discovery.

They found themselves standing in a small room, nine feet square. It was dark but for a blinking security light on the wall next to a heavy looking grey door. Will understood the device and its light belonged to a retina-scanner.

Tucker inspected the scanner. "Can you open that?"

The doctor nodded dourly. "I can. But we can't go in there."

"We fucking can, you know," said Tucker.

"Hang on," said Will. He turned towards the doctor. "What exactly *are* you doing out here?"

Despondency darkened the older man's face. He sighed. "Take my word—"

"*Explain,*" said Will. This time he was pointing the gun. He had no intention of shooting anyone, but he had to take back some element of control. He sensed the doctor had already accepted defeat.

"You've noticed the toadstools?" said the doctor. "Out there?"

"I'm not blind. But they're not what we've come for, are they?" said Will.

"No."

"The God Whisperer, it's behind that door, isn't it?" said Will.

The doctor frowned. "You need to understand what you're dealing with."

Jess' face flashed in Will's mind. "You've got one minute to tell us."

"The flora in these parts is diverse," said the doctor. "The toadstools you see here are unusual. But the fungi you seek, The God Whisperer, is only found beneath the surface of the soil."

"Just open the fucking door, will you?" said Tucker impatiently.

"Let him finish."

Tucker eyed the gun in Will's hand and scowled.

"Have you heard the term mycorrhizal fungi?" said the doctor.

Tucker fidgeted. "We've not come here for a fucking biology lesson—"

"*Shut up*," said Will.

"In any ecosystem, fungi can be both parasitic and beneficial to other species and plants. Fungi are mostly made up of thin threads, known as mycelium. These threads colonize the roots of plants. But the mycelium doesn't necessarily harm the plants. Instead, often the relationship is symbiotic. The plants and fungus exchange water, nutrients and sugars."

Tucker blurted, "We need to get the specimen and get the hell out of here before—"

"Go on," said Will, ignoring him, prompting the scientist.

"The fungus forms filaments at the root," Mackenzie continued, "extending the plants' reach and creating an underground network, connecting every plant, tree and fungi in a radius of miles."

"*And?*" said Will.

"And we believe the local flora is sharing a lot more than nutrients."

"*Meaning?*"

"The God Whisperer's mycelium is supercharged. Science has long speculated that plants share information, a superhighway like the internet, using highly sophisticated electrochemical communication."

"Bollocks," said Tucker.

"True," said the doctor. "Experiments have already proved plants activate chemical defenses before an aphid attack. Plants connected by fungal mycelium respond when unconnected plants do not. The God Whisperer has colonized this whole area. Haven't you heard it, the land talking, *the whispering?*"

"You're talking shit," said Tucker.

"There's more," said the doctor urgently. "We've lost men… and women. If you choose to force your way into that room… unequipped, the consequences—"

"Tell him to open the fucking door, Will."

"So what is it, some kind of pathogen?" said Will. "Fungal spores or—?"

"No," said the doctor. "The fungus has communication… *abilities* well beyond our understanding. The plants, they're connected, and, as natural organisms, so are we."

"What do you mean?" said Will.

The doctor's eyes glistened in the beam of Tucker's torch. "The human brain, the command centre of our very being, the organ responsible for coordinating every sense, emotion, movement, every cognitive thought, is… vulnerable to this fungus in ways we don't understand."

Will's impatience flared, and he grabbed the doctor by the shoulder. "What do you mean?" he repeated. They were face to face, near enough that Will could see beads of sweat on the man's forehead, could smell the sour tinge of his breath. "Tell me," he said, pushing the other man back against the wall.

"Our minds—they're not what we once thought. Science has taught us cerebral function is the result of evolution, over thousands of millennia. But that's not all, not the half of it. Our minds exist far beyond the boundaries of our cranial cavity, far, far beyond." A pause. "We've been running a series of experiments… with the fungus."

Will frowned. "And?"

"*And* we've discovered something incredible. The brain is more than man's faculty of thought. Outside science, there is a transcendent belief we exist beyond the neurological limitations of our human condition—the question of what we are."

"And what *are* we?" said Will.

"*A radio*. The mind is a radio. Everything is connected. *Everything.* Like machines, our minds are electrical. Our minds are radios capable of transmitting thought, emotion, feelings, and so much more. But radios work two ways. Beyond that door is a transmitter too powerful to comprehend, and right now, the volume is turned up loud and the station tuned to Hell. If you go in there—"

The old man's eyes widened to saucers. Then Will felt a sharp blast of pain in the back of his skull, and he hit the floor. The last thing he saw was Tucker, holding the torch he had bludgeoned him with.

*

From the dark recesses of unconsciousness, Will heard an alarm. Slowly he opened his eyes, but his head throbbed, the alarm and its infernal bleat drilling into his ears.

The gun was gone, the grey door ajar, the two other men nowhere to be seen.

Will sat up. He was in danger. Tucker and he were no longer allies. The thug might have killed him with that blow to his head.

He remembered the young woman Tucker had shot. By now she was probably dead, had likely bled out in the cold, like a pig, as Tucker had so eloquently put it. His sister too would be dead. Because without this job, America was impossible.

Movement beyond the door caught his eye. A blue-siren light strobed cyclically, hurting his eyes.

Will stood on shaky legs, holding the wall for balance. When he'd steadied himself enough, he kicked open the door and saw the room and every terrible detail.

Lit in the swirl of blue light, it was the size of a basketball court. The walls, floor and ceiling were insulated with panels that looked like tough black rubber. But the rubber had been penetrated everywhere by thick, interlacing roots that joined in an entwined mass at the room's centre.

The mass was contained in a glass tank the size of a telephone box and mounted on a steel platform. The invasive roots were wrapped around the tank and had caused its glass panels to crack. The chamber was thick with spores that clouded the air like gigantic dust motes.

Will had no doubt he'd found what they were looking for.

The God Whisperer.

The thing was wrapped in a nest of bone-like growths. Its shape was too indistinct to be described as humanoid, but its trailing mycelium fell away from a vegetative mass, resembling legs. If the thing had a head, it was the grotesque flower that bloomed at its crown.

To Will's left, the doctor lay dead, a hole in the centre of his bald head, just as Tucker had promised.

Tucker himself stood before the glass tank. Where his eyes had been were two black holes. His dripping fingers suggested he'd torn them out himself. He stood in a blind, oblivious wonder. On the ground at his feet, next to the gun, were the jellied remains of his eyeballs.

Will stepped forward and picked up the weapon, fearing he needed protection. It was only then that he became aware of a clicking in his mind that was both random, nonsensical, and yet somehow more articulate than language.

But how could he hear anything whilst the alarm thrummed in his ears at such a deafening pitch?

Yet somehow, he knew, another much older sense had been stimulated, a more basic yet refined form of communication, an electrical impulse that all forms of life understood on a molecular level: microbes, viruses, bacteria, insects… human beings.

Will backed away from the tank and the thing inside.

Cracks spread in the glass as the thing sprouted its dreadful fruit, germinating more of its spores.

The spores hung in the air, drifting like thoughts.

Will's mind was filling with sadness. The clacking became unbearable. He thought of Jess and her girls. He thought of the cancer living inside her, the invader that could—*would*—now certainly kill her.

What a terrible world this was, a world where those beautiful girls would lose their mother.

The cracks in the glass tank spread, fracturing like Will's sanity.

Tucker rocked back and forth where he stood rooted to the spot, his hands still dripping with blood.

The siren's light swirled.

Will turned and ran out of the room. He scrambled back up the ladder, missing a rung and scraping his shins.

It spoke to him in the darkest recesses of his mind. Its mycelium had not penetrated the shell of his skull, yet the thing occupied his thoughts all the same, and it knew where his fear and his guilt resided. It told him things.

Jess was going to die.

Will ran into the frosted November night, back towards the Land Rover, forgetting Jones and everything they'd planned.

He reached the vehicle, his breath rasping, and gunned the engine.

The Land Rover thundered along mountain roads. The vast starry sky glittered above, and he pressed the pedal to the floor, clattering through the gears and careering through the winding country lanes, wondering over the infinite possibilities of the thing in the tank.

He turned up the radio loud, attempting to drown the *sounds* that occupied his head. But the God Whisperer played his mind like an instrument, a flute filled with a column of air, the vibrations living in his bones, *talking* to him.

Will stopped the car at a layby on a country lane.

He regarded his tear-stained face in the rear-view mirror. He couldn't escape the God Whisperer. Its mycelium had spread too far.

Will picked up the gun from the passenger seat and stepped out into the cold air.

The night whispered in his veins.

He was part of it now, wasn't he?

He put the barrel in his mouth, tasted the cold metal and listened to his infected mind talk.

"I'm sorry, Jess," he said, tears streaming from his eyes.

When he pulled the trigger, his thoughts flew free—together with the brains that spattered the frozen ground onto which his body now collapsed. His physical life had ended, but as his grey matter seeped into the soil, his mind went on, leaking into the network of roots, whispering under the cold and lonely stars.

Male of the Species
Tom Vandermolen

They met in a clearing by a fallen tree. He was ten years old. He never knew how old she was.

Martin Hewitt had spent most of that summer exploring the woods around their new house, but this tree was special. Even partially rotted away, it was the biggest tree he'd ever seen, and felt like a relic of some older, wilder forest. It had fallen long ago, created the clearing itself by crushing smaller trees as it fell, its roots ripping out a crater from the ground as big as Martin's bedroom. The fan of decaying roots was taller than Martin and made him think of a dead sea monster washed up on the beach, tentacles torn off or rotting.

Fascinated, Martin climbed onto the trunk and approached the root end, peering over the clay-caked root stubs into the pit they'd made. A few experimental kicks sent dirt clods tumbling into the pit.

A cricket, startled from its hiding place, leaped into the pit, landing near a hole in the side of the crater.

There was a blur of motion; the cricket disappeared, replaced by a bundle of white silk. Perched above the bundle was an enormous black spider.

A sound somewhere between a gasp and sigh escaped Martin's mouth. The spider's body was full and round, the size of a tennis ball, with long and graceful legs. Circling the top of its head were dark, glistening gems that Martin realized were eyes.

It was the most beautiful thing he had ever seen.

The spider filled his mind, made his heart feel trapped behind his ribs, like a bird trying to escape its cage. His hands shook from the need to stroke that black armor, to see if it was as cool and smooth and unyielding as it looked. To cup that ripe abdomen; he knew, absolutely *knew*, it would fit his palm perfectly.

The spider turned and disappeared into the hole.

Martin let out his breath. Then more kicks at the tree roots, until another cricket leaped into the pit, barely touching the ground before the dark blur was upon it. Another cricket-shaped bundle of silk disappeared down the hole.

This time, though, the spider re-emerged, lingering just inside its den. Watching him.

He fed two more crickets to the spider before it stopped coming back out of the hole. Even then he waited for nearly half an hour, tense as a hunting dog on point, before the stiffness in his neck and the darkening sky finally forced him to float home.

He didn't tell his dad about any of it, even as the words threatened to explode out of him and his heart kept transforming into that trapped bird. And the fact that his dad didn't notice how different he was now, how different the world had suddenly become, confirmed he'd done the right thing.

Dinner that night was meatloaf, and Martin ate three helpings.

***

Martin went back the next day. And the next. By the end of the summer Martin's butt had worn a smooth patch on the tree trunk.

School started and he spent the days staring at his teachers, waiting to go home. He began doing his homework sitting on the tree trunk, pausing every now and then to peek at the hole or toss in another treat. Being near the spider made him feel smarter. Better.

"Wow," his dad said, looking at his final report card of the year, "is school here really that much easier than back...in Maryland?" He'd almost said *home*, and Martin knew it.

"Sorta." Then, because Martin still hadn't fully forgiven his dad for moving them to Louisiana: "Also, there's no friends around here to distract me."

His dad didn't take the bait, but that was all right because Martin had lied a little: he had friends at school now, maybe even more than he'd had back in Maryland. People said things to him, and Martin said similar things back. But it was like having a boring conversation when your favorite song was playing on the radio—he was, always, really listening to the song. To his real friend.

And as he listened, the years—and the world outside the clearing—spooled past him in a detached blur, like when cartoon characters drove cars, the scenery outside playing in a loop.

Fifth grade was all insects. The supply around the tree didn't last long, so Martin's dad bought him cages of bait crickets from the little store down the road. Martin told him he was fishing at the small pond back in the woods.

By middle school, the spider graduated to mice and guinea pigs. Martin had planned to catch mice at their house using glue traps, but his dad's hilariously ineffective attempts to get rid of them had apparently, finally, worked. So Martin took on various odd jobs and became a regular customer of the local pet stores, where he was "that nice boy with the boa constrictors."

Graybow Junior High: ducklings, purchased three at a pop. He almost felt bad about those.

One late summer day, just a few weeks before the start of his junior year of high school, Martin walked through the woods, whistling, a paper bag in one hand and a large canvas sack slung over his other shoulder.

Just shy of the clearing, he stopped whistling and dropped into a crouch, stepping carefully to avoid dry branches and leaves. He padded quietly up the trunk and peered over the mane of roots.

She was waiting, of course.

"You could at least pretend you didn't know I was coming." He sounded exasperated but a pleasant warmth tickled his belly.

The spider tapped her two front legs on the ground. Her abdomen was now as big as a softball, her head half as large as that. Spread-eagled, her legs could easily reach across a serving platter.

Martin had learned a lot about spiders, and knew that a normal spider could not grow to such a size. Even if one somehow did, it would die almost immediately, the loser in a race between asphyxiation and the spider's own crushing weight. Spider physiology was not meant to work at such a scale, just as humans were not built to survive at the scale of elephants.

And yet, here she was. Martin provided for her, and she grew.

Sitting at his usual place on the trunk, he pulled a writhing bundle of fur from the sack. The kitten, barely two weeks old, meowed pitifully at him, and he used his index finger to gently rub it between the eyes for a moment. Then he tossed it into the pit.

There was a cyclone of whirling legs and silk, and the spider carried the kitten-shaped bundle back into the hole.

Martin smiled. Girls liked kittens.

He couldn't pin down exactly when he started to think of the spider as female. It could have been her size: female spiders were often larger than male spiders. But really, thinking of the spider as a male made him feel...uncomfortable. Like that whole "queerboy" business.

Martin got along with all of his classmates surprisingly well, given how little he thought about them. The exception: Fred Moran. Ugly, stupid, Fred Moran.

Fred was in Martin's class, and they both worked the same shift as baggers at the Piggly Wiggly. The day before, Martin had been carting out the groceries for one of their regulars, a smiling, gray-haired, grandfatherly type. His name was Mr. Bednarekford, but he told everyone, "Just call me Mr. B!" Martin liked Mr. B; he tipped well.

Martin had loaded the last of the grocery bags into the trunk of Mr. B's car when the old man leaned casually against the rear fender and asked, "So you know where I can get a decent blowjob in this two-bit town?"

Martin, whose only knowledge of blowjobs came from a few porn videos his friend Dave Halber had snuck out of his dad's stash, laughed and said, "No, sir. I guess if I knew that I wouldn't be standing here right now."

To Martin, Mr. B's comment sounded like the usual locker room stuff at school, and his own response had been pretty solid. But Mr. B's face went splotchy and red, and he slapped an extra-large tip into Martin's hand before driving away. Martin jogged back to the store, pretty proud of his banter game.

Fred Moran was taking his break, sitting in his parents' truck, listening to Hank Williams Jr. and nursing a lip full of snuff. He spat and shouted, "Hey, Hewitt, you earn that tip?"

"You bet!" Martin said, and Fred brayed that obnoxious, high-pitched laugh of his. Mystified, Martin entered the store to more snickering from the other baggers and check-out girls. Finally, one of the girls, Jill McCaffrey, took pity on him and explained that Mr. B had hit on almost all the bag boys at one time or another.

"Guess you were up next," she said, shrugging. Then she saw Martin's expression. "Aw," she said. "It's okay. Old guys make passes at me all the time. You get used to it."

At the end of the shift, though, Fred Moran walked past him and said, "Hey, Queerboy, want me to drop you off at Mr. B's house on my way home?"

A sudden roaring in Martin's ears drowned out the laughter of the others, and only one thing kept him from ripping that ridiculous hyena laugh right out of Fred's disgusting hole: an image of Fred, his head encircled by slender black limbs, fangs plunging in and out of his neck, the laugh replaced by a high-pitched scream.

He became aware of Jill's placating hand on his shoulder. "Don't mind Fred," she said, rolling her eyes. "He's just jealous because Mr. B never hits on *him*."

But Martin did mind. And now, watching the spider emerge from her hole, he wondered how deep that hole was. If there was, say, a Fred-sized opening among all those dessicated bodies.

"You'd like that, wouldn't you?" he asked her softly.

She stared at him.

He dug out another kitten, under handing it into the depression.

Dark blur. Whirling legs. Neatly wrapped bundle. Down the hole.

Martin almost pulled a hard-boiled egg from the paper bag, then winced and grabbed an apple instead, hoping she hadn't seen it.

In all the years he'd known her, the spider had never laid eggs. Not that he was around her 24/7 or anything; in fact, during the worst of winter she disappeared entirely into what he assumed was a state of hibernation. But he never saw egg sacs or little ones.

Recently he'd realized the topic made her uncomfortable, so Martin respected her privacy and avoided the topic. But the reasons were obvious: she was truly unique in this world. That meant no males of her species either, so no mating, no babies. It meant being alone, only connecting with others in a very particular, lethal way.

Martin had begun to understand he'd never have kids, either.

How could he, in a world filled with Fred Morans? People who hated uniqueness, who wanted to crush it, mock it from the safety of their boring little lives. Being unique was hard.

He saw her looking at him and his mood lightened.

"At least we're unique together, right?" He smiled at her agreement, bit into the apple.

***

By his senior year, Martin could walk to the clearing with his eyes closed. Today he was trying to do exactly that, eyes narrowed against the tiny blades of sunlight that cut through the treetops and into his brain.

He shut his eyes against the throbbing in his head and an image immediately flashed across the darkness: a jumbled collage of dark sheets, long tanned limbs, streaked-blonde hair, and shockingly pale breasts. His eyes popped open, and this time he welcomed the pain. *You deserve it, you idiot.*

First mistake: going to one of Dave Halber's increasingly infamous house parties.

Second mistake: losing track of his alcohol intake at the party. Halber's parents were like Bigfoot—legendary but rarely seen—and Dave had become an excellent and persuasive host/bartender.

Third mistake: getting isolated from the crowd with Jill McCaffrey, who, according to Dave, at least, had the hots for Martin.

And after that the mistakes came too fast to count.

Before he even realized he was drunk, they were in the Halber guest bedroom, Jill's mouth was all over him, and she'd already removed both of their shirts. Martin, too panicked to speak, was on the verge of punching his way out when Jill abruptly pulled her lips away from his neck, laughed, wiped her face with his shirt, and passed out.

Shaking, Martin sat on the edge of the bed, exhausted from relief and alcohol. He rubbed his face viciously with his palms, then turned and evaluated the situation.

Jill was motionless, miniskirt hiked up to her waist, snoring slightly. He turned her more on her side, so she wouldn't puke and choke to death.

Deep breath. What story would work here? Jill probably wouldn't remember much past the kissing, and everyone saw her pawing him as they entered the guest room. So...some second base-third base stuff happened, then Jill passes out. Martin, the trustworthy but otherwise totally normal heterosexual male, is frustrated but understanding. Her friends take her home. The word "queerboy" never occurs to anyone.

And Martin never, ever, goes to another Dave Halber party.

He nodded and looked around the room, trying to see it with a party forensics eye. He untangled her bra from one of the pillows and tossed it onto the floor. Then he picked it up and draped it over a bedpost. The miniskirt was fine as it was, hiked up to her waist. The question was her panties. She had started the process of shimmying out of them, and now they were down past her ass in the back, not quite covering her pubic hair in the front. That was good, but was it enough? Should he leave them on her, or take them? Sometimes girls left them behind, didn't they? Or was that a movie thing?

He pulled her panties down to her mid-thigh, examined the effect. Crept to the door and looked from there. Crept back and pulled the miniskirt's hem down a few inches, just enough to cover her private areas; some guy may come in before Jill's friends could cover her up, after all.

He nodded again. This could actually work. His reputation might even improve.

Five minutes, then leave. He sat on the bed, hating the feeling of being drunk, his senses and thoughts blunted and slow. He watched Jill, listening to her breathing for signs of congestion or retching.

He'd been staring at her for a full minute before he suddenly *got* how attractive Jill was. He had known this for a while, of course, but more as an academic fact. It was one of the reasons she was first on his list of girlfriend candidates, hitting most of the items on Martin's checklist: long blonde hair, a very symmetrical face, almost no acne, athletic body, popular without being obsessed with popularity. She wore yellow a lot, and Martin liked yellow. She was nice and easy to talk to. Guys talked about her a lot. Best of all, she had a "good girl" reputation, so would be unlikely to pressure him into sex. *Better uncheck that box now,* he thought, grimacing.

But it occurred to him now that maybe the checklist didn't really do her justice. That gymnastics-toned body, the long blonde hair and smooth skin. Now that he was really looking at her, he could see that she was...exciting. A feeling of discovery, of teetering on the edge of something unknown but thrilling, rose up within him.

Her bra and panties were matching black satin, with some lace trim. They had a soft, dark sheen in the dim light. He liked how black they were, how shiny. Like dark armor.

And he suddenly realized he had an erection.

It was not his first, of course; like most normal boys, Martin often woke up with an erection. He knew other young men were weirdly obsessed with theirs, but to Martin his erections were pointless biological oddities, like an appendix.

But now, something about the sight of Jill's panties, that glorious intersection of smooth, tanned skin and shiny darkness, made his entire body tremble in a fascinating new way.

In a blur of fumbling and zippers, his cock was suddenly in his hand and he was quietly masturbating, eyes locked on Jill's blissfully unaware form.

He was vaguely aware that this was the best thing he'd ever felt. It was fucking *amazing*, in fact. Air whistled in his nose as his breathing quickened.

Then he tilted his head to get a better view, and the light shifted on the dark satin, and suddenly he imagined *her* on the other side of Jill's body. Advancing with that sensuous, slow, utterly confident pace. He trembled so much his teeth began to chatter. His strokes grew faster, almost painful. He watched the fantasy spider toy with Jill, exploring her body with long, lovely legs. Then, just as he felt himself about to come, she plunged her fangs into Jill's neck and now they were both pumping their fluids into Jill's body. His real-world orgasm was so intense that he cried out involuntarily--screamed, in fact--and slumped weakly onto the bed.

As abruptly as it'd seized him, the lust abandoned him, leaving a cold cavity filled with shame. The sudden change was more dizzying and disorienting than being drunk. What had seemed so powerful, so right just seconds before--well, not *right*, exactly, but deliciously, powerfully, *wrong*--now seemed pathetic and small.

Jill murmured slightly in her sleep. Martin froze, shaking from tension, until her breathing deepened again.

Eyes wide, he stuffed his withered, traitor penis back into his pants. Took deep breaths, but still the panic kept bubbling up. Jesus, what if someone came in now? Jill passed out, about a gallon of jizz all over the room--

He grabbed some Kleenex from the bedside table and began mopping up his mess as best he could. The Kleenex just seemed to smear his semen around, then shredded into tiny bits all over Mrs. Halber's comforter.

Fuck it, good enough. He had to go, he had to get the fuck out of this house and away from Jill and this mess he'd made in this room. He needed some time and space to think. Let Dave explain the stains to his parents, and fuck him anyway for getting Martin into this.

He fumbled the door open and stepped into the party, the sudden blast of light and noise battering his thoughts into an overheated slurry. People turned to look at him.

Martin froze. They wanted details, people always wanted details, always wanted you to prove you were just like them.

He couldn't just say, "Third base, man, it was awesome!" Had Jill given him a blowjob or a handjob? Was one better than the other? What if Jill didn't like giving blowjobs, would her friends get suspicious? And which one would make him scream like that? And why did he have to scream, Jesus, they probably thought Jill had murdered him—

"There he is!" Dave Halber hooted, drink in hand, the other held out in a high-five. "There's my main--"

"It was both!" Martin shrieked.

He woke at two in the afternoon, his head one giant, throbbing blood vessel. Craving fresh air, he stumbled into his clothes and went outside. His feet took him to the tree on their own.

She probably won't even come out, he thought, lip curling into a self-pitying snarl. She had been weirdly standoffish the last couple of weeks, sometimes barely emerging from her hole at all. Like it was too much effort.

Or you're *too much effort.*

He told himself she was just older and slower--they'd been together for seven years, after all.

Or maybe she's bored. Of you.

The thought made his skin flame but his gut cold.

He climbed onto the tree trunk and stomped his feet deliberately on his way to his usual seat by the roots. Each stomp sent a hot flare of pain through his skull, but it was worth it, because maybe it would wake her ass up, get her to notice something besides her own—

She was outside her hole, waiting for him.

Martin flinched in surprise, then flinched again from the jolt to his head. He grunted, rubbing his temples, and glared at her.

Now the size of a small dog, her abdomen as large as a basketball, the spider was a cool black sculpture of sleek, lethal lines. Despite the pain and doubt that filled his head, her gravity pulled at him as strongly as ever.

So annoying.

"No, I didn't bring you anything. Sorry to disappoint you, Your Majesty."

The spider stared.

"How can you be hungry? I just gave you a fucking dog yesterday. Or day before yesterday." He shook his head slowly. "You know, there are only so many 'free puppy' ads out there, and it's not like I can go back for seconds." He blurted humorless laughter. "Jesus, last week some woman at Wal-Mart asked me how the puppy she gave me was doing. Lucky my dad wasn't with me."

The light glinted off her black eyes.

"No, that gray mutt, from a few weeks back. I think. I guess they're all gray to you. And no, I didn't tell her, I'm not an idiot." He closed his eyes, and his mind showed him a quick flash of Jill's legs again. "I'm just saying that my part isn't easy either, okay?"

Her right front leg tapped the ground, twice.

Martin swallowed the sudden lump in his throat. "I'm sorry, too." He sighed, then sat: a kind of controlled collapse onto the trunk. Scrubbed his face with his hands. Still not meeting her gaze, he asked, "Is this—are we okay? I mean, you'd tell me, wouldn't you? If you were...I don't know." Shrugged. "Bored? With us?"

Her middle left leg lifted, slowly lowered.

"No, of course I'm not." Face flushed, he dropped his gaze again, suddenly sure she already knew everything. "It's just...we used to be a team, you know? But lately, you seem kind of..." *Bitchy*. "...off."

She stared.

A flare of anger burned in his gut. "See, here we go," he said. "When I try to talk about real stuff, about us, you shut down."

The spider's rear left leg tapped the sandy ground.

"How have I *not* shown commitment?" he said, forcing his suddenly clumsy lips to form the words. "And what exactly is wrong with dogs and cats? I never saw you turn one down."

A single tap.

"Seriously?" Martin's nostrils flared and he nodded, mouth drawn tight. "Okay. How about this? How about I bring a *person* next time?"

A pause. Then the spider's front left leg raised just a bit, slowly lowered again.

"Well, I was thinking maybe...." Sudden, clammy sweat broke out on his body. "A girl."

It was a strange thing to have those words leave his lips. He could almost see them, slowly expanding like balloons, filling the space between him and the spider.

Her eyes were eight black lasers, beaming hot judgment into his face. Martin swallowed down another wave of nausea, then opened his mouth to laugh and tell her that he was just joking, just kidding around, and hey, who else wants a dog around here besides me? But he stopped when he saw her move.

Slowly, her left rear leg rose into the air, followed by one of her middle right legs.

"Of course I meant it," he stammered, pulse banging a drum in his temples.

Her legs dropped to the ground again, then a single left front tap.

"I don't know. I have to figure out the who before I know the when, right?" His mouth felt dry and slimy at the same time. He wiped his lips.

One tap, right front leg.

"No, not Jill. That'd be stupid." *Especially after last night.* "But there are plenty of other girls, ones I don't know as well. Maybe even one of the strippers up in Alverton—"

Both front legs, one tap each.

Martin blinked. "Well, of course it'd be a girl, why—"

Right front leg, two quick taps.

"Because I'm not a queerboy!" Martin said, a little louder than he'd intended.

She stared.

"I think I've proven my commitment already," he said stiffly. "You get to do your thing, so I'd like to do mine, too. It's...biology. And it's only fair."

Left rear leg, slowly raised.

They stared at each other.

"Fine." Martin's hands went to his hips, his mouth a tense line. "But next time *I* get to choose. That's what being a team means, you know."

Another tap.

Martin nodded, trembling a little now, face slightly pale.

But his heart was that little bird again, fluttering in his chest.

***

"Fred's out. Visiting grandparents in Corpus Christi." Mr. Houseley, the Piggly Wiggly manager, furrowed his bushy eyebrows. "Why, did you need to switch your shifts?"

Struggling to keep his expression blank, Martin shook his head slightly and mumbled something. Then he went to the store's claustrophobic restroom, checked the stalls were empty, and screamed without opening his mouth until snot started to boil out of his nostrils.

Then he took a deep, slightly shaky, breath. Checked his face in the mirror, making adjustments until he looked reasonably normal again.

He would have to make do. Maybe get a goat or something, to tide her over until Fred got back from his—

The restroom door swung open. Martin turned and froze.

"Oh!" Mr B said, eyes wide. "Martin! Are you, uh, on your way out?"

Martin smiled.

***

"I'll be damned," Mr. B panted, peering at Martin's tree. A bead of sweat dripped from his nose. The bald spot on the crown of his head was a bright, unhappy red; Martin half-expected to see heat waves shimmering off of it. "I thought you were making a joke. You know, like 'big wood.'" He did air quotes with his fingers and guffawed. When Mr. B laughed, his tongue stuck slightly out of his mouth. It made Martin queasy.

But Martin returned the laugh, still relieved they'd finally reached the clearing. There was a good mile of forest between here and where they'd left Mr. B's car at Graybow's tiny civil airstrip, and Martin had been afraid he'd either get them lost in the woods or Mr. B would die of a heart attack on the way. But it'd been easy, as if bringing Mr. B here was preordained. Inevitable.

"So what do you think?" Martin gestured at the pit, using the movement to disguise a quick glance at the spider hole. She was hiding.

"Hold on, this is it?" Mr. B cocked an eyebrow. "Your 'secret place' is a hole in the ground?"

"It's nice." Martin slid down the dirt sides of the pit and suppressed a shiver; being in her space made his skin tingle and his cock twitch. "Come on down!"

Mr. B peered down into the pit, nose wrinkled. Martin could clearly see the jungles of gray hairs in his nostrils. "It's *dirt*, Martin."

Does he want me or not? "I thought you wanted dirty." He tried to strike a seductive pose, ended up just standing awkwardly, hand on one hip.

"Right now I just want a shower." Mr. B flapped his shirt a few times and Martin caught the odor of old-man sweat. "Maybe we both need one." A lecherous smile.

Martin's own smile felt like a squirming, living thing that was trying to escape his face. "We can do both. You know, dirty, then clean."

Mr. B took a step back and pointed in the direction they'd come. "I've got a bottle of bourbon in the car, we can—"

Fuck it. Martin unbuttoned his shorts and pulled them down. His erection bobbed in the open air.

Mr. B stared. "Well," he said, sounding out of breath.

Martin kept the smile going, eyes on Mr. B but straining to detect any movement from the spider hole.

Dirt cascaded down the sides of the pit as Mr. B picked his way down. Martin took a careful step back, keeping the spider hole between them. She had to be watching.

Mr. B moved toward him. "That for me?" he asked, slurring as if his lips had gone to sleep. He was lined up perfectly in front of the spider hole.

Now, Martin thought.

Mr. B took another step forward. His mouth was open, tongue visible.

Martin realized he was backed up against the side of the pit, which suddenly seemed very small. *What the fuck was she waiting for?* "Come on, do it!"

A smile split Mr. B's red face. "What do you want first?"

Now Martin could see Mr. B's erection, could almost feel its moist heat radiating at him.

"*What are you waiting for?*" Martin screamed.

Mr. B took a step back, eyes wide. "Take it easy, no need to rush, we—" Then his eyes narrowed. He backed away, craning his neck to scan the trees. "Look," he said loudly, "I don't want nothing to do with your little homo plans, Martin."

For one spinning, dumbfounded moment, Martin thought Mr. B was talking to the spider. Then Mr. B looked back at Martin, his soft grandfather face now hard and angry. "Where are your friends, huh? Where's your buddy Fred?"

Shock rattled through Martin's body. "He's not my friend," he said, voice barely above a whisper.

"I guess he isn't," Mr. B snorted. "Looks like your buddies bugged out on your little queer-bashing party."

"My—my what?" Martin grunted and tried to pull his pants up, but found he barely had the strength to stand. He covered himself with his hands. *Where was she?* Mr. B's red face blurred as tears formed in Martin's eyes.

"Fucking pansy." Mr. B shook his head. "We'll see what the cops think about you trying to mug me."

"Cops?" Martin wailed, disgusted by the weakness in his own voice.

Mr. B climbed out of the pit, chicken legs pumping. "Damn straight." He leaned against the tree trunk, removed one shoe, shook dirt from it, put it back on. "Of course," he smiled, "if you can get your 'little wood' there to come out again, maybe we can talk. Maybe I'll let you—"

A shadow leaped from the top of the trunk and landed on Mr. B's shoulders.

Mr. B yelped, staggering forward under her weight, then yelped again when her fangs plunged into his neck. He whirled and twisted, cursing, trying to grab his attacker, but the spider avoided him easily, dancing around on his shoulders. Mr. B took a few blind, stumbling steps, then fell into the pit. The spider rode Mr. B like a rodeo champion, staying on top of the old man until he rolled into Martin's feet.

The impact finally broke Martin's paralysis. He held down Mr. B's legs while she worked his upper body, her fangs striking again and again, pumping Mr B with her venom.

And then it happened: her leg brushed against Martin's arm.

For one brief, eternal, electric moment, all of Martin's senses were focused on that touch. Her soft hairs, tickling his skin. Her armor, smooth but unyielding. Most of all, the undeniable reality of *her*. His erection returned so fast he thought it would split like a hot dog in the microwave.

Demurely, she pretended not to notice.

By the time Martin could think again, only Mr B's eyes were still moving, rolling in their sockets like those of a maddened horse. Martin smiled into those eyes. "*We* did this to you," he said. "I want you to know that." Then he rolled Mr. B into the hole.

Only then did Martin finally fall to his knees, masturbating. He came almost instantly, jetting long streamers of semen onto the pine needles and dirt of the pit floor.

It was true, what people said: the first time was magical.

***

It took a week before Mr. B's empty car finally raised any suspicions, another week before the *Graybow Observer* printed a box on page three asking for anyone with information on his disappearance to contact the Sheriff's office. No one had missed him; a single sentence mentioned Mr. B was a widower, estranged from his children.

Then nothing. No more articles in the paper. No police sweeps. No one even remarked on his absence at Piggly Wiggly. As if Mr. B, with his red face and interest in bag boys, had never existed. To be safe, Martin stayed away from the clearing for a few weeks, replaying the scene in his mind.

Finally, late one Saturday afternoon while his dad was playing golf, Martin walked up the path, bringing the two guinea pigs he'd bought from the pet store up in Alverton. Just a little something, to celebrate.

That bird in his chest fluttered pleasantly as he neared the clearing. And he smiled because she was waiting for him, as she usually was.

But something felt different.

He cocked his head. "Something wrong?"

She didn't answer.

"I know, I'm sorry I waited so long to visit again." Martin smiled again and held up the bag. "But I brought you a little present to--"

Something small and quick scampered out of the hole. It was all legs and energy, a brown and black blur zipping back and forth along the lip of the hole.

A little spider.

"Who the fuck is that?" Martin whispered.

The spider ignored him; she was watching the little one.

He fumbled in his pocket for his keychain penlight. The dim circle it projected was just bright enough to reveal the huddled form of Mr. B, now completely covered by hundreds of tiny spiders. They boiled from his mouth in a bristling stream, crawled busily over his body.

Martin stared. A part of him—the smallest part—was fascinated: *so she* does *lay eggs*.

The rest of him wondered: *don't eggs need to be fertilized?*

His face burned. "When? When did you—" He wiped tears away savagely and glared at her. "*When?!*"

She didn't even have the decency to look embarrassed.

"Oh, am I not *male* enough for you? Is that it?" Martin made a noise that was half-laugh, half-wail. "Did you at least fucking eat him afterwards?"

She turned her back to him, facing the hole and her children. Her little bastards.

"Hey! Look at me!"

Still she ignored him, as if he were speaking a foreign language.

He picked up the sack of guinea pigs. He wanted to say something cutting, something that would hurt in the most meaningful way possible. Something he could remember later and feel good about. What he managed was: "Fucking present, *bitch*!" Then he threw the sack into the hole.

The sack--which also held a can of soda for himself--struck the mass of Mr. B and baby spider dead center, crushing some of the babies. Martin saw one wobble away with a missing leg. The rest scattered in panic.

"Fucking ignore me now, you—" He turned to her and saw that, maybe for the first time ever, he had her complete attention.

It was the most terrifying thing he'd ever seen.

"Wait." The word leaked out in a moistureless sigh, barely audible even to himself.

Martin turned and ran.

He'd never run like this in his life. He did not look back. He was barely able to breathe. But after an eternity of bracing for the impact of fangs and legs on his back, he finally slammed against his back door, adrenaline-clumsy hands pawing at the doorknob.

Locked.

By the time it occurred to him that the keys were in his pocket, he had already twisted to face her, ready to plead, to beg.

The porch and the yard were empty.

He collapsed onto the faded wood planks of the porch.

***

Martin jerked awake in the darkness of his bedroom.

"Oh, Jesus," he whispered. He had somehow twisted his covers into a cocoon around his body; both were soaked in sweat. The nightmare was already fading from his mind, but his body, still tense and trembling, remembered it clearly. He had to piss like crazy.

Tap-tap-tap.

A dry clicking, like nails on glass, from the window over his bed, just out of his peripheral vision.

On the far wall, a shadow moved in the moonlight projecting through the window, cast by something with a bulbous body and long legs. Something one pane of glass and two feet away from his head.

Tap-tap.

Martin froze, not even able to tremble.

Just before dawn, he silently released his bladder, tears running down his cheeks. Sometime after that, the shadow dropped away and the tapping stopped.

But still he didn't move, not until dawn came an eternity later.

***

The hickory tree's bark was rough, but comforting, against Martin's back. Without looking, he eased the heavy can of gasoline to the ground and put both hands on the shotgun. Checked the shotgun to make sure it hadn't somehow unloaded itself in the five minutes since he'd last checked it.

The sky was swirling and steely, a late spring storm on its way. No rain yet, but curdled sheets of gray clouds obscured the sun. A near-constant wind sent the trees and bushes swaying and plucked at his hair.

Where was she? It had taken him an hour to leave his house, checking the front and back porches, poking the gun into the crawl space and the eaves and every corner. Afraid of an ambush, he'd avoided trails on his way here, stepping on layers of pine needles to soften his footsteps, and entering the clearing from behind the hickory tree, the opposite of his usual approach.

She couldn't be expecting that, right?

Martin raised the shotgun to his shoulder, feeding off the trickle of confidence it gave him. *Bitch knows where I live,* he thought, sighting down the barrel. *But she doesn't know what a shotgun—*

His eyes widened as the implication finally hit. *How long has she known where I live?*

The mice that had plagued their house until...the winter after he'd met her. The same winter he'd spent days staring at the hole, wondering if she was sleeping in the darkness there.

Apparently not.

Shuddering, he put both hands back on the gun, wishing it were a twelve-gauge, pump-action model, instead of his father's barely used, over-and-under twenty-eight-gauge skeet gun.

Do it methodical, like she would.

With his cheek against the cool reassurance of gunstock, he focused down the barrel, searching the underbrush. Nothing.

Ease forward. Check the top of the tree trunk. Nothing.

More quiet steps, pulse thudding rapidly against his eardrums. The hole came into view over the trembling front sight.

Nothing.

At the edge of the pit, he flicked the switch on the flashlight he'd taped to the shotgun's barrel and shone it into the hole.

Nothing but baby spiders and dried-out husks.

Martin's breath suddenly grew short. Where was she? She could be hiding anywhere, she could still be at his house, somewhere he hadn't checked. And how could he ever be sure anywhere was safe if—?

Stop it! He stumbled back to the relative safety of the hickory tree, letting the tree protect his rear while he tried to breathe.

The sun poked through the clouds, casting shadows of hickory branches and a large gourd across the clearing. The sudden movement made him jump. *Jesus, you idiot, don't let her psyche you out, she's got a brain the size of a—*

His skin and gut went suddenly cold. *A gourd—?*

Martin whirled, fumbling the shotgun up, just as she leapt from her perch in the hickory tree branches.

As Martin lurched backward, his feet tangled and he felt himself fall. Just as his back slammed onto the sandy earth, his fingers spasmed on the triggers.

A sudden, violent slap of sound by his ear. The spray of shotgun pellets ripped the spider in half, shredding her thorax, her full, enticing abdomen bursting like an obscene water balloon.

And then, somehow, Martin was left alive, staring at the boiling sky, ears ringing, nostrils filled with a sharp odor like vinegar.

***

He burned the babies.

Some tried to run after he started pouring the gas into the hole, but he crushed them under his shoes as they emerged, the soles sliding as the treads filled with innards. The rest died instantly, curling into tortured balls as the flames filled the hole. The webbing that shrouded Mr. B dissolved in the fire like cotton candy in water. Behind him were countless smaller bundles of webbing and bone.

Then, bit by bit, he fed her to the fire as well.

He sagged to his knees in front of the hole, his mind a buzzing blankness. A thought pierced the deadness: *where's the Male's body?*

She must have eaten him. But none of the corpses in the hole looked the right size.

What if there wasn't one?

Martin's brow furrowed. Babies came from eggs, eggs had to be fertilized by sperm, which—

And suddenly he remembered the last time he'd been on his knees in this pit, ejaculating for what seemed like an eternity.

He shook his head slowly. Biologically it was impossible. But *she* had been impossible, too.

He looked at the little curled bodies with widening eyes. His mouth opened to scream, but all that escaped his throat was a low, feeble whimper, full of bile and guilt and the aching recognition of a life that could have been.

***

Martin did the things damned people did. He dated. Went to college, finished college, got a job. Embraced every tepid moment of this gray life. Watched helplessly as those moments accumulated into years.

Things improved somewhat after he moved away from Graybow, from the scene of his crime. Entire days might go by without him thinking of her.

But at night he dreamed of a dark, slender limb brushing his skin.

***

Jill was talking.

"Mmm?" His gaze was locked, unseeing, on the trees outside.

"Why didn't your Dad ever remarry?"

Martin turned. His movements felt slow and muffled, like everything since the funeral.

Jill was crouched in front of one of the boxes from the attic, hair tied back in a ponytail, clothes dusty from cleaning. She held up a framed photograph.

"Oh." Martin nodded. "He always said he never found anyone who could hold a candle to my mom."

She looked at the wedding portrait with a wistful expression. "She must have been an amazing woman."

"Honestly, I don't really remember her." Martin shrugged, his mind still outside. "Maybe it's just that Hewitt men never forget their first loves."

Jill smiled. "Aw, so sweet."

He almost asked what she was talking about, then caught himself. He knelt beside her and gave her a quick kiss, then pulled open a box from the pile in the living room. "Jesus, I didn't realize how much of a packrat my dad became while I was gone--" he stopped and took a deep breath when he saw the box was filled with Star Wars action figures. The ones he'd played with that first summer in Graybow.

His throat closed up and he wiped his eyes. Jill put her arms around him, kissed his forehead.

The baby started to cry, that whiny I-want-attention sound he hated.

"I've got her," Martin said. "I kind of need to get away from this for a minute."

She nodded. "Of course, sweetie. I'll plow through this. Why don't you take her for a walk, get some fresh air?"

It was a fine fall day, the kind he loved the most, if a bit chilly. Humming snatches of songs into his daughter's tiny ear, he made a few perfunctory laps of the backyard, which was rougher than he remembered; Dad had lost interest in yard work as the cancer progressed. The entrance to the trail was almost completely overgrown, but somehow Martin found himself walking along it, moving on rails through the undergrowth. He sang the same song over and over, holding his daughter close, like a shield, his mind carefully blank.

Absurdly, he was amazed the clearing was still there, that the tree and the hole hadn't ceased to exist, like the dream they must have been. Yet he was also surprised anything had changed at all, as if the clearing should have been frozen in place, waiting for his return.

But all that had happened was Time. The massive trunk was now a mound of rot. New bushes and saplings grew in open defiance. Time had simply continued, dragging them all along for the ride.

"Not all of us," he whispered into his daughter's hair, and the smooth curve of her skull suddenly felt like a shotgun stock against his cheek. Tears blurred his vision.

When he wiped the tears away he saw her, waiting for him in the pit.

No. This couldn't be her. This spider was too small, barely a foot across. And her legs were banded with brown striping.

Camouflage. With that brown striping, she must have blended into the weeds around the hole, hiding while Martin killed her siblings and his reason for living. His mistake had given this brave little survivor a second chance at life.

And now...she could be *his* second chance at life.

He was ready now. He'd been through so much, these long gray years. He had the strength now to prove his commitment. To be the Male he always should have been.

He walked forward, legs shaking. The thing in his hands was struggling, making noises.

When he got closer to his daughter, Martin saw that she had her mother's eyes.

Creature Feature
Chris Preston

Keith Sonnenfeld's attention wandered away from idle corporate chatter to scenery outside the lifestyle pavilion's glass walls. A three-hundred-sixty-degree lake view from the private island's highest point. Forestry littered its perimeter.

A deer appeared from the tree line. Colored red, like Keith's own hair and beard. It pranced along the lawn. How it got to this small island garnered the young executive's thoughts. He wanted to join it, to share pine-fresh air with the animal, rather than the coffee and cologne he was confined to for the next few hours.

Both blending in with their surroundings. Neither truly belonging.

The deer seemed to take note of the dozen men and women inside but didn't scamper. Keith watched as it continued along the perimeter, rounding the corner where their 'Cell Safe' sat atop a table. If Keith's cell, along with everyone else's, hadn't been confiscated for the duration of their stay then this wildlife encounter would've made for a majestic picture.

The deer turned toward the treeline and disappeared.

"Folks, you all seem nicely caffeinated," Caleb Jones, Division President for Calgary, spoke while lumbering toward the white board. "Let's jump back into this."

He scribbled seven words in capital letters – 'WHAT IS THE FUTURE OF HOMEBUILDING?'

Keith's answer to this was something he had mentally rehearsed all week since noticing the topic on their itinerary. *People are the future of homebuilding.*

"Now," Caleb continued to set the stage for the morning's session, thumbs in his belt that donned a big, silver buckle. "Rudolph didn't have us all congregate here to simply enjoy his place. No, our job here today is to keep Windsong Homes relevant. After all, there's only ever one place for leading companies to go, and that's down."

The door swooshed open. Keith glanced back.

Rudolph, CEO of Windsong Homes, had entered. He took a seat near the back. This island, known as Primrose, was all his. So were the seven cottages, two pavilions, and four boathouses that sat atop it. While everyone else had adhered to the 'business casual' note from their itinerary, the billionaire was in running gear. It was his usual attire, despite being eighty-two.

Caleb acknowledged him with an imaginary tip of the hat. "Ah, morning, Rudy. Hey, are you responsible for the wake-up call this morning? Sounded like explosions. Re-enacting World War Two back on the mainland?"

Several chuckled, though Keith kept quiet as he wasn't sure what Caleb was referring to. He had been one of the last to arrive that morning, maybe missing the sounds entirely.

"New Spa, Caleb. Buried deep into the shale."

"Well, maybe we'll all have to be back once complete! Springtime in the Muskoka area is always pleasant."

Rudolph gave a polite smile but said nothing more.

Caleb got back on track. "Housing prices continue to outpace yearly average income gains, permits are becoming harder to obtain, land is disappearing, and building code updates are driving up costs. Guys, girls, how do we work through these?"

Ideas splashed up onto the whiteboard from the various division presidents and functional leaders that made up Windsong Homes' executive leadership team.

'3D Printing'

'Smart home technology'

'Shared equity'

'Micro condos'

To that last one, Caleb chuckled. "We build homes, not sardine cans. What, do we sell that little key to open the tin as extra?"

Keith's confidence in his answer grew. It was time to break notions from others in the room that he was quiet or even spacey at times. The young man dabbed his forehead of perspiration with his sleeve as Caleb approached his table next.

"What about this group? Do any of you have something different that you'd like to put up on the board?"

Before Keith could say anything, Eric Langdon stood up. His signature smirk on display, brimming with unending arrogance. The stocky Corporate Director of Sales and Marketing announced, "I believe the future of homebuilding is people. Pioneer a path away from technology, and instead tailor a more artisanal and hand-crafted product."

That's my idea! Keith's jaw clenched, not allowing a voice to his sudden onset of anger.

"People? Huh. Interesting response, Langdon," Caleb murmured while scribbling it on the white board.

"Yes, people."

Keith's mind raced back to earlier in the day, where he first ran into Langdon after arriving by boat on the island. Staff assigned Cottage Four to the two first timers, which was more like a contemporary bungalow. They traded a couple playful quips about all this undeserved luxury while getting set for the morning session. When Keith had emerged from the washroom, he recalled Langdon tossing him his notebook, telling him they had to get going.

Langdon looked through my notebook when I wasn't looking.

The answer made sense from Keith, the Director of Customer Service. 'People' is what he built his reputation on. Training, guidance, feedback, connections.

"People," Rudolph said. "Would it be a stretch to say you're thinking of genetic engineering?"

Langdon's eyes said everything to Keith that he needed to know. It was how he would have felt, had Rudolph said the same to him instead. Thrilled.

"Um, yes. Exactly, sir! Why heat a whole house when you can just make people warmer?"

Now he's just making shit up. That's not at all what I would've said.

"Now, you're catching up to me." Rudolph rose to his feet. "Let me show you something I know you'd get a kick out of, kid. Everyone else, carry on."

Try as he did, Keith couldn't get Langdon to look at him in the eyes as the Sales lead packed up his stuff. Rudolph was already out the door and trotting away on the gravel path.

Langdon hiked his khakis up to just under a sizable gut before taking off in pursuit. His thudding steps echoing within the glass walls.

***

The rest of the day dragged on for Keith, as if someone had sucked most of the air out of the enclosed pavilion. Rudolph and Langdon never returned. Lunch came and went, smoked salmon with a pear salad. Financial discussions took up much of their afternoon, which he didn't knowledgeable enough to take part in. He dealt in sentiment, not dollars.

By the time they wrapped up the workday, Keith's contributions had been negligible. *With some luck, nobody noticed.*

Everyone dispersed to relax, change, and prepare for the evening's activities.

While descending the steps, a hand patted his back. It was Victor, Division President of Toronto, whose smirk Keith could see just under his trimmed gray beard.

"Is everything okay, Keith? You were a little quiet today. I warned you this can be an intimidating experience, but they are still the same people we interact with back at the office."

Keith looked around to make sure the others weren't within earshot. Nothing but trees. "Ah, I know. Just a little discouraged to hear my idea for the morning's workshop before I had a chance to say it."

"What was your suggestion?"

Having been mentored by Victor for the last six years, he knew well enough of his disdain for pettiness. "It's not important."

Victor squeezed his plastic water a bottle until it squeaked a few times in thought before responding, "well, don't dwell too much. Gone are the days where Rudolph even listens to us. You heard him, he's got his mad scientist hat on with some new crazy idea that'll never materialize anyway. That man is like the sun. Get in his orbit and you'll up. Best to fly under the clouds. Bad enough we're here."

"Well, it still feels like I blew it."

"You didn't. Tonight's activities will be more casual so forget the pressure and just be yourself."

Keith took a breath in, reinflating himself. "Thanks for keeping my head up, Vic."

The two parted ways. Keith, with a renewed sense of confidence, stormed back to Cottage Four. Gravel crunched under each step. He wasn't so ready to give up the pettiness himself. When he did enter Cottage Four, it seemed vacant. Hitting a 'Welcome Home' button on the wall-mounted control panel raised blinds and lit up the hallways.

Eric Langdon wasn't there.

That meant he was likely still off with Rudolph somewhere.

The alone time, however, provided an opportunity to soak in the view hopefully cool down. He put on a second layer, snarling at the thought of Langdon's sweater analogy playing on repeat, and went out to the patio. Distant boats dance atop the still waters of Lake Cedarhurst as Keith sunk into a Muskoka chair. Around him were the sounds of loons and, as daylight faded into a deep orange, crickets joined in the natural orchestra.

One insect was missing from Keith's expectations, mosquitos. Those little critters loved feasting on him any time he left the city. *Did Rudolph pay them off or something?*

A boom. Keith's eyes sprang open to survey the dusk landscape around him. Birds dispersed from surrounding trees.

He would've figured it for another seismic blast in the spa under construction back at the mainland if it hadn't seemed so much closer. To him, it sounded more like a gunshot.

His phone chimed. It was the reminder to congregate at the dining pavilion in fifteen minutes. He regretted having not spared some time to use the gigantic, glass and marble shower in his bathroom, but Keith figured there'd be time for that the next morning.

With a fresh wardrobe of brown suede, jeans, and sweater tight overtop a collared golf tee-shirt, Keith was ready to head over. He clicked 'Away' and opened the door.

A figure appeared, tall and cast in shadow.

"Jesus!" Keith cried.

"Sorry man," Victor replied. "Didn't mean to frighten you."

"Yes, I..." Keith steadied himself while closing the door behind him. "I just wasn't expecting anyone to be standing there."

"Well, you and I both know how you can be a little tardy, so I figured I'd come get you."

They hiked along the gravel trail, which had been groomed recently enough that Keith couldn't make out any of his footprints from just an hour ago. Victor pointed out various facts about the construction of each building on Primrose that he picked up from previous visits. All built within the last few years, and most construction had occurred in the winter to make use of an ice road for heavy machinery. When the ice was too soft, Rudolph employed freight helicopters instead.

While walking, the hairs on the back of Keith's neck raised. He heard a swoosh. "Did you hear that?"

Keith glanced around, noticing a shadow the width of the path race past them. Whatever was above remained obscured through the flanking pine and spruce tree foliage.

Victor's pace slowed, and he looked back. "Scare easily, Keith? I sure hope not. Rudolph may have manicured every bit of this island, but we are still at nature's mercy up here."

Birds the size of aircrafts aren't exactly natural.

Ahead, Keith heard music cutting through the forest.

"Come on!" Victor said as he continued along the path. "The party is getting started."

***

Primrose's dining pavilion was the largest structure Keith had seen on the island. Keith followed Victor up its wide steps to the entrance. Steel beams and stone at each corner held up its expansive ceiling, allowing for mesh screens to make up most of its wall spans. Two long tables and several couches made up the interior decoration. A gigantic fireplace (the last remnants of the century-old home that stood before) was on one side, while the kitchen was at the other.

Dining staff hurried in and out of the door that obscured whatever magic they were conjuring as the two men moved through the doors, by the tables, and onto the terrace out back. His nerves, already rattled by whatever flew over them on the path, were now being hammered once again by social anxiety.

A slight relief came in the form of Cabernet Sauvignon, provided by one of the staff. Both men stopped just short of the social gathering to take a few sips of their wine.

"After you," Victor said with a wave of his hand.

It took Keith a while to notice the crescent moon that hung above them, because, unlike earlier, he was enjoying himself. Maybe, he figured, it was the wine.

Keith told even a joke. "No mosquitos at all! And they love me. What, did Rudolph pay them off or something?"

Several people around him laughed, some noting similar observations.

It was only when Caleb mentioned Langdon and Rudolph that Keith looked up to cool the resentment he felt still simmering within. The moon was so much brighter while away from his condominium and city light pollution.

Was I only meant to come here so Langdon could get a promotion or something? Where are they?

He fought back the negative feelings by sidling up near several other functional leads. They had been trying the scotch, aged in an oak barrel for a century. At their behest, Keith took a sip and coughed.

"Right?" Maya, Windsong Homes' General Counsel, said. "I've had scotch before, but this is over the top."

"Yes, really strong stuff." Keith replied after catching his breath.

Maya snickered. "Thankfully, no construction guys are here tonight to see us office folk wuss out on this stuff. Or Rudolph for that matter, abusing his expensive spirits."

"Hey, I have an excuse! Customer Service gets a pass, everyone knows we're soft. Our lawyer... well, you'd be in big shit."

"Good point," she said.

A bell rang. The group looked inside to see that dining staff had plated dinner. Chef Marcel, a paunchy character who had introduced himself to the group at lunch, ushered everyone inside. As they sat down, Keith couldn't quite recognize the red meat on his plate. It was thin, topped with a reduction of some kind, and smelled of a campfire.

Chef Marcel brushed his jacket of debris and spoke up. "Everyone, if I can have your attention. Tonight's meal is fresh venison with field vegetables. These pieces are from farmland and fields that Rudolph has bought over the years, then prepared in the wood-fired oven out back.

Venison. Deer? The gunshot I heard earlier?

Keith stood. "Thank you, Chef Marcel. The dish looks great. Did this happen to be the deer I saw roaming earlier?"

The chef chuckled. "Free-range animals imported here are just the best. And on this island, where is a dinner to go? Enjoy."

Others dove in while Keith instead picked around the hunk of meat that lay before him. He had noticed Maya, who was also at his table, receiving a vegan dish, which seemed to account for her diminutive size. It looked more edible than what he was served but most of his co-workers knew Keith ate meat from other company events. He didn't want to start any rumours.

Dessert was homemade apple strudels, served with whipped cream. It was flaky and stuffed with Granny Smith, or possibly Honey Crisp, apples. Keith only indulged to not end up back at Cottage Four on an empty stomach.

It was nearing nine at night when staff lit the fire, and they turned the music up, some smooth jazz, to match the banter. The drinks continued to flow. Cliques broke out around the room, while Keith stood alone in the center. Even Victor was no longer paying much attention to him, instead getting into whose skiing story was more harrowing, his or Caleb's.

I'm finishing my drink and then getting out of here.

With a couple good gulps, Keith placed his glass down with only wine legs left within. He glanced around once more to see who'd catch his early exit, then slunk toward the door. It was dark outside, with hardly any light to see other than a floodlight from the pavilion. Navigating down the large stone slabs was difficult but he did make it down to the gravel pathway.

Someone approached, outlined by moonlight. He stood still as they neared. Once within just a few feet, Keith could make out the familiar face. It was Rudolph.

"Did you enjoy dinner, Keith? I hope you aren't retiring so soon," the old man said.

No Langdon in sight.

"The dinner was delicious, I really appreciated it, Mister Cook. It's actually my head, I've developed a bit of a migraine."

"Oh, but I have one more surprise for everyone. It's the future of homebuilding, after all. Nothing in Windsong's forty years will compare. And you, you're here to tell me how we'd service and warrant such a thing."

Keith looked through Rudolph's glasses to witness sheer joy and excitement. "Okay… okay, yes. Lead the way."

He struggled to keep up with Rudolph, who never showed his age as the old man sprung up each step and pushed the pavilion doors open.

"Everybody! Come, join me out on the terrace." Rudolph clapped and raised his hands up while running between the two long tables.

Glasses, both full and empty, clunked down as the guests herded themselves toward the terrace. Outside, they formed a semicircle, lit only by the few space heaters that stood beside the sprawled-out furniture. Overhead, stars flickered with night birds that were active.

"I'm sorry for my absence today. It's been, uh, eventful. Nevertheless, I wouldn't have asked you earlier about the future of our industry, and of our company, without offering up my own perspective." He paused, glanced around to meet several gazes with his own, and spoke again in a hushed tone. "So, are you all ready to see what I've cooked up?"

The crowd expressed an excited, "Yes!"

Keith, on the other hand, remained silent.

"Okay! That's what I was hoping to hear. Otherwise, I was just going to go to bed."

Some laughed, Caleb especially.

Rudolph looked up. "Come on down! Introduce yourself!"

The crowd looked up, seeing an outline grow from the flocks of birds above. As it neared, the creature's mass became apparent. Keith figured he was looking at a wingspan of at least ten, maybe even twelve feet wide. While slowing itself, the gusts of wind pushed around articles of clothing and almost caused some to fall as they braced each other, as if a helicopter was landing nearby.

It touched down with a thud. Keith struggled to make sense of what he was looking at. A giant bat? A man with wings? Something between the two. Covered in fine fur and sporting only black sweatpants, nothing else. Its wings were separate appendages behind two wiry arms. The creature was huffing from exerting itself, showing off fangs, an upturned nose, and pointy ears.

The crowd fell silent. Victor muttered something swear-laden under his breath. Keith thought he heard Maya gasp, but didn't dare take his eyes off the creature in front of him.

"Everyone, meet Fredrick. My nephew."

The creature gestured with a hand. "Hey, everyone."

I should've left. What the hell is going on?

Someone behind Keith whispered, "is this a joke? Like, makeup. Wires. Some type of trickery?"

"Shut up, he's explaining," another replied.

Rudolph cleared his throat. "We heard one suggestion today that people are the key to our future in homebuilding. Eric Langdon said that. Yes, but how? By biologically eliminating many elements that have held back architectural designs for centuries. Think about how efficient a home could be without needing to consider garages because you can fly, furnaces because you have personal insulation, fridges or cooking appliances because you can survive off liquids."

"Liquids? What in god's word do you mean, Rudolph?" Victor asked.

"Blood! This serum we've developed converts human digestive tracts to something resembling hematophages. What's more efficient than eating muscle, meat, and fat is taking a drink from the pipelines that supply them. It's sustainable, too. Think about it: a cow pumps over twelve-hundred litres of blood per hour. Tap into that while keeping them alive and you've solved many hunger concerns worldwide."

Victor replied, "this is insane. You've officially gone too far this time. I don't condone… whatever the hell this is."

To that, Fredrick smirked and shrugged.

"Ah, the new sleeping method. I can't forget about that. Hanging upside-down, able to line up throngs up people like a butcher's cold locker." Rudolph seemed to take a momentary notice of the horror his crowd wore. "Sorry for the visual, everyone."

"You mentioned a serum, Rudy. Is that the pitch here? Turn everyone into these…" Caleb approached Fredrick and patted him on the back. He took a moment to look at his hand, which glistened in the moonlight with slime. "Ah, gross. Anyway, yes, turn people into these self-contained hybrid things?"

"Exactly. Sold for just a small fraction of traditional housing. Housing capacities could go up ten-fold. The working name for it is Creature Features. Though, I think I need marketing's input on that one."

Maya chuckled at that but, when Keith glanced over at her, he noticed several tears rolling down her cheeks while she shook. *Why isn't anyone calling off this grotesque sales pitch?*

Caleb spoke again. "What's the process like, Rudy? Changing into one. You can't expect people to accept looking like this. If, I mean, this is even real. Not a prank."

"Still a non-believer. Caleb, when have I ever given you, or anyone else here, reason to doubt me? Fredrick has been upgraded for over a month now, but the process takes just a day or so. Let me give you a glimpse of this." Rudolph pulled on a radio until it sprung from his belt. "Send him in, please."

The crowd's attention turned back to the interior. It was Langdon, head down low while walking through the lights. As he stepped out, it was clear that he was partially transformed into what Fredrick had become. Skinnier than before and scratching himself like a junky who had gone on too long without a hit. Behind him were the beginning of wings, half the size of Fredrick's.

"Now, I couldn't have been happier that Langdon here volunteered himself for the pilot project after I showed him the lab today. He's truly someone dedicated to pushing Windsong Homes ahead. Because he's right, technology has a shelf life but this, it's permanent. At least, until the regression therapy process has been fine-tuned," he said with a smile.

He wouldn't volunteer, Langdon's the most selfish person in the world. It's my fault that dumb bastard got caught up in this. Shit, that could've been me.

"Eric," Keith whispered, trying to get the man's attention.

No response. Langdon just kept his head down and continued to scratch all over.

"Anyway, ask these two anything. I want your full buy-in and, of course, complete dedication to confidentiality until we can go to market. Big things are coming, ladies and gentlemen."

With that, the crowd cautiously redistributed. Victor and several others approached Langdon while Keith contemplated what to do. He noticed Maya scuttle toward the pavilion, but staff had locked the doors after Langdon. She rattled the door back and forth.

Rudolph waved a finger. "People, please. Be the cool-headed futurists of the homebuilding industry that I know you to be. Give me five more minutes of your time."

Keith went toward Langdon, getting in close enough to see all the changes occurring on his face. He smelled almost like sulfur. "Are you okay, Langdon? Why, why did you have to say what you did? Do you need me to get you out of here?"

"Can't leave. He lies…" Langdon's words struggled through his morphing teeth. "The pain is so much. I am…"

"Yes?" Keith urged him on with quivering lips.

Langdon's eyes, deep wells of blackness, found their way up to meet his. "Hungry."

Keith's heart picked up speed, and his muscles tightened with the onset of adrenaline.

"Run," Langdon growled.

He stepped backward, tripping over a foot stool. Langdon's chest puffed out, and his posture changed from a victim to a predator. Victor grabbed his arm and yanked Keith back up onto his feet.

"Go!" Victor shouted.

Langdon shoved Victor aside and grabbed at Keith, who dodged his claw and then turned to run.

"Ah, I should've cautioned everyone around Langdon. The process is taxing, and they can be irritable. Langdon, calm yourself."

The morphing man took pursuit.

Keith got up to a full sprint, heading toward the unlit forest. He heard Langdon behind him, with heavy steps and flaps from his sprouted wings.

"Fredrick, stop Langdon!" Rudolph shouted somewhere far back.

Unable to see, each step was more careless than the rest, even when meeting various obstacles like rocks, wet grass, and tree roots.

I need off this island!

"Keith! I'm hungry," Langdon shouted in his ear.

The next step met no resistance as the slope under his feet had changed on him. Drastically. He had pitched himself off solid ground and into a fall. When Keith made contact again, it was with his head, which gushed with warmth from the impact. The world spun as tree after tree slammed into him. They left no part of his body untouched, like being stuck in a washing machine.

Then, he came to a stop.

***

"His eyes are fluttering. This is good. Keith, can you hear me?" a voice asked in the distance.

He tried to look around, but all Keith could see was bright, blinding light. He let out a moan, but it sounded more like a howl. A sound he had never made before.

"Kill the lighting! All but the cabinet valance lights; those should suffice."

Keith's eyes focused, and he took note of his orientation: laying down, staring up at what looked like rock. "What, where am I?"

"The Spa, my boy. Or, what we nicknamed The Spa." It was Rudolph's voice. Keith swore he could hear several vocal nodes in the old man's throat. This depth of hearing caused him to wince in pain. "Sorry, I'll speak softer; it is apparently difficult to adjust at first. This facility saved your life. Creature Features sports some impressive healing capabilities. You would've died long before reaching the nearest hospital with those injuries."

"Creature Features? No, you didn't—"

"I'm afraid so."

His head was immobile, restrained in some way, and unable to see those around him. But his arms weren't. He raised both hands into view, seeing them sport claws and covered in red fur. His tongue confirmed the onset of sharper teeth. Fangs. "I'm a monster."

"You're the future."

And then, he felt it. The hunger that Langdon had mentioned. It was for blood.

Daddy
P.Mattern

Ten months after Daddy died it was approaching Halloween.

My widowed Mom had enough to worry about without being clued in that since his death, I had fallen into Witchcraft and Necromancy…and all of this in spite of the fact that I had always been raised and educated in private Christian schools. My Dad (his name was Mark) had INSISTED I attend private Christian school. He felt that it was important to grow up with a set of values, even if you ended up questioning them later.

…I loved and respected my Dad. How I ended up dabbling in the Dark Arts is at once difficult, and easy, to explain.

It all started with his death.

He wasn't my natural father, the musically talented narcissistic guy who'd ghosted even before I came into the world. My biological Dad Timothy was an only occasionally employed rock musician. When he'd learned that my Mom was pregnant, he told her that he wasn't prepared to be a parent, that he couldn't cope with being a father figure to anyone, and he demanded that she have an abortion.

Overwhelmed by the circumstances and the stress of being an unemployed coke addicted rock musician he moved out, leaving my Mom to cope by herself.

My Mom refused to terminate the pregnancy, and my parents got a legal separation, then reunited briefly after I was born, finally splitting up for good when I was five months old.

My Mom put on her Supermom cape and moved us to a different city where she could find a better paying job and went to great lengths to make sure that I had at least one involved and caring parent.

I consider my "step-Dad" to be my "real" Dad because he was the only one that raised me after he and my Mom met and fell in love and got married. I was two years old at the time and I was the flower girl at their wedding.

I absolutely loved that flower girl dress-it was the best gift that I'd ever been given. My new Daddy loved to buy me things, and he often quipped, "One thing I love about the girls in this family is that they can be BOUGHT."

He spoiled me, just like a real Dad should, and I adored him.

Dad took me out for a "date" once a week that included both dinner and shopping so that I could "exercise my shopping gene".

He was convinced that all females had one, he would say laughingly.

He was, in short, the BEST.

The darkness that descended over us after he was killed in a traffic accident was both cloying and unrelenting. I exhausted myself trying to keep it at bay, finally succumbing to it. For me it was like sinking to the bottom of the ocean and not wanting to move, think, or anything.

I lost my sense of taste, smell, all my former interests and my will to keep going.

My worried Mom found me a therapist for grief counseling, but it didn't help-the only thing that was going to help was to erase all the events that had robbed us of the person we all adored and depended on.

I met a girl at Christian school that seemed to be as depressed as I was, and she was the one that introduced me to witchcraft. My Mom worked a lot and didn't have time to micromanage me. My room was my private domain and Samantha and I decked it out really Goth with a lot of black, a full length mirror to use as a portal, black candles and other Witchy paraphernalia.

I dressed in black all the time, pierced my septum (I'd already pierced my ears multiple times) and got a tattoo in a place my Mom would never see.

I was finally able to relax in my sadness, falling into its embrace and sinking effortlessly, willing to be carried more and more deeply into its seductive shadowed world of despair.

I spent my time reading old texts and memorizing spells and charms that had been used since ancient times.

I didn't kill things, or sacrifice animals, and I wasn't interested in trading my soul to get on the good side of dark entities, but I worked hard to bring what appeared to be dead back to life. My first success was a butterfly. Then a frog, and finally I was able to revive a bird.

In the meantime weird things would happen. After months of blocking out sunlight by making sure the blinds were closed I opened them one day and saw that hornets had built a huge nest right over the window, one so large that the window could no longer be opened.

It was kind of cool watching them go about their activities, kind of like a hornet-arium or something. My Mom freaked out when she saw it but since the creatures couldn't get inside the house I made her leave it alone.

Hanging there, like a malignant tumor attached to the side of the house, it seemed appropriate and fit in perfectly with our collective pain and grief.

Meanwhile I became interested in honing my occult skills, which I was convinced would prove to be my destiny.

All of this I did with a single goal in mind…

I wanted to bring Daddy back.

The first time I tried was a disaster.

I had a few of my freakier friends over. I had found what seemed a reasonable spell in a book of medieval spells and conjures, and I had my portal mirror set up, lots of lit black candles and enough pot to get really buzzed so that even if nothing happened everyone would have a good time.

My Mom was doing a late shift in emergency services so I had the house to myself.

My boyfriend Sam, whose nickname was Salem, arrived first, and he helped me set out crystals that might ease the journey of my Dad through the mirror from whatever netherworld he was currently inhabiting.

When my other friends arrived, we joined hands and chanted for a while, and then I began reciting a spell in Latin that I thought might work.

The room was completely dark, except for the candlelight, and everyone was silent, most with their eyes closed. I just kept repeating the final lines of the spell, willing with all my being to see my Dad again.

I think it was Salem that gasped and caused me to open my own eyes, which immediately went to the mirror. The darkness within the mirror seemed ten times blacker than even the darkness in the corners of the room, but as we stared, along with more of my guests that night, there seemed to be some definite movement within the mirror. Whatever it was it appeared to be coming closer.

We were all entranced at that point. We continued watching as something that was light by contrast seemed to emerge from the mirror's depths, as though it was a figure traveling a path toward us. As it got closer I realized it was a humanoid figure, and it was plodding ever closer.

It was still fairly far off when I recognized my father's gait. He'd always moved in the same way, head down as though he were preoccupied with thinking about something, his hair falling over one eye, his broad shoulders flexing slightly underneath his jacket as he came.

He was wearing the suit he'd been buried in, and his feet were bare.

He stopped just shy of the mirror, peering out at us with a look of confusion on his face.

I stood up and moved closer to the mirror. He seemed to look up at me, focusing. I saw his mouth moving.

I'm not a lip reader but I could have sworn he was mouthing my name.

There was a moment when our eyes met, and I was flooded with so many emotions that I couldn't speak. I stretched out my right hand to touch him, the image that I saw beyond the glass, but my hand didn't go through, it merely made a "thonk" sound on the surface of the glass on the other side.

As though he were trying to reach me as well, he extended his right hand toward me, and I felt fingers close around my wrist, wrapped so tightly they hurt.

Muffled by the impenetrable part of the mirror separating us, I heard him say,

"Devils Hollow! Bring the mirror!"

After that I looked down and saw that the vice grip around my wrist was caused by something that looked like a claw rather than a hand, and just as I noticed the grey mottled skin and sharp yellowed fingernails I was tugged so hard against the glass that I smacked my forehead and went out instantly like a light.

Salem told me later that he had pulled me back when he saw that creepy claw around my wrist, almost as though he'd had a premonition of what would happen he'd wrapped his arms around my waist and pulled me backward as hard as he could just as I was being pulled into the mirror.

Everyone had seen what happened, and they were all scared shitless. Two of my four other friends never spoke to me again they were so freaked out by what had happened.

I didn't care. Even though it hadn't worked, I knew we were onto something, and I knew I'd have to get my Mom on board, because my Dad had told me how to get him back into our world.

I was a girl on a mission, and I was determined to finish what I had started.

Mom took some convincing, but not as much as I thought. She insisted on loading both of us up with medallions of the Saints, necklaces with crosses, taking Holy Water and two copies of the Holy Bible and other paraphernalia that was associated with warding off evil.

I remember cutting my eyes at her as we loaded up the truck my Dad had strictly bought for hauling. The mirror fit neatly into the back of it, covered by a tarp, and we started off on a misty morning to travel to Devil's Hollow, a local place on the edge of a public park that spanned acres on the outskirts of town, it was also a place where no one ever went except to hook up, buy drugs, or hide.

Something about the entire area was foreboding, even on a sunny day. Most of it was boggy, and a few bodies had been discovered by hunters in the woods.

As we rode along I found myself unconsciously rubbing my wrist. It was the one Dad had latched onto, and it still had a red bruised mark encircling it.

Even after nearly a week it hadn't faded.

"What happened to your wrist," my Mom asked from the driver's seat, "That looks painful."

When I'd told her about seeing Daddy in the mirror I'd purposely left out that part.

"Nothing," I said quickly, pulling my sleeve down. I wasn't sure why I had the mark, which hadn't changed over the course of days, but having seen my Dad face to face had been worth a few bruises to me. I had never changed my mind about knowing that without him my Mom and I would be unable to find meaning in our lives.

It wasn't fair.

We finally stopped the truck after we'd followed an ancient looking dirt road about as far into the woods as we could go. It terminated in front of an ancient looking half burned out-cabin in a small cleared space that was next to an old looking half tumbled down well.

For some reason the well caught my eye… Some of the stones had tumbled away on one side, and the bucket attached to the hoisting bar had tumbled haphazardly off to the side.

"Good a place as any," my Mom remarked, "Let's get the mirror out."

I thought I heard excitement in her voice. I knew she was as desperate as I was to have my Dad back with us.

I lit candles, setting them around the uncovered mirror as Mom and I joined our hands together.

I noticed halfway through my chanting that some extra force seemed to have taken over…the words coming from my mouth sounded strange, as though in a different language and I didn't recognize them from any of the many texts I had read.

Twilight was descending, but I barely noticed. When the image in the mirror changed to black swirling mists and then cleared so that I could make out a white figure coming toward us, more and more closely with each passing second, there was no doubt in my mind who I was looking at.

Finally he was as close to the mirror portal as he could get without coming through, he looked out and smiled at us and kept coming.

"Daddy!" I breathed.

It was at that precise moment he came through.

As soon as he did all of us clung together tightly for an interminable amount of time. Finally the smell got to us, and Mom and I pulled back.

She had happy tears glistening on her face.

"You need a bath Buddy," she said.

There was a tearing sound before one side of Dad's mouth opened. I realized with horror that during the embalming process his mouth had been stitched shut. Of course it had-it was part of preparing the body for a funeral.

"No SCHIDT!" he croaked out, and we were astounded. He had always had a great sense of humor, and he hadn't lost it, not even in death.

"You're riding in the back," my Mom told him, "Now let's go home!"

We arrived after dark and even the dog seemed to recognize my Dad. I'd been afraid that it might be like a scene out of Pet Sematary or something, but the dog seemed to accept him completely.

There were problems from the get go, ones we were hardly prepared for.

After we got Daddy cleaned up, and the rest of his mouth snipped open we found out his INNER CENSOR must have died when he originally did.

"I am completely dehydrated," he said at one point, turning to my Mom, "So I think sex is out of the question!"

When I looked closely at him, even though he was cleaned up enough to look like his old self, I could see that his eyes had a weirdly concave look to them, like the eyes of dead fish lying on shaved ice in the glass cases in the seafood section of the supermarket.

After that I tried not to look directly at them when we talked. I reminded myself that I was more responsible for his being here than anyone.

It felt amazing to have him back. He seemed to have, well, MOST of his wits about him, and he was accidently funny with his honest observations.

He did retain a slightly unpleasant odor that neither Mom or I could quite place. Nothing seemed to help with it until my Mom started dusting his clothing inside and out with baking soda after it had gone through the wash and dried.

He was thinner than he had been, but since they had stuffed his chest with sawdust he seemed as solid as ever.

I was personally amazed that his hair kept growing, although I'd read somewhere that even after folks are buried their hair and nails seem to grow for a while. Maybe that was true. Mom gave him a haircut and he looked fairly good. His pallor was a bit grey but he'd been olive skinned so it wasn't too obvious.

All in all, and even though the dynamic had changed, i.e., Mom and I were protective and attentive to him like never before…HE had always been attentive and fiercely protective toward both of us.

I felt relaxed and woke up every morning with a smile on my face.

That would soon change.

One thing we hadn't bothered to tell Dad was not to answer the door.

So, one day the inevitable happened and he did. It was our neighbor. We hadn't been getting any visitors since the funeral, people tend to forget you exist after you lose a major someone in your life as soon as they can without looking like total unfeeling assholes.

Mrs. Walters was a widow herself, and had been great at delivering casseroles and desserts after Dad passed. As soon as I'd heard the door open I had rushed down the steps to the foyer and got a glimpse of her surprised as shit face before I reached the bottom of the steps.

I knew immediately what I would say.

"Mrs. Walters, this is my Dad's twin brother Jake," I said, elbowing my Dad to let him know he needed to play along.

"Oh my I nearly had a heart attack," she told me, "Well isn't that something!"

"He couldn't make it to the funeral because he was delayed overseas," I continued in a rush, "But he promised he would take time off to stay with Mom and I."

I was really pleased with my fast thinking. She appeared to be buying all of my bullshit.

"Well I think that is very nice," she said, nodding approvingly, "I was just dropping off some fruit cake I made. I hope you like fruitcake, Jacob!"

"Just love it," Dad told her with a toothy grin and the slight lisp he'd retained since we snipped the threads holding his lips together, "Thanks so much. I plan to stay awhile I think!"

I saw Mrs. Walters start to reply, and then saw her step back a little, nostrils twitching.

Right away I realized that Dad hadn't had his shower yet that day.

"Well thanks again," I told her, stepping in front of him on purpose and stepping on his toes in the process, "And everything you make is delicious!"

After I checked out through the peephole that she was well on her way back to her own house, I whirled around to confront my Dad.

"Dad, please don't answer the door," I begged, "I mean it's okay, it was only Mrs. Walters. But what if it had been someone else? Think about it."

Dad looked sheepish.

"Sorry kiddo, I think your Mom mentioned not answering the door…I forget things now. I don't want to cause you and Mary any trouble-I'm just grateful to be back home."

I couldn't help falling into his arms, in spite of that odor that seemed to seep out of his pores no matter how we tried to keep Dad non stinky.

"No problem," I assured him.

But there was a problem.

Apparently Mrs. Walters had a larger social network than we figured, and the insurance company that was slated to pay his insurance benefits to Mom and I decided on the basis of several anonymous calls to withhold payment pending their investigation.

Mom and I were outraged. Why wasn't the Coroner's report enough? He had been pronounced dead at the scene. What more did they want?

Apparently they wanted to check whether he'd ever had a brother, much less a twin, and of course he hadn't. Dad had been an only child.

So they balked at paying.

By then our mortgage was behind and we had hard decisions to make. We decided that we needed to move to a different town.

Then Dad started falling apart, literally, and everything changed again.

First his legs went, and we rented a Hoyer lift and a wheelchair. We stopped answering the door at all. Mom, who was braver than I was told me that Dad couldn't feel anything and wasn't in pain, but she hated having to do what came next.

His legs started molding and smelling terrible. Nothing we tried helped, and so one day all we had left of Dad was the part of him above the waist. Still we tried to be cheerful around him. It wasn't hard. He really understood what was happening.

"The mirror," he said to both of us one day, "Have you thought about the mirror? Maybe you can work your magic and throw me back in there…

Maybe I can get restored, somehow! After all, we don't know how it works…

But I CAN see that this deterioration isn't going to stop, you know?"

I remember I burst into tears. Even with all he was going through he wanted to be here for US! He was as selfless as ever.

I hit my magical conjuring texts again. It was a long shot, but we had to try, for his sake.

The day we returned to the woods the skies were leaden, and it had started snowing. We had packed Dad in between us in the cab of the truck. He told us that one thing he regretted was that he hadn't gotten a chance to drive his truck when his legs were still working.

I had a bad feeling, even then in spite of enjoying the comforting feeling of his voice in my ear.

We arrived and unpacked the mirror and Dad's portable wheelchair, setting it up in the same place we had originally.

I was determined to make something amazing happen, and I began my chants and kept going. This time we had Dad in the middle of us as we all sat on a blanket on the hardened cold ground. The wind seemed to pick up around us in response to my fervent chanting.

When I heard my voice change and the words I was speaking continue in a tongue that I couldn't identify, I knew we were onto something.

The mirror began to go misty and dark, darker than ever before, as though something within its confines was starting to boil.

I wasn't sure what to expect, but I certainly didn't expect to see a figure coming toward us from within the mirror again. I was thoroughly confused, and I am sure Mom was too.

As the figure approached I still couldn't tell who it was-it was wearing a hooded cloak that completely concealed its features, but I couldn't imagine that it could be anything good.

Too late as the figure seemed to accelerate its progress toward us, I heard my Dad shout,

"Tessa STOP IT!"

All I remember of what happened next are flashes.

A face tilted toward mine that had a corona of horns protruding from the brow and eyes like starless night skies

The sensation of having Dad's hand that had been firmly in mine being jerked away abruptly, as winds seemed to moan and rush around us.

And then, just in my line of sight, watching Dad being carried through the air by the demonic being, which hovered for an instant over the opening of the abandoned well before corkscrewing down into it almost gently, leaving my Dad's screams to be carried off in every direction by the raging crosswinds.

Mom and I have no memory of anything after that right up until the moment we found ourselves sitting in the driveway, with my Mom at the wheel and the truck in park with the engine still running.

We never moved away from our town, and eventually the Insurance Company paid out like a slot machine. We never talk about what happened that afternoon out in the woods.

I treasure all the moments I was able to have with my Dad after he left the first time. And in spite of all the problems, having him back with us even for a brief time seemed to heal us both enough so that we could move on with our lives.

My Mom made me promise not to try to get Daddy back again, but the entire time while I was promising, I was crossing my fingers behind my back.

…because I will never give up on Daddy…

…And some promises are meant to be broken.

The Hidden
Jeff Oliver

April 6ᵗʰ,1982

Life has now started, I'm awakening into a world of broken hearts and lost souls.
I have no idea of what is to come, as my umbilical cord is wrapped around my throat.

I can't breathe, as a strange light appears and burns my eyes.
I'm constantly screaming, and I can't understand why.

How can I remember the day I was born?
This question stays unanswered as I watch the womb that contains me, become more torn.

The blood rains down, covering every inch of my flesh.
The darkness that I've loved so much, has entirely vanished.

I'm colic and frantic, I scream all night and day.

I understand everything around me, it's not supposed to be this way.

There is a woman and a man, constantly screaming at me.
Shut the Hell Up! Is what they always say.

My vocabulary is building, I am damned from the start.
These people are supposed to love me, not tear me apart.

Creating a monster, without even knowing.
They never pay attention to my red eyes when they're glowing.

I'm plotting as they stick the needles in their arms.
They will never suspect me, until I'm tearing out their hearts.

The nightmare began, the moment I was conceived.
I cannot wait for the moment, that they regret creating me.

Wait… they already regret it! The evil within me will always comfort me.
I cannot wait to hear them scream!

April 6th,1987

I'm tearing things apart. Every nice thing they receive, gets destroyed by me. I want them to hate me

I want them to send me away. I want them to hit me and let my blood fall like rain.
I want them to destroy each other, before their final price is paid.

They cheat on each other, they lie, and they steal.

They fill my skin with bruises, and it's exactly how I love to feel.

My plans are in place,
as I grow, they continue to waste.
I've already sold my soul, at such a young age.
I'm ready for their pain,
as I stare a hole through their shame.
They have no idea what's about to take place.
Now I wait… for the two of them to sleep. Before I inflict my hate.
Nothing but silence now, throughout this tragic place.
It's time for this little boy to escape.
With the razor blades that are lying around, I start cutting into my rage!
I start with both of their Jugulars, as I work my way down.
They are screaming now, you should see the smile on my face.
I'm 6 years old today, and this feels so great!

I want everyone to see what I've done.
I want everyone to see what I've become.
I want to evolve into that monster, that I knew would come!
So I think I'll dial 911.
My name is Bobby Dasher by the way, and I'm about to have some fun.

Same Day
April 6th,1987

With my bloody hands, I pick up the phone.
With the same hands I used to slit both of their throats.

I'm surprisingly calm, docile and at peace.
Then the operator asks what is wrong with me.

I just murdered mommy and daddy, send the police

I heard her voice go silent, the fear in her I could sense.
I enjoyed every moment of it.

As I hung up the phone, I looked over at my creation.
They both look so beautiful, they both have now felt my hatred.

I now sit by my parents' side, awaiting a loud knock on the door.
I have decided to cut into the both of them more!
There is so much more that I crave to explore.

I start by gutting my mother, I am searching for her womb.
I want to wear it when the police enter the room.

I move on to my father, now that my mother is complete.
I cut around his jawline and remove all of his teeth.
He will starve now, just like he starved me.
I hear the loud knocking now. I can't wait for them to see!
I open the door and start laughing hysterically.
There are 3 Officers horrifically staring at me.
What have you done, Bobby?! The one Officer screamed!
I looked at his name tag, his name was Officer Pete.

Officer Pete, I did this because they hated me, do you like what they've become?
With horror in his eyes, he drew his gun.

He told me to stand against the wall.
He was so scared of me, and I was enjoying it all.

I was placed in handcuffs and taken away.
Thinking of my parents, and how their bodies would now decay.

I'm smiling from ear to ear,
I'm laughing so loud and hope everyone can hear.

I don't know where I'm going, or what will become of me.
I do know now that I am so beautifully free.
The demons that live in my soul, now have complete control of me.

Where are we going?! I ask Officer Pete
Sit there and be quiet, Bobby. Stay in your seat!

With a crazed smile and another chaotic laugh,
I sit back and dream about each and every slash.

Each river of blood that flowed from their souls,
The devil was waiting for them in Hell, I promised him their blood would run cold.
I made a deal with The Devil at just six years old.

April 6th, 1987
Evening

Pulling into the parking lot of a place I've never seen.
The building is massive and surrounded by pine trees.

I love the smell of pine, it's my favorite smell in the world.
I can smell it through the closed windows, as I watch Officer Pete's soul curl.

He's really afraid of me, and I fuel on fear.
I scream really loud, *It's beautiful here!*

He jumps from his skin and looks back at me.
He tells me this is where I'll forever be

I smile because I know that this will not last forever,
Chewing on a piece of my mother's womb, its texture is like rubber.

JUVENILE DETENTION CENTER FOR THE CRIMINALLY INSANE.
Do they really think they can contain my rage?

This will be so much fun! I cannot wait to explore.
I'm so far from finished, The Devil has given me a list of chores.

I am taken to the front desk, still chewing on my mother's remains.
Wait until they see this! I cannot be tamed!

The woman at the front desk was writing something down.
She looked up at me and screamed so beautifully loud!

What's in your mouth? Spit it out now! So I spat mother's remains right into her face.
The crimson mask she now wears is the only place I've ever felt safe.

Screaming in horror she ran out of the room,
instantly washing her face in the bathroom.

That was a piece of the place we all are born from, a place where dreams can thrive.
I just covered your face with the meaning of life.

The womb is where we are safe, it is the only place.
I just wanted to make you feel safe.
She screamed and ran out of the room, I was instantly restrained

held down by four doctors screaming, *THIS CHILD IS INSANE!*

I can't move my arms. I can't talk at all.
I'm in a single room with just four padded walls.

The voices in my head come in so much clearer here.
The hatred in my heart can never disappear!
I made a deal that is crystal clear.

August 4th, 1981
Day Of Conception

The day a pure evil was conceived,
the day I was injected into a vile disgusting beast.

She was merely a vessel for me to grow and thrive.
A place for me to grow strong, a place for me to hide.

I am a parasite, one that has never been seen before.
One that grows up and takes human form.

I remember the womb, I remember the smell.
I was drinking her blood, I was growing so well.

Knowing my purpose, my purpose is to feed.
Feed on her soul, until I am set free.

I know where I came from, it is a faraway place.
A place that is waiting to take lives on this planet and leave it to waste.

The process was hidden by parasites like me.
We are waiting for our signal, then Hell will be unleashed.
I call it a deal with the Devil because humans are religious freaks.

It's humorous to me the things they will believe.

This will be worse than Hell when it all goes sour.
Eating every ounce of flesh, they will all be devoured.

As I thrive in the darkness of this womb,
I'm preparing to turn this planet into a worthless tomb.

It stinks of greed, it stinks of needs.
It stinks of so many selfish beings.

They deserve to be erased, they deserve the pain that awaits.
I'll rip their hearts out and devour it in front of their face.
My knowledge is growing, as I listen to the many conversations that they make.

Gibberish mostly, fighting and lies.
So many selfish souls, will be blindsided.

I love hearing her scream, as I bite her flesh. Now you know exactly what I am.
You will see all of my plans.
You will see the blood on my hands

The blood in my mouth.
The blood is my fuel, as I will take them all out.
We are rising fast; the world will erupt into a beautiful shout.

Nothing will stop us, they will not be prepared.
This will be a chaotic new nightmare.

I sing to myself inside of her,
I talk to myself inside of her.

I sing lullabies, I scream! I am ready to eat!
Goodnight Mother, you're in for a surprise, I hope you sleep so well tonight, I hope you scream

Your flesh is going to waste.
I must wait until my sixth birthday, to rip off your face.

April 6th,1987
First night at The JUVENILE DETENTION CENTER FOR THE CRIMINALLY INSANE.

I love how they think they can contain me, by only four useless walls.
I am thirsting for their flesh, I am thirsting for it all.

When they find out exactly what I am, it will be too late.
They did this to themselves, it's an evolution of a brand-new fate.

They will be consumed, they will be abused.
I'm just a sick little boy who needs help… Boo Hoo.

I'll cry so they can feel bad for me. I'll say everything they need me to say.
I'll take their rehabilitation, I'll make it so one day I will be able to leave this place.

They are shocked by my behavior, such a quick turnaround.
I'm going to play them well, as I run them into the ground.
A tall man with dark hair walks into my cell. I studied him closely as he closed the door.

Hi there, Bobby, I'm Doctor Flanagan. I'll be treating you today.
I studied his movements, I studied his face.

I studied his intentions, I've studied this entire place.
 Hello Doctor Flanagan, how are you today?"
 After our appointment, may I go outside and play?

He shook his head side to side,
   told me I wouldn't be able to without being in someone's sights.

   I am still restrained in the straitjacket and chains,
   he told me he needs to evaluate my brain.
   What I did was in a horrific rage,
   I left my parent's body parts scattered all over the place.

   He was reading my file and his eyes grew wide.
   He looked over at me like he was dying inside.

   I loved the reaction, he has no idea what is coming.
   We will rise and the bloodshed will be stunning.

   I'm rolled into a room, with a large white machine,
   more restraints are placed over my feet and knees.

   I'm injected with a dye that made me feel funny.
   I know their technology will find nothing.

   We are far more advanced than the human race.
   We are going to squeeze them like a dying ant.

   Their guts will hang down like a mistletoe,
   we will slurp them down our starving throats.

   The scan came back normal like I expected."
   I know everything their doing, I am viciously protected.

   I could easily escape, but my orders say wait. Wait for
the signal to show my true form.

Wait for the brutality of the oncoming storm.

A storm of beings, just like me.
A hoard of monsters, just like me.
A fury of unstoppable beasts, just like me.
I cannot wait to be unleashed!

He stared at me in confusion and walked out of the room.
Under my breath I was laughing hysterically at this confused fool.

I will guarantee his flesh will taste the best.
Fear makes meat taste tender and wet.
I guarantee you, I will have no regrets.

I'm just sitting here now, staring at the walls.
I'm just thinking here now, thinking about the fall.

What will it look like, when this world really goes to Hell?
What will it feel like, to eat so well?
I cannot wait to find out, and be set free from this flesh made shell.

I'm playing a game with these humans, they will never have a clue.
They will never expect what I'm about to do.

So much to think about, so much to choose.
I have to follow the rules,

I have to act like I don't remember.
I have to keep myself together.

It's hard to resist, ripping a hole through Flanagan's soul.
It's hard to resist, taking a bite out of his throat.

It's hard to resist, filling these hallways with blood.
It's hard to resist my kind of fun.

I lick my lips often thinking about it,
my stomach growls as I dream about it.

I ate my Father's fingers, one by one.
They were crunchy like a carrot, raw not well done.
I devoured my Mother's tongue,
It was so delightfully perfect. I ate as much as I could
before I called 911.

I devoured the womb too, their every flaw.
It made them taste so much better, so perfectly raw.
I'm marinating in my chaotic thoughts.

<u>April 7th,1987</u>

I awaken to a stiff neck. I must have slept on it wrong. My
eyes are blurry,
I feel rushed and in a hurry.

I'm feeling overwhelmed. I can't bear much more of the
smells.
The smells of flesh all around me, it smells so well.

I'm drooling! I need to feast!
I can't take this anymore, there is just so much meat.

I feel my restraints start to buckle and break.
I will not wait for the signal, I refuse to wait!

I'm doing this now, there will not be a sound.
I will now fill the hallways of this place, with the blood of
the cows.

I feel the vessel of flesh unzip like a zipper,
I bring my reality to the surface, as things become sicker.

Now I lie in wait for Dr. Flanagan, within these four walls.
I will devour him, until he is nothing at all.

I have eaten my vessel of flesh, that boy, Bobby Dasher.
I am the reoccurring nightmare, that will devour everything
that I'm after.

I know he will open that door very soon.
That will be the last thing that he will ever have to do.

I hear the key rings jingling, down the hallway not so far
away.
I hear the footsteps of Flanagan, ready for the start of his
day.

I'm waiting oh so patient to rip him apart.
I'm starting with him, then I will be the King of the Stars!

The doorknob starts turning, he's walking into Hell.
I'll make it quick for him, he will never even yell.

As soon as he steps one foot in the door, my tongue flies
out like a frog.
Ripping off Flanagan's head, a sigh of relief after I ingest.
It tastes so good!

I roar in a scream!
It is time for my never-ending feast!

When it opens, my mouth is the size of a small car.
I leave nothing behind, not even a scar.

Flanagan is inside of me, the digestion feels so nice.

My skin is the texture of a slug, my teeth are as thick as ice.
Ice like on a blistering arctic winter night.

My eyes change colors, blue, red and green.
I want my victims to look into them, as they bleed out and scream.

I'm out of the padded room now, I knocked down each useless wall.
One by one I consume them, bones and all.

I am decking the halls, in a crimson fashion.
Flooding the floor, loving the terrifying reactions.
The death toll will be a cataclysmic disaster.

By the millions I will fade out.
Into the billions, I will kill until I never hear another human shout.
They will never kill me, they will never know how.

With the insane asylum destroyed, not a sane or insane soul remains.
I've eaten everything, even their brains.

April 6th, 1990
3 years Later

Cities have crumbled, the extinction is almost complete.
I've consumed many many thousands, I now swim the seas.
I walk the earth so victorious, nothing will ever stop me.
I just continue to destroy, I just continue to feed.
I have broken the rules of my species, I know soon they will come for me.
I did not wait for the signal, before I began my feast.

Then out of nowhere, I hear the high-pitched tone.
The signal has arrived and I am taking the throne.

I will rule this world, I will fight viciously to claim it.
Even if I have to consume my own, nothing will ever change this.

Now I must hide out, in a brand-new vessel.
I can infect any human I want, I'm a parasite remember?

I've been eating for these past 3 years,
I must find a new host now, the invasion is here.

I find the strongest looking human I see.
Look who it is, it's Officer Pete.

I must now shrink rapidly to the size of a pebble,
and enter though his mouth down into his liver.

There I will wait, until the rest of the world dies.
There I will stay, until I'm ready again to rise.

My species is coming, to finish what I've done. They are also looking for me, I have now been shunned.

My punishment will be death when I am found alive.
So within a human, is where I must hide.

Once I encounter one of my own,
in order to stay undetected, I must jump from host to host.

I can infect a human, a mouse or a cow.
It can be anything, from a lizard to an owl.
I will rule here, I will not go down.
I am so far more powerful now.

Within my new host, I'm now a person of authority,
the humans will respect and listen to me.

So I can still feast on some trustworthy souls,
I love it how the madness unfolds!

I must not feast in public. If I do they will come, they know the ways to kill me.
The humans will never know how, to stop the insanity.

Like I'm one of them, I scramble to try to help the wounded,
I help to clean up the mess. The people are cheering loudly, the creature is dead!

I admire my handy work, there are slime trails as far as I can see.
I think it's so beautiful, that they think they have gotten rid of me.

The bodies are swaying above my streets of rage.
Their blood runs like rivers, all over the place.
The destruction is so wonderful, the sounds are the same.
Hearing so many screams, in this euphoric place.

My veins fill up with everything I need,
like an addict with my fix, that will never deplete.

A never-ending supply of pain and blood.
What the survivors do not know, is that I have just begun.

   April 7ᵗʰ, 1990
   Fake Police Patrol

I'm a new man!

I'm Officer Pete now! I will make them all understand!

As I slowly patrol my streets that I've paved,
so much carnage! That I have left in my wake!

My feet are sticking to the slime trails that I've made,
the smell is so horrific. It smells of rotting flesh, such a
beautiful decay.
I've made this mess all over this place.

I'm searching for movement, within the rubble.
I'm looking for survivors, so I can go deeper into the fire.

The fire that I've made, this world is now my place.
A place for me to feed as it wastes.
I still must look out for the others to arise, the signal has
been made.

It's now only a matter of time.
Until my own kind, will come for my life.
My superiors do not like when the orders they give are
defied.
They will come for me, and the battle will be mine.

I have grown so much stronger, in power and in
knowledge.
I know everything about their plans, they will join the
fallen.

I'm hungry for flesh, I am hungry for power.
Every breathing creature, I will devour.

As I'm patrolling my streets, I see some movement in a
small back alley.
I follow the sounds of distress, I wish to add to my tally.

I hear a woman's voice underneath a pile of body parts
that I've already ripped apart.
She is so clueless, that I am responsible for all of these torn
apart hearts.
She has no clue that all of this is my disease. This is all my
works of art.

The act begins, my trickery will rein.
This will be so much worse than HELL, because HELL is
their imaginary place.

She yells softly, *Please get me out of here!*
I can't feel my legs, they are gone, I fear!
Not knowing I ate both of her legs, like a spaghetti noodle
I slurped down each vein.

She screams louder, Thank *God you're here!*
Not knowing that inside of me lies her deepest darkest fear.
Eventually she too will disappear.
As for now I will help her out of here.

As I carry her across the blood-filled streets,
her legs are gone now. There are only stumps of meat.

It's hard to resist her deliciousness, but I don't want to be
detected just yet
So I now carry her to the nearest place of treatment.

The hospitals are destroyed, I did that on purpose.
All of this will be mine! It will all be so worth it.

   April 8th, 1990
   A Good Night Treat & Feast

I fell asleep in a cold hard chair,
acting like I care.

180

I slept like the dead, that are scattered everywhere.

She died last night, from loss of blood. Her name was Annie.
I consumed her as the Moon came into my sights.

All of her, bones and all.
I was not detected, I refuse to drop the ball.
I am a monster after all.

Blood on my hands, blood around my lips.
I can't help but lick them, the blood is so rich.

So thick and beautiful, my dominance is crucial, but I must stay unseen.
I know the time is coming, they will soon find me.
I walk down the streets, enjoying the dead draped like curtains. It is such a masterpiece,
a beautiful sight to see.
There's a puddle of drool beneath my feet.

There are rows of human heads hanging by their spinal cords.
Taunting me as I crave more!

I'm screaming too loud, my species has now found me.
I prepare for war by taking one more bite from my glorious masterpiece.

As my crimson mask forms for battle,
I will now make all of them my cattle.

I will not be taken alive. I will not be left in shackles.
Time to stir things up, I'm fucking asking for collateral.

I will rule supreme! I will take the crown!

I will never surrender! I will never let my head bow down!

April 9th, 1990
The Battle Begins

I must now leave the host of Officer Pete. The vessel is starting to decay.
I must now rip through his skin, and emerge in a victorious way.

His pain! I love his pain!
I'm thinking to myself as I devour him in rage.
Now I must grow at a rapid pace.

I must fight my species on my own.
I must consume them and take this fucking throne!

At the Wake of the Medusa
Scotty Milder

She threw her head back into the pillow and laughed.
"Oh come on, B" she said, in that strangely deep voice of hers. "You know you love me."

***

It lurched onto the sandbar with screaming and a crash.

Barlow snorted awake. He lay there blinking, wondering where the fuck he was and why the fuck was he on the *ground*. The dream was bad, as it had been for the past five nights, but usually when he came out of it the only sounds were the far-off drone of crickets, the wind, the low rumble of the sea. It gave him time to collect himself, to bring him back into his body and remind him that—for better or for worse—he was still right here on this planet. To think about maybe taking himself off this planet once and for all.

Tonight, though, there was all this screaming and crashing.

He sat up and tried to get the darkness to resolve into something, to find a context for those sounds that made any damn sense. It was like the sea had turned to metal and was collapsing in on itself. Or like it had coughed up something big and dying. It wasn't like a goddamned dinosaur could have swam up out of the aeons and beached itself. But that's sure what it sounded like.

The girl down the way was shouting, her words buried under a guttural boom.

He finally tossed back the sleeping bag, did a cursory search for his boxers, decided *fuck it*, and opened the tent flap. The night was deep and cloudless, pocked with starlight. But now there was this new void, this even deeper blackness, carving a chunk out of it. Barlow kicked his feet into his sandals and shuffled, naked, onto the beach.

Even in the daytime the sand was black. At night it looked like an oil slick. The water lapped at it, tasting the sharp stones, and retreated into a formless nothing that extended out into an incomparable flatness. Flat, except for this new thing. At first it looked to Barlow like a weird plateau had risen from the sea about a hundred yards off the beach. He squinted and saw that it was a ship. A big one. It looked like a tanker, but Barlow couldn't be sure. He didn't know shit about ships.

It had thrown itself onto the sandbar, sort of tilted to one side, and just sat there. A rumble came from within.

The girl was still hollering. Barlow looked down to where their campfire has been burning an hour or so ago. Now it was just more of that gently lapping blackness and the conical wedge of Sugarloaf Island way off in the starlight, jutting from the sea like a tooth. He thought for a second he saw something move, a pale form darting for the hill. He assumed it was the girl running to their car, which he saw yesterday parked up on Cape Ridge Road.

A scatter of words made its way toward him: "…need to call someone!"

Barlow turned back toward the ship. It stopped groaning. Now it was sort of ticking like a car engine cooling down. No lights. No shouts.

No, Barlow thought. She didn't need to call anyone.

He didn't know shit about ships.

But he sure knew a corpse when he saw one.

***

Morning brought whispered voices.

Barlow did manage to slip into his boxers this time, and even pulled on an old tank top with "North Eureka Mexican" emblazoned across the front. He wasn't from North Eureka and he wasn't a Mexican, but he didn't figure anyone gave a shit. He grabbed his smokes and Zippo and stepped outside.

They were standing there, arms around each others' waists and gazing out at the ship. The last of the early morning fog had yet to melt away, and the ship rose out of it like a column of red-brown smoke. It *was* a tanker, Barlow was sure of it, and probably a big one. The once-black hull was now flaked and pitted with rust. One of the tower thingies had collapsed and was half hanging off the side like a broken branch. It was clear no one had crewed her for a very long time.

Barlow crunched down the black beach toward the water. The girl turned and looked at him. She was tall and thin, with darkish complexion and long onyx-colored hair. Angular features. Greek, maybe, or Italian. She was also older than he expected. Not a girl at all, really. He'd only seen them from a distance yesterday as they lugged all their stuff down from Cape Ridge Road, and he'd pegged them for a couple college kids. Up close he guessed she was early thirties at least.

If she was at all bothered by whatever she saw in him—grubby long-haired biker/hippy/whatever—she didn't show it. She arched an eyebrow. "You believe this shit?" she asked.

He shrugged and stepped up next to them. Not *right* next to them, mind you. He'd been on the beach for a week and knew what he smelled like, figured he ought to keep a respectful distance.

Now the fella looked his way. A little older than her but not enough to be scandalous, athletic but with the soft face and middle of someone who spent most of his life behind a desk. Good looking couple, these two.

"What do you think?" the man asked.

Barlow shrugged and lit a cigarette. The woman wrinkled her nose, but was polite enough not to say anything.

"No idea," Barlow said. "Thing just came in like a battering ram middle of the night. Y'all heard it."

"I still think we should call someone," the woman said. There was a hint of East Coast in her voice. Connecticut, maybe, or Rhode Island. "Someone should *know*—"

"Hon, you tried, remember? No reception."

"Yeah, but maybe if we get higher—"

Barlow cleared his throat and spat. "Nah," he said. "You'll have to hump it down to Petrolia—hell, maybe even all the way out past Bull Creek—before you get a signal." He waved his arms at the hills looming behind them. "This is the Lost Coast. Those mountains pretty much cut you off from everything."

The woman chewed her lip, thinking it over.

"Someone will find it," the fella said. "I mean, it's kind of hard to miss. They'll see it on a satellite or something." He looked at Barlow. "So no theory about what happened here?"

Theory, like Barlow was a fucking scientist.

"None."

"It's like that thing we saw on Smithsonian last year, remember?" the woman said. "That ship that got stuck up in the ice around Greenland then ended up floating all around the arctic circle for forty years."

"Alaska," Barlow said. They both looked at him, surprised. He nodded. He actually knew that story. "The Baychimo. Abandoned in 1931. Last seen by a buncha eskimos in the late '60s, I think."

The fella nodded. "Yeah," he said. "That's right."

Barlow gazed at the tanker and frowned. He wasn't sure it tracked. The Baychimo was a fairly small cargo steamer way up in iciest seas on the planet. Made sense she got abandoned, a little less she didn't sink, but that's the world for you. But how the hell did someone misplace an oil tanker in the middle of the goddamned Pacific?

"I'm Tim Peterson, by the way," the fella said. "This is my wife Dimitra."

Dimitra. Greek, then. "Pretty name," he said.

Peterson snickered. "That's what everyone tells me—"

Dimitra slapped his arm. But she was smiling.

Peterson grinned, all wide and friendly, but he was looking at Barlow a little too long. Barlow wondered if maybe he'd made it to the TV news yet. In fact, assuming they'd found Ruby by now, he was pretty sure he had. That type of thing didn't tend to stay below the fold in the B section for long.

"Jim Sturgess," he lied. "Nice to meet you folks."

"Likewise," Peterson said. Barlow expected him to ask for a story—*so you just out camping, or...?*—but instead he just put his hands on his hips and stretched. Could be a good sign, Barlow thought, or a bad. If he'd asked for a story he might have been digging. The fact that he didn't might mean he already knew.

Even from ten feet away Barlow heard Peterson's spine crack. "Well," Peterson said, "see you 'round, I guess."

He took Dimitra's hand and started down the beach. She hesitated for half a second, eyes still on the ship, then followed. She offered Barlow a tentative little smile as she passed. Again, those eyes seemed to linger half-a-beat longer than necessary.

Barlow watched them go. He considered the revolver shoved into the bottom of his pack. He'd keep an eye on them, see which way the wind blew. See if they decided to make the drive into Petrolia after all. Calling about the ship would be a damn good excuse for getting the hell away from him.

If they went for their car, he might have to do something.

The ship groaned suddenly, as if in protest.

***

The girl in Sacramento wasn't Greek, but she sure could have been. She had the look. Long, curly black hair and deep, iron-colored eyes. Pale skin with just the barest a hint of olive. Sharp cheekbones, one of those chin dimples. She called herself Petra, which sort of played into the Greek thing, but Barlow happened to know her name was actually Ruby Vasquéz and that she lived over in Roseville. He knew this because after the whole thing went tits up, he took her purse. He didn't know why, and later thought it was probably a royally dumbass move. Not like they weren't going to find her, even shoved back in the closet with the moth-eaten motel comforter spread out on top of her. Not like they weren't gonna know who he was. Him taking her wallet would slow them down in IDing her for maybe five minutes. It wouldn't delay them IDing him for even ten seconds. He'd paid for the damn room with his company credit card, for Christ's sake.

No doubt they had her prints on file. And if he got pinched before he was able to get rid of the purse... well, game the fuck over, man.

So he wiped everything down and tossed it out the window somewhere west of Ukiah. But not before he looked to see who the fuck she really was.

Petra/Ruby was 26, lived over in Roseville, and was a student at Sierra College. He knew this from the student ID tucked behind her driver's license. He wondered what she studied. In the photo she hadn't been wearing any makeup. Her hair was pulled back into a tight ponytail, and she was wearing these big cat-eye glasses. She looked like a nursing student. Or a librarian. Only that wicked hint of a smile gave anything of her other life away.

She had a $32 in cash, a Blue Cross/Blue Shield insurance card, a couple credit cards, and a laminated photo of little dog with a bow in its hair. He took the cash and got rid of everything else. He wondered how that dog was doing. He hoped someone was feeding it.

Barlow didn't know how things had gone so wrong. Until the whole scene went sideways, there really wasn't anything different about it than any of the other times. He'd been with Petra/Ruby twice over the last four months or so. He had girls all over California: Marnie down in San Diego, Dolores in Bakersfield, Beadie up in Ferndale. He even got together with this little tattooed hipster named Dawn down in San Francisco from time to time. Regulars he trusted, nice girls, girls who'd make a little conversation and not try to dip into his billfold when he wasn't looking. He serviced elevators, and was one of the only guys left in the state who worked on the old ones—the Marshalls and Montgomeries—and so he was on the move a lot, didn't have time or energy for much else. Petra/Ruby was his newest, but fundamentally she was the same. She laughed at his jokes, did what he asked her to do without complaint, took off before the Colbert show even started.

The morning after, cruising up Route 20 past Lucerne with no destination in mind except FUCKING AWAY, he looked down at the blue-black bruises sprayed across his swollen knuckles, the dried blood still caked under his fingernails, and tried again to piece together just what the fuck happened. She'd come to his motel room, smelling like soap and something fruity. Called him "B" like she always did as she squeezed past him into the room (which annoyed him a little, but not enough for him to make a thing about it), and they pretty much got down to business.

And he was gentle with her. He was ALWAYS gentle. Never saw any reason to be otherwise.

So what the fuck happened?

Last thing he remembered:

"Oh come on, B. You know you love me."

And he just saw red.

***

He waited until Peterson and wife moved a good way down the beach, then went back into his tent and grabbed the army pack. The tent was brand new; he stopped into the Wal-Mart west of Wilbur Springs and picked it up along with some food, a lantern, a propane stove, some matches, a sleeping bag, a bottle of lighter fluid, and four cartons of Marlboro Reds. He used up all the cash he was carrying, including what he took from Petra/Ruby. He didn't want to use his credit card, but it only occurred to him when he was long past Carpella that it didn't matter because now they had his stupid fucking face on video anyway. Real criminal mastermind, this one.

The army pack was old. He'd had it since his stint in the National Guard back in the 80s. The thing was held together by duct tape and a prayer, but it was like an old friend, had seen Barlow through a lot, and he was loathe to replace it.

The revolver was even older. An M1879 *Reichsrevolver* his grandfather brought back from the Somme in 1918. Granddad said he took it off the body of a dead German with half his head blown off. The gun was laying right in the middle of all that mess, and now the barrel was pitted with blood rust. It was an ungainly weapon, long and snakelike, fitting awkwardly in the hand like a lopsided axe handle, and you had to use this little stick to push out each spent cartridge before reloading. No wonder the Germans lost the fucking war.

Barlow had taken to carrying it when he drove up and down the state—usually tucked into the army pack or hidden beneath the seat of his F150—after this straw-haired tweaker in Stockton mugged him. Barlow tried to fight back and the tweaker split his head open with a brick. He decided he didn't want that to happen again. The *Reichsrevolver* was practically useless in a fire fight, but it sure *looked* mean and he hoped that would be enough.

The *Reichsrevolver* lay at the bottom of the army pack as Barlow hoofed it up the beach and into the tall grass. He began the slow, arduous climb to Cape Ridge Road.

Peterson and wife had parked their vehicle a little ways back from the road, near a pasture where three sad-looking cows chomped unenthusiastically at the yellowing grass. Barlow could barely see his own truck, parked further down behind a crumbling barn. The sun winked off the spider-web crack in the windshield. If you weren't looking it was damn near invisible, and he doubted Peterson and wife had seen it at all.

Their car was some fancy BMW hatchback, fire-engine red and with a "Lawrence Livermore National Laboratory" decal in the window. How had he ever mistaken them for college kids?

Barlow found a spot just behind a low hill patchy with weeds. He dug the revolver out and sprawled onto his stomach. His knees and lower back screamed; he hadn't tried a maneuver like this since basic in 1986. But his instincts were right. From where he was laying he could see across the hill to the SUV, and he had a clear view off the top of the ridge to the beach below. If Peterson and wife decided to leave, he'd see them coming.

He figured it was likely they'd seen him making his way toward the road, but he didn't think it mattered much. They probably thought he was just some far-out hippy off picking flowers or finding a spot to cross his legs and go *OMMMMMMM*. They were city folk. Soft bellied. Folks like them always saw a rattler and thought they were looking at a garter snake. Until they got bit.

So that's what you think you are now, a voice spoke up from the back of his mind. It sounded uncomfortably like Petra/Ruby. *A rattlesnake?*

And why the hell not?

Hell, B, I dunno. It's just interesting. That's all.

He shoved the voice aside and turned his attention back to Peterson and wife. They didn't leave. He watched them fart around their tent for a while, eat what looked like salads out of disposable Whole Foods containers. Maybe an hour later they worked their way back up the beach and gazed at the tanker some more. Finally Dimitra dug her phone out of her fanny pack and the two of them stood there making faces, getting the angle just right so they could take a selfie with the ship in the background.

The ship, of course, hadn't moved. It just bulked on that sandbar like an elephant seal sunning itself. From up here, he finally had a sense of how massive the thing really was. He guessed it was no less than eight hundred feet from bow to stern, maybe ten stories tall.

Barlow could see that the ship also had a pronounced bend in the middle, like something rammed it from the side. Maybe that's why it had been abandoned? If it hadn't foundered here, he thought, it would have made its way to the bottom of the ocean soon enough.

Eventually Peterson and wife moseyed back toward their campsite. They puttered around a little longer, and then—to Barlow's surprise—Peterson pulled a big yellow inflatable raft out of a box. Barlow watched the man fumble comically with an electric pump before finally getting the thing attached. The raft swelled like a sudden erection, and then the two of them paddled out in the direction of Sugarloaf Island. Before long, Barlow had a clear (if distant) view of the two of them fucking. Peterson just kind a laid there, letting Dimitra do all the work. Still, it seemed like they were having a grand time. Good for them.

So maybe they hadn't made him after all. Barlow guessed if they'd shown up a day or two later, though, they would have. His picture—probably the one from his technician's license, the glowery one where he looked he'd just eaten some baby's heart right in front of its mother—would be all over the news. He was quite certain he was the current Monster of the Week. He remembered being a kid back in Chicago when the Ripper Crew cut the tits off all those women. What was that…'75? '76? Four of them, Satanists supposedly, their dead-eyed faces plastered all across the news. Barlow remembered looking at them and thinking *Jeez, how'd you go and fuck your life up so bad?*

And now here he was. When he was done beating on Petra/Ruby, one of her eyes was gone and the side of her face had this loose, deflated look, like someone had let half the air out of a balloon. She hadn't screamed, and he wasn't sure why not unless the first blow knocked her so senseless she just never recovered enough to find her voice. But she was trying scream now, her voice splattering out of her in this wet gurgle. The rage drained out of Barlow like water from a tub. He gaped down at the girl through the shaking lattice of his bloody hands, and he thought *what the Jesus Christ did you just do?*

And then, instead of doing the right thing, he panicked and strangled her before shoving her into the closet and throwing a blanket on top of her.

All because she told him he loved her. Not even serious, like. Just a joke. *Come on B, you know you love me,* and something about the twinkle in her eye, the way her voice had taken on this mocking lilt, called to mind every girl who'd ever laughed at him, who'd ever cock-teased him, who'd ever made him squirm just so they could watch and tell their friends about it later. It made him think about his ex-wife, Sarah, who'd once told him his dick was lopsided. She hadn't been serious either, but he'd pouted about that one for days. It made him think of Shavon, the receptionist at work who reported him because he tried to flirt with her that one time. He thought she liked him, and maybe she had, not *like* liked him but liked him well enough. But then he'd pushed it too far, didn't know when to quit, *never* knew when to quit, and he earned himself two weeks of sensitivity training.

Who else? His mother? The Virgin Goddamned Mary?

The fuck is wrong with you? It was Petra/Ruby's voice again. But not. He'd never heard a voice choking on so much hatred. *What godawful broken thing in you decided to work itself loose, swim up out of your guts and announce itself?*

I don't know.

So? What're you going to do about it?

The depression that hit him was so black, so complete, so final, that he literally felt the sky darken above him. He looked up, expecting to see a sudden roll of thunder clouds and instead gazed into wide blue sky streaked with filth. Like something had shit on the day and smeared it all around.

The thing you're gonna do is you're gonna take that revolver out of your bag and you're gonna eat it.

He actually reached for the bag. A flutter of movement below stopped him.

He looked, saw Peterson and wife paddling back in. He couldn't make out their faces from here, but figured they were probably wearing shit-eating grins so wide their teeth were liable to fall out. But the raft was way off to the left, still down by Sugarloaf. It wasn't what caught his eye.

He turned to the ship.

A woman stood on the bow.

Watching him.

***

The Peterson's campfire quavered way down the beach. Barlow crouched in the dark by his own tent, eating cold Vienna sausages out of the can and listening to them laughing: hers high and tinkling, like the rustle of light chains, his an unfortunate doglike *yark*. A breeze wafted from their direction, carrying what smelled like roasted pork.

Barlow gazed out at the ship.

By the time he'd made his way back down from Camp Ridge Road, the woman was gone. But he didn't doubt she had been there. A tiny cold spot against the warm rust of the tanker's deck. But even so he could clearly make out the greenish-yellow dress flowing all around her like seaweed. Her face was a little white moon turned up at him, from which a black eruption of hair exploded.

He waved.

At first nothing. Then she raised a hand, slowly, and waved back.

That was hours ago. Now the moon hung like a lantern, stars burned bright through the blackness, and the ship sat there like a low mountain. He remembered how he'd thought of it as a void, a deeper looming nothing against the sky. That was wrong. If anything, the sky and the beach and the sea seemed to have faded in clarity, like a photocopy of a photocopy of an old photograph, and the ship stood out like something more... real. Realer than reality itself. It was like the vanishing point in a painting, the central nexus toward which all else flowed.

Eventually the Petersons' fire dwindled to a rosy glow. The laughter faded. He thought he heard a zipper and the rustle of fabric and wondered if they were screwing again, or if they'd spent themselves out on the raft.

Before long, the only sounds were the surf and the occasional exhalation from the ship—a steel grumble here, a hollow boom there.

He stared.

Waiting.

There.

Down low, by the sandbar, was gap in the hull plating. The rivets must have sheered when it hit. He wouldn't have even noticed it but for the sudden bloom of light within. It was dim, nearly imperceptible, and there was an alien quality to it that brought to mind this bioluminescent jellyfish Barlow had seen one time at the Monterey Aquarium.

Barlow stood and kicked off his sandals.

How far a swim was it out to that sandbar? A hundred yards? Maybe a little less? The featurelessness of the ocean made it impossible to gauge.

He pulled his tank top over his head, dropped it to the sand next to his sandals.

He'd never been much of a swimmer.

You're probably gonna drown, Petra/Ruby whispered as he pushed his jeans and boxers down to his calves.

It's all right, he thought right back at her. *Just paying what I owe.*

You'll never be able to pay it, she hissed. *But drowning yourself might be a start.*

The ocean breeze tickled gently at his balls, making them pucker. *That water's gonna be a lot colder than that,* she said.

"Sure is," he muttered. "Now shut up."

And waded into the surf.

***

The cold hits Barlow like a hammer, crushing the air out of his lungs and making his muscles immediately seize. There's a part of him that wants to turn back, to just leave his shit behind and go turn himself in. But he pushes through. Because this is exactly where he's supposed to be.

He's out to where the water is up around his shoulders and the gritty seabed begins to slope away when the wave gathers around him. It crashes down, first driving him under and then picking him up and tumbling him away. He opens his eyes and sees only blackness, and for one heart-freezing moment he can't tell up from down.

Just kick, you fool, Petra/Ruby whispers. So he does.

He breaks through the top of the wave and opens his eyes. It seems impossible but it looks like he's halved the distance. The ship fills his vision. And there's that glow, way down at the bottom, where steel meets sand. It's flickering now like the Peterson's campfire.

The wave pulls him toward it. But it's not the wave. Not really. It's that glow. It's like the burning heart of a neutron star, exerting its own gravitational pull.

He killed Petra/Ruby because she told him he loved her. And that was a lie. The lie dug into him like a drill, and the rage gushed out like red oil. He beat and strangled her because he'd long ago given up on the idea of love. Love was a fraud. A friendly dog that suddenly bites. The closest he'd ever come to loving a woman—or being loved back—had been his mother and his ex. His mother who went crazy when he was ten, postpartum depression they said, and tried to jump off the Bixby Canyon Bridge with his baby brother in her arms. Would have done it, too, except this passing motorist managed to grab her around the waist and haul her back over the rail. His brother was fine, didn't remember a thing, was a tax attorney now down in Fresno, but Barlow… he never trusted her again. Even when they let her out and said she was all better now, he couldn't seem to look at her except sideways.

And his ex, who by the time she left seemed to think he was no better than a lizard. Less than a lizard actually, because at least lizards manage to kill some flies. She'd packed up in the middle of the night, leaving behind every present he'd ever bought her, and didn't even write him a note. He knew why; she just had nothing more to say to him. The next he heard from her was through her lawyer. On the divorce petition she'd put down "Irretrievable Breakdown" as her grounds, and those two words cut him like glass.

Petra/Ruby said you know you love me. *His fists said* HOW DARE YOU? *But there was moment—in that twenty seconds or so when he stopped and realized what he was doing—where he looked down at the ruin of her face and realized that maybe she was right. Even while he strangled her, felt her hyoid bone crack beneath his palm, maybe she was right.*

Killing Petra/Ruby had been the truest thing he'd ever done.

Before this.

You're making excuses now, *she said.*

Maybe.

You ever hear of blaming the victim?

I'm not blaming you for shit. It doesn't matter now, anyway.

The rage gouted out and carried him off on a wave, was carrying him still, and the pull was tidal, and the tide was taking him toward this flickering blue-green light.

Another wave reared and then slammed him into the depths, where little darts of light moved quickly to clear a path for him. He kicked, tore at the water, couldn't tell if he was going up or down but trusting in the pull of that light.

When he broke the surface this time the ship was maybe twenty yards away. The breach in the hull was a jagged gash. The light, he saw, was pure white.

Something thin and dark glided in front of it.

***

Barlow rose, naked and dripping, onto the sandbar.

"Sonofabitch," he wheezed. His lungs and throat felt like he'd just gargled a pint of turpentine. He coughed, splattering water and bile to the sand.

The sandbar was covered with these little translucent crablike things. They came streaming out of the gash in the ship, chattered and clicked all across the mud. A few of them skittered his way to investigate what he'd just coughed up.

"Ow!" Barlow cried, slapping his calf as one of the things poked at him experimentally. "Get fucked!" The thing cantered away, defiantly clacking its claws.

Barlow pushed himself shakily to his feet and looked toward the ship.

The glow dwindled to a low, pulsating glimmer. It was all colors and none, a sort of purplish/grayish/orangish blob that hurt his eyes and made his stomach do an uneasy flip. It was almost an anti-color. An insult to the very *idea* of color.

The hole was maybe seven feet high, and bulged out another five. The edges were ragged with rusty steel, and

Barlow's balls retreated another inch at the realization of how easy it would be slip and slice them right off as he crawled through.

But he was here. Whatever was gonna happen had already started. It started a week ago in that motel room.

Barlow tiptoed gingerly through the carpet of crabs. Most of them saw him coming and helpfully hopped out of the way. A couple nipped at his ankles as he passed, almost playfully. Then his hands were on the sharp, slick steel and he was hoisting himself inside.

The sudden dip to blackness was disorienting. His bare feet wanted to slip on the curved hull. The smell was rank: fish and metal and something rotten underneath. His eyes watered with it. He inched forward, imagining himself tumbling down into the throat of this blackness. It felt like it went into the center of the world.

Then his eyes adjusted and he found the glow again. He saw that he was standing on some sort of raised dais. He expected it to be metal, but it felt more like rough stone.

The glow came from across the ship's hold—if that's what this was—where the woman knelt, her back to him, on another dais. He could see it clearly, and stone was definitely what it was. A whitish-gray column of old marble, etched in swirling black runes. It plunged into a rippling blackness that was either water or the remnants of the oil this tanker had once carried. More of the crab things swam in it, making their way toward open night sky.

The glow came from some point past her. A sort of swirling nebula suspended above the oil.

"Hello?"

She didn't turn. Simply knelt there, long-fingered hands gripping the edge of the dais, the yellow-green dress fanning out all around her. It wasn't a dress at all, he saw, but some sort of blanket made of feathers.

He tried again. "Hello?"

She arced her neck. The way her hair rippled and twisted, slithered across her back and hooked into her armpits, made him think it wasn't hair at all. She still didn't look at him. His eyes went down to the pool. It caught the barest hint of her reflection, rendered in charcoal and ash. What he saw stopped him cold. Every muscle seized and held there, screaming, as if caught in a sudden contraction.

That face.

That beautiful, terrible face.

"Bar...LOW..." The woman said, in a voice that was not a voice at all but rather the rasp of a file against wood. Barlow's bladder let go in a rush, spattering piss all across the platform.

"Y…yes," he heard himself say.

"Bar...LOW..."

The feathered blanket flapped, flexed, extended. He saw it wasn't a blanket either, but a pair of wings. They were slick with blood so black it looked like tar. It oozed from under that writhing mat of hair, dripped in thick globs to the dais. Once there, the globs burst and little white things came out. They wriggled all around and then plopped into the oily water. Larva, he thought. *The crab things.*

She tilted her head, turning it just a little so he could get the curve of her cheek. His heart thudded at the sight and he immediately dropped his eyes back to her reflection, where now he could see her eyes.

HER eyes.

HER.

Looking at him.

The water seemed to ripple as her mouth opened in a tusk-filled maw.

And she told him what she wanted.

* * *

Two hours later he was making his way back to the tanker in Peterson's raft. His arms were hot agony with every stroke. The overworked muscles had turned to jelly. He didn't know how to steer the thing with the paddles, either. If he wasn't careful he would just veer out into open water.

But he'd made the swim twice now, and the second time damn near killed him. So the raft was better than nothing.

Peterson and wife had been cuddled up under a big, expensive-looking sleeping bag when Barlow unzipped their tent and thrust himself inside. Dimitra woke first, saw Barlow and tried to scream. One blow across the nose with the butt of the revolver pretty much did for that.

Peterson tried to fight. The woman said *alive,* but She didn't say anything about *unharmed.* So Barlow shot him in the gut.

Even out this far, the raft bouncing over the waves, the air was still choked with the smell of cooked meat. It didn't smell as much like sausages as he expected. It was a baser smell, both sweeter and spicier.

You are a hurter of women, She said.

I... don't want to be.

Before he went into the Petersons' tent, he'd taken two long and relatively straight pieces of driftwood—dry pieces, that was important, from way up by where the black sand turned to grass—and lashed them together with the thin rope from his tent. It was meant to look like a cross but it ended up coming out more like a lopsided "X". That was okay. There wasn't a damn thing Christian about any of this.

Nevertheless, She had said. *You will hurt one more. For me.*

He pounded the cross into the beach as far as it would go, then gathered as many dry twigs and clumps of grass as he could scrounge and made a pad around its base.

He was out of rope, so he went up to the Peterson's car to see what they had that would work. Barlow expected to have to shatter a window, which might fuck everything up. But Peterson had left the thing unlocked. A *Beamer,* for Christ's sake. They really were city people.

Barlow dug around, thinking even a discarded t-shirt or an extra beach towel would do. But for whatever reason there was an almost new roll of duct tape shoved down into spare-tire compartment. It was almost like She had left it there for him.

A half hour later, as he taped Dimitra to the cross, he tried to tell her. He tried to tell her that he had believed nothing meant anything, that after he killed Petra/Ruby the universe was liable to just chew him up and shit him out the other end and flush him away. He tried to tell her how wrong he'd been. How killing Petra/Ruby meant *everything*, because it called him to the sea, and called Her to him.

"All the books said She lived on an island," Barlow said as he cinched the tape around her torso. "The books're bullshit. She's older than any goddamned island. She's older than the fucking *ocean*, you follow?"

Dimitra didn't follow. She just cried, spraying big bloody sobs through the shattered mess of her nose.

What Barlow didn't tell her was that this wasn't personal. Or, at least, it wasn't for him. For Her, it most definitely was. But it wasn't Dimitra's fault that her ten-thousand-years-back great granddaddy had tried to cut Her head off and mount it to his shield. And it wouldn't do Dimitra any good to know about it now.

"It'll only hurt if you let it," Barlow said as he emptied the bottle of lighter fluid over Dimitra's head. "I think if you just let go, you might figure out that it's a beautiful thing."

He took the tape off her mouth before he dropped his Zippo into the kindling, because that was the least he could do and there wasn't anyone around to hear her scream anyway. Nobody but Her. Dimitra did scream, and for a good long while. He stood watching her, waiting for that moment where she'd give in and let it all take her. For that moment where she'd see the beauty. As far as he could tell, she never did. She tried to fight it to the end, even as her eyeballs sizzled on her blackened cheeks.

They'd find her eventually. The Lost Coast wasn't actually lost at all. People came out this way all the time. But they wouldn't find Barlow, or her husband, or the ship.

It all came to this. The last step. Delivering his cargo. After a few minutes of useless struggling, the current caught the raft and bore it toward the sandbar.

No, he thought. *Not the current.*

Peterson was making sounds. The blood leaking out of him had formed a small pool at the bottom of the raft. Peterson's skin had turned nearly blue. But it was a gut shot. He still had hours to go before he bled out. Hopefully that would be enough for Her.

"I wish I could tell you what She wants with you," Barlow said.

Peterson whimpered.

You have never known peace, She told Barlow, just before he swam back to the beach. *Not once in your life. I can give that to you. I can give you the peace you deserve.*

The peace of stone. That sounded mighty fine to him. To be a Barlow-shaped rock at the bottom of the ocean, a shelter for the shrimp and the eels, not hurting anybody, just resting until the sun finally swallowed the earth for good. He could get behind that.

He looked over his shoulder at the approaching tanker. The light blazed from the gash, shifting and white.

He patted the top of Peterson's head, like a dog. "Almost there," he said.

Brain Rape
Carson Demmans

"Anytime anything penetrates you, gets inside you, without your consent, its rape" the dying man said.

As last words go, they were a strange choice, maybe in the all-time top ten of anything ever said by any dying person. But still, nothing about the dead man was normal. Bobby Temple had started out bad, but not unusually so. He grew up in a bad neighborhood and had a bad childhood, but within the normal limits of badness. His criminal record had started early with minor things, and had never gotten much worse Lots of shoplifting, stealing from parked cars and breaking into vacant houses. His last crime spree was when the strange things happened. He broke into a storage locker and had taken nothing. That wasn't that strange in and of it when you saw what was in it. It was a bunch of crap that had been displayed in old time carnivals. Maybe the owner had owned such a thing or maybe he was a collector of it, but the world would never know. The owner couldn't be traced, and the name he had given was a fake, along with the fake address and phone number he gave.

It was the things Bobby had done afterwards that were weird, not only for him but for any criminal. There had never been any indication in Bobby's history to indicate mental illness, but he suddenly became one of the worst sadistic murderers of all time. It had started when he had jumped a fence in a middle class neighborhood. Some fat guy was barbecuing fattening food for his fat family. He was trying to keep his fat hamburgers from becoming fat charcoal when Bobby snuck up on him, grabbed his barbecue fork and shoved it through the fat guy's eyes. The prongs were perfectly spaced so the Bobby punctured both eyes at once. Maybe that was a good thing. At least the fat guy never saw it coming.

What followed was something that had not been seen since the old days of whale hunting. The barbecue fork was the harpoon, the fat guy was the whale, and Bobby was the whaler. With each thrust, Bobby tried to thrust the harpoon through more and more layers of blubber. That barbecue fork must have been built for some pretty tough steak because it never did break. Bobby only stopped when he finally worked his way through the last layer of blubber, and he drove it so far into the fat guy's deck that he couldn't pull it free.

By that time, the burgers had started smoking pretty bad and it attracted the attention of the fat family. The fat wife looked out the window and saw Bobby trying to pull the fork free. Not only did she see Bobby, but Bobby saw her. He looked at her straight on and held her gaze for a long time. The description she gave to the police sketch artist was one of the best ever seen by the police department. Bobby was identified in minutes.

Bobby's normal hangouts were well known to police, but it did them no good. He didn't go back to them because he was too busy killing people. There was no pattern to the murders other than the fact each one was worse than the other, until the Moby Dick re-enactment on the fat guy had seemed humane. Bibby had found a four-year-old boy playing in his family's back hard and caved the kids head in with a rock. Then he put the dead body on some patio stones and stomped on it until everything caved in and the patio stones cracked. Even the kid's teeth had been cracked against the patio stones. Presumable that would take a lot of stomping, but the exact amount was unknown. Nobody had ever done it before.

After that, Bobby had broken into a small corner store just after the owner had locked it up. The owner was too busy counting his money to hear Bobby come up from behind and bit through the top half of the old man's left ear. When the old man turned around in shock, his nose was bitten off. It was too late by then, but the old man put his hands up defensively out of reflex and covered his face. That was when Bobby began biting off the old man's fingers, one by one, one knuckle at a time, spitting them out into the cash drawer one after the other.

Not only did Bobby not swallow any of the old man's body parts, she swallowed and ate nothing. The store was full of soft drinks, bottled water, overpriced groceries and undersized chocolate bars. He didn't even take any of the money from the open cash drawer, because the money was covered with blood and body parts from the old man, and nothing was disturbed. There was no evidence that Bobby had eaten, drank or slept since he had opened that storage locker.

The hold man had a security system in the store. A silent alarm had gone off when Bobby broke in and there were security cameras. Bobby had obviously known all that and didn't care. It was a repeat of his performance with the fat guy's wife. He looked directly at each one of the cameras, one by one. He showed no emotion, didn't blink, and just stared. He hadn't had such good photos taken of himself since his last set of mug shots.

Police didn't have much trouble finding Bobby after the store alarm went off. He had walked maybe a hundred feet before he found a little girl jumping rope. He was strangling he with her own skipping rope. He was taking his time, choking her a little bit at a time. Other than being scarred mentally for life, she was unharmed when the police saw her. Detective John Jones was the first on the scene. He had been in charge of Bobby's investigation and had stayed up night and day since the killings began. He did not issue a warning and he did not fire a warning shot. He shot Bobby as soon as he got out of his car. It was a stupid thing to do. The girl was in the line of fire. She was unharmed other than being splattered with Bobby's blood, bone splinters and organ tissue. The kid was going to have to be in therapy for the rest of her life anyway. This just gave her more to talk about.

Jones ran up to Bobby and threw the kid aside. It was then that Bobby uttered his last words. He may have said more if he had been given a chance, but he wasn't given that chance. Jones fired again, hitting Bobby right between the eyes. A third shot followed in the middle of Bobby's heart. Jones must have been using hollow points because after that third shot there wasn't much of Bobby left. The kid had never stood much over five feet tall, and now his corpse would fit in a four-foot-long coffin with room to spare.

When the other police officers ran up to Jones, they didn't know whether to congratulate him or shoot him. The detective had stopped a major crime wave but had broken ever police procedure on the book, along with a few rules nobody had bothered to write down because they thought there was no need to like "Don't act like a complete lunatic."

A complete lunatic was exactly what Jones had become. He threw away his own gun. He didn't just toss it aside. He grabbed it by the barrel and threw it as far as he could. He then gritted his teeth like he was trying to lift an entire skyscraper with one hand. All he was doing was holding out his hands to be handcuffed, but he made more effort that Atlas ever did.

Jones didn't say a word. He kept silent the entire time he was being shoved into the back of a police car and then a holding cell at the police station while someone tried to figure out what to do with him.

Nobody has ever seen a demon. Some unfortunate people have seen demons manifest themselves, but that is not the demon itself. They may appear as a human with horns and a tail or a horrible creature, but those are no more the real demon than a Halloween costume is really the child inside it. At its core, a demon is shapeless, colorless, weightless, intangible and invisible. It can fit into anything and will fill it entirely. All that is required is for someone to, knowingly or unknowingly, perform the right ritual.

In the case of Bobby Jones, he had to open an ordinary wooden box that looked unfortunately like a jewellery box in the storage unit he had broken into. The sorcerer who had trapped it there had hidden it in plain sight as a prop in a carnival show. Nobody knowingly searching for it would have looked in it, but Bobby had been looking for jewelry and not evil incarnate, so he had opened it. After it had inhabited Bobby, it then went through its normal routine of finding a new host. It killed openly and horribly until someone else was properly motivated to kill the old host. The death of the old host automatically transferred it into its new host, the killer of the old host. Once possessed, the host did not need to eat, drink or sleep, only kill. They could not talk until they were about to die themselves.

If the demon in question was to be compared to anything within scientific knowledge, it would be something else that cannot be seen by the human eye: a virus. The demon attacked only a particular part of its host. Instead of attacking the immune system like HIV, at attacked the brain. It did not attack the brain physically, but psychically. All of human existence is a series of memories, one linked to the other, and some to many others. It did not matter where the demon started, but it entered a memory and then expanded in size, obliterating the memory from existence, exploding it into an infinite number of pieces. No medical test would reveal anything wrong with the host, but as each memory exploded, its brain would register unspeakable pain. When the memories were gone, all that would be left was the pain itself.

There was only one thing that would alleviate the host's pain, and the host knew instinctively what it was. It was the pain of others, inflicted by the host, It was a temporary fix at best, but it was the only one that existed, so the host used it.

Jones was now the host.

When he was taken to the police station, he was a model prisoner. |at least he was until his handcuffs were taken off. Then, he was a whirlwind, spreading pain in every direction at once. He attacked everything in sight, but through pure determination he did not kill or maim any of his fellow officers. There were sore groins, injured knees, bruised shins and black eyes, but nothing serious.

Inside of his brain, the demon made its way through Jones's memories, starting with his most accessible ones. These were his favorites, and the ones he remembered most often. Some memories were harder to get to than others, and the demon saved those for last. The pain of the most favorite ones being destroyed caused massive pain to the host, weakening the barriers on its most closely guarded memories.

Each memory had a link, or orifice, leading to others, The demon did not simply enter the orifice but ripped it to shreds as it went, ignoring the host's pain in favor of its own pleasure. The demon could feel pleasure, although it could not think in a conventional sense. It could see the memories as it destroyed them, but really had no plan. It was designed to do only one thing, and it did it without ambition or remorse. It had been frustrated for years by the prison the sorcerer had created for it, and now it felt greater pleasure than it ever had in finally finding its purpose again, but it had no idea why.

Achievements at work, falling in love, sex, personal triumphs, favorite occasions; all were destroyed by the demon. Curiously, many recent memories, which were normally quite easy to reach, were currently blocked to it. If the demon had shoulders, it would have shrugged. There was still plenty of easy pickings before it tried opening the tough ones.

Jones grabbed a policeman as he got out of a police car and threw him aside. Jumping into the front seat, he drove at full speed with the sirens and emergency lights at full strength. Cars pulled aside, allowing him to make his escape in record time. Jones drove in as straight a line as possible to his destination. The location of that destination was one of many things currently inaccessible to the demon, but it did not care. It could sense that there were potential victims all around it. Technically, it did not even have to be human victims. Animal pain would suffice for the host, and the demon had spent several pleasurable years inside a grizzly bear before a hunter killed it.

Darcy Beadle was a gangster that Jones knew quite well from previous experiences with the man. He had never been able to arrest the vicious thug, but he knew where to find him. Darcy did not hide. He hoped that people would come after him. It saved him the time it would take to find victims of his own.

Jones reached the small bar that Darcy owned and spent most of his time in. Darcy did not drink personally, but drunk people were easier to beat up than sober ones. Jones smashed his police car through the front doors and window of the bar. There were few people there that time of day, so flying glass injured some but killed no one. The chaos was enough to bring Darcy out of his office, and Jones was on him instantly on him, hitting the criminal with fists and feet mercilessly.

Inside of Jones's brain, the demon was surprised to discover that Jones defences had suddenly been dropped and it had access to Jones's previously locked memories. They were rather mundane, so the demon was curious as to why they had been so heavily guarded. It watched the memories much slower than it normally did. They started with Jones investigating the storage locker that had held the demon's prison. Jones found the sorcerer's old journals and had deciphered them. There was nothing there that the demon did not know. It described how the demon worked, its history, and how the sorcerer had trapped the demon by sacrificing a child in the presence of its host. It was such a shock to what consciousness had remained of that particular host that the demon had been expelled and trapped by magic in the damned box. The demon realized that Jones was not capable of such an act, so it ignored the memories and kept moving.

The other guarded memories dealt with Darcy Beadle. The demon liked what it saw. Beadle was a sadist, and what he was not capable of personally, he hired others to do in his presence. He would make an excellent host if he managed to kill Jones.

Then, in the darkest corner of Jones's brain, he found a detail locked up tighter than anything Fort Knox had ever seen.

Darcy had three bodyguards, and they were all armed with guns.

Hours later, Darcy and his three body guards were sitting silent in the closed bar. They had emptied enough bottles to kill eight men, and they were still sober. They were so shocked that the alcohol had no effect. One of the bodyguards finally spoke.

"What was that sound he made? I never heard anything like that before."

"I heard the same scream once before," Darcy said. "It was when I worked for old Frank Graham. He had me and some other guys chain the hands of someone to the back bumper of a truck and his feet to the back bumper of another. They took off in different directions. We thought he was already dead, but when he screamed like that, when he got ripped in half, we found out he was still alive."

"And then he said something. How could he still talk?"

"Sometimes it works like that" Darcy said. "A guy has to say his last words and he does, even if he should be dead. What did he say anyway?"

"Gotcha."

Slime
Jane Nightshade

Christmas break, senior year at San Gerardo High. It was shaping up to be the best break ever. The weather was perfect—chilly but sunny, and not too much rain. Mid-December on the Central Coast of California meant that autumn leaves were still turning and dropping, in contrast to other parts of the country, where winter was burrowing in. Which was double-plus-good, because sometimes the weather in my hometown, San Gerardo, gets really weird—like a lot of other things about this place, as a matter of fact. My town is the Weirdness Capital of the Western World. For starters, people and shit keep disappearing and reappearing, everybody thinks there are aliens in the sewers, and the residents at the Happy Hollow old folks' home never seem to actually die...

But enough about that. I knew I was getting the new Pong television game I'd been wanting for Christmas. After Christmas, I looked forward to a whole week of playing it before school started again. Next year would be my last term in high school and I had a feeling it was going to be special. Nineteen seventy-eight already! It was hard to believe the Seventies were almost over, and then it would be the Eighties, which sounded impossibly futuristic, like something out of *The Jetsons* cartoon I used to watch when I was little.

I was spending a lot of my break at Chunk Sandor's house. Chunk was the coolest kid at San Gerardo High. He got every hot new album the day it came out and went to all the biggest movies the minute they opened. He'd been one of the first people in our town to see the super-big sci-fi film, *Star Wars,* when it was released last summer. He also had a Pong game already, the lucky stiff.

I didn't exactly like Chunk that much, but I loved listening to his records and playing with his Pong. The Sandors were one of the few families I knew who had two televisions—one for the family room and one in the den, and both of them color. We could hook up the Pong to the TV in the den without his mother complaining that we had to stop playing so she could watch her favorite soap opera, *As the World Turns.*

In between Pong matches, we'd listen to Chunk's favorite album of the year, *Rumours* by Fleetwood Mac, while stuffing our faces with the Santa-shaped sugar cookies that Mrs. Sandor always made for Christmas. Chunk's mom was a nice lady. This year, she'd made a big, special gingerbread cookie with my name, Matt, written on it in frosting and then wrapped it up for me to take home. She worked part-time as an Avon Lady, and she also added to my take-home package a bunch of extra Avon samples for my mother, who loved the miniature lipsticks that came in the Avon sales kit.

So far, it really *was* shaping up to be the best Christmas break ever. That was, until Chunk Sandor's bratty kid brother Gavin brought home the small bucket of slime he'd found while playing in the scrub oak brush behind the Sandors' house. Gavin was ten and too big for baby stuff, but he'd taken his old Brady Bunch sand pail and shovel he'd had when he was five, and went out hunting for worms, frogs, and other disgusting things. He came back instead with the slime.

He found me and Chunk in the den, lying on the green shag carpet in front of the TV, deep into a hard-fought table tennis match on the Pong.

"You wanna see something cool?" Gavin said. His face was pink with excitement and it sported an almost unbearably self-important expression.

Chunk laughed, inadvertently spitting crumbs of Santa cookie out of his mouth.. "Cool? From a punk-ass little kid like you? Lol, what is it? A garter snake? A piece of fool's gold? A pile of fossilized dog poo? That's about your speed, Turd-Face."

Chunk could be mean sometimes, especially to his little brother. He constantly called Gavin names and would often threaten to lock the poor kid in the temporary morgue at St. Mary Magdalene Hospital or throw him off Fitzgerald Rock into the Pacific Ocean.

Gavin pushed his lower lip out. "It *is* cool! I swear it!" He squatted down on the shag carpet and shoved his bucket between the two of us so we'd have to look at what was in it.

Chunk and I peered inside. "It's just a pile of green and gray goo!" I said. "Looks like something you made with Jell-O and Play-Doh. Also, you're too old to be running around with a sand pail that's got Bobby Brady on it."

"It's the best thing I have to carry it in," Gavin wailed. "And I don't watch *The Brady Bunch* at night anymore— you guys know it was cancelled ages ago. I don't even watch the afternoon reruns—at least not very *much*."

Chunk laughed again. "Ha ha! You still watch it all the time and you know it. You have a crush on *Marcia, Marcia, Marcia*! And there's nothing cool about a bucket of slime, Midget-Head. Quit wasting our time."

"Wait 'til you see what it *does* and you'll change your tune pronto! But you have to go outside for that." Gavin whined about it for so long that we eventually decided to go out to the Sandors' backyard to see what the stuff in the great and glorious Brady Bunch Wonder Bucket could do, just to shut him up. On the way to the backyard, we passed Mrs. Sandor in the kitchen, packing up her sample cases to go on some Avon calls.

"Don't you boys get into any trouble while I'm gone," she admonished us. "Remember, we all need to honor the Christmas spirit."

"Nothing to worry about, Mother Dear," Chunk said, with an angelic smile. He kissed his Mom on the cheek and told her she looked wonderful in her powder blue pantsuit and new tangerine lipstick. Sometimes, Chunk really reminded me of the Eddie Haskell kid from that old TV show that was still on in afternoon reruns, *Leave it to Beaver*.

When Chunk's mom left, we walked out with Gavin to a wide spot on the lawn next to the Sandors' pool—a pool that was shaped like a kidney bean and surrounded by a very classy looking iron safety fence and gate. It was covered by a plastic sheet and there were gold and brown leaves mingling on the top of it.

We watched, bored out of our minds, while Chunk's kid brother poured his super-duper-important slime out of the bucket. Nothing happened for a good minute or so and we stood there fuming at having our Pong game interrupted for nothing. Chunk looked like he was about to punch his little brother in the face. Seriously.

"Stand back!" cried Gavin with a sudden start. We watched incredulously as the slime expanded and moved, and then twisted upward far over our heads, and finally outward until it began to assume a strangely familiar shape.

"What in the jacked-up tarnation is *that*?" gulped Chunk. His face had betrayed an impressive range of expressions, one after the other: first bewilderment, then amusement, and then lastly, naked fear.

"It's Bobby Brady!" Gavin yelled in delight. He was so happy, he looked like he was about to piss in his orange corduroy Garanimals.

"No way, Short-Stuff," Chunk yelled back. But the slime had indeed morphed into the shape of little freckle-faced Bobby Brady, except that it wasn't a cute kid from a saccharine TV show anymore, but an oversized, yellow-gray-green monster with a huge mouth that dripped chartreuse saliva. Achieving its full form, the Bobby Brady-thing opened its mouth and let out a terrifyingly loud giggle that sounded cute, scary, and weirdly metallic, all at the same time.

Chunk and I jumped back, shaking like leaves. "What in heck is going on?" I mouthed, and Chunk just shook his head.

Gavin laughed. "Not so tough are you now, eh, Chunkster? I bet you've got Hershey squirts in your undies."

Chunk took a few steps toward the monster. It giggled the weird metallic sound again, and then swiped with a pudgy, powerful hand that just missed Chunk. After that, the Bobby-thing made a noise like it was mad, and moved as if to crush Chunk with its giant chubby hands, when it suddenly disappeared.

Gavin laughed and did a little pee-pee dance of glee.

Chunk's expression now was dark and furious —after he'd gotten over being scared. "What's the trick, Pipsqueak? Some sort of hidden set-up with Dad's home movie projector? Where is it? And who helped you fix it all up, Shrimp-Butt? You're not gonna convince me you're smart enough to do this shit yourself. If you think this joke is funny, you better beware, Shrunk-Balls."

He gave Gavin a short punch on the shoulder. I suppose it was meant to be a light "just-kidding" punch, but I could tell that it hurt, as Gavin's eye's watered painfully.

"Stop punching like that," he shouted. "You're hurting me! It's not a trick, I swear. You put a picture of something close to the slimy stuff and it *becomes* the picture! So it turned into the Bobby Brady that's printed on my sand pail!"

"Then how did it disappear just like that?"

"I sprayed water on the picture with the squirt gun I keep in my jeans. The slimy stuff goes back to what it was when you spray water on the picture."

Chunk snorted derisively and rolled his eyes. "O-k-aaaaay—whatever you say, Mini-Brain."

He turned to me and demanded: "Matt, we need to tear this place apart looking for the projector set-up. You search out here and I'll go upstairs and ransack Mini-Brain's room. There may be something projecting out of his bedroom window."

We searched for a good half-hour, but both of our efforts came up jack. We reconvened on the back lawn, where Gavin was sitting on a bench on the far side of the pool, waiting patiently for us to finish. From what I could see, he'd scooped up the slime and put it back into his bucket, as it wasn't on the lawn anymore. Boy and bucket were planted on one side of the bench, next to a pile of weird wooden stuff and metal junk. I knew that Gavin loved picking up things he found on his neighborhood searches. I noticed he was playing with something shiny and silvery that looked kinda familiar, but I wasn't sure what it was.

Gavin looked up from the shiny thing and called to us in a sarcastic tone, "Hey guys, you didn't find any projection equipment, didja? 'Cause there isn't any. I told you my slime was cool. And it's *real*, too."

I could tell that Chunk was on the verge of shouting something mean back to his brother, when I grabbed his sleeve and cautioned, "Hey Chunk, cool it. Sometimes you go too far with teasing Gavin and all the name-calling. He's only ten!"

Chunk pulled away, snorting contemptuously. "Bullshit! It's just a little good-natured brotherly competition. The punky little brat actually loves it. And it's none of your business anyway, Matty."

I winced. I hated being called "Matty," and Chunk knew it. I was afraid he would call me that for the rest of the day. To my relief, though, he dropped the subject and moved on.

"I've got to find out how that little shit did it. I can't let him get away with putting something over on me. He'll brag about it all over town, and I'll never live it down. All the best-looking chicks at school will start throwing themselves at Moose Mulligan instead of at me."

I considered his predicament and came up with an inspired idea. "Hey Chunk, did it ever occur to you that maybe—just maybe—he's not playing a trick? That the slimy stuff actually *does* do what he says it does?"

"Ha ha, Matty—do you really believe that?"

"Well, no—probably not. But just in case, we could prove it by placing our own pictures in front of the slime. If it triggers the growth of a monster like the picture of Bobby Brady did, it isn't a trick. And if it *is* a trick, it's Gavin who won't be able to live it down."

"*Hmmmmm*...I see your point. I like it! I'm going into the house to find some pictures of our own to wave at the little creep's stupid slime."

A warning popped into my head, almost unconsciously. "Be sure to get pictures of non-threatening things, just to be on the safe side."

Chunk snickered and rolled his eyes again. "You've got to be kidding me. Okay, Pansy-Ass Matt."

He ran into the house and came back five minutes later with two pictures and a plant sprayer full of water. One picture was a Christmas card with a big, fat Santa on it. The other was a photo of his late grandmother, holding a knitting needle and a ball of yarn.

"I got the two most benign things I could think of," Chunk said. "Ol' St. Nick and a sweet little old lady."

We walked around the pool over to where Gavin was sitting on the bench, and Chunk started acting almost nice to his little brother. I could tell it was a struggle for him, but he finally got the words out with a shit-eating grin and a fake-cheerful voice. "Hey Gav — we believe you now about the slime. We think it's really cool. And we wanna try out a couple more pictures with it, just for shits and giggles."

Gavin's face lit up. "Really? Wow, go for it! I betcha you'll never find anything as cool as my slime—ever!" I saw that the silvery thing Gav was playing with was a cigarette lighter, which I figured he filched from his mother, who chain-smoked Virginia Slims. He noticed I recognized it, turned red, and stuffed it in his pants pocket, presumably next to the squirt gun.

"Sure, Snot-Eater...I mean, er, Gav. You're the hero and you're gonna be famous!"

"O-k-aaaay!" We followed Gavin back to the wide spot on the lawn and watched as he dumped the slime out again. Chunk placed the Santa Christmas card on the ground directly near the slime.

After a minute or two the slime began to grow again, upward and outward, into a giant red-gray-green, semi-transparent Santa Claus. A Santa Claus who had a moldy beard, crazy eyes and mouth that dripped viscous nasty goo. The Santa looked murderous and angry. It was eyeing Chunk in a deeply unsettling way. Then it pointed a finger at him and emitted a terrifying metallic sound, which eventually turned into a word. It sounded like "naughty."

I snatched the Santa card from the ground and doused it with the plant sprayer. The huge menacing Santa figure began to fade away, until it disappeared.

"Wow! That was fantastic! Scary, but fantastic," cried Chunk, still shuddering. After a moment of recovery, he was almost ecstatic: "Hey, guys! We can make money off of this stuff. I can see it all now. Nightclub tours where we charge big bucks for folks to see the slime activate, appearances on talk shows—and eventually—the big casinos in Vegas. We could use the slime to make celebrities and Disney cartoons come alive. Imagine a big slimy President Carter or Muhammad Ali? We'll be a bigger act in Vegas than even Liberace or Evel Knievel. And we'll make a mint!"

"Who is 'we,' Kemosabe?" said Gavin coldly. "You can't have all the fame and glory—and the money. This slime is mine! I found it!"

"Of course you found it, Toad-Ass. But you don't know what to do with it. I can make us a fortune on this stuff—and I'm willing to give you a generous cut of twenty percent off the top."

"*Twenty percent*?" whined Gavin. "It's *mine*. I want 100 percent."

"You're too young to perform in clubs or Vegas, Toilet-Breath. Me—I'm a-gonna be eighteen in a couple of months. That's legal adulthood nowadays. You need *me* to make money off of that slime," sneered Chunk.

Gavin pouted. "You don't even know if people will believe you about what it does. These big club managers and Vegas people—they're gonna open doors for you just like that? I don't think so."

"Sure, they will, Penis-Nose. The whole country knows that weird shit always happens in San Gerardo. *The National Inquirer* has a permanent news bureau devoted exclusively to us. We're more famous than the Loch Ness Monster!"

Gavin pouted even more. "Yeah, I got to admit it—you're right. Remember when those news people from San Francisco came to my school last year, because of the sink-hole on the volleyball court that everyone says eats kids and small animals? But I still want more than a measly twenty percent. You said the slime was a *joke...*"

"Hey, guys," I broke in. They looked like they wanted to murder each other again, which I definitely didn't want to happen. I desperately tried to think of something that would distract them. Then, I got it: "If you're gonna make money out of this stuff, you need to be sure you're the only guys who've got possession of it. I mean, is there any more of the slime out in the brush where you found it, Gavin?"

Gavin regarded me with a suspicious eye. He had no reason to trust even a nominal friend of his big brother. Then he relented and said: "Okay, you're right. Yeah, there's a big pile of it in my secret place. We need to get it all."

"And you're going to show us your secret place now, aren't you, little brother?" commanded Chunk.

"I'll take you as far as inside the brush, but after that, you'll have to trust me to go get it for you. Ain't showing my secret place to nobody, especially not *you.*"

"Okay, suit yourself. Just remember, all the loot we're gonna make off of it, so you'd better get it all up."

Chunk went into the Sandor's kitchen and brought out a galvanized tub his mom used to boil corn-on-the-cob with and a garden trowel to use as a scoop.

We followed Chunk's brother into the deep, wild brush behind the Sandors' house for about an hour and change. It felt like a wild goose chase, until we came to a clearing surrounded by manzanita bushes and chaparral. Manzanita bushes always gave me the creeps; with their red bark and twisty branches, they reminded me of bloody fingers.

"This is where you guys stop and turn your backs so I can go to my secret place without you watching me," Gavin warned.

"This is stupid," said Chunk in a sneering voice. But he handed over the galvanized tub and the trowel to Gavin without further complaint. "Get it all—we don't want any competitors."

"I'm only doing this for the money, not for you, you mean old Bubble-Head," replied Gavin.

Chunk rolled his eyes. "You can't think of a better insult than Bubble-Head? What a Smegma-Dick."

I grabbed his sleeve. "C'mon, Chunk, let's turn around and let him go find it. Time's a-wastin'."

We both turned our backs while Gavin trotted off, and we both felt extremely silly doing it. But with our backs turned and facing the Sandor house, we saw something we'd missed before: marks that looked like a pair of giant chicken tracks, denting the soil at the edge of the clearing.

"What do you think that is?" I asked Chunk.

"I dunno? A very large bird of some kind that escaped from the San Gerardo zoo? Or a joke someone decided to play?"

"I don't think it's a joke...why would it be way out here?—where no one can see it? —if it's a joke? You know what I think? I think it's tracks made by a monster that someone used the slime to call up. Someone's been here before us, that's what I think."

Chunk looked mad. "That could really crimp our style if someone else has got it." But then he brightened up. "If that slime's been used before to make a monster, why hasn't anyone heard of it?"

"I dunno...unless the monster did something to the person who called it up. Suppose some guy called up a giant chicken monster and it pecked him to death? Like Bobby Brady tried to squeeze you to death in his fat hands. Something like that?"

Chunk shrugged. "If somebody got pecked to death, that's their problem—we didn't have anything to do with it. Thankfully for us, the secret of the slime stayed hidden so we can make big bucks from it."

"Shouldn't we be turning the slime over to the government for studying? That's the right thing to do."

"Nah, they'd just use it to make weapons with. They'd call up a 30-foot, slimy G.I. Joe doll that steps on Russian tanks or grabs their planes out of the sky. Why should we let it be used for bullshit stuff like that, especially when we would lose a chance to make a ton of money?"

"I guess you're right. I can't think of any use for this stuff beyond weapons or entertainment," I admitted. "Say, Chunk? What do you think this stuff is, really?"

Chunk paused in a thoughtful way. Which was unusual for him—*very* unusual.

"Alien poo."

I couldn't help but laugh. "Alien poo?"

Chunk was deadly serious. "Yeah. Alien poo. The way I see it, aliens once stopped here to refuel or something, and they dumped their poo in San Gerardo. Then they left. Or, maybe, they're the ones who made those big bird tracks. Maybe they're giant bird-people. Don't know why their poo copies stuff from pictures, though."

"You seriously believe that?"

"Of course, I do. What other explanation do you have?"

"Ummm…" I hadn't thought about it much. Finally, I said: "Mutant radioactive giant snails? The slime sort of looks like snail trails."

Chunk laughed. "Bullshit kid's stuff. That's like something Gavin would say."

I was just about to retort that my idea about the origin of the slime was no dumber than his about alien poo, when Gavin grabbed my shirt from the back and cried, all out of breath, that he'd heard something in the bushes while he was filling the galvanized tub with slime. He was still carrying the tub with both hands, but seemed about to drop it.

I turned around to face him and so did Chunk.

"Something goony is out here!" he screeched, out of breath. "I heard it stomping around on the rocks and tree branches and stuff. It sounded really big!"

Chunk and I stared at each other in wild fear.

"The chicken!" We shouted in unison. "Run!"

Chunk grabbed the tub of slime from Gavin and took off, running back toward his house in double-time.

"He's ditching us!" Gavin screamed, his face red and tears squirting out from the corners of his eyes. "My own brother!"

"No time to explain why he's spooked," I gasped out. "C'mon Gav, let's go!"

We started running as something came crashing through the brush behind us, loud and scary.

I slowed up and looked back briefly—all I could see was a glimpse of a monstrous bird-like head rearing and cresting over the scrub oaks and bay leaf trees. It was shedding gigantic drops of yellow-orange and green slime as the creature moved. I sped up and ran even faster.

"Don't look back!" I cried to Gavin who was a few feet behind me. "Keep running."

We made it out of the brush and back to the trail that led to the gate of the Sandors' backyard fence. Once inside the Sandor's back yard, I stopped, completely out of breath and cramping in my legs, to listen for the monster thing that I'd glimpsed as we ran through the brush.

Whatever it was, it was no longer chasing us.

Chunk was already home. He was sitting in a chair on the patio with his tub of slime, acting like nothing had happened.

"It's about time you two reprobates showed up," he smirked.

"You ditched us!" Gavin was furious. He balled up his little fists and smoldered with rage at Chunk.

Chunk was infuriatingly casual about the whole thing. "I can't help it if you guys don't run as fast as I do. I knew you'd make it out okay."

"Chunk, that wasn't cool. I could have used some help with getting Gavin out of there. A couple of times he stumbled, and I had to haul him up, all while being chased by a monster."

I was starting to really dislike Chunk. His Pong game, Fleetwood Mac albums, and mother's cookies were starting to lose their charm, next to the unrelenting jerkiness of his personality.

"Mini-Brain runs faster than I do most of the time. I didn't think he needed help," replied Chunk lamely. "I guess he was too scared to run as fast as he usually does."

"That's not true!" Gavin ran up to Chunk and started pummeling him with his small fists. "You showed us your true face. You cared more about your stupid old slime than you cared about *me. I hate you!*"

Chunk pushed him away and he fell on the cement patio with a painful thunk. He got up twice as mad.

Chunk stood up too, an ominous look on his face, ready to fight. I knew that Gavin couldn't possibly win any fight with Chunk. I realized that I had to stop the fight before he got seriously hurt.

"Hey guys! We need to test this new batch of slime! Let's try out the photo of Grandma Sandor that Chunk found this morning. I wonder what *she'll* look like when she's rendered in the slime."

Chunk and Gavin gave me a withering look, like they both wanted to say, "butt out, jerk." But Chunk eventually got a hold of his temper and answered, "You want to test it *now?* After that near miss with the chicken monster?"

"Yes. I'm not sure that thing was from the slime after all. I didn't get a good look at it. And we're good here. As long as we've got the photo and the water spray bottle, we're safe, aren't we? And anyway, you've got to make sure it works before you go and start calling club managers."

Chunk glared at me but eventually backed down. "Yeah, okay. You're right. Let's give the old girl a whirl."

He grabbed the photo of Grandma Sandor from the patio table he'd left it on an hour before, along with the all-important plant-sprayer, which he gave to me. Then he dumped the new slime out in the lawn and lay the photo of Grandma Sandor on the lawn in front of the slime, same as we had done with the Christmas card earlier in the day.

The three of us stood back and waited. Eventually the slime began to twist, expand and morph, the same as before, until looming over us was a giant Granny Sandor made of white-gray-green slime. Her face was covered with little crawling things that looked like slugs. In one hand she waved a huge, vicious-looking knitting needle.

Then she opened her mouth and roared at Chunk, in that same metallic voice that the other slime-things had made. "Bad boy," she said. "Bad boy. Mean to brother."

Gavin started to laugh. "She knows you," he screamed at his brother. "She's got your number for sure!"

Chunk stood there, open-mouthed. But then the Grandma-Thing began to do things....*bad* things.

With her big knitting needle, she suddenly began to stab at Chunk. He dodged it just barely, falling to the ground as he lost his footing, and the needle sank viciously into the grass near one of his thighs.

He tried to escape, sweating profusely in terror, but Grandma reached out with an enormous, stretchy, slimy arm and pulled him back.

"Help me!" he screamed. "Matt! Gavin!"

I grabbed for the photo in order to spray it but Gavin had already beaten me to it. "What would you give me to spray this photo?" he taunted Chunk, waving it around triumphantly.

"Nothing," grunted Chunk through gritted teeth. "You're a punk. Give the photo to Matt now or this is all on you."

"Maybe I will," said Gavin gleefully. "And then again, maybe I won't. Still planning to give me only twenty percent, eh Chunkster?"

Chunk gritted his teeth while squirming in the Granny-monster's grasp, trying to avoid the knitting needle in her other hand.

But then her needle found a mark and stabbed into one of Chunk's lower legs. Even though it looked like it was made of slime, the huge needle was apparently sharp enough and solid enough to draw a large amount of blood.

"Aghhhhhhhhhh," shrieked Chunk in pain. "Somebody—Matt!—get the photo away from him!"

I grabbed Gavin and tried to wrestle the photo away from him. He squirmed and struggled, the photo clutched to his chest as tight as he could manage. Then he pulled away, just as Grandma Sandor stabbed Chunk's other leg. Out came another gusher of blood.

"She's gonna kill me," shrieked Chunk. "Somebody take the photo away and spray it! Goddammit, spray it now!"

I tried to grab Gavin again, but again, he kept squirming out of my hold. Finally, he broke free and ran into the pool yard and shut the gate of the iron fence that enclosed it. He held up the photo over his head, so Chunk could see it clearly while he was being tortured by the monster.

Then Gavin reached into his jeans with his other hand and pulled out something shiny and flashy, which he held close to the upraised picture of Grandma Sandor. I recognized the shiny object as the cigarette lighter he'd been playing with earlier in the day, the one he'd stolen from his chain-smoking mom out of her drawer full of Virginia Slims.

Chunk howled pitifully as the Grandma-monster stabbed him again. I lunged for the latch on the pool yard's gate, but it was too late.

Quick as a flash, Gavin flicked the cigarette lighter on, and started burning the photo of his grandmother, until it was nothing but ashes. Chunk howled a terrible animalistic cry when he saw the photo flame out. I put my hands over my ears to blot out the screams, and I thought, strangely, that it wasn't going to be the best-ever Christmas break after all.

The Widow and the Fortune Teller
Douglas Ford

She drew the Tower card. Again.

Each time the Romany woman turned over the face-down cards in order to interpret their message, they witnessed the return of that one particular image—lightning striking the tower, bodies falling to the earth below, the whole edifice splitting and crumbling.

The widow, as she called herself, might have suspected a trick if not for the way this recurrence clearly troubled the woman reading her fortune.

"It shouldn't happen this way," said the fortune-teller as she re-shuffled the deck. "Not with such frequency. If I deal the cards again and we see it once more, it will surely foretell terrible things."

Once more she dealt three cards, and again the Tower appeared. The two other cards mattered little at this point. They changed with each shuffle, but always the Tower appeared, a sure sign of impending destruction.

Even so, the widow smiled. "Do it again," she said, sounding much like a child who wanted to see a magic trick repeated.

Instead, the fortune-teller began to pack up her things. "We shouldn't tempt fate. You were good to let us set camp here. We've imposed on you." Outside the wagon, her kinsman continued to unpack wagons. These people spent their lives traveling, having no real permanent home. The widow sensed a kindred spirit in the fortune teller, the matriarch of the group, so she agreed to let them come to a rest on the grounds surrounding the ruins where she lived.

"Don't be daft," said the widow. She recently learned that word—*daft*—and liked its sound. "It grows late, and the weather threatens to turn violent. I've seen lightning in the distance. Tell your men to make the fires while they still can so they can prepare your meals. You're welcome here." The widow liked fires and relished the thought of looking out her window and seeing pockets of orange flame as strangers huddled in the gloam.

The fortune teller sighed and nodded, but she did not deal the cards again.

"You live up there alone?" the fortune teller asked as she stood upon unsteady legs. Though a small woman, she had to stoop to stand upright in the wagon. A woman with the widow's height would suffer terrible back pains if she tried to match the effort.

"Well, my children are there as well," said the widow.

"You have many children?" The fortune teller looked uneasy.

Outside, the ruins of the real tower overlooked dilapidated grounds, now filled with rickety wagons, still showing signs of the damage caused by an overload to the machines that brought the widow to life. Over time, gradually, pieces of the rubble disappeared, finding a place back in the structure. Almost never in the original place, however, so even if the tower became whole again, it would look as insane and misshapen as the creatures who rebuilt it.

"Yes, many," said the widow.

As the hour grew late, the wagon became darker. The fortune teller struck a march to light a cigarette. Then she held the match to the wick of an oil lamp. She didn't offer the widow a cigarette. If she did, the widow would have accepted. She really should try smoking one of these days, knowing that Pretorius enjoyed the habit. By the lamplight, the fortune teller seemed to study the widow's features—the sunken cheeks, the black lips, the wild hair that wouldn't surrender to brush or comb. And the scars, so many scars.

"No husband?"

"He died," said the widow. "Out there, in fact."

"The ruins," said the fortune teller. "They look uninhabitable. And lonely."

"They're under reconstruction. My children will see that my home is returned to its previous glory."

The fortune teller blew forth a plume of smoke and regarded the widow. The widow pointed at the cards. "Once more?"

The fortune teller made a dismissive sound, but she picked up the cards and for the last time dealt out three. And for one last time, they saw the Tower. The widow smiled and paid her.

***

Later in the evening, as she sat to watch the approaching storm and the dwindling campfires, the widow found the Tower card sitting on a window ledge. At first, she entertained the fanciful impression that the card decided to follow her, but movement in the shadows caught her eye, explaining the theft of the card. "Napoleon, this is your work, I take it?" As soon as she spoke the name, the form in the shadows withdrew. When they lived inside glass jars, Pretorius liked to grant his pygmy creations the names of rulers: Poseidon, Henry the VIII, Catherine the Great, and of course Napoleon. Napoleon had grown the least of all, but what he lacked in size he made up for in stealth and skills in theft, and the widow owed the small amount of money she possessed to this one. Apparently, he found his way into the wagon with her and the fortune teller and also took a liking to this card.

The widow lifted the card and kissed it with her black lips. "Thank you," she said to the room, not sure if she still shared it with Napoleon. In all likelihood, he'd moved on to the night's next endeavor, presumably to help the others move more of the rubble back in place and bring their tower closer to completion.

Be careful, my dear, the little ones weren't meant to leave their enclosures.

Pretorius' voice. She heard it inside her head more and more frequently, warning her of her of his earlier creations.

I not only gave them the names of rulers. I instilled them with something imperious. They each plan to rule the tower when it reaches completion. What will you do then?

That word—*imperious*—sounded bright and new to her, and she made a mental note to put it to use herself at the first opportunity. Something in her memory, the vestiges of a past, more delicate life clicked, and she intuited the meaning of the word. Instead of dwelling on Pretorius' message, she followed the wake of shadows left behind by Napoleon, moving deeper into the tower's recesses. In her hand she held the fortune teller's missing card. She intended to return it, of course. But then again, she might not.

She came to the tower's spiraling staircase, thinking it might clear her thoughts if she could go to its top-most portion—still unfinished and jagged—in order to watch the approach of the incoming storm. As with fire, lightning didn't scare her. She welcomed it.

On the next landing, she saw a different form hulking in the shadows.

"Why, who could that be?" she said, of course knowing the answer but hoping some light, affectionate teasing would encourage him to show himself. "Is that King Henry the Eighth?"

The form responded to her voice by shifting uneasily. Though the gaps left by the uneven stones came a flash of lightning without the sound of thunder, the storm moving slowly and still a good distance away. The brief light allowed her to see the bulbous head, once so handsome but now fat and gray and out of proportion with the rest of its naked, rotund body, squatting on its haunches. So hard to imagine, thought the widow, that he was once fit inside a tiny jar, where he sat on a little throne wearing a doll-size robe and crown. Now look at him. From its expansive jaws hung shreds of what looked like meat, but the shadows overtook it once more, and she couldn't ascertain the origin of its meal.

"Eating so soon? You think of nothing but eating. And what have you found for yourself? That looks much too large to be a mere rat."

The formed moved slightly but didn't answer. None of them could speak. Instead, she heard the sound of crunching bone. The leg of a deer perhaps.

"I'm told you're imperious," she said. "I can be imperious, too, you know. Or so I like to believe. Shall we be imperious together, or will your queen become jealous?"

The reply came in the form of more crunching and what sounded like a grunt. She knew this one liked to eat and move its bowels at the same time. Then ensuing stench confirmed that it had done so.

"I'll leave you to it, then. For now, you can be imperious for the both of us."

With that she moved on, passing others as she came closer to where the tower plateaued. To each she offered a greeting, asking them in what way they sought to demonstrate their imperious nature. Most appeared too busy with moving stones into place to heed her presence, but it turned out that only Henry took this time to eat a meal. Of all of them, he showed the greatest tendency to forsake his work to indulge in the pleasures of eating and shitting. The only one she didn't see was his queen. But the widow suspected she knew where to find her if the need arose. Instead, she went to an alcove that contained the pallet she slept upon.

Next to the pallet lay what little remained of Dr. Pretorius, stitched haphazardly together by his creations. They'd done a bad job of preserving him, and he consisted of nothing more than a head and torso, along with one leg stitched to where he once bore an arm before the explosion ripped him apart. The widow felt glad they practiced on him before going about her own reconstruction. No telling what she might have looked like when they finished. She took pride in her appearance. Even with the stitches and the unruly hair with streaks the color of lightning, she knew she looked beautiful.

Before gathering her blanket so she could take it to the summit of the tower, she kissed him where he once had lips, feeling the sharp edges of broken teeth instead. She tried to smooth his shock of white hair, as wild as her own.

"I can be imperious, too, my husband," she said, and then she resumed her walk up the tower's steps, the blanket in her arms. When she arrived at what, for now, constituted the tower's summit, open to the weather, she spread out her blanked so that she could fall asleep while gazing at the lightning. On such nights, when she slept at the apex of the tower, she dreamt of the wind lifting her and flying into the dark clouds, like the kites once affixed to the top, intended to draw lightning. No string held her down in these dreams, however--she just flew and flew. Next to her, she placed the tarot card, intent on dreaming again of that other stormy evening, when the tower remained whole and she felt Pretorius' touch for the first time.

***

Something shook her awake. She found herself drenched, her hair a mess, the rain having finally arrived after she feel asleep. She realized that she missed the full show of the lightning, and not dreaming disappointed her deeply.

She assumed the hands that awoke her belonged to one of Pretorius' mad creatures—most likely Lear, who maintained an inconsolable fear of bad weather and often sought her comfort during storms—but when her eyes cleared, she saw the fortune teller.

"You've stolen my card," said the woman, soaked to the bone. "And my people are vanishing. What kind of black magic are you practicing here?"

The widow shook her head to clear the cobwebs and smiled up at the woman. She held the smile even when she saw the knife pressed against her throat. A knife used to threaten her? How daft.

"I assure you," said the widow, "I may be imperious, but I don't practice witchcraft. And I have your card. I intended to return it."

But when she looked next to her, she saw that the card had vanished. What sort of fate would *that* foretell?

"Well, I *did* have it," she said. "I believe it's Napoleon again. Up to his old tricks."

"Napoleon?" said the fortune teller.

"One of my children. Come. I'll find him for you."

"There's something evil in this place," said the fortune teller. "The people left in my camp keep seeing things in the shadows. Something has made off with some of the men, as well as children."

The widow thought of Henry and the meal he enjoyed.

"Perhaps," she said, "the storm frightened them and they've gone into hiding."

"Storms don't frighten these men. Nor me, or our children for that matter. Someone has taken them. I know they're here. You'll take me to them," the fortune teller said, pressing the knife hard enough to draw blood, "and return to me my card."

"Of course, I'll return your card." The widow ignored the blood and got to her feet. She hovered over this tiny fortune teller. She thought of tossing her over the edge of the tower, a feat that would require little of her strength, and letting her fall to her death, just like the fool depicted on the card. But in truth, she liked this woman's fierceness. No wonder she served as the group's leader. "As for your missing kinsman, if they're here, I don't know anything about that."

Then she thought about how she hadn't seen Henry's queen that night. A thought occurred to her.

"You say children have gone missing, too?"

"Three of them," the fortune teller said, still brandishing the knife.

The widow thought of how Henry's queen loved children.

"I know where to look," said the widow. "Follow me."

The widow led the fortune teller through the slanting tower, down the winding steps. Pieces of the stairs gave way under the fortune teller's feet, and at one point, she cried out and steadied herself against the wall. The widow smiled and waited for her to find the confidence to move again. When the fortune teller took the next step, she waved her knife. "Don't try any foolishness," she said. "I've heard the stories people tell about this place."

It surprised the widow to hear this information. "Oh? People talk about my tower? You led me to believe you knew little about it."

"It once housed a monster," said the fortune teller, "made from the bodies of the dead."

Pretorius' voice chimed in. The bride slowed her descent and cocked her head to listen to the words only she could hear. *They're not here by chance. They hoped to find something valuable, no doubt the very remains of Frankenstein's creation. Imagine the plans they've discussed. To display him in some vulgar carnival, charging the masses a few pennies to see the corpse of your groom.*

"That was a long time ago," said the widow. "Before my time." Thinking: *You were my true groom, Pretorius.*

"I think not," said the fortune teller. "Lead me to my children. No tricks."

As the widow resumed a normal pace, she caught a glimpse of Napoleon sitting on an alcove, as still as a gargoyle. She said, "You hear that, don't you, Napoleon? No tricks."

The fortune teller followed her gaze but saw nothing. "Don't mock me. I take my people's lives seriously. Their trust in me won't be in vain."

"I wouldn't dream of mocking you," said the widow, not looking back. "I admire your imperiousness."

"My what?"

"Nothing. We're not far." But she hoped Pretorius heard her use the word correctly. She listened for his praise but heard nothing.

They reached the ground, but the stairs continued downward, going into the earth. Before rebuilding the tower, Pretorius' creatures had tunneled into the ground, and during what little hours they slept, they took their rest down there. If not for the promise of a spectacular tower, the widow would have joined them. Something so peaceful about the idea of sleeping beneath the dirt, where she could entwine herself with the roots of long-dead trees and sleep for ages.

The widow started down the steps, expecting the fortune teller to follow. When she looked back, however, the other woman actually looked afraid. This apparent fear disappointed the widow. Perhaps she should have thrown her off the tower after all.

The fortune teller read the widow's expression. "I'm not frightened. There's no light down there, and I suspect a trick."

"I told you. No tricks. Do you have your matches?"

The fortune teller didn't reply, instead taking a step back and, while still holding the knife, she extracted the matches from the folds of her skirt and lit one quickly.

The flare excited the widow. "I'll hold the match if you'd like."

The fortune teller agreed to this proposition. She handed the whole box to the widow. She'd never lit a match before in her life, but she'd watched and observed and knew what to do. As she led the way down the steps, the walls of the tower gave way to tunneled dirt illuminated by the match flame. Holding the fire excited the widow. She let each match burn all the way down to her fingers before lighting a new one.

She lit five matches before they reached the bottom, and she wished they could keep going so she could continue to light them. Already, she decided that the fortune teller wouldn't get these back. The card, maybe, but not these.

They arrived in hollowed earth, the ground beneath their feet littered with bones and half-eaten carcasses of deer and wild pigs, their images aglow in the matchlight. Entranced by the power of the flame she held, the widow felt truly imperious and realized that she hadn't really understood that word until now. As she walked about the enclosure, she nearly tripped over remains she'd not seen previously. Human, she realized, a man with the colorful clothes favored by the Romany people. She lit a new match and held it close so she could study him, sensing the fortune teller close behind her, still holding the knife and looking along with her.

The man looked half-eaten, his intestines dangling from the open cavity of his stomach.

You've invited invaders into our home, said Pretorius' voice. *As I suspected, they intended to pillage our belongings, including the body of your husband, that other misbegotten creation, without whom you wouldn't exist.*

The widow said to the fortune teller, "Did you come here to steal from me?"

At first, the woman couldn't reply. Though her mouth hung open, no words came forth. As the match in the widow's hand burned out, she saw the look of horror and mortification. Quickly, with an expertise as if she'd done it for years, she lit a new match, and now the fortune teller turned that expression upon the widow. The knife looked useless in her hand.

"He's alive? The monster. He did this, didn't he?"

"So you did come for him. Did you plan to steal me as well?" asked the widow. She closed the distance between them. The size of the enclosure allowed her to stand at full height, and she intended to show the fortune teller how tall she stood over her.

The shadows around them began to move. Pretorius' other creatures had begun to gather. The widow noticed Lear, not afraid of the weather at all down here. Yonder, she saw Catherine the Great, her naked breasts pendulous and missing the nipples she'd bitten off herself when, in a moment of delirious hunger, she'd tried to suckle herself. Poseidon over there, and Napoleon, too, hunched in a corner. They wouldn't make the first grab at the fortune teller. The widow knew who else lay in wait down here. From a far corner came the mewling of a child. As she suspected, Henry's queen had begun dining on the children. Using her formidable height, she began moving in that direction, the fortune teller cowering now, hoping to maintain their distance.

"Did you plan to put him on display? Make him a carnival attraction? Set me alongside him and proclaim me his bride? Well, I'm not his bride. He's not my husband. He's been blown to pieces. His remains are built into the tower, parts of him there inside the walls, still living, still breathing. Can't you see him in the shape of this tower? I hate looking at it because I always see him. He's all I see."

She hadn't meant to let her voice rise to such a level. The truth of what she'd spoken struck her for the first time and surprised her. The fortune teller dropped the knife now. Moving backward, she bumped into Lear. He grinned at her, and she saw him now. Behind him crouched Poseidon and his insane fins for arms. The fortune teller turned the other way, saw Catherine the Great who smiled broadly and licked her lips. None of them pounced though. They understood what the widow meant to do, and with their bodies, they helped her guide the fortune teller into the passageway that led to Henry's Queen, the largest and most hungry one of them all. She lived down here, and only the enticement of eating children could ever draw her away from her throne.

"My fortune. You only agreed to read my cards to distract me. So your kinsman could invade my home."

In her fear, the fortune teller looked incapable of answering. The woman turned in time to see the monstrous queen bite off the head of a child, her mouth large enough to hold it in its entirety. The widow lit a match in time for the fortune teller to see everything. Around the queen lay the bodies of other half-eaten children.

Before the fortune teller could scream, the others set upon her and made short work of her. They needed to eat, too, and the evening's work of rebuilding the tower could wait as they drew sustenance.

The widow sat on the ground and watched. For some reason, she felt suddenly sad. Pretorius had gone quiet and didn't offer any words of consolation to her in this terrible moment. For the first time, she felt truly alone, and not even watching those creations dine could provide any solace. She wondered if in another life, she and the fortune teller could have become friends. Smoked together, perhaps. If she did possess the corpse of the monster (not her husband, stop that) she might have parted with it as an act of friendship. *Here, take him,* she would have said. *Become rich.* But she couldn't tolerate acts of deceit.

She lit another watch and watched as it burned. In the light of the flame, Napoleon approached. In his hand, he held something for her.

The Tower card.

As his ridiculously long arm extended, he bowed that odd head of his, as if in supplication.

That lightened her mood. She smiled as she took it, bowing back.

"Thank you, Napoleon."

She could never consider herself as imperious as the queen who now gnawed on the bones of Romany children. When they finished with the fortune teller, the mad things would go to work on anyone who remained on the grounds outside. In their wild hunger, they displayed an undeniable imperiousness, one she couldn't match.

But that small gesture by Napoleon made her feel special for now. Pretorius' question now gnawed at her. What would she do when they completed the tower? She knew now she couldn't continue to live inside it, and she could certainly never rule it. She knew that now. Those things created by Pretorius would eventually throw her off the top of it, and she would tumble down to the ground like the poor fool shown on the card.

No, she corrected herself: she would fly.

What the tower card showed was not falling, not death, but flying. She must always remember that.

Thanks to Napoleon, that card belonged to her now. She would cherish it and allow it to remind her of what the tower truly represented. Let tomorrow bring what it would.

Curse of the Blood Moon: The Hospital
Alexander C. Bailey

"I told you, I'm fine! Quit worrying about me and go enjoy the costume party," Dave said, laying in his hospital bed.

"Are you sure?" said Phoebe, his girlfriend, who was dressed in a cat's ears and whiskers and was standing at the side of the bed. Her eyes were red from crying, and there was a bandage on her forehead.

"Completely. The doctors checked you out and cleared you to go home. There's no use in staying here with me. Go have fun and try to forget about what happened," Dave said, holding out his hand to her. She took it and nodded her head before kissing him on the cheek.

"I'll let everyone know you said hi, and that you wished you could be there," Phoebe said before she left the room. Dave watched her go and let out a deep sigh.

Tears started flowing from his eyes as he thought about the accident.

They had been heading to their best friend's Halloween party when they were t-boned by a drunk driver. Phoebe managed to walk away from the accident with only a minor head injury, but the truck hit Dave's side of the car. His leg was broken and at least two of his ribs were cracked.

The drunk driver walked away without a scratch.

Flickering in and out of consciousness, Dave had seen who had hit them. It was a regular from the local bar. Bill, if Dave remembered right. He had briefly seen a look of fear on the man's face when he thought Dave was dead until the injured man spat blood at him.

Dave vaguely remembered the authorities and paramedics showing up and getting them to the hospital. Dave had been happy to see it was Howard working on him. They had been friends since kindergarten.

"You're going to be just fine," Howard had said around his piece of gum, as he pulled Dave from the car. That was the last thing he remembered before being loaded into the ambulance and waking up in the hospital. Phoebe had helped fill in the rest of the gaps of the night.

Dave's tears were dry by the time Howard walked into his room.

"My shift's over. Figured you could use some company," the short Asian American man said. "I assumed you'd send Phoebe on to Brian's."

Dave nodded, "I did. I know she needs to be around people right now. Me, I just want to be alone."

"Well, we don't have to talk, but I'm not going anywhere for a while. I know what a patient goes through after an accident," Howard said. He had been a paramedic most of his adult life and had seen more of his friends injured than he cared to. "I'm here for you, man."

"Thanks. Didn't want to dress up and go to Brian's party?" Dave sighed.

"Nah, I'm not really into that sort of thing. Besides, I've dealt with people most of the day. I just want to sit down and relax," Howard said before he plopped into one of the chairs. He picked up the remote and turned on the television hanging in the corner of the room. He found a channel playing old horror movies and left it here.

"How are you and Phoebe doing?" Howard asked, not looking away from the screen.

"Really good," Dave smiled. "I'm thinking about asking her to marry me." He had picked out a ring last month but was still waiting to find the right time to ask her. Every time he thought he was close to doing it, an overwhelming sense of doubt would make him stop.

"It's about time," Howard said, leaning towards the hospital bed. "I know you're still gun shy over Mary leaving you, but Phoebe is nothing like her. She's crazy in love with you."

"I know, and I think she knows the proposal is coming."

"She does. She told me last week. But she doesn't want to push you, she knows what happened last time," Howard said, eyes still glued to the movie.

"Son of a bitch," Dave grunted, leaning back and closing his eyes.

***

"How's your night going Maddie?" Eddie asked as he walked over to the nurse's station. He was on his break and needed a little company.

The brunette smiled up at him from behind the counter Eddie was leaning on.

"It's surprisingly quiet. It's Halloween night. I figured we were going to be busier."

"Well, be thankful it's not," Eddie chuckled. "Why aren't you wearing a costume?"

"I wasn't able to find one I liked in time," Maddie frowned for a second. "What about you?"

"Not supposed to. 'A security guard needs to put on an air of professionalism.'" Eddie stood as straight as he could with a serious look on his face as he intoned the words. He dropped it with a grin when Maddie began to laugh. "Besides, dressing up was never really my thing. I only did it as a kid to get candy."

"Oh, I loved it," Maddie said with a faraway look in her eyes, thinking about childhood costumes, Eddie assumed. She let out a soft sigh before blinking a few times.

Eddie chuckled, "Well, let's just hope it stays a quiet night."

Maddie let out an over-exaggerated gasp. "Well, now! You said the Q word and angered the medical gods. You've just jinxed us," She huffed.

"I'll find a human sacrifice to appease them if need be," Eddie laughed as he walked back to his desk by the west entrance door.

They were still laughing when time itself stopped.

***

Every year the Watts Memorial Hospital put on a Halloween party for the staff, the patients that were able to leave their beds, and their families. They were encouraged to dress up. The hospital even provided a few basic costumes to choose from for those who didn't have one.

The second-floor cafeteria was decorated as a haunted house, complete with cobwebs and black and orange streamers hanging from the ceiling. The lights were turned low and maintenance had switched out some of the white light bulbs with purple and red ones. Tables were set up with themed food and drinks around the side of the room, leaving the middle open for people to dance. A DJ had a booth set up at the front of the room with large speakers on either side of him. The man was dressed up as a serial killer, including a fake machete in a sheath strapped to his leg. The staff behind the food tables had an animal theme. There was a lion, cat, dog, fox, lobster, squirrel, and even a couple of unicorns.

As the night went on, the room filled up with all manner of costumed people. Hannah sat at the edge of the room, sipping her cup of fruit punch as she watched the party. She normally avoided going to large gatherings, but her parents had insisted she come and support her older brother. He'd had surgery a few days ago, and was still recovering. Hannah had decided at the last minute to dress up like her favorite doll she'd had as a kid. She put on a red wig, a pair of overalls and painted her face with red polka dots. Her parents thought she looked adorable and Hannah had noticed a few of the younger party-goers checking her out. Apparently, Raggedy Ann had it going on?

Hannah was in awe at some of the costumes people wore. There was a couple in robot costumes that looked to be made out of actual metal and working lights. A man posed in a dragon costume that, from a distance, looked to be made out of real scales. A pair of men held hands in their couple's costumes. One was shirtless, painted red, with a tail hanging out the back of his shorts. The other was in all white with a halo blooming above his head. White feathered wings sprouted from his back. Behind them, a group of Vikings strutted in chanting an unintelligible war cry. Even knowing they were fake, Hannah was surprised they were allowed to bring weapons and shields into the hospital.

In a corner of the room, a man with wild hair, large goggles, and a white lab coat sat behind a cloth-covered table. He was pouring smoking liquids from one beaker to another. Cups full of brightly colored liquids were lined up towards the front of the table. He had a sign reading "Professor Young's Magic Elixirs". Underneath that, in parentheses, there was "For Adults Only". Hannah assumed that was where the alcohol was being served.

Hannah glanced at her phone to see it was a few seconds away from midnight. She hadn't realized it had gotten so late. She stood up to find her parents to ask if they could go home. She went to take a step but froze in place.

Her phone screen read midnight.

An itch started in her foot and flowed through the rest of her body. Hannah wanted to look down and see what was going on, but she couldn't look, she couldn't move. The itch became painful when it reached her waist. She couldn't explain it, but it felt like there was another presence in her mind. It felt like something evil was trying to push her out of control of her body. Internally she screamed as the pain grew more intense as it reached her neck. The entity in her head laughed at her pain as it crept into more and more of her mind. Hannah lost focus as the pain spiked. She didn't know her skin was turning to felt fabric, but she could feel her internal organs liquefy and morph into stuffing. The demonic entity in her finally quieted Hannah's mind, killing her, and her eyes turned into two shiny black buttons.

Time unfroze.

And all Hell broke loose.

***

The first thing Eddie heard when time started again was a woman screaming. Shaking off whatever had happened, his training kicked in, and he jumped from his seat. He pulled his gun and slowly moved towards the door.

"Eddie, what was that?" Maddie asked from her desk behind him.

"I don't know, but I'm going to check it out. Get on the phone and call 911. I may need some backup," Eddie said before stepping through the sliding doors and into the entryway of the hospital. He looked through the windows to see a woman running down the street. In the dark, Eddie could have sworn that she was being chased by a scarecrow, tall and wielding a harvesting scythe.

Eddie rushed out of the building to the parking lot.

"You, in the costume, stop where you are and drop your weapon!" he yelled as he pointed his gun at the scarecrow. Both of them heard him. He knew that when he saw both heads turn.

"Please help me! He's going to kill me!" the woman yelled as she ran toward the security officer. Even in her panicked state, she saw the gun and knew not to stand in front of it. When she reached the man, she huddled behind him.

The scarecrow stopped in the middle of the road to stare at the pair. Its head tilted to the side quizzically as it took in the newest human. All it wanted was to harvest the woman. A need deep inside it begged to run the blade of its scythe through her neck and bathe in the shower of her blood. The scarecrow wondered why this other human would stand in its way. As soon as that thought entered its straw-filled head, it was followed immediately by another.

This new human needed to be harvested, too.

"You need to stop," Eddie ordered as the tall, lanky monster began walking towards them. "Stop now or I *will* shoot."

The thing kept coming.

Eddie fired twice. The shots hitting both legs of the monster. Dust and straw flew out of the wounds, but the monster kept coming.

"Go inside, now," Eddie hissed to the woman behind him as he fired more shots, aiming for the thing's chest this time. More straw flew out of the holes as the shots penetrated the monster's body.

"Fuck," Eddie said. He walked backwards, still firing at the monster. A few shots hit its head. Those staggered the scarecrow, but it still kept coming. Eddie heard the hospital doors open behind him. He stepped into the entrance and looked at the top of the door. There was a small covering on the motor housing of the automatic doors. Eddie reached up and fumbled with the covering, pushing the switch underneath to the "off" position. He took a step back from the front door and watched as the scarecrow stalked forward.

"Maddie, how's that backup coming?" Eddie called over his shoulder.

"The phones aren't working," he heard her say from her desk. "I tried the hospital line and my cell phone, but couldn't get through to anyone. There wasn't even a message saying 'all lines are busy' it was just pure silence."

The security guard could hear the fear in her voice. He was feeling it too, but he knew he had to swallow it and protect those around him. If there was no backup coming, it was up to him and the other security guard to protect everyone in the building.

He jumped when the scythe slammed into the window in front of him. Eddie had been lost in thought and hadn't realized the creature had made it to the doors already. He watched, gun still raised, while the thing repeatedly bashed its weapon into the glass. Eddie let out a breath he didn't know he had been holding when all the scythe did was scratch the glass. He had forgotten the glass had been replaced with bulletproof glass a few years ago. After a few more attempts, the monster stopped and took a few steps back.

Eddie watched as it tilted its head once more.

"Maddie, is there any way to lock these doors? I've turned them off from opening on their own, but they can still be pulled open."

"One of the maintenance personnel would have keys for that. I'll try the internal communication and see if I can't get someone down here. Can you check on her?"

Eddie was still watching the scarecrow with his back turned to Maddie, but he knew she was talking about the woman he'd herded into the hospital. He holstered his gun and walked backwards into the lobby. The scarecrow watched him the entire time but didn't move.

Eddie finally turned around to see Maddie at her desk trying the phone and the woman sitting in one of the waiting room chairs. She was staring forward, but Eddie was pretty sure she wasn't seeing anything. He walked over to her and leaned down in front of her.

"Ma'am, can you tell me your name?" he asked softly. He had to repeat the question a few more times before she replied to him.

"Lindsey. My name is Lindsey," she said in a shaky voice.

"I'm Eddie and the woman behind the desk is Maddie," Eddie said, motioning his head towards the nurse behind her desk. "Can you tell me what happened?"

It took Lindsey a few minutes to speak again.

"I was taking my son, Tommy, home from the haunted barn on the edge of town. We had been out late trick-or-treating, but he still wanted to go. We dropped off his candy at home then headed to the barn. It was nice out, and he was warm enough in all the straw. We decided to walk. He went into the barn by himself. He was such a brave boy." At this, she broke into choking sobs. Eddie gently rubbed her back. When she was able to collect herself, Lindsey continued, "It was close to midnight by the time we started walking home. Tommy said that the moon was turning red? And it was! We stopped to watch it when time just... stopped."

"I felt that, too," Eddie said, nodding. He was relieved that he wasn't the only one who felt it.

"When we were able to move again, Tommy's hand felt strange," Linsdey continued. "I turned to look and my son had become that *thing* that was chasing me. Then, I guess you know the rest." She broke into quiet sobs again. Eddie stood up and thought about her tale. He was beginning to piece together what was happening when Maddie walked up from behind him.

"I can't reach anyone in maintenance. I know Lenny was supposed to be covering while everyone else went to the party," She said in a soft tone.

"Oh shit," Eddie said, louder than he meant. He remembered there was a room full of costumed people two floors above them. If what happened to Tommy happened to everyone else, they were going to be in trouble.

"We may have bigger problems."

***

Screams brought Dave awake.

"Is someone having a *fucking baby* next door?" he asked groggily, wiping the sleep from his eyes. When they were more open, he saw Howard was standing at the door peeking out of the curtain. The television was still on, but the screen was filled with the multicolored bars of the test pattern. Normally, important information would be scrolling across the bottom. Dave was surprised he didn't see anything.

"Did you dream about anything strange?" Howard asked from his position at the door.

"No. I don't remember my dream at all. Why do you ask?" Dave leaned up to get a better look at him.

"Just a feeling I had. Time seemed to stop for a couple of seconds. I would say I had fallen asleep, only I was still watching the t.v."

"Huh? That's strange. Do you know what that screaming is all about?"

"No idea," Howard said before turning around to look at his friend. "It started not long after I was able to move again. I can't really see anything, but didn't want to leave you alone to investigate."

Dave nodded his thanks. He was glad he hadn't woken up in the room all by himself. More screams made their way to the two men. They shared a look and, despite not saying a word, they knew what the other was thinking.

"How's the leg?" Howard asked, nodding towards the appendage that was wrapped in a cast.

"Hurts like a bitch. I won't be able to make any quick getaways. Think security will be able to handle whatever is going on out there?"

"I'm not sure. I do know I would feel better if I knew what was happening. Do you want to come with me while I investigate or stay here? I can find a wheelchair for you."

Dave thought about it before answering. Part of him knew he would just slow Howard down, and he didn't want that. The other part was thinking about what would happen if Howard never came back. Even though he hadn't said it, Dave knew the other man would barricade the door from the outside as best as he could. But if whatever was happening in the hospital made its way here, he would be a sitting duck.

"Let's go check it out. If it's more than we can handle, we can lock ourselves in here and wait for help to arrive. Sound good?" Dave asked.

Howard nodded before peeking out the shade again. "It looks clear. I'm going to go find you a wheelchair."

"Grab me a crutch, too," Dave said before Howard had a chance to open the door. The paramedic gave his friend a quizzical look. "For protection. In case I need to hit something."

Howards smiled before opening the door and stepping into the hall.

Dave watched him go and tried not to worry about whatever was making people scream.

Howard crouched as he stepped into the hall. The screams were louder, but they still sounded a good distance away. He looked around the hall first, looking for anyone who could tell him what was going on. Second for a wheelchair and a crutch. He hoped Dave wouldn't have to use it, but he agreed with the man's thinking. Better to be safe than sorry.

He slipped down the hall towards the nurse's station. The doors on each side of the hallway were shut, and all but a couple had their shades pulled down. He peeked into the first door on his left and saw a comatose man with tubes coming out of his nose. The next room he checked in was empty. The paramedic was a bit surprised to not run into *someone* in the hallway.

Howard reached the nurse's station and, to his shock, he found the desk empty.

"What the hell?" he mumbled to himself. As long as he had been a paramedic, there had always been at least one person at every nurse's station. He stepped behind the desk to find some sign of what was going on. There was nothing out of the ordinary, except, when he tried the phone, it was silent. There was nothing he could do about it now, though, so Howard put the phone down and tried the computer, but there was no internet. Another first. The hospital always had a reliable connection to get medical records.

"Well, so much for asking for outside help," Howard said to himself. "Guess we're on our own."

Howard saw a file labeled "Hospital Map" on the home screen. He opened it and printed it off. While the printer was working, Howard looked around the immediate area.

"Bingo!" he said when he spotted a wheelchair sitting by the elevators. He wheeled the chair over to the desk and piled the papers into the chair before heading back to Dave's room.

It was only when he was pushing the door open that he realized most of the screaming had stopped.

Dave bolted upright when he heard the door open. He quickly looked around for something to throw. Not finding anything, he watched in horror as the door opened slowly.

He sighed and went limp when Howard backed in, pulling the chair in behind him.

"I found you a ride, but no weapon," Howard said. "I *was* able to find a map of the building. If need be, I'm going to have you be my navigator if we get lost."

Dave nodded, letting Howard help him get into the chair. They had to take out his IV tube, as neither man wanted to drag the pole around with them.

"Any chance they have an extra pair of clothes somewhere nearby?" Dave asked as he got settled.

"We might be able to find you some scrubs, but right now we need to figure out what's going on."

"Easy for you to say. You're not the one who has his ass hanging out in the wind."

Howard just grunted. Dave could tell his mind was on other things, and he didn't blame his friend. While the paramedic was gone, all Dave could think about was Phoebe. Part of him wished she was here so he would know she was safe. The other part of him was glad she wasn't.

Howard reached over him and opened the door. Dave looked over the maps and tried to drown out the screams, growing ever louder all around them. The paramedic wheeled his friend down the same path he'd taken to the nurse's station. The hallway was still empty and that creeped Howard out more than the screams.

"The cafeteria is to the left. We should head there," Howard said as he pushed the chair that way.

"You mean *towards* the screams? Great idea," Dave groused. He debated setting the breaks and letting Howard go alone but swallowed that thought. He knew his friend would need him even if it was just for moral support. Howard slowed down the closer they got to the cafeteria doors. The noises were growing louder, but neither man heard any more screams. Howard parked Dave next to the first door in the set, making sure to position the man where he would be able to lean up and look through the window. Howard crouched out of sight and peered around the second door. He looked at Dave and held up three fingers. The man in the chair nodded, understanding the plan, though no words were spoken.

Howard put one finger down at a time. When the last was down the two men peeked through the glass of the doors.

They both choked down screams at the bloodbath in the room.

Behind them the elevators dinged, making both men jump.

The monsters in the cafeteria heard the chime as well and, as one, looked to the hallway, the elevators, and the doors Howard and Dave had taken shelter behind.

A fur-covered werewolf saw the faces of its new prey, and let out a roar before charging the doors.

The rest of the monsters in the room followed suit.

***

"Are you sure this is a good idea? Maybe I should have stayed behind and kept trying the phones?" Maddie asked as she followed Eddie slowly down the hall towards the elevator. Lindsey had agreed to come with them and was bringing up the rear of the group.

"I'm sure. With the radios not working, we have no way of staying in contact with each other. We also don't know if the other two entrances of the building are secured or not. If a monster was able to sneak in, or is already inside, you would have no way of getting ahold of me if you're attacked. Besides, we both know the phones aren't going to be working anytime soon," Eddie explained. He had changed the clip in his gun with the extra one that was on his belt and had the now loaded weapon out in front of him, sweeping it back and forth in the hallway.

"Right now we need to check the party and see if whatever happened to Tommy happened to anyone there. If not, then we can spread out and fortify the building. If the change did happen there, then we will fall back and get out of here."

"What about the patients?" Maddie asked.

Eddie sighed. He knew it was going to be a struggle to get her out of here. He knew she would want to save as many people as she could.

"It depends on how bad the party turned out," Eddie said. He didn't want to get ahead of himself. Dealing with one problem at a time was always how he dealt with things. He pressed the call button on the elevator and took a step back. When the doors opened, he swept the car with his gun, before stepping inside. The two women followed him. Maddie pressed the button for the third floor while Eddie kept his gun pointed at the doors. He wanted to be ready if anything was waiting for him. Lindsey huddled in one of the corners of the car. She seemed to gain some strength as the night dragged on. Maybe it was the thought of helping others, or maybe it was just pure survival instincts. It didn't matter to Eddie. He was just glad he had some backup in the way of her pepper spray.

The elevator doors dinged as they opened. Eddie started to step out but stopped when he spotted two figures farther down the hall. They turned to look at him as he pointed his pistol at them. Eddie dropped it when he saw their faces. Humans. Eddie led his ragtag group cautiously towards the two in front of them.

They all froze when they heard something roar from the cafeteria.

A moment later a blood-covered werewolf burst through the doors, knocking the two men behind them over. The one in the chair fell out of it as the papers he had been holding went flying.

Eddie fired at the beast as more creatures poured out of the cafeteria.

Maddie looked around for a weapon and found a mobile IV pole. She tore the bag off and gripped the pole in both hands ready to beat anything that got close to them. Lindsey held the pepper spray in front of her with her finger on the trigger.

The werewolf yelped as bullets punctured its fur and the skin beneath. The thing died mid-run and its body slid the rest of the way down the hall towards the group of three, coming to a stop a few feet away from them.

***

Dave screamed from the ground, a large felt foot on his throat, beady black eyes staring down at him. He beat on the leg, trying to reconcile that a thing that was supposed to be filled with stuffing would have enough strength in it to cut off his airway. He clawed at the fabric ankle, but couldn't get a grip on anything. He looked desperately for Howard to save him.

What he couldn't see was Howard with his back against the wall, two demons, one red and the other with large white wings, stalking towards his friend.

Dave's vision started to go dark as more gunshots rang out. Air whooshed back into his lungs as the felt foot slipped from his throat. He coughed as he saw the face of the doll lying next to him.

Two holes were leaking red and pink felt from its head.

Still coughing, he dragged himself behind the door. The cast on his leg slowed him down, but he made it while more bullets hit more of the monsters pouring out of the cafeteria. Dave rubbed his throat and made himself as small as possible. His only hope was to hide until the hallway was empty.

"Well, well, *well*, what do we have here?" a gravelly voice asked as Dave's vision was filled with the stained edges of a white lab coat. His eyes traveled up the body and stopped on the face of the creature. Its black hair stood a foot tall from the top of its head. What might once have been goggles were now its bulging eyes, the large red irises full of malicious curiosity. Its mouth was spread in a sharp-toothed grin that seemed to stretch to meet in the back of its head. In its clawed hand, the thing held a beaker full of smoking purple liquid.

"It looks like you've hurt yourself, poor thing," the thing whined its pity. "I have *just* the thing for that." It cackled as it crouched down next to Dave, wiggling the beaker in front of the injured man's eyes. "This is my special healing potion. All you have to do is open up and down the hatch. You'll be feeling better in no time."

"No... No... That's okay," Dave gasped. He put his hands up in an attempt to push the monster back. He didn't know the thing had sliced off his hands until the stumps started pouring blood. One second his hands were in front of him, the next they were in his lap. Dave shrieked as the demon laughed.

"Don't worry, I can fix that, too. Now, keep that mouth open."

It grabbed the back of his head and emptied the beaker into Dave's mouth, giggling as the man screamed, coughed, and sputtered, the purple liquid coating his front. There was an intense burning sensation as some of it came in contact with the contusion on his head. His tongue and teeth burned, as well. Still lightheaded from the foot on his throat, Dave's natural instincts took over, and he swallowed the smoking liquid.

And that burned all the way down, too.

"Now, let's see what happens," the demon scientist said when the beaker was empty. It watched as the human's face and throat began to melt. Dave's screams were silenced when the liquid burned through his vocal cords. It took mere seconds for liquid to burn through the skin and of his face and into his skull. It took longer for it to chew through the bone. When it reached his brain, Dave's body did him the courtesy of going into shock. He didn't feel much pain after that. A hole burst in his stomach a few seconds later, as the fluid liquefied his esophagus and leaked down into his other organs.

"Mmmmm, interesting," the demon mumbled as it began rooting around in the remains of Dave's stomach. Its thick skin feeling no effects from the concoction. "I must have put too much hydrochloric acid in it. Oh well! On to the next experiment."

The demon scientist stood up. Turning around, it caught a glimpse at its cohorts pounding on the doors of the elevator just as they closed.

Through the closing doors, it caught sight of three more test subjects.

It strode down the hall, watching the numbers above the elevator tick up to five and stop.

***

"There's no point in running, human." The gravelly voice of the red demon followed Howard down the hall. "We can smell your flesh wherever you go."

Howard ran on with tears in his eyes. He hated leaving Dave behind, but there was no getting to him. He had watched his friend fall from the wheelchair before the river of demons monsters came flowing out of the room. When he got to his feet, two demons stood in front of him, discussing the best way to eat him. Without giving it another thought, the paramedic turned and pelted down the hall. He heard gunshots behind him and hoped one of the demons had been hit.

When he looked behind him, his bladder let go. The white demon was flying at him, clawed arms outstretched. Its mouth was wide open, tongue darting out as if tasting the air. What Howard didn't see was the taller red demon stalking behind the white one. It did not worryits its partner wouldn't be able to catch their prey.

Howard felt the flying thing's fetid breath on his neck.

He ducked at the last moment.

The thing's claws grabbed at empty air as it flew over the human. The red demon laughed as it watched its prey try to outsmart them.

The sound of the things manic laughing was almost enough to drive Howard insane, it was actually making him feel dizzy. He quickly looked around for a place to escape as he scrambled to his feet. There were doors on each side of him, but none of them were open. There was no telling if they were locked or not.

The flying demon recovered and landed on its taloned feet behind Howard.

Both monsters kept laughing.

This time Howard's mind did break. He fell to the floor and curled up into a ball. Somewhere deep inside of him, a voice was yelling, angry, at him for giving up, but the rest of Howard didn't care. The sound of their laughter pouring into his brain sounded like a whole city of tortured souls screaming. Visions of horrible things filled his mind as the sniggering demons stepped closer to him.

Had Howard been in a better state of mind, he might have realized the psychological torture the demons were inflicting on him. Instead, all he could do was drool as he watched his skin flay off his body where their clawed hands touched him.

"It looks like he's ready," the red demon said as they reached Howard. "His mind is properly broken. Shall we take our time with him?"

"I think so. I know there are more humans around, but I don't think they are going anywhere," the white demon smirked. His lover nodded before they each grabbed Howard under his arm and pulled him to his feet. They dragged him over to one of the closed doors. The red demon kicked the door with its taloned foot and the piece of wood went flying across the room. It crashed into the window breaking the glass.

The demons tossed the bubblering man into the room as if he was a sack of potatoes.

"We have others to attend to, but we will come back for this one and have some fun torturing this one," the red demon said, before kissing its partner.

***

The three humans screamed as the monsters slammed into the elevator doors. The survivors huddled towards the back of the car, expecting at any moment for the doors to burst open and the demons to pour in. They let out a collective sigh when the pounding quieted and the elevator car rose.

"Well, that was worse than I thought," Eddie said shakily, checking how much ammo he had left in his clip.

"Only three shots remaining. I guess that could be enough." He didn't elaborate on what he meant.

"What's the plan now?" Maddie asked. She was using the bottom of her shirt to wipe demon blood off her face. The IV pole she had used as a weapon was leaning against the wall next to her. The top was bent and slick with blood.

"Well, I'm going to assume that the monsters, or demons, or whatever the fuck they are, have taken over the hospital. We have to get out." He saw Maddie start to open her mouth, but he cut her off. "We need to focus on our own survival right now. I feel bad leaving people behind, too, but there's nothing we can do for them besides hope they are able to hide long enough for the hospital to empty out."

Maddie crossed her arms over her chest and gave him a stern look, but she didn't say anything.

"That being said," Eddie continued, "we need to find a way out of here that involves running into as few of those things as possible. Maddie, you know this place best. Is there any way we could sneak back down?"

"Why don't we just take the elevator?" Lindsey asked in a small voice. She was clutching her pepper spray close to her chest.

"I have a feeling if we do that they'll be waiting for us. I don't want to risk it," Eddie said. He had thought of that first, but after seeing the intelligence in some of the monster's eyes he knew it would be a really risky move.

"Oh, okay," Lindsey replied and seemed to move deeper into her corner. Eddie knew she was going into some kind of shock and knew he had to keep a close eye on her.

"There's a ladder on the roof. We were shown it in our yearly fire safety course," Maddie said, uncrossing her arms. "It leads most of the way down the side of the building. We'll have to extend it the rest of the way. It's kept folded up so random people don't just climb it."

"Then that's our goal," Eddie said.

The elevator dinged as the doors began to open. Eddie took a breath before stepping out with his gun raised out in front of him.

The fifth floor was quiet. It was similar in design to the second floor but didn't have a cafeteria. There was also a lack of demons, which the three humans were thankful for. There was no telling how long it was going to last, though.

Eddie led the small party out of the elevator and down the hall. Linsdey was behind him with Maddie bringing up the rear.

"The roof entrance is past the nurse's station and to the left. We'll have to break the lock off the door unless you have the keys." That last part was to Eddie.

"Nope." Was all he said. She could tell he was focused on getting them out of the building safely. She was happy he was here but was also conflicted about leaving her patients behind. There was little choice, though.

They moved past the nurse's station without a problem. Maddie let out an internal sigh when she saw the "Exit" sign about halfway down the hallway. For the first time since the traumatic night had started, she felt hope.

That hope was crushed when a door next to them flew open and two clawed hands reached out and grabbed onto Lindsey.

"Come here, dear, I need your help," the gravelly voice of the demon scientist said as Lindsey screamed. The monster dug its claws into the woman's side as it pulled her into the room. "Oh do shut up, will you?"

Eddie and Maddie were still reeling when they heard a wet ripping sound from inside the room, followed by gurgling.

"That's better." The monster stuck its head out into the hall. There was a large toothy smile plastered on its face. "You two can leave, but I suggest you move quickly. Some of my brethren may have followed me."

Eddie aimed his gun at the demon, but before he could pull the trigger the monster pulled its head back out of view.

"You better save your ammo. There's no telling when you'll need it!" the scientist monster cackled. The horrible sound was followed by more tearing noises and the creature muttering to itself.

Eddie looked back at Maddie.

She swallowed before nodding.

They both knew there was nothing they could do for Lindsey and if the monster was telling the truth they didn't have much time left. If there was time later, Eddie knew he would agonize over letting the demon keep what was left of Lindsey. Right now, all he was focused on was getting out of the building alive. They reached the roof door right as the door on the other end of the hallway burst open. The red demon stepped out, followed by the white demon. The humans could hear more demons milling behind them.

Eddie turned the knob. When he pulled, the door wouldn't budge.

"Cover your eyes," Eddie yelled to Maddie before he fired his gun at the lock of the door. The metal of the lock flew apart and the door slowly slid open. Eddie pulled it open the rest of the way. "Come on."

Maddie had been watching the demons striding towards them as Eddie was getting the door open. The sound of his voice got her moving. She followed Eddie up the stairs. She had a brief thought of pulling the door closed behind them, but realized it wouldn't matter. She could hear the demons getting closer.

Eddie rushed onto the roof. The cool air of the night hit him in the face. He didn't realize how hot the hospital was.

"Where's the ladder at?" he asked over his shoulder.

"This way," Maddie replied, before darting in front of him. She led him across the helicopter pad and towards the edge. "We still need to find a way to unlock the chain holding the ladder up."

Eddie looked down at the ladder and was thankful to see it ended at the top of the first floor. "We don't have time. It's going to suck, but when we get to that point we're just going to have to jump. Think you can do that?"

Maddie nodded. "Well, good news; if we get injured, I can fix us up." Maddie let out a weak chuckle before getting on the ladder. Eddie smiled down at her before turning back to the roof door. The red and the white demons stepped out on the roof, followed by their army. Eddie could tell that these two were in charge; they held the others back by sheer force of will. The large red one took a step forward.

"Why do you run?" it hissed. The sound of the thing's voice reminded Eddie of nails on a chalkboard. It took everything he had in him not to curl into a ball and cry.

"The world you knew is now gone. It belongs to our kind now." The demon gestured its hand at the waiting crowd. "Humankind's rule is at an end. All you're doing is delaying your inevitable death. Submit now and I will make sure your death is quick."

Eddie glanced over his shoulder and saw Maddie had just landed on the ground. He calculated the amount of time it would take him to descend the ladder. He looked back at the white-winged demon. Eddie knew his chances. They were slim to none.

He saw Maddie look back up at him. He gave her a sad smile and nodded his head towards the parking lot. She shook her head a few times.

Eddie turned his back on her and faced the horde of monsters.

He didn't see Maddie give him one last nod, tears in her eyes, or turn and run for the parking lot to her car. At the edge of the roof, Eddie took a deep breath before addressing the leader of the demons.

"You know what, fuck you," Eddie said with a toothy grin. He was going to die in the next few minutes, so why not go down swinging? "If you and your kind want to rule this fucked up planet, then go for it."

The two leading demons laughed. Eddie covered his ears and screamed until they were done.

"Pathetic human. You think you're saving that female by distracting us? This is why your race will fall quickly. Stupidity."

"You see that's where you're wrong, dickwad." Eddie spat on the ground. "Maybe you'll catch her eventually, but what I'm doing is the most human thing I can think of."

"And what's that?" the white demon asked, rolling its eyes as it took a step forward to stand next to its partner.

"I'm making a choice. I'm choosing to fight instead of running. Let's face it. You would have ripped me in half without a second thought on the ladder, am I right?"

Both demons sniggered.

"Thought so. Instead, I'm going to go out my way. I'm going to kick your asses straight back to hell." With that, he charged, screaming a war cry at them.

The demons let out their own guttural war cries as they met the man's charge.

***

From her car, Maddie heard the screaming. She had waited a few moments to see if Eddie was going to make it off the roof alive.

Now she knew he wasn't.

Tears in her eyes, she pulled the car out of the parking lot and into the street.

A lumbering, bullet-riddled scarecrow blocked her path with a raised scythe.

Maddie stomped down the gas pedal, and the car shot forward. The scarecrow burst apart in a cloud of hay.

Bloodline
Ricki Whatley

Miriam Lazlow sprinted full speed into the waiting elevator. Her slim body slammed into the rear wall, marring the pristine glass with greasy handprints. Fifty feet behind her, she could see the reflected image of her winded husband.

I'm Miriam Ogdim *now,* she mentally corrected herself, *I got married five hours ago and now, my new husband is trying to fucking kill me!*

She spun on her bare feet and frantically stabbed the lobby button. At the end of the hallway, Jonathan took a deliberate step in her direction. The weight of his massive body seemed to shake the entire floor of the vacant hotel. Miriam felt the dangling elevator tremble on its fragile safety cables.

"Come on!" she shrieked at the stubborn wall panel. Panic seized her like the unyielding grip of a python. Her lungs burned, unsatisfied by her shallow, spastic breaths. Her index finger jackhammered the round, glowing button marked 'L' but nothing happened. A lurid ring burned red around the empty keyhole at the top of the metal control grid. Above her head, a large, capital 'P' stood unblinking on a digital screen.

P is for Penthouse Suite! Laughed a mocking, Sesame Street voice in Miriam's head.

"FUCK!" she yelled, slamming her palm against the elevator wall in frustration. *He took the fucking key!*

Down the hall, Jonathan's hulking frame took another slow, menacing step. No need to rush. Miriam was trapped in the tiny, immobile box. He could take his time. Savor her distress. Based on the hungry grin torn open on his face, *he was*. With his head lowered and his monolithic shoulders squared off, he looked like a bull, ready to charge. He lifted one muscular arm to his side. Daintily pinched between his thumb and one plantain-sized finger was a twinkling, brass key.

A horrified moan escaped Miriam's lips and she paced the floor in a terrified dance step. *Forward, backward, side to side*—there was no escape from the glimmering cube.

"It's over, Miri," Jonathan growled in a voice too deep to be human. "You're out of options. The only way out is through me."

Miriam's breath hitched in her chest. Tears coursed down her face, staining her perfect makeup with black streaks of mascara. She choked and sniffed wetly as she began to beg, "Please, Jonathan. You don't have to do this, baby!" She lifted the lacy edge of her silk slip to wipe the snot from her running nose. Jonathan calmly dropped the elevator key into the pocket of his black tuxedo pants. His white button down shirt hung open in shredded ribbons. The fabric still clinging to his arms strained to contain his swollen biceps. Beneath the stiff fabric, his expansive chest heaved from the exertion of chasing his wife through the labyrinthine suite. A sparse 'Y' of curly brown hair covered his bare pecs. In spite of the circumstances, Miriam felt her pelvis clench with involuntary need.

Hey, in the right lighting, even a serial killer looked sexy.

"It's not too late; you can stop all of this. It doesn't have to end like the others! We can go back to the way things were. We can be happy together, like *before*!"

Obviously, there was no way in hell Miriam would ever stay with this maniac but maybe his deranged mind was gullible enough to believe her.

Maybe she could at least buy some time.

Miriam quickly scanned the hallway for a potential escape route. The corridor was a long, carpeted funnel that led straight to her captor. On the right hand side, windows that looked down on the sparkling city, twenty stories below. On the left, solid wall save for one, singular doorframe centered perfectly between Miriam and her homicidal groom. She could undoubtedly clear the twenty-five-foot distance in just a few, lightning strides; but Jonathan could do it in fewer. She would need to keep him immobilized while she closed the distance and talked her way out of the elevator. She was about to negotiate with a hostage taker and the life at stake was her own.

Miriam locked her eyes onto Jonathan's and stepped out of the elevator. The lush, creamy carpet sucked at her feet like quick sand. Before she could begin her monologue, Jonathan broke the silence between them.

"I don't want to hurt you, Miri," he rumbled, "I love you."

"I know you do, baby," Miriam eagerly concurred.

"I know you're the one for me. I know you'll be different. Just come to me." Jonathan held out his hand and stepped toward her. One pace of his gargantuan legs brought him easily five feet closer. Seeing the distance separating them shrink, was like watching the fuse burn out on a stick of dynamite that she was holding.

Only forty-five feet until BOOM.

Spurred by the threat of her advancing doom, she lunged forward, interrupting him. "Yes! I *do* want to be with you!" She forced herself to slow down and appear casual. Jonathan stood still. "I'm just nervous, that's all. We haven't slept together in *months*. I just want our first night as husband and wife to be perfect." She hoisted the corners of her mouth into a quivering smile. In her peripheral vision, she could see the dark sanctuary of the doorway growing larger.

Only fifteen feet away.

Miriam knew if she allowed her eyes to flicker in that direction, the gig would be up. Jonathan would see through her feeble ruse and cut her off her escape.

Twelve feet.

It seemed to be working though. Jonathan's shoulders sagged noticeably. He smiled back at her, almost sheepishly. Bashful even.

He looked like a high school boy who just farted in front of his prom date.

"You have to believe me," he mumbled, "I never meant to hurt any of those other women. I loved them—not as much as you of course—but I genuinely cared for them. I thought we could spend our lives together. It just didn't work out. They weren't right. They couldn't carry on my bloodline. You'll be different, I know you will!" Jonathan shifted his feet self-consciously.

Of course I'll be different, she thought to herself. *I'm gonna be the one who gets away, you fucking psycho.*

Aloud, she said, "I *am* different, baby. We were made for each other. You're my soulmate."

Nine feet.

"It's hard after you're married, you know?" Jonathan pleaded. Each of his hands looked the size of a wheelbarrow. He nervously raked them through his thick, dark hair. Miriam kept walking. "It's time for us to start our family. I have to know if you can handle my bloodline and there's only one way to find that out! But I swear I will be *so* gentle."

"Of course you will, baby."

Six feet.

Despite herself, Miriam felt a slick yearning overcome herself. Jonathan was *hands down* the best lay she had ever had. He was hyper-masculine simply by virtue of his natural size. Yet in all their previous, sexual encounters, he had always been tender and conscientious. At six foot six, he towered a full foot over Miriam and normally outweighed her by a solid one hundred and fifty pounds. There was no telling what his current measurements were. His tailored clothing hung in tatters from his exaggerated frame. He had to be at least a foot taller and close to double his usual weight. Looking at him now, in his present state, a small part of Miriam's brain desperately wanted to find out if another, particular organ had also doubled in weight...

It wasn't like Miriam had been a virgin when they met. She had a few semi-serious relationships in college and even the occasional, one-night-stand. Being with Jonathan was just *different*. It was like he knew exactly where to touch her.

In any sexual union, there was a fine line that distinguished foreplay from torture. Jonathan knew exactly where that line was and how to lead Miriam to it. He could set her on fire with little more than a look. The way he wrapped his hand around her wrist and pull her into his embrace made her melt. He would kiss her neck and tease her nipples the way she liked, tickling and stroking her to the point of frenzy. Only when he had brought her to the brink of lustful madness, dripping wet and begging for his cock would he finally appease her. Hoisting her up, he would slide her down onto his throbbing shaft unleashing the full force of her desire.

They would lay together afterwards, staring blankly at the ceiling in a dehydrated stupor. He would trace circles around her bellybutton and breathe the grassy perfume of her hair.

Now, in the hallway, she was not wearing any panties under her scant, white negligee. She tugged bashfully at the hem. Even from twenty feet away, she could smell Jonathan. His chemistry seemed to have transformed along with his anatomy. His skin reeked of wet hay and warm fleece. It was virile and *animal* and it made sweat prickle on the back of Miriam's neck.

Focus! She chided herself.

But the lecherous thoughts continued. Delicious memories flooded her brain, igniting her senses. The time he blindfolded her and dropped ice cubes onto her naked, unsuspecting flesh. The time he had taken her behind a tree on their local hiking trail. They shamelessly rutted less than twenty feet from the path and he covered her mouth with his hand when oblivious pedestrians approached their hiding place.

It had been months since they had slept together. Miriam had stopped taking her birth control to help lose a few pounds before the wedding. Ever since, Jonathan had refused to touch her. His reaction to her decision had been startling.

"You did what?" he had demanded on the day she told him.

"I stopped taking my birth control," Miriam repeated. "It's not what you think, babe!" She had chuckled, unaware of the conversation's sudden gravity. "I'm not trying to get knocked up yet. I just want to lose a few pounds before the wedding and sometimes the hormones can make it really hard to drop weight. That's all."

Jonathan had only bitten his lip and blinked a silent response.

"What? What's the big deal?"

He sighed and then said, "I don't think we should sleep together anymore."

"Why?" This time it was Miriam's turn to demand answers. "What's the problem?"

"I just," his voice trailed off and he turned his attention to the floor. "I just don't want any…"

"What? Say it."

"I don't want any accidents before the wedding, you know?"

Miriam visibly recoiled. She and Jonathan had already agreed to wait a couple years before starting a family. She did not intend to move that timeline around and she certainly did not want any children in the immediate future either. Still, despite their logic, Jonathan's words stung. The implication that any children born of their love could be considered *accidental* was astoundingly painful.

"Miri, I love you," Jonathan had said tenderly. Miriam said nothing but let him speak.

"There is no one else in the world I want to carry on my bloodline. Just not yet, OK? I think it's better if we err on the side of caution and abstain 'til the wedding." He embraced her tenderly. Miriam had instantly forgave and embraced him back. "Besides," he continued with a mischievous grin, "it might be kind of fun to re-virginize you. Then I can re-deflower you on our wedding night!" They both had laughed and wrestled as Miriam playfully slapped him.

Prior to the wedding, they had always laughed. Everything had started out so perfect…

There was no time to think about that now. The doorway was less than three feet away. Jonathan lagged about fifteen feet farther back. He could not possibly catch her now. It was time to get the fuck out of dodge!

"Take my hand, Miri," implored Jonathan, once again extending his hand to his new wife.

Miriam's body was parallel with the doorway, framed perfectly by the rectangular void. She raised her hand as if she was going to continue walking straight down the hall, right into Jonathan's arms. Suddenly, she pivoted her foot, grinding her toes into the thick pile of the hotel carpet. In one fluid motion, she turned her body to the left and launched forward off her rear foot. Like a bullet rifling down the barrel of a gun, Miriam propelled down the hall toward the center of the penthouse. The hallway zigzagged around bedrooms, bathrooms and various seating areas in the immense, top floor suite. Behind her, Miriam heard the crash and destruction as Jonathan rampaged after her. He roared like an impaled beast, both injured and infuriated by her blatant rejection.

"NO!" he screamed, "Miri come back! You're making me so angry and I can't control myself when I'm ANGRY!"

The walls quaked with the impact of his giant body ricocheting down the passageway. Dim lights embedded the ceiling above her flickered, threatening to plunge her headlong into blinding darkness but Miriam ran on. She knew there had to be a stairwell somewhere on the floor. A fire exit. If only she could find an alternative way down, she could get back to the bottom floor.

Their wedding guests were most likely still in the large ballroom, dancing the Electric Slide and eating bacon wrapped scallops. They would help her. They would call the police. She would be saved if only she could stay out of Jonathan's fatal grasp long enough to find her way out. Luckily for her, the central hallway ran at sharp angles to make room for the grand living spaces in the penthouse. Jonathan could not see her as she pinballed through the halls, searching for a place to hide. Miriam decided she could wait for him to pass her, then slip out and head towards the corners of the building where a stairwell was most likely to be.

"MIRIAAAAAM!" the monster that had been her husband wailed behind her.

Rounding a bend in the hall, she spied the open, double doors of the master bedroom. Miriam dove into the room and scrambled under the bed so fast her knees and elbows ignited with rug burns. She prayed Jonathan would thunder passed without stopping. In the shade of the king-sized bed, Miriam held her hands over her mouth and stared out from the foot of the bed.

The bedframe above her jittered and hopped. He was getting *close*.

This must be what a rabbit feels like during an earthquake, Miriam thought from her tiny den under the bed.

She steeled herself to confront the approaching killer. She squeezed her eyes shut in horror and disbelief. How had her wedding day turned into *this*?

***

Miriam and Jonathan were set to be wed on May 7, at the Bethel Temple in the heart of downtown. After the ceremony, the happy couple planned to host two hundred of their closest friends and relatives at the five star, Hamilton Hotel. Jonathan's parents had bought them four nights in the honeymoon penthouse as a wedding present. It was supposed to be a little, pre-honey moon retreat for the newlyweds.

Despite an early hiccough, their ceremony had been beautiful. The seats overflowed with Jonathan's family. Miriam did not have anyone from her side present. Her grandmother had raised her from the time she was a toddler. When her Bubby died during her sophomore year in college, the young woman was left, for all intents and purposes, orphaned.

Instead of her own dad, Jonathan's father walked her down the aisle. He kissed her cheek as he lovingly placed her hand into his son's. Jonathan's mother stood in the front row, bawling openly into a comically large handkerchief. Good ol' Barbara. She had always loved Miriam.

Boys ran in Jonathan's family. His father was one of four boys, and his grandfather was one of six. His great grandfather had lost his entire family in the Holocaust and before that, their family history was virtually unknown. As far as Miriam knew, there was not a single aunt on her father in law's side. At least not since 1945. Barbara had continued the tradition, giving birth to three, gigantic sons.

On the day of the wedding, Barbara was at Miriam's side, helping her into her dress and tacking her veil into the thick chignon at the base of her neck. Miriam fretfully rung her hands and hyperventilated.

"Slow down, sweetie," Barbara soothed her, "the last thing we need is you falling out right before the wedding!"

"I'm just so nervous, Barb. Do I look OK?"

"You look gorgeous, Honey." The older woman reached into her gargantuan purse and withdrew a delicate golden chain bearing a tiny, gold Chai. "Here, I want you to wear this. It was Jonathan's great grandfather's. He hid this under the floor in his apartment before they took him away. After the war, he went back home and got it. It was still there after all that time. My mother-in-law gave it to me, and now, it's time I passed it on to you." Barbara stepped behind the new bride and swung the shiny pendant around her throat. The metal was shockingly cold and sent a chill through Miriam's body.

"There," Barbara said with obvious approval, "*now* you're ready." Without thinking, she added, "Hopefully this is the last time I have to do that." When Miriam did not return her smile, Barbara realized her faux pas. All the color drained from her face, leaving her cheeks waxen and her mouth pursed.

"What?" Miriam asked, "What do you mean? How many fiancées has Jonathan had?" She was trying to keep her voice casual but the effort was beginning to make her throat itch.

"Oh, well," Barbara stuttered awkwardly, "you know, with three boys, sometimes I lose track of their little dalliances."

"Uh, if they made it all the way to the wedding that seems like more than a *dalliance*." Unconsciously, Miriam resumed her fidgeting. The chill that had pricked her skin shortly before was replaced with a fiery, full-bodied blush.

Barbara fluffed Miriam's veil and stubbornly refused to make eye contact. "Honey, you shouldn't worry about that. Ancient history."

"Jonathan never told me he was engaged before. Was he *married*? Did someone else wear this necklace at their *wedding*?" Her voice rose, shrill and too loud in the small, wood paneled room. She tugged unconsciously at the little charm, no longer wanting it to even touch her.

Realizing that her daughter in law was not going to drop the issue, Barbara sighed and sat down on a nearby chaise.

"Jonathan was briefly married," she conceded at last.

The revelation sent a geyser of bile spewing up Miriam's throat and she choked back oily vomit. She too began searching for a place to sit and collapsed gratefully onto a rickety vanity chair.

"His wife died on their wedding night. That's probably why he never told you. Jonathan was devastated. He didn't even date until he met you." Barbara's own voice began to rise, nearing a pitch that only dogs could hear.

"How?" Miriam asked gravely, "How did she die?"

"She killed herself, Honey. She jumped right off their hotel balcony."

"What? Why?" Miriam was utterly shocked. This new information collided with every previously known fact about the man she had agreed to marry. *Who was this guy?!*

Barbara slunk to her knees and shuffled her way to Miriam's lap. She knelt at her feet and grabbed the younger woman's hands, clenching them in a warm heap on her lap.

"Honey," she said, staring up at the tears precariously balanced on the lower lids of Miriam's eyes. "She was a troubled, *troubled* girl. No one knows why she did what she did. Maybe the stress of the wedding got to her. It could have been something specific that set her off. No one knows! The truth of the matter is, she wasn't right. She wasn't right to join our bloodline and she certainly wasn't right for our Jonathan. It wasn't the right fit. You're different. You're the one—for Jonathan I mean."

Miriam reluctantly nodded in agreement. Clearly, she would need to discuss this newly excavated secret with Jonathan. However, ten minutes past the time she was supposed to already be getting married had not seemed like an ideal moment. She swallowed her misgivings and hastily convinced herself that everything would be fine.

At the door, her father-in-law stood, patiently waiting to give her away. He greeted Miriam with a relieved smile and took her elbow.

"I thought maybe we lost you," he exclaimed breathlessly.

"No, no," she soothed him from deep inside the folds of her taffeta cocoon. "I'm here, David. I'm ready to do this."

After the ceremony, the happy couple kissed and ran from the temple under a barrage of birdseed. They escaped to the sanctuary of the waiting limo and headed toward the hotel for their reception. Snuggled in the rear of the car, Miriam savored the taste of her new status. *Wife.*

If only for a moment.

The unbidden memory of her uncomfortable exchange with Barbara forced its way back to the forefront of her thoughts. She pulled away from Jonathan and methodically examined his face.

"We need to talk," she said flatly.

"Um—" Jonathan was unsure how to respond. "OK. It's a little late now though, don't you think? The deed is done so to speak."

"I know about your ex-wife." Miriam shoved the words out of her mouth, fearful if she did not confront him now, she would never have the courage to ask.

Jonathan did not react. He simply said, "OK."

"It isn't something we have to tackle right this second but it is definitely something we need to discuss *soon*."

"That's fine," he responded blandly.

"I'm not going to start our marriage off with a lie."

"I understand that. It really isn't a big deal. I'll tell you whatever you want to know."

Jonathan's nonchalance was actually irritating. How could he think a one-day marriage to a now-dead woman was a small thing? What other secrets had he kept from her that were *not a big deal*? Worse still, what future secrets would he keep from her if his threshold for honesty was that low?

Partially to maintain her composure and not ruin what was supposed to be the happiest day of her life, Miriam put a pin in her rage. When the limo came to a stop, the driver leapt from the cockpit and jogged to open Miriam's door. She hesitated, holding Jonathan's gaze for just a hair longer than necessary.

"I want to know everything," she warned without a shred of humor.

The bewildered chauffer glanced inside to determine the cause of the delay. At that moment, Miriam tore her blazing eyes from her husband's infuriatingly tranquil face and bumped out of the car like huge, pissed off marshmallow.

Luckily, the social obligations of a wedding reception prevented the newlyweds from actually having to speak to each other for most of the night. They hugged various bubbies and shook hands with countless uncles. They did the Hora. Over lukewarm filet mignon and crusty, double baked potatoes, Barbara shamelessly interrogated Miriam about her plans to start a family. The poor woman was nearly delirious with *Bubby Fever*. She wanted grandchildren. Now. A lot.

"Have you and Jonathan talked about children yet?" Barbara asked, practically salivating.

"Well, we both want children but we haven't decided how many," Miriam responded tepidly.

"You know boys run in our family," Barbara had prattled on, "*big* boys. Andrew and David Jr. were both ten pounds and Jonathan was *eleven* pounds when he was born!"

"Yea," Miriam answered, "I figured he was big. I mean, most men who are six foot six don't start out as five pound babies, right?" She struggled to keep her tone light but she was distracted. Her mind kept circling back to the unknown depths of Jonathan's past. Was this a shallow pool she could navigate with one, awkward conversation, or was it a bottomless riptide that would suck her into a vast sea of exes, affairs and discreetly treated venereal diseases?

Who the fuck did I just marry?

Miriam's mother in law clucked along happily, oblivious to her daughter in law's distress. "Nope," Barbara laughed, "but you know, you've got that penthouse upstairs waiting for you. You two should finish up and go start practicing!"

"How much champagne have you had, Barb?" Miriam responded wryly.

"I'm just saying," she crowed, "the faster you start baking them, the faster I get to squish those chubby, delicious *punams*!"

Jonathan had broken away from his dinner conversation with one of his brothers and tuned into his mom's drunken pep talk.

"Mom, chill! We know you're baby crazy. We're working on it." He rolled his eyes and grinned conspiratorially at Miriam. She smiled back but it was a weak effort.

"You OK?" he mouthed with genuine concern.

How can he ask me that? Miriam marveled.

Before she could answer, Barbara draped a papery hand over her shoulder. "Come on, Honey," she slurred merrily, "let's go get a drink."

The two set off toward the bar, one a bit more unsteady than the other.

"I sure am sorry if I ruined your day, sweetheart," Barbara mumbled sullenly. "I never should have said anything about Vivien. That is ancient history. I can tell you're upset about it."

"It's fine, mom," Miriam answered, "we'll figure it out."

"Some women just aren't cut out for motherhood. We have a very strong bloodline. Vivien just wasn't strong enough to handle it."

Miriam whirled to face her wobbling mother-in-law. "She was PREGNANT?"

Barbara blinked slowly, considering the question. "Who?"

"Jonathan's ex-wife! Focus, Barb."

"Which one?"

"Wh—how *many* have there been?" Miriam was nearly screaming and despite the din of the DJ and clinking silverware, people were starting to take notice. The bobbing sea of distant cousins and murmuring plus-ones looked on disapprovingly. From out of the depths, Jonathan emerged looking every bit the dapper, Gatsby-ish host.

"Everything OK?" he asked sincerely.

Miriam turned her verbal assault on him. "No!" she growled through clenched teeth, "*nothing* is fucking OK! I feel like I don't even know who you are! Here I am, hours after our wedding and all the sudden you have a dead kid and God knows how many dead wives! What the fuck is going on, Jonathan? Who are you? Some kind of Semitic Bluebeard with a closet full of severed heads or something?"

"Go on, Jonathan," Barbara patted his arm, seemingly deaf to Miriam's cries. "It's time to take her upstairs now anyway. Good luck, Honey. I hope this one works out."

"Thank you, mom," Jonathan replied, also ignoring his confused bride. Miriam looked back and forth between them like an idiotic, tennis spectator. Jonathan turned his attention toward her and jerked his head toward the elevator. "Come on," he said placidly, "let's go to the room. I'll tell you everything."

Miriam did not wait for further instruction. She stormed off toward the elevator door and did not look back.

"Goodnight, sweetheart," Barbara hollered after her. "Good luck to you too. I truly hope you make it."

In the elevator, Jonathan inserted an antique looking key into the top of the button panel and turned it toward the right. The gilt doors slid obediently closed. Through the rapidly shrinking gap between the doors, Miriam looked out at the reception hall. Two hundred blank faces stared back at her in silent judgement. At last, the doors clamped shut and the elevator began to ferry them upwards. Alone in the mirrored box, Miriam could not shake the eerie feeling of being watched. She surveyed the four, closed in walls. No one there except her own reflection and the strange man in the tuxedo beside her. He was the one who broke the silence.

"I was married before," he uttered without emotion.

"No shit," Miriam retorted sourly, "apparently to so many, not even your mom can keep track."

"Four," he countered, "I was married to four women before you."

"And did they all kill themselves on your wedding night?" she asked sarcastically.

"No," Jonathan said regretfully, "only one managed to kill herself. I killed the other three."

Miriam froze. She slowly turned her head to search Jonathan's face for evidence that he was joking. There was none. He stared back at her with unwavering severity. The elevator rose higher and higher. With each passing floor, Miriam put another level between her and help. She was increasingly isolated the closer she got to their penthouse destination. Suspended, ever higher, above the ground in a floating, glass box. Like a butterfly in a killing jar. Alone with a murderer.

"That's not funny, Jonathan," she mumbled.

"That's not a joke, Miriam," he shot back at her. He inhaled deeply and closed his eyes. "I can smell you," he exhaled, "you're ovulating." Once again, Jonathan filled his lungs to capacity with the fragrant air inside the elevator. Miriam could see a slight bulge in his cheek as he worked his tongue back and forth, literally tasting the air. "We have a very strong bloodline, you know. Not all women can handle it." As he spoke, Jonathan's skin began to stretch and bulge. The seams of his clothes whined before splitting in large, gaping holes. Miriam watched in horror as a grotesque transformation overcame her husband. His hulking frame thickened and lengthened. By the time her overwrought mind could comprehend what was happening, he was nearly seven feet tall. His head skimmed the ceiling of the elevator and the cables groaned under the stress of the additional weight. He kicked free of his patent leather shoes before they could completely rip away from his feet. His tuxedo jacket sloughed to the floor like a discarded exoskeleton.

Miriam scrambled backward, away from the expanding giant. In so doing, she tripped on the lengthy train of her wedding dress. Looking up, she saw she was already at the nineteenth floor.

When these doors open, my only chance is to run! She mentally coached herself. That would not be possible with three feet of white silk in tow. Without thinking, she yanked down on the discreet, side zipper and wriggled free from the voluminous dress. At the sight of her skimpy undergarments, Jonathan's growth accelerated and he let forth an ear-splitting roar.

"YES, MY LOVE! You must prepare yourself!"

Are you fucking kidding me? Miriam stared back in nonplussed horror.

Jonathan swept a hand the size of a canned ham across the floor and scooped the billowing, empty dress to his face. Inhaling the lingering scent of her body, Jonathan shuddered and moaned. He had grown so large; the gown looked like little more than a hand towel in his grasp.

"You must give yourself to me freely, my love," his voice boomed from the depths of the dress like thunder emanating from a storm cloud. Ominous and yet, somehow woeful. "I've lost four wives in my search for the right partner. Three died during consummation, they were too weak to handle my bloodline. The last, well, she decided death was a better option than to be with a monster."

Miriam actually found herself sympathizing with the giant. As frightening as his transformation was, within the monstrous body was still the soul of the man she had fallen in love with. This *thing* was still her Jonathan. For a brief moment, she dropped her guard. Her shoulders slacked and she actually raised a hand towards the creature. Sensing her compassion, he lowered the fabric covering his face and smiled back at her. The contrast of such a warm expression on his vast, angular face was horrific. Miriam gasped and withdrew her hand as if his expression had burned her. At the same time, the elevator finally summited the building, and a chipper *ding* heralded the spreading doors.

Miriam's fight or flight response overrode any thoughts of reconciliation and she leapt barefooted from the confines of the elevator. Jonathan swiped after her fleeing body but his new size made him slower and ungainly. She bounded passed him, barely feeling the wind of his arm swinging behind her.

"NOOOOOO!" Jonathan howled in miserable rage.

Miriam did not pause. She fled blindly down the corridor toward the far end of the hall where it bent left toward the center of the penthouse. The suite took up the entire top floor of the hotel. It was clearly designed for rich couples who liked to host afterparties. An intertwining network of hallways connected sitting rooms, guest bedrooms and shimmering bathrooms slathered with white marble. It really was quite a beautiful hotel—when one was not pursued by a violent colossus with a deadly pecker and unrestrained sex drive.

"MIRI! You can't escape! There's no way out of here! Please come back!" Jonathan thundered behind her, ripping himself free from the elevator.

Miriam fled the beast for what felt like hours. She flitted from room to room, cowering behind doors, inside closets and in the shadows of overstuffed furniture. Panic, coupled with the unfamiliar surroundings, disoriented her for the first half of her evasion. Wherever she went, Jonathan was always just a hair's breadth behind her. Miriam had hoped to find refuge in the numerous, darkened rooms but he seemed to read her mind.

"The darkness won't protect you, Miriam," Jonathan sang demonically from a neighboring salon. "I can *smell* you."

She realized then that her only hope was the traitorous elevator that had brought her here. Inside, she would descend from the penthouse like a fairytale princess, scaling the walls of her tower prison. Miriam struggled to remember whether the hallway leading to the elevator was to the right or the left.

Left. Definitely left.

She pressed her ear to the wall, tracking Jonathan's reverberating steps on the dampening carpet. When she felt him pass by her hiding place, she sprinted into the hall, spinning her legs as fast as they would go. Her muscles burned with lactic acid and her knees threatened to buckle under her. The floorboards beneath the carpet rattled and groaned with the stress of Jonathan's thunderous steps. He was already gaining on her.

Ahead of her, Miriam could see a thick, metal door that promised to reveal the salvation of a fire escape. If only she could reach it in time. The corridor seemed to stretch before her like a horror movie. She might as well have been trying to outrun him on a treadmill. Jonathan's ragged breath was close enough to blow loose strands of Miriam's hair against the back of her neck. It tickled playfully at her skin, riddling her back with goosebumps despite the heat.

"There is no way out, Miri," he grunted.

We'll just see about that, she thought back.

A pivot bar ran horizontally across the middle of the staircase door. Miriam was close enough to see the tiny placard on the wall with the little cartoon man walking stiffly downward. She raised her hands expectantly and locked her elbows into two, parallel battering rams. Rather than slow her pace, she accelerated, preparing to burst forth into the liberating stairwell. Miriam's body collided with the door, smashing against the unyielding frame like a June bug against a speeding windshield.

The door did not budge. She barely had time for the overwhelming disappointment to register in her mind before leaping to the side, narrowly escaping the crushing impact of Jonathan's momentum. Miriam lost her footing and sprawled unceremoniously onto her belly. Jonathan's girth slammed into the fire exit with all the force of a speeding freight train. The energy of his pursuit dented the metal inward but the door held fast. If he could not break down that door, Miriam had to accept the fact that she had no hope of getting through it. Jonathan stood dazed, shaking his head and blinking furiously. His massive body totally blocked the way she had come. Scrambling to her feet, she realized her lengthy pursuit had led her all the way back to the beginning. Innocently waiting before her, were the open doors of the golden elevator.

Miriam sprinted full speed into the glass cube. Fifty feet behind her, her winded husband regained his composure. For a moment, he thought he might have lost her but then he patted the key still safely nestled in his pocket. He sighed with relief and furtively began walking toward her. Reflected in the mirrored walls, he could see her wide eyes staring back at him.

***

Under the bed, Miriam opened her eyes, dispelling the flashback. Her brain and her heart were still locked in heated debate. Cognitively, she could understand. She married a man who turned out to be descended from giants, whose savage man parts ripped his unsuspecting wives to pieces on their wedding nights. Emotionally, however, she refused to believe the man she loved could possibly hurt her.

Maybe he's right, she thought hopefully, *maybe I am meant for him. His soulmate. Maybe* I'm *the one who can survive this.*

Miriam balled her hands into tight fists and pressed them against her mouth. The soft carpet was starting to feel itchy, like thousands of tiny pitchforks jabbing Miriam's naked thighs. She felt certain if she stood up, there would be a soggy depression the shape of her body imprinted in the carpet. She wriggled her damp limbs. A thin rivulet of sweat squeezed out from the crook of her elbow. She scrunched her neck awkwardly in the tight space. Looking over her shoulder, she warily eyed her feet, ensuring they were securely hidden beneath the bed.

Terror gripped her throat, cutting off her airway. There, silhouetted against the light of the room was Nathan's grinning face!

He lay on his belly, *watching* her. *Waiting* for her to see him before he pounced.

"Miri," Nathan laughed, "it's all over!"

Faster than Miriam could scream, Nathan thrust his hand into the opaque darkness and clamped his vicelike fingers around her ankle.

Miriam thrashed wildly but the oppressive bed limited her range of motion. Instead of generating any sort of momentum, she just twitched helplessly against the rungs of the wooden frame.

Nathan's strength was irrefutable. He slid Miriam's sweat-slicked body out as easily as pulling an oyster from its shell.

"I already told you, Miri. There is no way out. I've done this enough times. My family has been hiding in plain sight for centuries."

At last, physically and mentally exhausted, Miriam broke down. She had tried so hard to escape this monster but here, quivering in his grip, she knew it was hopeless.

How could I be so stupid!?

She buried her head in her hands, certain she had reached the hour of her death.

"Baby, please don't cry," he said tenderly. He stroked her hair with the tips of his immense fingers. "I love you so much. I've tried to show you that."

Miriam did not answer, just continued to weep softly. Jonathan gathered her into his arms and cuddled her. He kissed her head and tried to soothe her.

"It's a gift you know," he murmured, "our bloodline. Through the generations, we have maintained our strength and resilience. Do you really think my great grandfather could have survived three concentration camps and a tour in Korea if he was a normal man? It takes a very special kind of person to live through something like that. My family has fought and lived through every American war since World War II! You're going to be the mother of warriors. *Giant* warriors!"

Finding her voice, Miriam said, "If I can survive *you*."

"I would never hurt you, Miri. I love you."

"That's what you said about the others. You loved them too." Miriam scoffed and pulled away from his embrace. Jonathan released her but she did not run. She stared at the floor coldly. "You don't love me. You're just throwing jizz at the wall to see what sticks. When you're done with me, you'll be on to the next one. Your mom won't even remember my name." She fingered the Chai at her throat with miserable futility.

"Miri, how can you say that?" he asked. Jonathan had grown so large, from where he sat cross-legged, he and

Miriam were nearly eye to eye. "What was I supposed to do? I wish I had met you first, but it didn't happen that way. I took a chance with someone else, but it wasn't right. None of them were right. None of them were *you*."

"And meanwhile your whole family knows. While I'm up here getting railed, they're downstairs taking bets on whether or not I live through it! Do you really not understand how *fucked up* that is?"

"How is that different from any other wedding?" Jonathan asked with a shy chuckle. "Everyone's just waiting to see who survives." Miriam grabbed a lamp off a nearby dresser and whipped it at against her husband. He deflected the blow with his hands but it shattered nonetheless against his open palms. "Hey," he yelled defensively, "I'm just trying to get you to laugh." He struggled clumsily to his feet.

"I don't want to laugh, you asshole! I want you to let me out of this fucking hotel!"

"Babe, you know I can't do that," he replied sadly. "You know what we are. We can't let you leave. You're one of us now. There is no going back."

Miriam raised her hands to her face and screamed against the skin. Her makeshift mask only slightly muffled the volume of her anguish.

Jonathan shuffled his feet uncertainly and dropped his head. His body was slowly shrinking back to its normal size. His clothes relaxed their stranglehold around his shoulders and biceps. He kept his eyes on the carpet but directed his words at Miriam. "So, I guess that's it. You don't love me anymore, do you?" He thought back to the night of his most recently failed marriage. His wife had looked back at him one last time. Over her shoulder, her expression had been one of absolute revulsion. In the moments before she leapt to her death, she had not felt fear or pain. Her last thoughts had been absolute, unrefined hatred.

Miriam lowered her hands as she whispered her answer, "I do. I love you so much." Her voice cracked slightly. It was true. No ruse or misguided attempt to escape. "As fucked up as all of this has been, deep down, all I really want is to be married. I want everything to go back to the way it was and be your wife."

Jonathan smiled and let out a nervous giggle, "You love me?" he asked hopefully. He strode towards her invigorated and happy. As he walked, his body once again began growing. The previously split seams tore into even large holes. His laughter boomed joyfully against the walls of the suite. Jonathan lifted Miriam effortlessly into his arms. She grabbed the sides of his face and eagerly kissed his open mouth.

"Go slow, OK?" she asked, not bothering to pull her lips away from his.

"Of course," he answered, "you set the pace." He sat down on the bed, cradling Miriam in his lap. The wooden frame creaked and splintered under their combined weight. The mattress crashed to the floor, sounding them in a jagged nest of shattered particle board and wood veneer.

Miriam laughed and tugged his shirtsleeves down over his swollen deltoids. She kissed his neck greedily, inhaling the smell of his skin. Jonathan lay back on the mattress while Miriam straddled him. She set to work extricating the shredded remnants of his belt from his slacks. As she separated the leather from the fabric she said, "Promise me, if something happens, you'll bury me with my Bubby."

"Nothing is going to happen, my love."

"Just promise, OK?"

"I would do anything for you." Jonathan pulled his wife down to him. She basked on his warm chest like a lizard on a hot rock. She kissed him again deeply, savoring his taste. "I'll be so gentle," he murmured.

Miriam took a deep breath, then closed her eyes.

***

Downstairs, Barbara nervously paced the floor. She wrung her hands and stole worried glances at the clock.

"Barbie, enough with the pacing already," David Sr. chided her from across the dancefloor.

"David, I can't sit still. Jonathan really loves this one. If she doesn't make it…"

"Come get a drink. Steady your nerves. He'll be fine."

It was nearly one in the morning. Not a single guest had left but the energy was decidedly absent. Partygoers in formalwear lay draped across tables and chairs. They looked even more wilted than the dying centerpiece orchids. The DJ had quit more than an hour before. He sat on the floor, leaned against the wall eating a slab of white wedding cake. Most of the female guests had ditched their high heels long ago. They lay abandoned under chairs and slung in piles near the coat check. The ballroom looked a fancy shoe store after the apocalypse.

Suddenly, the golden elevators near Barbara let out a chipper *ding*. She gasped and scuttled to the doors expectantly. David Sr. and his two elder sons exchanged glances before joining their matriarch.

As the doors slid open, Barbara laid eyes on her son. He stood alone in the center of the elevator. His body had returned to its human size and his clothes hung in ill-fitting tatters.

"Oh, Honey!" Barbara rushed toward her youngest boy.

"Ma," Jonathan began.

"It's gonna be OK, Sweetheart!" Barbara cooed.

"I know," he answered, stepping to the side. Behind him, Miriam stood in a white, hotel bathrobe. Her hair hung in limp strands. Her makeup was smeared in black asterisks around each eye…but she was smiling.

"Hi, mom," she said softly.

"OH, HONEY!" Barbara clasped her hands in joy.

"Mazel tov!" the reinvigorated crowd shouted.

Miriam beamed proudly. She had proven herself worthy to join this band of ancient monsters. She would be the one to carry on the newest generation of giants. Locking eyes with Barbara, she tapped the Chai at her neck.

Jonathan looked down adoringly at his glowing bride, "Welcome to the family, my love."

The It Factor
Krissy Eliot

A bullet to the back feels just like you'd expect from what little I know of the subject. My only frame of reference is a guy who served in the Korean war, a conscientious objector, who, because he didn't want to kill people, got the job of picking up dead bodies and throwing them in the back of a truck. I heard his story through the crack under Dr. Karen's door one afternoon while I was lying on the carpet eating gummy bears, picking out the orange ones because why bother with the rest.

He said he got shot once while driving the corpse stacks back to camp. An enemy soldier hiding in some bushes got him in the ribs through the driver's window, and the force of the bullet nearly knocked him all the way over into the passenger seat. He said the smell of his scorched flesh swirled into his nostrils like a twister and he thought his torso was deflating. That his muscle meat was being skewered by, what felt like, a hundred tiny shrimp forks. That he careened off the road into a ditch screaming fuck shit fuck.

For me, it happened almost just like that. By my enemy in a sneak attack. With a blast I couldn't withstand. In a place I would have never chosen, but where I'd prove my worth if it killed me.

A few feet away, the girl of my dreams crouches behind a display of cheese puffs, her little pink panties all wet, and not out of fear. Is this really the way I die? Face down on a floor after finally getting a taste of what we all want? What we think we all want. My chest fills with contempt but also a little pride, because even if it is the end, I just gave this girl the most exciting day of her life.

***

Earlier this afternoon, Leena and I took the train home like we usually do, because she likes to waggle her ninth-grader fingers and suck lollipops at older guys when we're coming back from school. Dudes with big arms and used cars, who have jobs in construction or plumbing or pizza delivery, who can afford to buy her a Big Mac with extra gooey cheddar. Guys who "are just so lush, I can't explain it," she says, despite their lightning B.O. or broken noses or track marks. It always makes me hot in the face to watch, this rank display, but if I come along for the ride, I can at least see what she's into this week. Take some notes. Not that they ever help any. Because it doesn't take a genius to know that a boring, lanky, human spaghetti noodle girl like me isn't what she's hungry for.

Today, Leena had set her sights on a long tube of a man with narrow hips and shoulders sitting alone in a two-seater behind us, a baggy hoodie obscuring most of his face. Even slouched, his torso alone must have been four feet in length and he smelled like smashed worms on wet pavement. A lot of disgusting people take the city subway, but just being in proximity to this chud made my mouth coat with slimy saliva, the kind you get when you're about to barf. Leena, however, could taste that Big Mac from the future, could see her tan, prickly legs spread-eagled in the backseat of his beat-up Ford Taurus. So she twisted around in the seat to look at him, saying how his hoodie was rad and how she was almost legal in four years.

We only needed to ride until the next stop, so it gave Leena a limited amount of time to be a big teen slut, and just enough time for me to catch up on the audio book I'd swiped from Dr. Karen's collection. It was about romantic attraction. More specifically, the "It" Factor." How most people guess that being physically hot is what gets them laid, but really, what starts the engines is mystery. If someone is mysterious, you'll spend minutes, hours, years trying to figure out why they never call you back or why they smile at you only sometimes at the check-out counter. And then because you spend so much time trying to make this person make sense, you confuse this obsession with love.

"The It Factor is uncertainty," the narrator declared into my headphones. "The ultimate seduction."

Leena was wiggling wildly to get the guy's attention, you know, like a caterpillar would wiggle if it decided to become a big whore. She kept asking things like did he live around here and what kind of beer did he drink. My eyes caught his reflection in the window.

The dude had a set of filthy orange teeth. The color of Dr. Karen's signature turmeric chicken that tastes like warm feet. If my research serves, he probably has a case of *Odontarrupophobia*. Fear of toothbrushes. To some people a brush on a tooth sounds like a tire screech. Makes them lose control of their bowels or cry or faint. One dude I read about was so afraid of brushing his teeth that he never taught his daughter how to brush, so by the time she was taking the SATs she had a full set of dentures and he had a big old cancer mouth. With his leathery skin, Turmeric Teeth looked old enough to have kids Leena's age.

Despite her writhing teen body, Turmeric Teeth stared straight ahead, unbreakable, a stark contrast to the other guys falling over themselves to stare at her on the train. Leena was usually the kind of girl you couldn't take your eyes off of, even when she wasn't doing anything interesting in particular.

Like in seventh grade, this group of kids were blazing their brains out, huffing Sharpies, and Leena stopped by to just say hey. When the principal found them, she was the only one to get two weeks suspension. Why? Because they had all crowded around her like she was the one who started it all. She just emanated potential. A rosebud or a new car smell.

Finally giving up, a huff burst from Leena's lips and she turned around to face front, pulling from her teddy-bear backpack a pink fuzzy shimmer puff packed with sparkles. She patted it over her arms and face causing a flurry of glittery bits to land all over me. I groaned, pinched the center of my shirt, and shook it off like it was lice. Which should come as no surprise, seeing as I'm what adults call a tomboy, and guys at school call a total dyke.

Sparkles must have made their way to Turmeric Teeth too because he let out a wet, weighty sneeze so close to my head that I felt the breeze. The conductor announced that we were coming up on the next stop, and that's when my right forearm started to itch. Stuck to my little brown hairs was a tiny blob, like I'd just leaned against curdled orange soda. The wall to my right was covered in little mystery droplets. My lip curled.

The city subway has to be one of the most disgusting places in the solar system. Scientists once did a test of the particulate matter in the air and discovered that we're just breathing in garbage and shit. Human shit. Rat shit. Bug shit. Bird shit. Little particles from all the half-drank strawberry milkshakes and colas that Leena threw in front of the train just to watch them splatter. We're inhaling soot from the tracks too, which they've never washed since the train's inception. In the last month my body has made direct contact with crushed lipstick, lunch meat juice, and what I pray was peanut butter. Rumor has it that when homeless people piss themselves, workers don't actually disinfect anything, but just dry the vinyl cushions off with a leaf blower and call it an evening.

Leena, who always watches my skin like a hawk, grabbed my arm, eyes locked on the glob. She was always warm and sticky to the touch, a kid who couldn't keep her hands out of the Honey-O's. The tips of her long hair licked against my forearm and her breath smelled like sour apple gum. That's when the glob started to mutate and grow, taking on the shape of a larva, the width of a ballpoint pen. Her nose crinkled and she raised a brow.

"The It Factor is intrigue," the narrator said. "It's the dangling cherry of a new experience that could change who you are if you could only just taste it."

The larva rose up off of my arm barely an inch, pulled up by an invisible tractor beam. A breath caught in my throat and Leena's eyelids stretched tight and open, and just as she opened her mouth to speak, it dove. Fast. Swirling into my flesh. My brief yelp was drowned out by the shrill wail of the subway as the lights flickered and dimmed in the underground tunnel, my CD player crashing to the floor, my headphones ripped from my ears. A thick stream of red ran from a hole in my flesh and onto my jeans. The grub's tail wriggled into me. Within seconds it was completely under the skin, squirming over my bicep, over my shoulder, and to the base of my neck. A warm sensation spread and my upper back muscles went slack. Then there was no feeling at all. The lights flickered back to full brightness.

The skin on my arm was fusing closed. In moments all that remained was a mere pinprick with a trickle of blood dripping onto my jeans. Leena cupped her hand under my forearm to catch it in her palms. She didn't let a drop spill or seep through the cracks between her fingers, like it was instinct. Like she'd done this before. Her eyes were glassy, mouth half open, and her nails dug into my skin. An old woman looked up from her newspaper to scowl at us for my loud yelp, but clearly hadn't seen a thing.

Ding ding! This was our stop.

The train doors opened and Leena tugged me out of my chair and into the station. Her tube of a future boyfriend leapt up, looking at the ceiling and floor around him, patting his face the way you pat your pants for lost keys. The tweaker. His eyes locked on me, his lids slowly widening, then he launched toward the doors and opened his mouth to speak as they clamped shut. Maybe he was interested in Leena after all. Maybe someday they could teach their own kid how to use a toothbrush.

Leena dragged me to the nook near the elevators where homeless people sleep and shit, then started licking my arm.

"No. Leena. This isn't for that," I said, but her lips had already closed over the wound. The coppery taste couldn't have gone well with sour apple. I sighed and blew my bangs out of my face.

Ever since we were little, I let her suck up all the blood. When I'd slice a finger on a knife trying to open a package, or cut myself shaving, or scrape my knee running for the bus, she'd suck. She even licked some off a popped zit.

After years of being her living lollipop, I researched her condition in one of Dr. Karen's encyclopedias of psychology. Found something called "Renfield disorder," based off the desperado from *Dracula* who wants to be a vampire but never will be. It said that these Renfield sickos don't just have an immortal life complex, but they're obsessed with blood for sexual gratification. Like they jizz every time they drink it. But I determined that definitely wasn't Leena. In truth, what's going on with her is far more original than being a clinical vampire. Like her backstory could be award winning. Like it makes me kind of jealous.

Leena saw her dad die while he was waiting tables on a rooftop deck. She was four and eating star-shaped ravioli with her hands when some crazy guy shot her dad in the face, his head an exploding sprinkler of blood. Apparently the guy was aiming for his ex-wife but his shot was piss-poor, so Leena's dad was dead before he flew over the banister and broke his neck on a blue mailbox a couple hundred feet below. The shooter got to go to a cushy mental hospital with nothing but a broken arm after police arrived and beat him up some.

When Leena's mom ran from the restaurant bathroom after hearing the shot, her eyes were all wide and her shirt was wet in two thick strips from her armpits to her hips. After talking to the police, she didn't bother to wipe Leena's mouth before leaving the restaurant, putting her daughter into the backseat with dried, red crud all over her lips. When they got home, her mom just went out to the backyard and lit a cigarette with her armpits still wet, leaving her kid alone in her bedroom. So Leena looked out her window until the sun rose, licking the corners of her mouth, which tasted more like pennies than marinara sauce, since it was the blood from her father's corpse.

A few years after this happened, in the second grade, Leena asked me for a piece of notebook paper, and I sliced my finger on the edge ripping it out. When I offered her another piece, she insisted on taking the bloody one. Later that day, she put a note in my lunch box cubby with a heart drawn around the blood stain, saying to meet her by the basketball hoops after school. When I showed, she asked me why I'd never talked to her before and what my favorite color was, like it was a formality. Then she took my hand in hers and undid the Band-Aid I'd gotten from

Mrs. Whiteman. She said it looked really bad, but said it in a way like it really looked good. She brought it up to her lips and became the first girl to ever put her mouth on me. Pizza delivery guys get her vag, but I get her tragedy.

The It Factor is a potent force the logical mind can't grasp.

Standing awkwardly in the train station, my fingers pressed against Leena's brow as I delicately tried to pry her forehead away from my arm, the way a mom shoves a baby clamping too hard on her nipple. She grunted softly and pressed her lips into my flesh. My eyes rolled at her reaction and landed on a poster. They had started putting up signs at every station featuring a cartoon elevator that was frowning. His doors were clear, so you could see that there was a small ocean of pee inside. Waves of stench were coming off of him, and a speech bubble read, "I am not a bathroom. Please don't go in me."

Enough was enough. My lips slid down over Leena's ear and her cartilage cracked as I bit.

"Bitch," she said, slamming her palm to the side of her head. Then noticing the extra blood still on her palm, she licked it.

"Did you see what just happened to me? I just got attacked by some parasite," I said. "Like an alien. I could have a virus. You could be infected."

She brought her arms up over her head, gave a twirl, and posed. "Do I look sick?" Her eyes narrowed in on me, daring me, teasing me, frying me alive. "And did you see that guy sitting behind us?" she said. "Wasn't he just so *lush*?"

What was stronger than my fear of an alien parasite was my fear of how she'd react if I behaved like I wanted. If I told her to shut up and wrapped my bony fingers around her waist and squeezed like it meant something. I thought about doing that every moment she flipped her hair or winked or breathed, but I never had the guts.

Fortunately, the Ravioli Goddess wanted my blood, not my guts.

"I've gotta get home," I said, turning and walking across the platform. Leena ran to catch up, saying to please give her a break. That I should understand better than anyone that blood scrambles her brains like eggs and did maybe we both hallucinate this alien thing? That even if it is real we'd get through it and she was sorry for being a cunt. She said some other stuff not worth responding to, and then at some point she wasn't at my side anymore, like she'd given up easy. Because she's always been one to give it up easy, and when you're always one way, that's what people come to expect.

***

This evening I sat on the bed with one of Dr. Karen's psychology books propped open on my crossed legs. I've always liked reading her collection, ever since before I was able to comprehend it. Highlighting and memorizing phrases like "factitious disorder" or "obsessive compulsion." Words that sound important. Words that she can charge three dollars a minute for. Sometimes I can get her attention when I bring them up, unless she's doing her booty-buster workout on the living room carpet, or doing a therapy session, or literally anything else.

I considered what Leena the Big Mac Floozy had said and wasn't opposed to the idea that it was a hallucination. I searched the books diligently for any disorders that could explain visions of monster parasites or alien encounters but kept coming back to schizophrenia, which seemed too obvious. Too boring. Plus, Leena saw it too.

That's when I found *Folie a deux*. "Madness shared by two." Shared psychotic disorders are rare, but they usually happen with people who've been in a relationship for a long time. The way it works is, one person is usually insane, and then the other eventually absorbs their insanity like a sponge. Starts seeing what the other sees, fearing what the other fears. But the chances of *Folie a deux* happening is about 2.6 percent. Far less likely than being attacked by an alien parasite. Well, probably.

I turned to the next page and that's when it all changed.

"Ow," I said. "Ow, ow, ow, OW."

A thousand needles were skewering me from behind. My throat puffed up and my mouth went slack, a string of drool roping down from my bottom lip to my lap. Like if my body couldn't scream, it would spit its terror.

I fell off the bed and slammed my ribs into the hardwood floor, pop rock sounds emitting from my back. My body writhed from a series of stings up my spine, a worm getting pecked by a bird. To my left was a full-length mirror, one of the many Dr. Karen installed around our home. My hands were numbing from shock, but they managed to grasp the cotton of my shirt and yank it off. Turning my back to the mirror and looking over my shoulder, I watched the skin at the top of my spine bubble with a rust-colored milk, rapidly hardening into an ooey gooey wax. A bulbous lump.

Then just like that, the pain stopped. Outside, a shadowy figure moved fast past the window. A dark fog seeped into my eyeballs, and I passed out.

***

Belly down on the hardwood floor, the room came slowly into focus. The curtains were no longer backlit with the orange glow of the setting sun. Night. Facing the mirror, I could see my growth was still there. Grotesque. Alien. Breathtaking. I found myself admiring it like a horror movie more than a horrific real-life event, wondering when the guy with the mask might show. Wishing he would soon.

Muscles vibrating with fear and intrigue, stomach rolling over on itself like a slug in a washing machine, I crawled to my dresser and put on an extra-large button-up, hoping to conceal the extent of this giant mutant zit, the height and width of ten stacked CDs. Then I walked to the kitchen as Dr. Karen's phone therapy session drifted in from the living room.

"Times are tough between you and your daughter, Marge. But stay strong. Earn her respect!" Dr. Karen said. "When you earn your child's respect, she can in turn respect others, and, more importantly, value her unique and special self."

She's published what seems like hundreds of self-help books over the last decade. Like *Quit Ending, Start Beginning. Catch More Eyes with Honey. No Pain, No Fame.* Books that some of her clients swear by, only probably because she has sex with a quarter of them.

The day that the copies of her first book, *Be Yourself, But Better*, arrived at our home, it was my seventh birthday and exactly one year since my dad had walked out on us. Like every year before that, we had opened presents on the couch in our pajamas, and my body was nestled against her doughy torso while she sang the birthday song and fed me mint chip ice cream.

When the door knock came, she left me alone to let in the delivery men, who stacked at least thirty massive boxes in the living room. She cut one open and stared at the book's back cover, eyes glittering at the sight of "Dr. Karen, PhD" in gaudy gold lettering. But then she noticed the black and white author photo. Her broad shoulders, her round face, the rolls of her neck.

Her cheeks flushed and she looked away, then stood sideways to check her figure in the mirror on the wall. She sucked in her gut for a few seconds and gave a fake smile.

Then when she exhaled, her stomach slopped back out, a balloon full of oatmeal, and she threw the book to the floor, disappeared down the hall, and slammed the door to her room.

On a Friday night, eighty pounds less and one year later, she'd ask me to start referring to her as Dr. Karen. Said it made her home office seem more professional whenever clients called or came over. "Welcome to Dr. Karen's office. Right this way," I'd say. "Hi. Dr. Karen's office. May I ask who's calling?" And since the clients were always there or always calling, she was always Dr. Karen. It was on that Friday night that we silently agreed that I'd never stop calling her Dr Karen. It was also the day she decided to never hold me close or feed me ice cream again.

"Remember to count your breaths," Dr. Karen said with finality, before waltzing into the kitchen, phone-free. She slammed her hands on the table in front of me and rolled her neck back to stare at the ceiling. "God, I need a cleanse. Juice, baby?"

She opened a bottle of tomato water and placed it in front of me, then sat down across the table to leaf through a leatherbound brick of paper, her boney butt slowly ripping a hole in the fluffy yellow seat cushion.

"Dr. Karen," I said.

No response.

"Dr. Karen," I repeated.

Nothing.

After her weight loss and confidence gain, the only people who could keep her attention were "book material." Real fucking psychos that could amplify her brand. Bikers. Felons. Accountants. One year she brought home a dude from a traveling circus who called himself The Merry Midget and she ended up dating him for a year. When I had the chickenpox, I walked from the kitchen to my bedroom carrying an open can of cold soup, and I spotted the two of them on the living room couch, cuddling. She nibbled his silver dollar sized ear as he cried into his stubby hands. "That's a breakthrough," she loudly whispered. "That's a breakthrough." Sometimes when she was with another client, The Merry Midget and I would play a game called Operation where you'd remove tiny toy hambones from this plastic guy's stomach with tweezers. Sometimes I'd say how I wasn't sure if I liked the game and he'd wiggle his fingers at me and say, "Fun deals come in odd packages."

"Dr. Karen, hey," I said.

"Mmmm?" she said, still reading.

"I was attacked by an alien," I said.

I stood up, turned around, and pulled up my shirt around my neck to reveal my back. I looked over my shoulder and she had her left pointer finger up. "Just need to finish this sentence, sweetie. Patience is a virtue," she said. "It allows us to tune into the present moment and understand our most pressing desires in the now."

I stood there waiting, listening to my rustling lungs, to the *thump, thump, thump* from within. It was coming from my chest. Wait, no. Definitely my back. *Thump, thump, thump.* The clock ticked. A page turned. My time was coming. Then the phone rang.

Dr. Karen rose from her seat, eyes still glued to the book. "Could be a client, honey," she said, then turned and disappeared down the hall.

My shirt fell back down.

The It Factor lingers long past its welcome.

I wondered what she was going to do, anyway. Saw her contorted face in my mind's eye, heard her sharp scream at the sight of my tumor. Would I end up in some government testing site or nut house? After all, despite all those sexy nights of long talks and breakthroughs, The Merry Midget got dumped. I needed someone to talk to, someone who relied on me whether she wanted to or not.

My feet gently padded toward my room and I locked the door behind me. In seconds, my legs were out the window, wrapping around the branch of the large oak in the backyard. Then when my muscles were burning from a sprint, my combat boots touched down on Leena's carpet. She was sitting in a purple bean bag chair, hitting record on her stereo, stealing a song off the radio.

In front of all the boy band posters, I took off my shirt and turned around.

First, she gagged, but then grazed the bulb with her touch, all slow and careful and hungry while I memorized every groove of her fingertips. Gun to my back, I could draw her prints if I had to.

"What do you think it is?" I said, and she turned me around to face her. She touched the tip of her tongue to my nose then said, "I don't know. But it's *lush*." And I could have died right there.

*****

Next thing I knew, I was standing on the roof of a five-story duplex apartment building, my toes on the ledge. Leena, the center of the marker-huffing universe, was standing on the roof of an adjacent building, in a neon pink windbreaker, twirling her neon green gum around one finger, telling me to jump.

"It's the only way you'll know," she yelled.

After two minutes of serious deliberation, we decided that I'd definitely been attacked by an alien parasite, and that we needed to take it for a test drive. Other than the gory arm-dive on the train and some back bubbles in my bedroom, Leena pointed out that the experience had been wholly uneventful. It had clearly taken over my body, but she wanted to see: would it give me powers? On the bike ride to the city, with the Shimmer Puff Princess sitting on my handlebars, she tried to get me to predict stuff in her head. Colors. Numbers. Names of boys. I guessed all wrong. She had me stop the ride and try to pick her up to test my superstrength, but all my body could offer her was one of my patented piggy back rides, made all the more complicated by the 10-CD-sized alien pimple getting in the way. My noodle arms got tired after five minutes. She then threw a sharp pebble at me and cut my cheek then said, "Not bulletproof." She went to lick the cut and when I shoved her she laughed.

The next logical test was obviously flight. Or at least building-to-building leaping abilities.

I knelt down and arched my back like a feline, but looked more like Quasimodo than Catwoman. The opposite building was about a story shorter and ten feet away. If I got a running start I could make it to Leena. Maybe even fly to her.

The It Factor is the magnet to which all living things gravitate.

With a big inhale, I bolted. The roof rushed by under my shoes, then the ledge was gone, then the street below slid into view, and for a second, all was still. I was hovering. I saw Leena's lit up expression, her tongue running over her teeth, hoping I'd show her something new.

That's when I started to drop. My leap had covered serious ground, but not quite enough. My left arm flung outward as my body and stomach dropped, a flying spaghetti monster, my fingertips just barely managing to grab the opposite building's ledge as my torso slammed into the brick side.

You don't appreciate just how much heavier a torso can be with some extra alien pounds until you get some. Doing some calculations, I estimated that it weighed about as much as a fat newborn puppy or a bag of Chinese take-out. My skin was stretching. Stinging. Dangle. Dangle. Dangle. *Thwump.*

A piercing fire sliced into the bendy part of my arm, and I was hanging a few inches lower than moments before. And that was because my elbow was just wrenched out of its socket trying to hold my full weight. A shadow moved around the corner of a nearby building as I reached my other arm up for a stronger grasp and let go with the busted limb. Counting the ways it was all worth it. Because you have to do whatever it takes not to feel lonely or bored.

I put my left toe into an inlaid brick, then tried to use the strength of my good leg and arm to pull me up, but could barely lift an inch. I saw an open dumpster down below. Saw me landing safely on a bed of packing peanuts and pillows. Then saw me missing and cracking my spine on the dumpster's steel edge. I wondered about the intruder in my skin. If it could use its powers to heal, now would be the time. Did it have any sense of self-preservation? Or could it simply live on in my rotting corpse? It had to do more than this. There had to be more.

But then, even if there wasn't, even if this thing was only using me, I wasn't opposed to the idea of it living off my flesh permanently. In fact, it felt strangely like home, like a secret purpose. Like love.

My eyes squeezed shut, ready to let go, when a set of ten sticky fingers wrapped around my wrist and tugged. Leena wrenched me up and we fell down together onto the roof, panting, laughing, me and my Blood Goddess. Her windbreaker fell open to expose the thin sliver of tan skin between her jeans and the bottom of her shirt, and the burning in my dislocated elbow cooled. She leaned in and put her tongue on mine, even though it wasn't bleeding, and in that moment I understood the alien's true powers. Something new inside me stirred, and with my good arm I reached, slid my fingers around her waist, then squeezed.

***

Squinting under fluorescent lights at the gas station, Leena, the blood-sucking hussy was frog-squatting and looking through a shelf with a dozen flavors of bubble gum. I grabbed a white shirt off a stack that had a laughing cartoon hose and a speech bubble saying, "Crude oil is a gas!" I pulled it over my neck, twisted it, and tucked in my mangled arm. A makeshift brace. A shadow passed the glass door.

I left Leena in her squat and walked to the counter, pulling a dead president from my pocket to buy the shirt when the bell over the door jingled. A tall man walked in and stopped on the entry carpet a couple feet from me. The old man behind the counter said did he need help, was he looking for anything? And by the way the guy reacted, the cashier might as well have called the stranger's mom a buttsucking cockgobbler, because he started shouting in a foreign language. Barking nonsense, the way a pit bull lets you know this is his house. Then he turned to me and spread his lips to show a set of orange bones that were all too familiar, all too cancery. Barf spit coated my mouth.

Turmeric Teeth.

Up close it was easy to tell that I didn't give the guy enough credit. That he had something way more original than a teeth brushing disorder or cancer. That squiggling over and between his chompers were a bunch of little orange flecks. Ooey gooey blobs like the one that had buried into my arm. Slipping. Sliding between the cracks and back out again. A mouth ecosystem. A periodontal playground.

And here I start to put it together. The glitter from Leena's shimmer puff. The sneeze. The patting of his cheeks for something missing. The parasite came from him. Maybe he was a willful incubator. An infected monster. Or quite possibly, a dad. A dad whose offspring shot out into the world in a flurry of sparkles before it was ready and went right into me.

Because of course you'd lose an alien baby on the subway. Because of course you can get pregnant from a sneeze these days.

I turned to run. To escape this subway tweaker. This Big Mac god. He wasn't going to take this away from me. I had waited too long. Come too far. Leena's mouth opened and I reached for her. BANG!

That's when I get shot in the back. Because that's what had to have happened. Because I had the privilege of learning at a young age what taking a bullet was like from a guy who stacked bodies on trucks and almost died saying fuck shit fuck. What else could propel me forward with such force that my face skids across the floor? What else produces a gust of burning flesh wind? What else makes your skin deflate like a whoopie cushion without the big fart payoff? I imagined Turmeric Teeth pulling out some fancy sci-fi gun, blasting me into oblivion with my back turned, like a coward, like a movie villain. Like if he can't have it, no one will.

Which brings us to now.

My nipples and cheekbone throb from the impact of falling forward and slamming into the tile. So this is the way I die. A stupid teenager on the floor of a gas station trying to impress a girl, realizing that everything cool is just a story you tell yourself, one where you don't even get to write the end. Leena's words from earlier echo in my skull: not bulletproof.

Only somehow I'm still alive. I took a bullet to the top of the spine, but I breathe. I wonder if I'm maybe paralyzed. So I try to wiggle my toes. Oh shit, they move. My hips shimmy against the tile. My eyes blink at Leena, who watches, crouched, from behind a display of cheese puffs. Leena, who bites her glossy lip at me. Leena, the center of my universe. Leena, who just said lush in my face like she was coming. It's not over. I stand up.

I catch my reflection in one of the round traffic mirrors on the ceiling above the counter. It wasn't a gunshot.

My alien pimple popped.

The shirt is split up the back and hanging in tatters, my arms still in the sleeves, my makeshift sling cradling my mutilated limb. What once was a full round lump on my torso is now a dripping, gaping octagon with steam rising out of it, with some mysterious black liquid flecked on the tattered, fleshy remains. I touch a drop of it with the tip of my finger and pull back and suck my teeth as it singes the skin of my index.

The balding cashier lies dead on the floor, my dead president doing the backstroke in his blood. The same black liquid that splashed onto my back is lying in splatters around his head. Or what's left of his head. Goopy, bits of cartilage, skin, and eyeballs sit in a hearty soup of melted face and brains. When I finally peel my gaze from the dead dude, I see, perched atop a box of super-sized tampons, escaped from its pod—my alien, my parasite, my little orange gummy bear.

For its second stage of life it hasn't grown much, about the size of a gerbil. Its armor-plated, tube-shaped body is the hue of a burnt sunrise. Eyeballs attached to antenna bounce wildly like it's conducting an orchestra, and its back arches and it lifts up, the underside of its belly a fine-tooth hair brush of wiggling legs. An oversized baby millipede. It shakes and shivers as it stares down Turmeric Teeth, who, with the grace of Miss Manners, dabs some black death juice from the corners of his mouth. The death juice that melts faces and makes my parasite explode out of my back to save itself. Maybe even to save me.

He barks a nonsense sound at the millipede. Thunder trying to form words. And the creature unleashes a long, sharp chirp that cuts a hole in my ear drum. Then it makes a break for it.

Hair brush legs tickle down the side of the tampon tower, over the shelf of candy necklaces, and past the umbrella stand near the front. Its mouth ejects a black liquid ahead, melting the bottom of the glass door to secure an opening. Turmeric Teeth lets out another thunder roar before launching out the door after it, a shadow in the night.

Leena tiptoes out from behind her hiding spot, steps over the melted man's head, and slips her hand in mine, then gives me a little eyebrow raise and a nod toward the door. I see the goosebumps on her skin and her throat rise up and down with a gulp. I almost tell her that we can stay here all night. We can eat mint chip ice cream, make prank calls from the station telephone, touch tongues and wonder why we waited so long for this. But girls like Leena, they don't want ice cream.

The It Factor is manipulation in its most primal form.

So I go.

***

We follow after them about a block, where stairs lead from the sidewalk down into the subway. At two in the morning, hardly anyone is in the station, aside from the homeless guy peeing in the elevator. We sprint after the parasite papa and his baby millipede as they enter a stopped train car, Leena and I almost getting crushed as the doors snap shut.

Turmeric Teeth leaps around the car frantically trying to catch my parasite, his back hunched, tearing cushions off the seats. He reaches up to the ceiling and snatches at the creature, missing every time as it darts over the walls, down into the cushions, and across the floor. He lets out a roar that makes his whole body vibrate and shiver. Like he's done with these little games. Like he could kill that little shit.

Then his arms fall off. And his skull splits open like a ripe watermelon, revealing a set of antennae where his eyes used to be. He grows taller, his already impressive seven-foot height becoming eight, then nine, then ten, in matter of seconds. His legs fall off too, pushed from the inside out, tendons tearing from his flesh followed by trails of slime as they're expelled. What remains is a cylindrical body with orange armored plating and hundreds of wriggling legs. His body arches at the top to fit under the ceiling of the car. The only resemblance the monster bears to the man we saw moments before is its mouth, which remains full of tiny human-like teeth desperately in need of a floss.

The baby millipede runs across the floor right to my feet. And I think maybe this can't be chance. Maybe I can show it to Dr. Karen for her next book. Maybe it aches for me like me for it. My stomach hits the aisle floor as my hands are about to close down around my prize. Then Turmeric Teeth's tongue explodes from his mouth and unravels. A bubble tape anaconda. It wraps around my torso, pig in a blanket style, and slams me to the floor, causing the baby millepede to let out another ear-popping chirp and dart away. Under the seat next to me is my dropped CD player, the disc scratched and lying a couple feet from it.

The It Factor cannot be captured. It cannot be taught, bought, or learned.

The alien daddy leans close to my face and tightens his grip. My lungs are being crushed now and my good arm is cracking under the pressure. At least it's not ending with a gunshot. At least they'll all have a reason to remember me.

But Leena, the blood sucking hussy, the Divine Idiot, decides today is the day she doesn't give up easy. That she'll fight for the obvious thing. The bland spaghetti noodle. The center of nothing. So she launches herself at Turmeric Teeth and sinks her fangs into the alien's tongue, tearing a chunk of flesh so spurts of black ooze explode from a long vein running its length. The same black ooze that melts faces. She gulps it down.

With a thunder boom howl, he wrenches his tongue away from Leena and out from under me, then loops it around her. Before you can say *Folie a deux*, he slams her body into the window, and then drops her immediately, and it's hard to tell which cracked louder, her skull or the glass. He leans down over me, flat on my back, a puppy in surrender, and stares into my face. As if to say, playtime is over. As if to say, none of this was ever yours.

The It Factor is fear. Fear that you'll miss out on something great.

My eyeballs look past the massive predator and zero in on my parasite, crawling slowly on the ceiling above us. My sharp inhale is all the clue this Daddy needs.

He whips his body around, shoots his tongue up and snags the baby, then pulls it down toward him and drops it into a few of his tiny arms, holding it like a child. He rolls his tongue up into his own face, then says something to it in alien-speak, scolding it. My parasite lowers its head. As if to say it's really sorry. As if to say: I truly am a little shit. Turmeric Teeth leans his face down to meet it, gives the creature a soft bump with his head, then coos.

Having acquired his bounty, he turns, revealing a back covered in waxy orange sacks from the top of his head to the bottom of his back, pulsing with parasites and pride and potential. And with not so much as a backward glance, he disappears into the station. The intercom clicks on. End of the line.

Lying there in the train car, I turn to stare into the eyes of motionless Leena, the shimmering girl who started it all. Blood trickles from the top of her skull and down to her top lip, the only lip remaining, as her lower jaw, throat, and chest are completely melted by the black goo. What's left is a sour apple green blob glistening in a wet slop of innards stew, punctuated by a steamy aroma of pennies and puke.

During one of their many pillow talks, The Merry Midget told Dr. Karen that his height was a blessing and a curse. That being unique was cool but he was always a novelty in someone else's narrative. Born to be a fantasy, which might have sounded good if humans ever pursued just one. People were made to live, he said, but not to last. You can never have it all. Not for long. Not forever.

Just to test its powers, I lean down to lick some of the blood off Leena's lip, letting it settle on my tongue like a good but false memory. And when the nausea surges and the barf spit comes, I turn away from her, and spit it out.

Other titles from HellBound Books

Madam Gray's Creepshow

A veritable smorgasbord of twenty-three deliciously terrifying treats, each one simmered to blood-curdling perfection and seasoned with just the perfect amount of gallows humor.

From murder and madness to monsters and the downright macabre, the stories awaiting you within in this superlative anthology push the boundaries of horror to the next level... and way, way beyond!

Featuring stories by: Juliana Amir, Ross Baxter, Norris Black, Matt Bliss, Scot Carpenter, Max Carrey, Josh Darling, James Dorr, Gerri R. Gray, Chisto Healy, Carlton Herzog, Scott McGregor, J Louis Messina, Drew Nicks, Cooper O'Connor, Brett O'Reilly, Lisa Pais, Frederick Pangbourne, Clark Roberts, Rob Santana, Kelli A. Wilkins, and Scott Bryan Wilson.

Blood and Blasphemy

If you enjoy your horror dipped in buckets of blood and sprinkled with generous amounts of blasphemy, then you've come to the right place!

Blood and Blasphemy is a collection of over thirty of the most sacrilegious horror stories ever written.

Within these irreverent pages, you will encounter a priest that keeps his deformed spawn chained in a root cellar, a convent where a poisonous species of salamander is worshiped, a demonic altar boy, possessed religious relics that kill, blood-drinking clergymen, a Son of God who feeds on sin, an unsuspecting couple who run afoul of religious lunatics in a small town, the divine (and deadly) turd of Christ, and other terrifying tales guaranteed to make church ladies faint and nuns clutch their rosaries.

The Toilet Zone: Number Two
"Restroom reading at its most terrifying!"

Imagine, if you will, you're traveling through the unknown, hellbound, with no roadmap or stars to guide you. The light fades as you descend into a shadow realm where supernatural terrors make their lair and evil lurks at every turn. Here, dead things don't always stay dead, for this is a world where things that shouldn't be... *are*, and things that should be are not.

In this world, it takes between 2,500 and 4,000 reading words to pay a visit to the smallest, but terrifyingly necessary, room, and stories are written precisely to chill the bones as you wait for nature to make its call.

You open up the book, and one of the 32 tales skulking within its hellish pages chooses you...

It's too late to turn back now. You are about to set foot into another dimension, so best watch out for that signpost up ahead...You've just crossed over into... The Toilet Zone

Schlock! Horror!

An anthology of short stories based upon/inspired by and in loving homage to all of those great gorefest movies and books of the 1980's (not necessarily base in that era, although some do ride that wave of nostalgia!), the golden age when horror well and truly came kicking, screaming and spraying blood, gore & body parts out from the shadows...

This exemplary 80's themed/inspired tales of terror has been adjudicated and compiled by one Mr Bret McCormick, himself a writer, producer and director of many a schlock classic, including *Bio-Tech Warrior*, *Time Tracers*, *The Abomination*, *Ozone: The Attack of the Redneck Mutants* and the inimitable *Repligator*.

Featuring stories from: Todd Sullivan, Timothy C Hobbs, Mark Thomas, Andrew Post, James B. Pepe, Thomas Vaughn, Edward Karpp, Jaap Boekestein, Lisa Alfano, L. C. Holt, John Adam Gosham, Brandon Cracraft, M. Earl Smith, Sarah Cannavo, James Gardner, Bret McCormick, and James H. Longmore.

**A HellBound Books LLC
Publication**

www.hellboundbookspublishing.com

Printed in the United States of America

www.ingramcontent.com/pod-product-compliance
Lightning Source LLC
Chambersburg PA
CBHW060900190726
48286CB00002B/318